specular

 sovareign

SCION SAGA BOOK THREE

specular

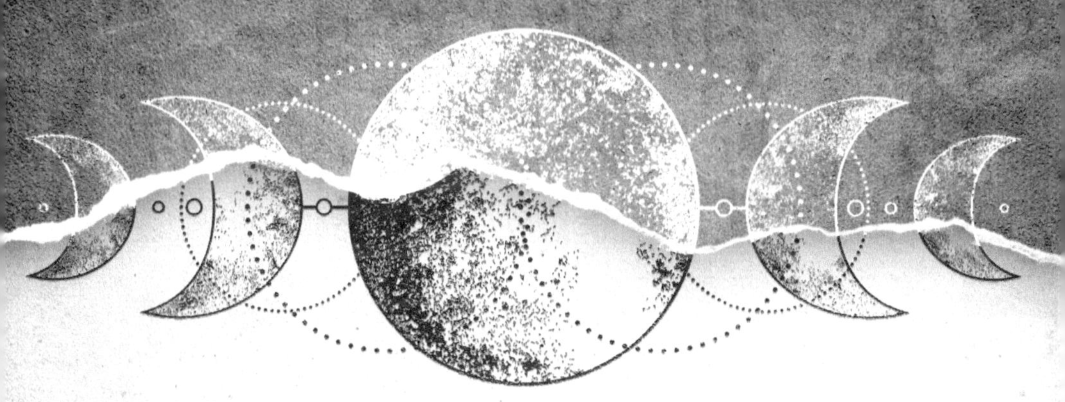

CĀLIX LEIGH-REIGN

Specular: Scion Saga Book 3
by Cālix Leigh-Reign

www.ScionSaga.com
www.Calix.co

Copyright © 2023 by Cālix Leigh-Reign

For permission requests, contact publisher below:

Sovareign Publishing

www.Sovareign.com

For permission requests, contact the publisher below:

Sovareign Publishing

California USA

www.Sovareign.com

Cover Concept by Calix Leigh-Reign
Cover Art by Carlos Quevedo
Descendant illustrations by Wasi Ahmed - Owned by Calix Leigh-Reign
Interior Design & Typesetting by Ampersand Book Interiors
Edited by Norahs Ltd.
ISBN: 978-0-9979239-0-2 [hardback]
ISBN: 978-0-9979239-5-7 [paperback]
ISBN: 978-0-9979239-6-4 [ebook]

First Edition
10 9 8 7 6 5 4 3 2

CONTENTS

My most beloved mommy,

I was beyond blessed to have you here with me for as long as I did. An ending was nothing more than a non-existent space that my mind refused. Your life, sacrifice, and legacy are eternal. You live inside me, your surviving children, grandchildren, and great-grandchildren. These human words will never sufficiently express my eternal love nor the pain of missing you the way I do. I'll hold you again, mommy. I will.

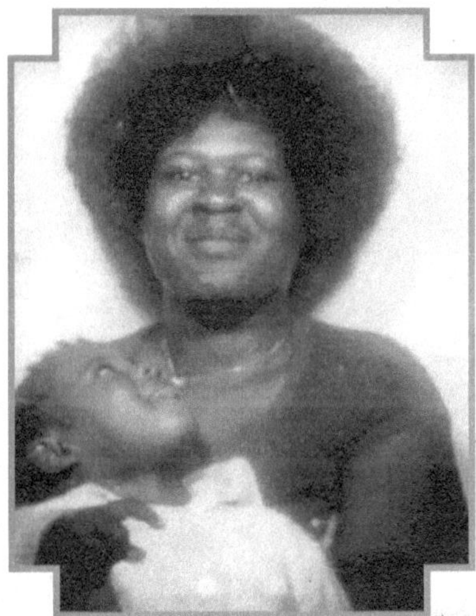

Eternally, your
legacy middle child,

Calix Lorraine

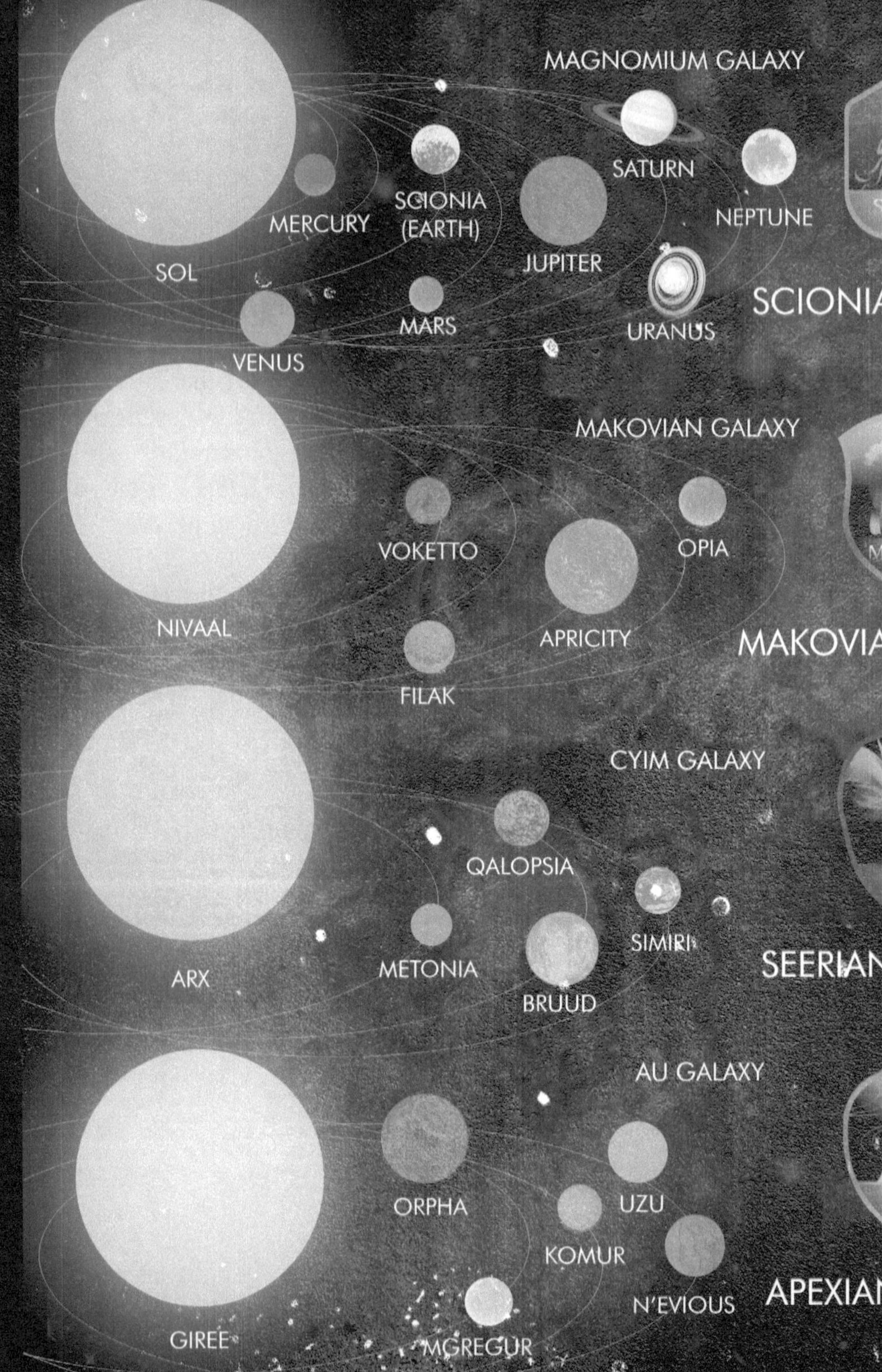
MAGNOMIUM GALAXY
SATURN
NEPTUNE
SCIONIA
(EARTH)
MERCURY
JUPITER
URANUS
SOL
MARS
VENUS
SCIONIA
MAKOVIAN GALAXY
VOKETTO
OPIA
NIVAAL
APRICITY
MAKOVIA
FILAK
CYIM GALAXY
QALOPSIA
SIMIRI
ARX
METONIA
SEERIAN
BRUUD
AU GALAXY
ORPHA
UZU
KOMUR
N'EVIOUS
APEXIAN
GIREE
MGREGUR

RIP GALAXY
ORIGA
ARCANIA
NABAT
YEUTON
JEXUXA
SHAREN
UNIVERSE
AEONIA GALAXY
HUREX
VYUN
SXULIT
THYIMA
OBLE
UNIVERSE
DUENDEN GALAXY
DESA
GEHZ
BERRONYA
CAVA
LEIN
NIVERSE
KLIPP GALAXY
ILLAYIA
WREIYN
GIJI
ELYSIA
VELLUN
NIVERSE
KROO

PROLOGUE

consanguineous

CARLY SLEPT AS peacefully as she could, though she tossed and turned with anxiety. Adam normally would've grabbed her close, but he still hadn't returned. In her slumber, the toil of existence and expanse pulled her into its depths.

An indescribable pulling of disconnect jolted Carly closer to an unreachable consciousness. The only feeling she registered was Rye's flesh…until it was cruelly ripped from her. Her lids refused to allow the blaring light inside, though it threatened to slice through. Several whirling nightmarish eternities passed before tiny foreign electrical charges connected to her core.

Had she been ported to Afrax?

Feeling it was safe enough to wake from her nightmare, she opened her eyes and gawked at an unbelievable sight. Convinced she must still be asleep, she blinked rapidly while pinching herself. Neither changed the scene. The faces surrounding her weren't the human ones she had experienced for a lifetime. Hundreds upon hundreds of onyx ovular eyes punctured her long-standing reality.

growing pains

carly

CARLY WIT'S MOTHER taught her there was a difference between a truth and *the* truth. As a new adult, she constantly battled with which one she encountered on a regular. Her fiancée, Adam, had been regularly checking on her like he was anticipating her non-existent regret to reveal itself over the life they were building together.

It was difficult to explain her relationship with regret in a way he'd understand, so she'd left him to his own devices in that regard. At just 19-years-old, Carly reserved regret for the most extreme of uncontrollable circumstances. For instance, killing Chandler, her own cousin, versus rendering him unconscious when he'd tried to kill them all after he was inadvertently poisoned with a tainted strand of V. She was fairly certain she'd regret that for the rest of her life. It didn't matter how many others disagreed with their cushiony words. She could've made a better decision if she'd embraced her calm the way her mother had always taught her. She pushed that regret aside, yet again, until redemption could be had.

The sunrise filled her as she meditated on the patio of her and Adam's cozy home at Meridian — the above-ground housing community the Descendants had built for themselves. The sun was more alive in her than it had ever been, bursting inside her cells in the most fulfilling ways. With her eyes closed, she sighed. Her life was changing and her relationships were growing.

After a few more precious moments of introspection, she hit the shower. As the warm water cascaded down her face, her chest hummed and sang to her in the most unfamiliar way. It wasn't her mom's song, and certainly not Adam's. This rumble was different. It was a simultaneous pull and influx that worried her simply because it was new. If she didn't know any better, she'd think her cells were growing abnormally. She was no doctor, but she knew her body.

THE PROMENADE

CARLY AND JO spent the afternoon flower-shopping for the wedding. Though Jo had tried to get everything finalized weeks prior, Carly hadn't found herself to be in a celebratory shopping mood. She preferred something simpler, but Jo wouldn't hear of it.

"What do you think of these, honey?" Jo asked her.

"They're pretty."

"You've said that about every flower."

"Because they're all pretty," she chuckled indifferently.

"Well, when you know, you know…come with me." Jo escorted her to the back of the flower shop where most customers rarely made it to before falling in love with the traditional arrangements displayed on the main showroom floor.

Jo didn't say a word and hushed the shop attendant as well when she'd attempted to assist them further. Instead, she allowed Carly to feel her way through. After a few seconds, Carly paused in front of the flowerbed of orange and yellow California poppies, and smiled wistfully.

"Should've guessed that," Jo huffed with a grin. She turned to the sales representative to request options.

After paying for their selections, they strolled along the street. The sun warmed their shoulders nicely as Zsita refreshed their skin.

"Thank you…for…everything." Carly said.

Jo reached over and embraced her future daughter-in-love. "Every event is just an excuse to spend more time with you without appearing clingy."

"Jo," Carly paused her stride, "you don't need an excuse. I love you and I love spending time with you." "*Please, don't read my thoughts,*" she thought, near tears.

Jo silently grasped her hands. They interlocked fingers and continued walking along the Promenade.

"*I'm with you Карли,*" Dauma spoke from a part of Carly she couldn't seem to reach. Jo decided not to relay the message and squeezed Carly's hand a bit tighter before they entered a restaurant for some lunch.

"*Why are we taught that losing a parent at an early age is normal?*" Jo thought.

"*I'm tired of watching the world be normal. I'll never wake up one day and not miss them. Half of who I am is gone away from me forever and I'll never accept that as natural,*" Carly thought in a grievous tone as they were seated.

Jo was a tad taken aback since she hadn't spoken. "Let's scratch this Meridian ceremony and you two can elope."

"Nah. Grief robs me of the simplest joys on most days, but I won't rob anyone else."

Jo rubbed her back.

"I once imagined exchanging vows on the beach, but with Adam's latest inherited ability, that might not work out too well," Carly giggled.

"Are you sure, honey? He can fly you anywhere in the world. Not to mention Mariah can…"

"Even if we ported to another planet, they wouldn't be there, so—" She wouldn't deny Jo the opportunity to see her son wedded in fairytale bliss just because she grieved over the loss of her parents. The depth of her pain told her she'd grieve until the life left her body, so she searched her soul to find a way to manage it, but there was no explaining that to anyone. It wasn't anyone else's time to grieve.

Jo kissed her on the cheek.

Carly was so much younger than the average person was when they lost their parents. Not to mention, it was usually due to slow progressing illnesses versus a sudden hijack without any closure or goodbye.

Carly's father, Erik, was acquired by the Iksha just months before Dauma had forcefully merged herself with Carly. Within a small span of time, Carly's entire world came crashing down.

"I've gotta grow up just as much as Adam does," Carly finalized when their food arrived.

They shared a smile and held each other tight.

CARLY SAT IN her living room gazing at the college acceptance letters splayed across the coffee table. She'd delayed starting her first semester after the Dylan fiasco because she'd felt needed around Meridian until their daily lives normalized. Well, it was now time to move on to the next stage of her life.

She snatched the letters up and glared at them before shuffling them again. She knew immediately she wouldn't leave the state. Ivy Leagues were ideal for the best jobs and such, but she preferred to make her own way career-wise, so she tossed those acceptances aside and slouched backwards. The nearest Uni was Mojave, where Crystal was now a sophomore. It didn't have the best programs for Law majors, but she knew it was the smartest choice.

"Hey, Carly." Vikki plopped down on the sofa.

"Hey, Vik."

"You hungry?"

"Not really."

"You're never hungry, but you've gotta eat. I'll make you something light." Vikki patted her knee and started towards the kitchen.

"Hey, Vik. Have you ever attended college?"

"Yeah. Graduated with honors comparable to Summa cum laude."

"Really?" Carly sat up, intrigued.

"Uh huh."

"What was it like?"

"Well," Vikki breathed, reclaiming her seat, "it wasn't as laxed as American universities. You know, frat parties and such, but it was where I grew the most in my early adult life."

Carly nodded. "Like, self-discovery?"

"Exactly. My studies were there, but more as plain ole duty. Whereas, the environment and the people helped me navigate myself and learn adult humanity in ways I didn't know before. It was a very important step in my life."

"Wow, that's so awesome. What was your major?"

"I double-majored in Sociology and Business."

"Oh my gosh, Vik. I can't believe I never thought to ask you these things before."

"It's okay. Most people thought I was truly a blonde airhead. Apparently, many still do. Guess I played the role a little too well," she laughed.

"Not as well as you might've thought because I knew you were smarter than you put off."

Vikki smirked and glanced at the college acceptance letters on the table. "Don't let anyone make your decisions for you. It's a self-journey. Not a joint one." She winked and sauntered off.

Carly grabbed the University of Mojave letter and levitated the others into the trash. She'd made her decision and was grateful that she had someone like Crys already matriculated to guide her along.

But first, the wedding.

tapestry

adam

ANOTHER DAWN PURIFIED Adam's cyclonal life as he ogled the swirling sky from his bedroom window. His days were saturated with people who likely wouldn't bother to brush the dust of frustration from his shoulders if he hadn't proven himself to be a token of exotic rarity. Of course, Carly, his mother, and Vikki were the exceptions.

He inhaled the moisture in the air while he motioned the terrace jacuzzi waters vertically with his biokenretic energy; a sight any normal person would flee in terror from, but it comforted him.

The whispering clouds didn't know which way they were going or where they'd end up until their master commanded them. It was a peace that owned his heart until just under a year ago when adulthood responsibilities slapped him out of the pretense of high school afterglow. He was getting married soon, so his time was now devoted to bettering himself for the next chapter of life.

His thoughts scattered once again into the what-if realm. Where would he be if Carly hadn't moved to Piure during fall semester of his senior year at Keetering High? If she hadn't come, that would've left his twin brother, Dylan, roaming free, torturing him and others.

God had certainly moved the chess pieces of their lives intricately from birth. Adam managed to be adopted by a family who just happened to reside in the same city as Carly's Aunt Vera, which lead him to believe they were destined before they could form thoughts. What if Carly had run away instead of obeying her parents? They never would've met, and if they'd never met, what kind of monster would Dylan have turned him into? Would he have drowned in darkness? Most importantly, would he know how to love or even be willing to?

Adam's 18-year-old mind was once so dark, very little light passed through it, and instead of fighting it, he'd accepted what he once thought was his fate. He'd once resented humanity so intensely that he regularly envisioned mass exterminations as the best cure for a fresh start, second only to evolution. The day Carly Wit breezed into his English class is the day he decided to try and reach the light. It was through her he'd discovered his Russian lineage and mutated genes that gave him supernatural abilities.

Finding that evolution had already begun, he'd abandoned his dark thoughts for the sake of joy and hope. For a while, all he'd wanted was simply to love Carly and reprogram his thought processes to allow a little light inside, no matter how much it stung. It didn't happen overnight, and he was still adjusting while he learned to make better choices. Although, still a fierce introvert, Adam surrounded himself with people who didn't trigger his anxieties, and that's a hell of an accomplishment.

He rolled over onto his side to absorb the rising sun, the humblest boss in existence. It gently made its way to the forefront of the sky without offending other energies or scaring off the moon. He neatly flattened the cooled jacuzzi waters and sighed.

While young at heart, death was so distant, almost like it was never going to happen. It was tucked far away where a person could gloriously take their mortality for granted. But with each passing day, he felt the Descendants inched closer to an end, if nothing changed.

Descendants were the offspring of women who bore children with extraordinary abilities over a thousand years ago in Sintashta, Russia. No one knew what caused the mutation or why it only existed in seven bloodlines. Adam descended from the seventh; the Rozovsky Bloodline.

Since discovering his origin, his heart had aged a thousand years, and a thousand more after rediscovering bits of a past he was never meant to learn about, but wanted so desperately to.

It has now been nearly two years since Carly rejoined him and his twin. With their merger, Dylan's memories randomly surfaced in his mind as if they were his own. They triggered Adam's own childhood memories, and the two swayed back and forth on a teeter-totter tapestry where Dylan told him all the truths he would never have believed had Dylan spoken them in the flesh. It was easier to believe someone when their ability to lie was reduced to zero.

Though he had once despised the thought of having any of Dylan's darkness inside him, he now grieved the loss of his brother because Dylan gained his freedom only to lose his life to his own family. The betrayal of that was maddening.

Carly had insisted they were never meant to split and the only way to *cure* them, was to rejoin them. Rather than wasting time being angry or resentful of something he couldn't change, he learned to be grateful that he could now protect Dylan eternally, and they would now exist together, rather than be divided by the evils of the Iksha or a humanity that detested them.

He rested his head against the pillow, preparing to empty his introverted mind, so he could be as open as possible, in a private community of evolved, mutated Descendants.

leighton, california

the poppy field

ADAM AND CARLY laid swaddled in fleece blankets amidst the orange poppies in Leighton. With the Hex Ksenyia had casted around the city for protection, only Adam and Rye could pass through it freely. Today, their moment was owed to a port, courtesy of Rye.

Carly's thoughts were a burning mystery to Adam, so he nuzzled his face against hers and sighed, wishing desperately to one day gain access to her memories.

"Before you moved to California, did you ever imagine you'd be getting married at 18?" he asked, hoping she hadn't developed a case of cold feet.

"*You're* 18. I'm 19, and I didn't even imagine I'd ever have a boyfriend. So, nah, never in a zillion years. But 18 or 48, it doesn't really matter. Your own mother has proven that to you."

"I'm 18 and ¾," he corrected her, "and of course it matters."

"In what way?"

"Statistically speaking—"

"Pause. Not interested in those. The world should've lost count long ago with how many times humans have been wrong, especially about other humans."

"I just don't want you to regret it," he said.

She tugged his face to hers. "I will never regret spending my life with you. It's the mere thought to the contrary I can't bear. I don't need a man-made government to validate us."

He didn't want her to change her mind, but he needed her to be sure, and that involved imagining the worst. "I think my mom is more excited about it than we are."

"I love her just the way she is," Carly giggled. "A shopaholic with minimal sales resistance, and a credit card that never gets declined."

"Yeah, but buying a private jet is somehow a frivolous purchase?" he moaned.

"For a teenager, it is. The chopper is good enough for now."

"It wouldn't just be for me. It'd be for everyone at Meridian. They only look like teens, but they're very much adults. Way older than we are." Adam's mind was still blown by the age gaps.

"Only Sage, Evan, and Val are trained to pilot aircraft," Carly shrugged. "Imagine the squabbles."

"You mean, besides the regular ones?"

"Err, right. You've got a point. None of our friends are good at pacing themselves."

"Right, like 'let's take this relationship nice and slow,' said no teen ever," Adam mocked.

"They're not teens, remember?"

"They act like teens." Adam rolled his eyes.

"Another good point."

Gazing around, he envisioned one day building Carly a home in her favorite place in the world, the poppy field. As a kid, he'd always fantasized about leaving Piure behind. Well, Earth really. He'd dreamt of floating among the cosmos in outer space where an interplanetary pull told him he belonged — lightyears away. He forced that impossibility from his thoughts.

Growing up sure can suck the fun out of things, he thought.

They enjoyed laughter and wonderful solitude while waiting for Rye to retrieve them, though they were in no hurry.

"Adam, there's something else I've been meaning to tell you—"

Rye appeared with her hands on her hips, immediately impatient. "Are you two lovebirds ready to go?"

"Hi, Mariah. How are you?" Adam teased, eager to aggravate her.

"Ready to get back to Kane." She stuck her tongue out at him.

Carly snickered.

Rye grabbed their wrists and they were back home in the gardens of Meridian.

CARLY WAS CURLED up in the corner with a book, wearing the reading gloves Jo had gifted her a few years back, with Maroon 5 on repeat in the background. One would think they didn't own real furniture by the way she preferred the floor pillows.

"Babe, I'm really tired of his voice," Adam bemoaned. "Just because I share name and likeness with this dude doesn't mean…"

"How sad for you," she uttered with a sullen expression, neglecting to lift her eyes from her book.

He smacked his lips and covered his ears with his palms.

She smirked, completely unbothered.

He decided to practice extending his cloak when a thought materialized in his mind. Lately, he'd identified with everyone else's cores individually. With ease, in fact. He tinkered with her source while she obliviously read her book in the corner, almost like nudging his forefinger against a dense substance. He blanketed her with his energy—absorbing, amplifying, and ultimately, suppressing…or attempting to.

She glowered up at him with her LR blazing and revolving like a reactor. "Adam, what are you doing?"

"I don't really even know. What does it feel like?"

"Like you're trying to drain my energy."

"Am I hurting you?"

"It tingles, but no."

"Wait, you said *trying*. Is it not working?"

"We're synced, remember?"

"Oh yeah, duh."

"You have to be careful. You don't know how it'll affect other Descendants."

"That's precisely why I need to practice this—whatever *this* is."

"I'm sure it's suppression, and you can't just experiment on someone without their consent."

He punched himself in the thigh. She was right, as usual. He could've hurt her. He could be so absent-minded, he scared himself sometimes. They didn't have any Descendant prisoners at Meridian to practice on, so he couldn't properly develop Dylan's amplification or suppression abilities.

"We're not even sure Dylan had the ability to suppress. It was a working theory," Carly reminded him.

"A very logical one," he countered as a light bulb illuminated in his mind. "I wonder if the Afrax council has any detainees I can experiment on."

"Adam!"

"What? It's not like they're innocent."

"What if it were Vikki?"

"It *was* Vikki."

"Yes, and it was wrong to torture her. You'd be just as wrong to experiment on a captive."

"Babe, let's keep it all the way real. We're talking about Iksha militants who tried or even possibly succeeded at killing Descendants. How innocent could they be?"

"Allegedly."

"Come *on!*" he stood and threw his arms towards the ceiling.

"You asked me to keep it real. What's real is we know the council lies. As far as we know, the captives are innocent of any wrongdoing."

"If they've ever sided with the Iksha, they couldn't be, and you know it."

"Vikki once did."

"That's different."

"The difference is our knowing her story versus not knowing others' stories of how they were deceived into siding with the Iksha."

He sighed. "You once said you wanted them all dead no matter their story. Now you don't want me to practice a trait that could possibly save all our lives in battle? You're confusing me."

"I just—the thought of harming innocent people doesn't sit right with me. I said a lot through my grief, but really, I just want to be sure."

Adam recalled when Dauma had told him Carly would revert back to the wholesome girl she'd raised her to be.

"And Fenyx?" Adam asked.

Her heat upsurged. "She confessed and there was irrefutable evidence. I just…"

"There's a way to be sure. I can access their memories and my mom can listen to their thoughts. We're not helpless to discover the truth."

"Okay, fine. I just don't want to think about it right now."

"Well, that's new. She usually thinks herself into a stupor," he thought.

"What's wrong?"

"I don't know. I just—I'm going for a walk." She tossed her book and hastily dove off their balcony.

He remained seated, confused. Maybe she was having second thoughts about getting married. Or maybe she —*Jesus, Adam!* He flew out of the bedroom after her, scooping her into his arms before swooping deeper into the budding brush.

"I'm so stupid and I can't apologize enough for that."

"Adam, I…" Tears fell from her eyes and her hands shook.

He grabbed them and wrapped his arms around her. "Never mind a ridiculous ceremony. We don't need one. We don't even need to get married. All I need is you. As long as I have you…"

"I tell myself I'm fine without them every day, but it's a lie. I don't think I'll ever be okay. I don't. I'll always be broken." She hyperventilated.

"It's okay." He wished he could calm her the way she calmed everyone else. He pummeled her face with kisses while allowing her to express her emotions. He rarely thought of the absence of his own father during the ceremony because he'd made his peace with Mark's passing, but it was wrong of him to expect Carly to do the same. He wasn't as close with Mark and had buried that regret where it couldn't stab him. Carly and Dauma may as well had been one person as close as they were. His heart ached for her.

Rye appeared out of thin air, per her usual. "Hey, Car. Adam. What the… why are you…why is she crying? What the hell did you do to her?"

"As if I'd ever hurt her."

"He didn't do anything, Rye. Just going through the motions. What's up?"

Mariah scowled at him. "Sorry to pop up but Jo's looking for you."

"Why didn't she call us? Why'd she send you?" Adam asked.

"Don't know. Didn't ask. Why does a billionaire dress like a bum every day? We'll never know." She shrugged, glaring at his jeans and hoodie.

"Rye, your face is doing that thing I so despise," Adam said.

"What? Being fabulous?"

"No, emitting sound."

"Whatever."

Carly giggled.

Adam just wanted Rye to shut her stupid perfect face for once.

They grabbed her hand and she ported them to Evan and Rye's living room before zipping up the stairs, back into Kane's arms.

Jo bounced down with a conflicted expression on her face, revealing that she hadn't expected Adam to tag along.

"Mom, are you okay? What's going on?" Adam tried checking her over, presuming something to be physically wrong, but she wouldn't let him touch her.

"Well, we have counseling in a bit and…"

"Mom, that couldn't have been an emergency."

"Rye isn't taking us, so we'll need to leave much earlier. But um, I needed Carly."

"What's wrong, Jo?" Carly grabbed her hand.

"Can we go for a quick walk?"

"Sure."

They looked back at a bewildered Adam on their way out the rear patio door. As soon as they were out of earshot, Carly asked if she was okay again.

"I need your mom's advice about something that I'm not ready to discuss with Adam yet. That's all."

"But…"

"I know and I'm sorry to involve you, honey. I just…I know no one else but Dauma can help me with this. I trust her."

Carly nodded. They traveled to their favorite flower bed of purple cosmos where Jo had an in-depth conversation with Dauma, leaving Carly gloriously in the dark on her mother's responses.

On their brief walk back, Jo made small talk because she understood the predicament she'd put Carly in.

"So many people assume I named Adam after the first man or some ancestor, but I named him for adamantine."

"Really?"

"Yeah," she chuckled. "From the moment I held him, he exuberated this aura of strength. He rarely ever cried and was beyond adept. Looking back on it, I know why…but then, I was surprised, proud, and…so scared."

"Scared of what?"

"That he wouldn't need me or that I'd fail him. I never felt good enough for him. He had this special energy about him and I was just regular ole JoAnn."

Carly stopped and faced her. "Descendant parents who share the same genetic code as their children haven't done even half as good a job as you did raising Adam. If it weren't for you, his fate might've been…well, grim."

They embraced and hastened their stride, arriving at the house, where Adam sat on the sofa. His grimacing expression deepened at the sight of their interlocked hands. He was annoyed with being left out of their rendezvous. He bounced up and headed for the front door.

"I'll be back with the truck." He didn't wait for Carly this time. He hastily sauntered off, leaving Evan's front door ajar.

"Adam," Carly whispered.

"Let him go, honey. It's a part of him growing up. He has to learn that he doesn't have the right to know everything."

Carly outwardly expressed her uncertainty about not going after him because he came for her every time she was conflicted or hurt. "This feels like abandonment and I'll never do that." She darted out after him, catching him as he rounded the block.

"Adam, wait!"

"It's okay," he said without looking back or slowing down.

"Can you slow down and talk to me?"

He considered ignoring her request for a millisecond before turning around. "Look, I'm sorry I left like that."

"I'm sorry about the thing with your mom, I…"

"No, no. You don't owe me any apologies. You didn't do anything wrong and neither did she. This is just me learning to change. It isn't easy, but I'm doing it."

"I'm not keeping secrets. I promise."

"I know. I trust you. I'm just ready to be better. I'm tired of feeling the wrong thing. That's why I rushed out the door. I wanted to get the truck so we can get to counseling."

"You sure?"

"Yeah." He wished he could fly them there.

They linked fingers and walked the rest of the way home together.

He'd told a half-truth. He was jealous *and* angry. When he'd approached his mother, ready to make right whatever was wrong, only to hear he wasn't needed, it made him feel useless. Replaced.

So much was piling up on him emotionally, but he was unwilling to mess up anymore when it came to he and Carly's relationship. He was already still holding on to what he'd thought was a harmless omission in the beginning, but could now cause damage if revealed. He'd wanted to tell her he was a virgin. He knew it wasn't the worst thing in the world to be, but it was just so embarrassing. He'd refrained from correcting her for so long, it was beginning to feel like he was betraying her.

He was furious enough to tsunami the entire community, but for now, he'd settle for psychotherapy.

dual healing

adam

ADAM DROVE Jo to their weekly joint counseling session in midtown. The two-hour ride was silent, which was torturous for him. He'd always enjoyed conversing with her without the others around but that had become rarer as of late. Not to mention, he was starting to feel she didn't want him around as much. He gulped down his heartache.

She stared out of the window, looking through the scenery, at whatever was on her mind. She didn't even register their arrival until Adam opened her door.

"Mom?"

"Oh." She unbuckled her seatbelt and dragged herself behind him into the building.

Their therapist, Dr. Hiram Sonner, greeted them, and dove right into their session.

"Adam, how are you feeling today?"

He swiftly glanced at Jo before responding. "I'm good."

"JoAnn, how are you?"

"Fine, thanks."

"Okay, well let's pick up where we left off last."

Dr. Sonner's thoughts were frightfully boring, so Jo easily ignored them. He narrated the session instead of welcoming interaction, which escaped her completely.

"JoAnn?"

"Oh, I'm sorry. I zoned out."

"Does that happen often when you're at home?" Dr. Sonner asked.

"What?"

"You zoning out."

"Oh, no. Just so much has happened lately and…" she sighed, regretting the slip, but was ready to release the beast of secrecy.

"Mom," Adam sighed, presuming to know what was bothering her. "Turning 19 doesn't mean I'm leaving you, just like turning 18 didn't." *But getting married might*, he thought.

"Mm," she managed in response.

"JoAnn, is that what's on your mind?"

"Not at the moment, no."

"What's pulling your attention away from this session?"

She sucked in a breath. "Evan asked me to marry him."

The room fell silent, but her head was annoyingly full of the doctor's *oh boy* thoughts.

Dr. Sonner waited patiently for a response from Adam. When no one said anything, he reopened the lines of communication. "Adam, how do you feel about that?"

"I'm happy for them. I just…I really wish this had been a private moment." Adam smiled uncomfortably.

"I didn't know how to tell you. I know you don't…"

"Mom, you always taught me to allow others to grow from what I think I know about them. I don't need to like Evan because I love you." He paused to be more careful with his words when a thought hit him. "You announced your engagement in counseling because you were afraid of how I'd react?" His own presumptions hurt him.

"JoAnn, is that true?"

"No, maybe, I don't…know." She didn't make eye contact with anyone, still stoically peering out the window. She mindlessly fiddled with her fingers.

"Mom?"

"Hmm."

"What's wrong?"

"Nothing is wrong. Ksshhh, we should've rescheduled. Can we end this session early? I need some time alone, to think."

"Sure," Dr. Sonner agreed. "I'll see you both the same time next week."

"Thank you, Doctor." Adam shook his hand before silently escorting his mother to the truck. He swiftly blinked the doctor's bland memories away to focus on her.

He didn't understand why she seemed solemn, given how much she loved Evan. He secured her in the passenger seat, hopped in, and sped out of the parking lot. She continued glaring silently out of the window until he couldn't take it anymore and pulled over.

"Mom, please talk to me. What's really wrong? Why are you pulling away from me?"

This was as good a place as any, and after a full minute, she responded.

"I haven't told him yes."

"What? Why?"

"Now that I've taken too long to give him an answer, he's heartbroken."

"How long ago did he propose?"

"Almost a year…and again a few months ago."

"Mom!"

"You wouldn't understand, honey. You're not a parent, barely an adult, and I can't even talk to you about your father."

"I'm sorry. I'm trying. I can…let me try."

She sighed because she hadn't meant to hurt him. She never wanted to hurt her baby boy, but he reached out for her hand and she jerked away again.

"What don't you want me to see?"

"They're my personal memories and no child should see their parent… um, parenting."

"Can you help me understand then?"

"Well, at the time, I didn't know how to tell him I wanted to wait until after your wedding and honeymoon. I'm having so much fun helping Carly plan everything. By the time I managed the words, he was already hurt. Now I don't think he even wants to marry me anymore." She valiantly restrained her tears.

"Trust me mom, he does. But why didn't you say yes and then delay the ceremony, if you…"

"Because my answer wasn't yes…isn't yes. The timing of the entire proposal seemed to be a stab at you and Carly's moment. I'm a thousand percent sure of him, just not of the proposal." A tear escaped her.

Adam needed context, so he rubbed her hand silently.

She allowed him, accepting that her memories were her best hope of him understanding her predicament.

Images of Evan's solemn face overtook his vision. The man was truly crushed by her hesitance. He watched as Evan kissed her goodbye before she'd jumped in Adam's truck. He maintained contact, hoping to see more, but she snatched her hand away before he travelled too far back in her mind.

Instead of internalizing the actions she took, he opted for understanding. Her happiness meant more to him than his own.

"Is that what you needed to talk to Carly about?"

"No." It wasn't a lie because she had needed to talk to Dauma. Not Carly.

"What are you thinking and feeling, Mom?"

"I want to be sure that anyone I marry will get along with my son, and I don't feel the two of you like each other. It'd be like before with—"

"That's not fair. Dad didn't know who I'd grow up to be…I didn't know about BK puberty, Dylan was in my head, something was wrong with me then and I didn't know…"

"It wasn't just about you. It was an entire situation involving three people. Well, more if you count his mistresses."

"Mom."

"That's neither here nor there, but Evan is…different. I'm different. I'm not a 19-year-old kid this time. I'm not doing what the world tells me I should. I'm irrevocably in love, but I don't need to marry him."

"But you want to."

"I do, but I won't choo…look, it's okay if you don't like him."

"I don't like him or dislike him."

"Indifference is the equivalent of not liking him. It means you don't care. I can't hear his thoughts, so I don't know if he likes you either, and I'm not forcing the two of you to play nice. Either it happens or it doesn't. I'll make my decisions accordingly." She patted his clothed forearm and smiled. "Now let's go home."

"Mom—"

"Home, son."

After dropping her off at Evan's, he made a beeline for his personal therapist, Dr. Aubrey Blake, requiring an emergency solo session.

THE DAYS AND weeks that followed Adam's and Jo's revealing therapy session, she'd fought to maintain her jolly glow, but Adam wasn't fooled one bit. With Dr. Blake's help, he finally understood his mother's confliction. He couldn't be a better person if he didn't apply what he learned.

Though he was prepared to simply force a relationship with Evan for his mother's sake, he knew it would hurt her more to learn he'd faked it when his cloak failed him, as it occasionally did. Plus, he wouldn't have bettered himself, and would only have wasted everyone's time, including his own.

He slowly, but ultimately, banished his resistance against Evan. The smooth transition was owed in part to Dr. Sonner, who'd helped him understand his jealousy of his mother and why it intensified with the absence of his father. Turned out it wasn't jealousy at all. It was merely a son's love, amplified after loss of life. Although he regretted rejecting Mark's love, his mother was indeed in love with her late husband, and it shattered her world to lose him, first to other women, and then completely.

Adam felt it was his duty to step up in Mark's absence. Though Dr. Sonner said it was honorable of him, he reminded him that for anyone else it wouldn't be a problem to step back into the role of the son, but Adam's psychological irregularities made him a special case.

At any rate, he was now ready to allow Evan to exist in their lives on his own merit. Given how resistant he had been the past two years, it was only right that he made the first move. To his delight, Carly agreed with everything he shared with her, and she was fully supportive of the entire healing process.

After showering and dressing, he walked over to Evan and Rye's. He knocked while swallowing his nerves.

Evan yanked the door open. "Hey, your mother's upstairs. Come in."

Adam stepped into the foyer. Evan closed the door and turned to walk away.

"Uh, actually…I'm here to see you."

Evan pivoted around on his heels.

"Okayyy…what's up?" His brow furrowed and he was on guard.

"All pretense aside, we haven't gotten along much and I'm fully to blame for it. I didn't want to confuse you by suddenly warming up to you while delaying an apology. I'm sorry for being so selfish about your relationship with my mom."

Evan was floored, speechless. For two years, he had endured the jealous emotional tantrums of a little boy who now stood before him as a mature young man. Evan's pessimism leaned towards owing this scene to Adam's engagement to Carly or a guilty conscience, but when Adam's eyes remained on his, he decided not to resist the change. He'd hoped for this moment for a long time.

"We can talk about it here, go out, or never talk about it again. The ball is in your court."

Instead of offering Adam a handshake, he hugged him. "Let's go out and get some fresh air."

"Where to?"

"Well, I can't take you to a bar. 18 is a far cry from 21."

"I'm 18 ¾ and she doesn't have to know." A mischievous grin spread across Adam's impossibly perfect face.

"Uh yeah, not happ'nin. In 2.75 years, we can revisit this conversation."

Adam laughed.

"Let's just grab a bite to eat."

"Sounds good."

"I'll run up and tell her. Be right back."

"Sure thing."

Adam listened to his mother gasp disbelief with a smirk on his face. Evan reappeared with his jacket and car keys. Jo slowly descended the staircase, worried they'd end up punching each other out with no one to break them up.

"Adam?" She approached him with caution.

"Adam, I'll meet you out front," Evan said while shooting Jo a glance to warn her not to coddle Adam's feelings.

When the inner door leading to the garage slammed closed, Adam responded by grabbing her hands. "Mom, this is what I want."

"But do you want it because I want it? Or because…"

"Mom, you're overthinking."

"Well, my brain is kinda wired that way."

"Tuh, truly," he joked.

"Oh hush."

"Obviously, I want you to be happy, but I've always wanted that," he said. "What's changed?"

"Me. You. Us. We're all changing. Our family dynamic is different and I've finally accepted that's okay. I loved…love Mark…Dad, more than I was willing to admit because that would've meant I'd have to accept how horrible I was to him the few years before he died. I was so lost in anger over him hurting you, and frustrated with BK puberty. It was easier when things were in limbo because I didn't have to face the regret of how things ended. I don't know when I stopped being afraid of the pain, but I'm just glad to face it now because I can grow. We can."

"Wow." She allowed a tear to gather in the corner of her eye.

"Save those for another day. This is just the beginning." He kissed her cheek.

"Gotta send Dr. Blake some flowers," she said.

They shared a laugh, embraced, and then he vanished faster than she'd ever seen.

"Guess I don't need to call shotgun," Adam said as he slapped the dashboard of Evan's muscle sports car. "Let's go!"

Evan sped off out of the community like a mad man to a diner several miles away. Their conversation flowed like water the entire ride. After they were seated in a comfy booth, Evan slaughtered the elephant squeezing its way into the room.

"I owe you an apology too."

"No, you don't. I…"

"Yes, I do. I was childish in the beginning and stubborn for the stretch."

Adam opened his mouth to interject but Evan stopped him.

"I'm 58 years old."

Adam relaxed, grateful that Evan finally felt comfortable enough to be open and forthcoming. Learning his age for the first time was shocking because Evan could easily pass for twenty-one, depending on who was judging.

"I'm no expert on anything but I've been alive much longer than you. Long enough for me to have handled the situation much differently. It's just…I never thought I'd meet your mother or anyone like her, so I didn't care how anyone else felt about us being together. I was too happy to have her in my life.

"After my mother was captured, life just became something to endure until it was over, ya know? The only reason I lived was for Mariah. I couldn't leave her alone in this place called Earth. A place I had come to despise because everyone was so selfish. Descendants had evolved into an egotistical mess and I didn't wanna have anything to do with the BK gene or any abilities. I was ready to die of old age and be done with it all."

A theory formulated in Adam's mind, but he repressed it so he could just listen; not simply wait for his turn to talk.

"Being around humans and Descendants alike drained my energy for decades until I arrived at a crossroad. Survive for Mariah or live for me. I chose to live. Making that one decision led to…um, to my um…"

Adam leaned forward. "Take your time."

"My absorption ability." He paused for backlash.

"Whoa," is all Adam managed. It wasn't the trait that paused him. "How did you know what it was when it happened?"

"I wound up in space, suffocating. No B.S." He chuckled.

"Wow, that had to be scary! I can't even grasp it. How…wha-what did you do?"

The server interrupted them to take their orders.

"Man, I can't even tell you how scared I was. Thought it was a dream until I couldn't wake up. Every time I thought of a place, I wound up there until I accepted I was porting. After puking my guts out, I focused on our dorm at Afrax and poof, I was back. Mariah was still asleep right where I'd left her on the couch. I had dozed off with her head in my lap."

"Is it involuntary?"

"The first time it seemed so because I had no idea I pulled on her core, but no."

"So, it wasn't just her energy?"

"It was her entire primary ability. I was so relieved when it wore off. I jumped away from her for months afterwards." He laughed at the memory. "I eventually got over my fear when I learned to return the grab but needless to say, she threatened to beat it out of me if I didn't tell her why I wouldn't let her near me, so I did. I never divulged it to the council, so it still isn't on record."

"Then how does Carly kno — never mind."

"Right. Those two with their vow of honesty. At first, I was upset. Like, be honest about yourselves, not about business that isn't yours. But then I grew to trust Carly and accepted she'd eventually tell you."

Adam smirked because Carly had only hinted about it, but she'd never told him the story behind it. She likely didn't know that part.

"Sooo, Rye's always been a grouchy bully huh?"

"Since the womb, man."

They shared a laugh.

Adam saw Evan for the empath he was. Carly was the only other empath he'd ever met. They seemed to be rare gems. Jealousy is truly a disease because it robbed him of getting to know a decent guy who sincerely loved his mom.

"I don't want to 20-question you about your ability, but I'm damned curious."

"Okay, let's trade off then."

"Oh, bet. What do you wanna know?"

"How I've longed for this day!"

The server filled their table with plates of food and refreshed their beverages.

"Let's start high. Did Carly really kill your twin?" Evan dipped a steak fry into ketchup.

"Kind of, but not really."

Evan took a huge bite of his cheeseburger and smacked loudly. "What do you mean? Did he trip and fall into death?"

"Haha, no. She merged us."

"What?" His mouth hung open.

"Yeah, we began as one and we were abnormally split as embryos, so Carly put us back together again."

"Honestly that wasn't anywhere near what I expected to hear. That is just… mind blowing. Unbelievable, really."

"How can I prove it to you?"

"I don't think you can because I never witnessed his abilities. I'm more amazed Carly is capable of something like that." Evan's eyes wistfully wandered off.

"Does it scare you?"

"No, it comforts me that she's so powerful, like her mother. I'd always believed someone like Carly would eventually exist. Besides Rye and your mother, Carly is my closest friend. I'm glad it's her."

Adam wasn't surprised by that. He actually wondered if they'd make better friends for each other than her and Kane, though Evan seemed to be more of a father figure than friend, in his opinion. Nevertheless, Evan was safer than Kane.

"Okay, my turn then." Adam shoved French fries into his mouth. "You never wondered how your trait showed up so long after puberty?"

"Of course, I wondered until wondering wasted my time. It seemed to have spontaneously flourished. Don't know if I always could but just never tried or what."

"So, all you have to do is touch someone and you absorb their abilities?"

"Short answer, yes. But it doesn't work the same from person to person. For instance, I've hugged Carly many times and I get nada from her. With Krill, I absorbed his weapons but not his DLC titanium skin. Got Dauma's bio-scan for a few and skipped around Afrax silently assessing everyone's power levels, which was how our little clique formed, but I'll tell you about that another time. That was fun until she snatched it back and banned me."

"Wait what?" Adam leaned in closer.

"Yeah, man. That woman played no games and she was the only one who noticed my pilfering. She told me if I did it again, she'd melt me. Needless to say, I avoided her like the plague so there'd be no mishaps."

Adam erupted in roaring laughter.

"One day I accidentally grazed her and thought for sure I was dead meat, but then nothing happened. She'd effectively banned me so I couldn't grab from her, even by accident. All she did was grin at me and I nearly pissed myself."

Adam laughed even louder.

"Yeah, I miss her. Anyway, the process only lasts for a few minutes at a time. Not long enough for a Descendant to get too worried, but it does make absorbing Mariah's port extremely dangerous because it could've worn off while I was floating in space and then boom, dead ass Ev."

"Wanna take Zsita for a ride?"

"As tempting as that sounds, it might wear off while I'm midair."

"Then don't go too far. Just float. Come on!"

Up for the challenge, Evan slammed a large bill down on the table and brushed the crumbs from his lap.

"Let's go, young buck."

Evan drove them back towards Meridian, where there was an abundance of vacant land, and brush they'd bought out to ensure they'd never have neighbors. They stepped out of the car and faced each other. Adam bravely offered Evan his palms.

Evan playfully did a few jumping jacks, wrung his hands, and shook his head free of fear.

"Okay, I got this."

Both wondered which ability Evan would hijack, but Adam was hopeful he got Zsita because she was a force like no other, and it'd be awesome for another Descendant to witness just how much power it took to control her. He was beyond curious to see Evan take her on, and excited to share this experience with him.

Evan grabbed his palms and waited to be surprised by the gift he received.

Adam's energy level took a dip but he couldn't decide what was missing. He communicated with Zsita, and she responded, so that wasn't it. He hurled a burst of atomic breath into a tree.

Evan ducked. "Damn, that one would've been cool to play with."

"You'd think. How do you feel? Any different?"

"A spike but nothing else."

"Okay, touch me."

"Can you reword that, please?"

"I meant, grab my hand."

"Well, if I do that, whatever I absorbed will return to you, then we'll never know."

"Okay, so you didn't see any visions or any hallucinations?"

"Nope."

Adam snickered when he realized what Evan's likely absorbed. "You've got my cloak."

"No shit? How do you know?"

"Process of elimination. I mean, if you feel nothing else, it has to be that."

"One way to know for sure," Evan taunted mischievously.

Everything went black for Adam.

"Dammit, man! Really?" Adam groaned.

"YES!" Evan hopped up and down like a kid, ecstatic to finally blind the one he never could. "Woot, woot!" He danced the shoot until Adam brought him back to reality.

"Okay, can you let me see again?"

"Well, since you asked nicely."

The first thing Adam saw was a cheesing Evan in a goofy pose.

"And here I thought you'd be disappointed," Adam said.

"Heck no. Can't believe that little nothing you can't even feel protects you from so much. Better learn to appreciate it."

"Trust me, I do. You're marrying the main reason why I'm grateful."

Evan's facial expression morphed. "Yeah, man about that. I…"

"Congratulations, Ev. For real."

"Thanks. I mean, she hasn't…well anyway, I'm sorry I didn't…"

"We're past that."

"Are we?"

"Let's shake on it."

Evan grabbed his hand.

"Ha! Got'cha!" Adam danced backwards.

Evan rumbled in laughter. "Nice one." He smacked Adam upside the head, stole his cloak again, and ran.

"You can't outrun me, remember?"

"I can if you can't see. Take that!" Evan jutted his fingers.

A blind Adam fumbled around in the darkness for a minute until he closed his eyes and focused.

"Oh my," Adam grinned.

Evan slowed down and turned around, wondering what Adam was smiling about. In a split second, Adam was floating directly in front of him.

"Hello there."

"But…how?"

"Return my energy and I'll gladly tell you all about it."

Evan touched him, prematurely ending the absorption. "Okay, spill it."

"The merger gave me Dylan's abilities too. Well, his control of water and amplification."

"Amplification, right! What he used to help Ksenyia cast the Hex in Russia."

"Exactly."

"So, how did that give you sight?"

"It didn't. But amplification requires identification of energy, so I didn't need to see you with my eyes. And Zsita carries me where I think, feel, and speak."

"Did you really need to kill my vibe like that though?"

Adam giggled. He realized the two of them could've had this comradery a long time ago. He had forsaken regret for growth, and tapped his forefinger against his lips. "You know what I wonder?"

"What's that?"

"If we can control this thing. Like, what if I can choose what to give you or you control what you grab?"

"I've tried that so many damn times on my end. You'd have to stop my core from automatically grabbing what it calls out for."

"Maybe. We need to keep doing this until we figure it out."

It was a major enigma that Evan could take the one tiny thing of Adam's that existed solely to protect him but could only take his sister's primary ability, which rendered her all but powerless.

They spent hours in the brush trying to control the outcome before eventually returning home, exhausted, but optimistic.

defamation

early

J O TOSSED AND turned in a pool of clammy sweat as nightmares of her deceased ex-husband plagued her. When Jo had first began hearing other people's thoughts, she'd dismissed the occurrences as fatigue. One day she was at work and thought she'd heard her boss make a sexual comment about her, but he was in his office, where his voice sounded so close. That same day, on her lunch break at the Promenade, voices swirled around her. Their lips were moving, so she couldn't be sure what was going on. Anxious to know if she was imagining things, she'd eaten inside the pizzeria, and watched everyone around her as they chewed but still seemed to talk.

Then she'd rushed home in a panic and waited for Mark to return.

"Mark," she'd exclaimed, flying into his arms as he walked through the door.

"Whoa, whoa. What's that for? Are you okay?"

"Something weird is happening and I…I don't know, I can't explain it."

"Okay, slow down. Calm down. Let's talk about it," he'd said, guiding her to the sofa. "What happened? Is Adam okay?"

"He's fine. I don't know to say this without sounding crazy, but you've gotta promise me that you won't dismiss it."

"Honey, I promise. Now, what is it?"

"I…I think I can hear people's thoughts."

He paused and gazed intently into her eyes before smiling. "Now, honey. You know that's impossible. Have you been injured?" He checked her over.

"No. At first it was like whispers, then full on talking, like we're talking to each other right now…except I paid attention today and their lips weren't moving or their words didn't match their lip movement. Like double-talking with the same voice! That's when I realized…"

"Realized what exactly? I think you're overworked and stressed. I've told you to quit that job until Adam's older. You don't need it and it's running you ragged."

"Mark, please! Listen to me." She was exhausted with his insecurities.

"Okay, okay…for the sake of your sanity, I'll believe you if you can prove it to me. Can you do that, honey?"

"I…I…"

"Let's do this. I'll think of a number between one and one-million. If you can guess the number, I'll believe you."

"Um, okay."

"387,517," he'd thought.

"387,517," she'd uttered aloud.

His eyes bulged and he gasped.

"Was I right? Did I guess it right?" she'd probed.

"No, honey. No," he'd lied, terrified that his wife might just hear the sinful thoughts and secrets he was harboring. "You need help, JoAnn. Professional help, and I'll see to it that you get it immediately."

"Professional help? What do you mean?"

"Yes, immediately. You're scaring me, I'm out of town for work often, and I'm afraid for Adam's safety."

"I would never hurt my baby. What are you saying, Mark?"

"I'm saying that you're having an episode and I can't…before this gets out of control, you need to quit that job and get psychiatric help."

"You're serious? You can't be serious. We've known each other…"

"Yes, my darling wife, which is why I'm getting you help instead of…"

"Instead of what?" she'd demanded.

"It's my duty to keep our son safe. If you were in my shoes, you'd do the same thing. Tell me you wouldn't?"

She gazed down at the floor, worried about her precious baby boy and how she was likely losing her grip on reality.

"Okay," she'd acquiesced. "I'll do whatever it takes to get better. For you, and for Adam."

"Oh, thank God," Mark breathed, hugging her far too tightly, which struck her as dramatic and forced.

"I'll set up your first appointment right away and call your boss as well."

"Thank God she agreed," Mark thought to himself.

She'd nodded. "I might be fired anyway, but sure."

"It's going to be okay, honey. Everything's going to be okay," Mark coaxed.

Jo sprang up from her dream.

THE COOL AIR enveloped Adam and Carly's patio deck as the duo relaxed in the hot tub. They inhaled steam, and exhaled contentment.

Carly's cell phone jingled, snapping her from a daze where she'd envisioned Jo reliving hurtful memories.

"Whatever it is, it can wait," Adam pled.

"Might be an emergency, but hopefully not." She pecked him on the cheek before levitating her phone into her hand. "Adam, look. The Afrax council actually summoned me to collect the last of my parent's things. I don't see why they didn't let me take them the many times I was there since she…this feels like an excuse to get me back there."

"Hmm," Adam huffed. "I'll go with you. We'll be in and out in no time."

"I'd never go without Jo and Rye. I need to know what they're thinking, and Rye can get us out in a hurry. If you go too, they'll be unnecessarily suspicious, and likely hostile." Not to mention she didn't want them both to be at risk. She just didn't trust the council.

"If they're suspicious of anything, they'd be questioning why my mom's always with you. I'd be more careful of that."

"I won't go without her," Carly repeated defiantly. "And I'd never let any-thing happen to her."

Adam nodded confidently. "When are you thinking of going?"

"They want me there tonight, but I likely won't bother until tomorrow. I need to talk to Rye and Jo about it first."

"Then get back in here." He summoned Zsita to nudge her over the side of jacuzzi.

Carly fell into his arms with a smile.

He took her breath away with kisses.

Her hand slipped down his chest.

He grabbed it. "If we start, I won't stop."

"That's the point." She bit her bottom lip and straddled him.

He carefully moved her damp curls from her face. "Only a few more weeks before the wedding. We can be strong until then."

"I guess." She rolled her eyes to contain the ridiculous tears forming on her lids. "I'm going to Rye's." She angrily sprung from the fizzing water and grabbed her phone on her way inside the bedroom.

Adam sighed, resting his head back.

afrax safehouse

"You're late," a Leeailia Kashirin admonished Carly as she exited Afrax's corridor and entered the common area, flanked by Rye and Jo. "We were expecting you yesterday, without an entourage."

Carly folded her arms across her chest, daring her to approach Jo or Rye. She noticed the way Leeailia's eyes roved over Jo, and shot Rye a cursory glance, but she didn't care. She wanted to get it over with, so they could get out of there and back to safety.

Something was off. She felt it.

"This way please," the Leeailia motioned.

Carly clenched her jaw. As far as she was concerned, they were lucky

she'd had enough manners to pass through their corridor at all. Rye could've ported them right into the conference room, but she chose to be respectful of the Descendants who lived there.

They entered the modest hall where the fully assembled council awaited them. Each chair was filled, except the Rosovsky seat.

"Why have I been summoned to retrieve my parent's belongings so suddenly?" Carly asked, her voice unwavering. *Don't let go of Rye's hand,* she communicated to Jo when the nuclei of her cells warbled like angry ocean waves.

"Carly Wit, of the Wit Bloodline, the evidence against you is insurmountable. You are hereby charged with—"

"Rye, now," Jo mumbled.

Rye touched Carly's arm, and before she could hear the rest, they were back at Meridian, in Carly's sitting room.

"What happened?" Carly asked Rye and Jo.

"They were going to detain you," Jo exclaimed. "They were all thinking horrid thoughts. They want you…neutralized."

Carly's LR flashed, and her insides thundered. The only reason she didn't take it further was because she didn't want to ruin the foundation of their home.

"How dare they!" Adam yelped, appearing in a flash, wrapping Carly in his arms.

She had to fight, like she never had to before, to prevent a complete meltdown. They couldn't wait until her mother was gone before attacking her. She wondered why they were so committed to destroying each other.

"Dauma says remember your training," Jo relayed.

Upon hearing her mother's name, she pulled herself back from the ledge. Her LR dimmed.

"What did you hear, Jo? I need to know everything." Carly trembled with anger.

"They were looking forward to feeling safe again, once you had been *disposed of.* How your relations with a Rozovsky was bringing too much heat down on them. As soon as I heard that, I knew we needed to leave." Jo rushed.

"Why not just kill me then since I'm the only Rozovsky left?" Adam offered. "Why are they going after Carly?"

"Because they fear you less," Jo replied. "I don't think they want her dead. They seem to want something from her."

Carly's phone pinged, then Rye's, and Adam's. But before they could look, they were interrupted by a loud banging on the front door. Krill, Ksenyia, and Jude marched in, all talking at once, aiming at Carly.

"Whoa…whoa…whoa…one at a time please." *I'm not Jo,* Carly thought to herself.

Jo smiled at her.

"What the hell did you do?" Krill boomed. He was definitely pro-Carly, but was damned curious about the entire situation.

"Exist, apparently. How did you know about—?"

"Here…look," he said, showing Carly his phone.

Descendent,

Carly Wit, of the Wit Bloodline, has absconded from custody. The Wit Descendant is a threat to our security, and any Descendant aiding her has been deemed a threat through their association with her. The Wit Descendant is a danger to us all.
All access to Descendant Facilities and any protections the Wit Descendant and her known accomplices had, have been revoked.
All Descendants are hereby charged with presenting Carly Wit at any Descendant facility for processing. Any known accomplices who present the Wit Descendant shall have their access and protections restored without question, trial, or investigation.

— The Afrax Panel

Everyone checked their phones. Each one displayed the same message, except Carly, whose message notified her that her access and protections had been revoked, and she was required to surrender herself immediately.

"Why do they think they have ultimate authority over our lives?" Carly said while staring at her phone in bewilderment.

Val and Evan had walked in, and that's when the bickering really started, as they all attempted to gain understanding and clarification of the unfolding situation.

If only we could tell them all everything, Carly thought. But it was too dangerous, and if she had to choose between Jo and any of them, she knew she'd choose Jo. It angered her, so she decided she'd never be forced to choose.

Jo whistled through her fingers.

Everyone glared at her.

"You guys, stop!" Jo yelled. "Bickering will get us nowhere. How can we protect each other if we are fighting among ourselves? This is the time we should be pulling together."

"Us?" Jude sneered at Jo's use of the word. Her blatant contempt for those she considered outsiders poured from her eyes and poisoned the atmosphere.

"Just tell us one thing, oh mighty leader," Krill said to Carly, with a sarcastic snarl, unable to resist laughing at his own mild humor. "Did Mariah port you out?"

"I'm not your leader, dum cuff." Carly stuck her tongue out at him, which amused him and angered Jude. "Yes, of course, she did."

"Hmm, Mariah, I think they're really going to gun hard for you over this," Krill said.

"They've already been trying to find ways to cage me, which is why I will never return underground to live," Rye retorted.

"Hey guys, what's happening?" Vikki asked as she entered the living room. "I just got back and saw everyone's doors wide open. Who died?"

"Nobody died," Adam told her. "But Afrax tried to detain Carly."

Vikki was stunned into silence as the others continued to argue over the current situation. She approached Carly, concerned. "Carly, what happened?"

"They've accused me of something, but we didn't stick around to find out what it was," Carly explained.

"Why didn't you stay long enough to at least hear what the allegations were?" Jude added. "How are you supposed to defend yourself without knowing? There's more to this, and I want to know it all. You are always keeping things from us like we're children and we're sick of it. Aren't we?" Jude looked to the others for backup.

No one supported her, including Krill, which angered her.

"Like, why is JoAnn always included in everything, even more than us? Always right by your side when you've visited Afrax, but none of us? What's the deal?" Jude pressed.

"It doesn't matter what they've accused me of because I haven't done anything. Would you rather I allowed them to detain me, keep me there under lock and key until they could kill me? Or worse, kill all of you? And Jo is by my side because I want her there," Carly stepped closer, daring Jude to challenge her regarding Jo or threaten her in any way.

"It's their democratic process, and it's in place for a reason," Jude said, slightly cowering.

"Then why aren't you there, Jude? Huh? Why are you here with us?" Carly asked her, exhausted with her negativity.

"I'm here for Krill," she inadvertently confessed.

No one seemed surprised by her revelation.

Krill sighed with disappointment, but remained by her side. "She didn't mean it like that. She meant…"

"I know exactly what she meant, Krill," Carly interrupted.

"She loves all of you and she's on our side, you guys," Krill declared, attempting to minimize the damage.

"Rye, Carly, and Jo — you made the right decision," Val added. "The Afrax council is corrupt and can't be trusted. I'm sure whatever accusations they created are faux smokescreens to conceal their true agenda, whatever that may be, and it's always something with them. The Afrax council is the very dirtiest of all safehouses. They're likely plotting against the rest of us because that's what they do when Descendants try to go their own way and live their lives on their own terms."

"But why bother though?" Sage asked.

"Look at us," Val said. "We've dared to live openly in the free world, a group of us, together in a community. The Afrax council doesn't like change. They want us underground where they can control our every move and implant every thought we have. Control what we believe, and how we act."

Evan and Rye nodded.

"Plenty of Descendants don't live in safehouses, Val," Jude said. "Does that mean they plotted against all of them too? Be reasonable."

Val squinted in disbelief. "Whatever your inner demons, you need to vanquish them because they're blinding you. I won't argue with you. No one has been in the safehouses longer than I have, nor have any of you been to all of them, which is also by design. They don't like Descendants who live in the free world. It goes against everything they stand for, and they believe it risks the safety of all of them. Reason and logic are tools to use when facts are missing. I'm not missing any facts."

"If I had to a guess, their guilty conscience is the culprit," Sage said. "They've committed so many atrocities, and they're afraid of being exposed to the other facilities. The Rozovsky Bloodline was hunted into near extinction as the council sat by and let it happen, and now all of a sudden, a Wit is a threat? Why do they *really* want her?"

Evan uncrossed his arms. "I think it's pretty obvious the council wants to neutralize Carly because she's the most powerful among us."

"And she barely recognizes her own abilities for what they are," Jo snooped from Val's thoughts.

Carly quietly remembered Jo telling her they would feel safe after her relationship with Adam was neutralized. Nobody knew why the Rozovsky-Wit alliance was forbidden, and the council existed to conceal it at every turn. Layers upon layers of secrets, lies, and betrayal. She wondered why her mother had decided on Afrax versus the other safehouses, distance notwithstanding.

"I think there's some unexplained Afrax violation they need a fall guy for," Ksenyia offered.

Everyone snatched their heads her way.

"That's literally their trademark M.O." Ksenyia shrugged. "Fenyx never resurfaced and they might've had something to do with her disappearance."

Carly and Rye swiftly exchanged remorseful glances.

Sage briefly dipped his head and exhaled. Vikki noticed, but kept quiet.

Adam sighed. "I honestly can't spend too much time caring about why a corrupt Descendant council wants my fiancée captured and/or killed when the Iksha wants the same. Enemies on both sides! My only concern is to keep her, and all of you, safe. We may never know the whys, and we have our own problems here to deal with. That was the point of you all leaving that place, wasn't it? *We're* a family now. Let's focus on protecting each other from *anyone* who tries to harm us. Any of us."

They all agreed, except for Jude, who crossed her arms defiantly.

Carly glowered, utterly annoyed by all that had transpired recently. When she thought to pull Jude aside to have a private conversation with her, her chest nearly leapt from her torso. An infinite number of chattering voices filled her head until she backed away, into the bathroom, slamming the door.

"Shhh," she whispered to herself as she attempted to calm down. She closed her eyes and focused.

The echoing voices fell like waterfalls.

You are the Light.

Come home.

We need you here.

It's your time.

The time has come.

You are the Light.

"Quiet!" When she opened her eyes, the voices had simmered, and her energy levels stabilized.

She wondered what was going on and why she'd felt like her core has been pried from her chest, which increased her power. She had no time to be afraid. Her life was changing before her very eyes. She was now a wanted woman by her own people.

spar

adam

Adam soared out of bed, through the French doors of their bedroom patio, to the sound of his blaring car alarm, where Carly was already leaning over the railing of their open balcony.

"What the heck is going on?" he asked through a dipped brow and squinted eyes.

"Your car…it's possessed," Carly anxiously replied.

They watched, wide-eyed, as his truck spun, on an axis, five feet in the air.

"I—is that, Vikki?" His eyes bulged. He swiftly summoned Zsita to carry him gracefully downstairs. "Vik?"

Carly landed close beside him.

He ducked as he was nearly smacked in the face with his half-ton truck, as Vikki swung it around like cheerleader's spirit flag.

"Do you like my new powers little brother?" Vikki chirped, bright-eyed.

"I-I do, but at what cost?"

"Don't start," she mildly replied. "I just wonder why it took so long to happen."

"You're sweating, Vik." He inched closer, suddenly recalling when Vikki had begun breaking escrima sticks, weight bars, and punching holes in walls without trying.

"Well, I am holding a truck in my hands right now."

"We need to get you checked out," he said.

"Are you blind? Look at what I can do! I'm better than fine! I'm fantastic!" She toggled the bumper and front end of the truck between her palms like a ball. "I've already told Sage I won't be seeing any creepy doctors either, so forget it."

Adam and Carly exchanged worried glances. He was upset that Sage had clearly learned of Vikki's abilities and discussed them with her, but had not kept him in the loop.

"You two worry like you're old parents or something. Look how strong I am, little brother! Can't you just be happy for me?" She slowly put the truck down, undamaged.

Other Descendants had gathered on scene, still in their nightwear. Vikki slowly glowered at their expressions of horror.

Adam breathed deeply, doubtful that logic would penetrate the endorphins clearly spreading inside Vikki's brain.

"I thought you'd be happy I wasn't helpless anymore," Vikki uttered in a low but pleading whisper.

"You were never helpless, and I am. I'm just worried about you," Adam countered. "Please, let me get you a doctor we can trust."

"I said no." She turned towards the others. "Would any of you had come if I was in distress? If I needed help, would you have bothered?" Tears welled up in her impossibly blue eyes when they didn't answer, but instead, dipped their heads and shuffled their feet.

"Of course, Vik," Adam responded, appalled by the others' lack of empathy.

Carly clutched her chest as the other Descendants silently looked on. "You know *I* would, Vikki."

Vikki huffed in disbelief. "So, only my newfound brother, who likely only pities me, and his fiancée, who clearly feels obligated, are the only ones who'd help me if I needed it?"

The heartbreaking silence thickened.

She dipped her head. "Right, exactly." She stormed back into the house, shoulders slumped, sad and defeated.

Adam and Carly assured the others everything was fine before they went inside.

"I'll go talk to her," Adam told Carly as they huddled in the foyer.

"Maybe you should let her calm down first."

"I don't want her to feel alone right now. Nobody is warming up to her here. Not in the way they are to Kane, and it's not fair. She's proven herself time and again."

"It's because Kane doesn't insert himself in Descendant matters or try to be something and someone he isn't," Carly responded.

"As far as you know," he thought. "He's a tag-a-long, babe. Vikki was raised by an Iksha scientist. This *IS* her life and it has been long before we knew her. There's no comparison."

Carly's silence served to concede his point.

"Vik trains with us, plans with us, and fights with us."

"It still doesn't make her a Descendant, and I think the others may resent her for it."

"So, because she made an informed decision this time, they resent her?"

"Likely, yes, because none of them were afforded that opportunity."

"Well, that's really stupid of them because she was tricked into taking the V the first time, and was used as a pawn. So, she didn't have much choice in this, same as they didn't. And Kane is ornamental until he proves otherwise." His cheeks had fully flushed as he dismissed further conversation on the matter.

Carly merely nodded.

"I'm going to talk to her because being alone right now will only cement her broken heart."

"I understand, but if she breaks even one thing in this house, I'll fry her hair off," Carly warned as she headed to the staircase.

"Babe?" He puckered his lips in disbelief.

"Just letting you know. I'm here if you need me." She floated upstairs, plopped down on the bed, and turned on the T.V.

He gently tapped on Vikki's room door.

"Go away, Adam."

He cracked the door ajar. "How'd you know it was me?"

She was laying on her bed, turned on her side, facing the wall. "Because you're the only one who would care. Pity or not. I'm going to sleep. We can talk later." She didn't turn around.

He sat on the edge of her bed. "Look at me, Vik."

She sighed loudly before turning over. As she did, she fell backwards. He caught her before she hit the floor. "See, this is why I want you to see a doctor."

"I just lost my balance is all. I'm fine."

"No, you're not!" He sat her on the bed. "You're seeing a doctor, end of discussion."

"Fine," she breathed. "But we're banished from the safehouses, and I also don't want to end up a lab monkey of the US Government, so good luck with that."

"I'll find a way."

"Not like me dying would make any difference around here." The tormenting heat in her face spread its wings.

"I admit they're a tough sell, but …"

"Tough sell, my ass. This is real adult life! Not a high school popularity contest. They like Kane just fine, and he does nothing but sit up under Mariah all day long. At least I contribute. I train and help the others hone their combat skills. You know, just in case their cores get depleted. I shop, I cook, and I clean. I'm supportive and assist with operations. I'm always ready and willing to throw myself in front of a bullet for everybody here, and they still don't give a damn about me, just like my wanna-be father didn't. Maybe that's just my lot in this life."

Adam embraced and squeezed her tightly. "Some of them are intimidated by you, which isn't the same as disliking you. A whole human who was basically buried underground and tortured in a Descendant prison came through fighting and kicking the butts of beings with superpowers. Can you imagine being them?"

She chuckled through her budding tears. "Well…"

"And you aren't shy about flexing your skills at all, which rubs it in their faces even more."

"Well, I …"

"I'm not saying you should be ashamed of your accomplishments, or your new abilities. Just don't be so flashy all the time."

"Nobody likes a show-off," they chimed in unison.

"Yeah, I know," she said. "I get it. That's just … all I have. I don't have friends to hang out with. Nobody to talk to. Nobody to shop with. I have no social life."

"You have me."

"And you have Carly. Three's a crowd."

"Don't ever say anything stupid like that. You're my sister, my family."

She acquiesced. "I get it, Adam. You don't want me to feel hurt, like any caring brother, but I'm still lonely and sad most days."

"You have Sage."

"Right. Did you see him in the crowd outside anywhere?"

"He was probably at home sleeping like you should've been instead of twirling trucks in the air at 1 a.m."

"Oooh, you're funny," she crooned. "Look, we like each other, but Sage isn't lovey-dovey like people think. He's still mourning that girl who left. Fenyx. I can tell he's holding out for her, waiting for her to come back one day. I feel it every time we're near each other. It's like, I feel his despair or something."

"Well, she's not coming back," Adam retorted before he could stop himself. He shoved his fist into his mouth, and cursed his tongue.

"How do you know that? She might. And then I'll be tossed to the side like spare parts. No thanks. I've had that all my life and I refuse to settle for it ever again."

"You might just be overthinking this, Vik."

"Adam, I'm no dummy. I wasn't born yesterday. I'd love to pursue something more with Sage, but he just isn't emotionally available. He was simply smitten two years ago by a new girl who just happened to have been his private lab monkey at the time. Now that he's gotten used to having me around, he's returned to pining over that girl. Carly would dump your ass too if she found out there was some other girl you were pining over."

"Uh, she'd do more than that, but I hear ya. Look, I'm sorry you're going through this. I wish I could solve it all and make it all better. Just know that you do have the option of …"

"Of what? Leaving Meridian?"

He nodded solemnly.

"Is that what you want?" she asked.

"No." He flashed his LR. "I want you here, but I want you happy."

She paused for a spell before hugging him. "Thanks, little brother. I'm going to sleep now."

"Okay, you know where I'll be if you need anything."

"Mmm hmm." She rolled herself up like a burrito inside the fleece blankets and turned over.

"I love you, Vik." He paused by the door.

She didn't reply.

He left her alone to rest and padded back up the stairs. "Babe, I've gotta find a private doctor for Vikki."

"Okay. How was she feeling?"

"Hurt, lost, lonely … and a little sick."

"Sick how?" She leaned forward and turned off the T.V.

"She lost her balance while turning over and fell off the bed. Who loses their balance while laying down? This is her second time taking V in her lifetime, as far as we know, and she gulped the entire test vial."

"A worldly doctor won't know what to look for nor how to treat her," Carly said. "We have to get her a Descendant doctor."

"She's refusing that."

"All you have to do is not tell her. You have all the money in the world to make it happen."

"But, aren't we cut off from the Descendant facilities?"

"Maybe the safehouses, but…you should talk to Val about it. She seems to have all the connections. Maybe she could make some recommendations."

"I'll go ask her," he said as he headed for the terrace.

"Adam, no."

"What? Why not?" he asked as he prepared to defend his friendship.

"It's the middle of the night and everyone's in their pajamas. It can wait 'til morning."

"Oh, right." He tossed his pajamas into the hamper, jumped in bed, and cradled Carly.

"Maybe she's looking for love, or friends, or both. But you're the last family she's got, so nothing anyone else does will matter more to her than what you do."

He nuzzled his face against ear. "You'd think that, but she figures everything I do or say is out of pity or obligation, so it's hard to…"

"Don't let the challenge of proving your love stop you from proving it. She's redeemed herself from her past, as far as I'm concerned. You know her best. There's gotta be a way to tip the scales away from her feeling unappreciated."

"Yeah," he quietly replied, just as an idea came to him.

ADAM BURST INTO Vikki's loft and yanked the white sheer curtains apart. "Wake up."

"Are you insane," Vikki said in a gravelly voice. "The damn house better be on fire or…"

"You've got 10 minutes to get dressed and meet me upstairs on the patio."

"What? Why?" She sat up halfway.

"10 minutes." He went back upstairs.

When she marched out onto Adam and Carly's terrace, she gripped her firm hips in aggravation. "So, what was so—"

Before she could finish her gripe, Adam snatched her and darted off into the skies.

She held on for dear life as he flew faster. "Adam, slow down."

He chuckled at her burying her face into his chest while tightening her legs and arms around him. After a while, they landed in a brush of desiccated trees and dirt.

She leaned over and puked. "What the hell is wrong with you?" She punched him in the chest.

He just grinned wider while removing his hoodie.

"Where are we?"

"It doesn't matter where."

"Well, then why are we here?"

"To spar."

"You can't be serious," she smirked, catching her breath.

"Oh, I certainly am. You have all these new superpowers and you need to let loose with them."

"Let loose?"

"Yeah! Go wild, get crazy."

She smiled wider than he'd ever seen.

"So, you're challenging me? Is that what you're saying?"

"Yeah, I guess I am."

"But you can just fly away, so…"

"I promise you that I won't. Zsita is off the table, but I won't hold back otherwise…and you shouldn't either."

"Right, as if—"

He kicked her backwards before she could finish. "Less talk, more fight."

She pulled her sweater off and cracked her neck. "Well, alright."

She lunged at him with both fists, sending him skidding backwards. Dust flurries surrounded them as they went blow-for-blow, besting each other. After she'd warmed her muscles knocking knuckles with him, she summoned a ball of energy from the bottom of her rib cage, and pushed it into her arms. She grabbed him by his ankles, and spun him in a vortex before thrusting him so far away, she'd lost sight of him.

She hopped up and down gleefully. "Uh oh." She ran blindly in the direction she'd tossed him, adrenaline pumping.

She searched everywhere and couldn't find him. "Little turd. Where are you?"

"Looking for me?" Adam levitated her into the air, hurled her across the cactus-ridden plain, and dashed towards her.

She dusted herself off while scrambling to her feet. "Uh huh, I knew you'd cheat and use Zsita. You're no match for me without her."

"I didn't. I don't need her to whoop your butt."

"Then how'd you—"

He thrust an elbow forward, knocking her chin upward. "Stop holding back. Fight me!"

"I am fighting you," she said between blows and breaths.

"You're afraid of letting go," he said with a punch to her gut. "You wanna be the best so bad, but you're too scared to take it!"

With three quick moves, she put him on his butt. "I'm not afraid of shit, little brother." She glowered down at him.

He focused for an instant, and summoned all the moisture from the ground and trees. He spiraled himself into a vortex that grew bigger by the second.

She backed up in fear.

"All that fancy super strength is nothing compared to natural Descendant traits," Adam taunted.

"Adam, I get it okay. You can stop now."

"No holds barred, remember? Either stop me or die. I'm tired of babying your feelings." His golden LR glowed brighter as he charged his core.

"I said you win. I concede. Are you happy now?"

"No." He floated towards her.

"Adam, stop. That's enough." She inched backwards with moist eyelids.

"I guess you don't deserve to be among us," he shrugged as he hurled the whirlpool at her.

Different energies in her body jerked and tugged painfully into her chest. She thrust her arms out in a last-ditch attempt to save herself from what she'd apparently perceived was sudden death. A shockwave of energy rushed from her upper body, obliterating the maelstrom, and nearly Adam. He had no choice but to summon Zsita to create a protective barrier around him when he'd felt the burn of the shockwave singe his skin.

Spent and out of breath, Vikki fainted.

Adam quickly scooped her up. "Vik? Vik, are you alright?"

She glanced up at him, dazed, with blood oozing from her nostrils. "Did I win?"

He couldn't believe what he'd just witnessed, and he couldn't wait to tell Carly.

"You sure did." He tearfully smiled before she went limp.

the virgin confessions

adam

BACK AT MERIDIAN, the ground rattled, and Carly's chest tugged her in a foreign manner. She sat forward on the bed, rubbed her heart, and glanced around the bedroom. Several moments later, Adam landed on the terrace with Vikki in his arms.

Carly tossed her book aside and rushed over when she saw blood. "What happened to her?"

"The most amazing thing you can imagine."

"Adam, she's bleeding."

"Let me put her to bed and I'll be right back."

"I'm coming with you."

They rushed into Vikki's room where Adam laid her down.

"You should've seen her, babe. She…"

"Her pulse is faint," Carly said, interrupting him. "Stand back." She summoned her reddish-gold dust, allowing it to sink into Vikki's skin.

Vikki groaned before dipping into a comfortable slumber.

Carly turned to Adam. "Tell me what happened."

He took her by the waist and guided her into the living room. "Babe,

Vikki's more powerful than we ever imagined."

"What do you mean? What happened? Why was she bleeding?"

He sat on the sofa and pulled her down with him. "What we thought was just super strength last night, was just a part of her abilities."

"Adam."

"Okay, I took her out to a safe spot to spar with her."

"Spar? Fighting was your gift to her to make her feel better?"

"Carly, yes. Now listen to me. Vikki's a fighter. The best fighter here. So good, she trains everyone else. I figured if I allowed her to fight without restraint, it would make her happy, and it did."

"So, why was she bleeding then?"

"When we hit an impasse, there was only one way to go. I sent a whirlpool at her, full force, because she was holding back."

"Adam, you could've killed her!" she bounded to her feet before he pulled her back down.

"Don't ask me how, but I just felt like I wouldn't."

"But you didn't know, and you were willing to take that chance?"

"Babe, she actually nearly killed *me*," Adam finally divulged.

Carly's eyes bulged from their sockets. "Whaaat? But…how?"

"She sent some sort of shockwave that destroyed the whirlpool and singed my skin. Look!" He rolled back the sleeve of his black hoodie sweatshirt and shoved his bruised forearm at her. "The only rule of the spar was that I wouldn't use Zsita. But, babe, when she hit me with that sonic wave, I had no choice or I would've been blown to bits."

Carly whooshed out a breath as she calmly healed his forearm. "Holy cow."

"I know. Can you believe it?"

"I think that's what I felt a few minutes before you got home." She angled her body sideways, away from him.

"I really think Vik's ability surpasses many Descendants here," he went on.

"It's not a competition, Adam."

"I know, I know, but if they could see how powerful she's become, I think they'd respect her more."

"We need to get her checked out before we even think about telling the others," Carly drove.

"I disagree with waiting to tell them, given Jude's outburst. We should tell them asap."

"The V she took was a byproduct of your mom, Adam. This could get complicated quickly. Especially with Rye wanting it for Kane."

"My mom won't be drained like an animal. We can't just go around turning people like vampires," Adam boomed.

"Yes, I know, which is why we need to think this through before we tell people just for the sake of them accepting her as one of their own." She eyed him intently.

"If Vik displays her abilities the way she did with me today, and we haven't told the others, there will be more division here. Likely the kind that'll send everyone their separate ways. There's little time to waste. We need to decide quickly."

"You're right," Carly agreed.

THE BUDDING FAMILY of five enjoyed a peaceful afternoon in Meridian's gardens when Evan found himself bored with Carly and Jo's wedding plan conversation.

Adam, once annoyed by Evan's overly playful shenanigans, had grown to like him, but Evan's absorption ability kept him on edge. Especially since Evan's humor often blurred the lines between laughable jokes, and fight-worthy embarrassment.

"You guys need to liven up a bit," Evan said as he cranked up the music and began dancing.

"Who taught you how to dance?" Adam teased with a raised brow.

"Ya mama."

"Ohhh!" Vikki sang.

"Ouch!" Carly added. "Jo, you gonna take that?"

Jo bounced onto her feet and pushed Evan backward. "Let me show you a few things, old man."

Adam then pulled Carly and Vikki up, and soon they all danced around the garden.

Evan swayed closer to Adam. "Nice cloak you've got there. Be a shame if someone were to…absorb it," he chuckled mischievously.

"Evan, dude. I'll bop the shit out of you if you don't back off."

Evan doubled over laughing, tumbling to the ground in hysterics.

Adam shook his head and murmured, "just remember, as of right now, my boring cloak is all you get, leaving me with all of my other abilities. I could fly you out of the atmosphere and drop you."

"I mean you could, but you'd never hurt your mother like that. So, gimme some different incentive not to enjoy this."

"Dammit," Adam grumbled under his breath.

Before he could move to a safe distance, Evan knocked his wrist and darted away with his cloak.

Jo immediately jumped for joy at the thoughts she snooped. "I'm the greatest mother in the world!"

"Jo, are you okay?" Carly asked, bewildered.

Adam swooped over and slapped Evan on the shoulder, retrieving his cloak. He then swiftly whisked Jo off into the skies before she had the chance to utter another word to anyone.

Carly and Vikki remained below, gazing confusingly above, as Jo's giggles trailed off.

They landed several miles away in a wooded brush.

"Mom, you can't just snoop in my head like that."

She clutched her stomach in roaring laughter. "Seriously? Coming from someone who pirates people's memories?"

"Whatever, Mom. You can't — CANNOT — tell Carly." He sliced the air with his arms.

She slapped him on the back of his neck. "Don't raise your voice to me."

"Sorry, mom, but please." He rubbed his stinging skin where she smacked him.

"Don't tell me she believes you're not a virgin and you just let her?"

He shrugged.

"That's so ridiculous. Why shouldn't she know she isn't alone in this?"

"Because I'm a man...and...I'm supposed to have experience."

"Who made that stupid rule? Being a man isn't synonymous with sexual experiences, and being 18 doesn't make you a man. Enjoy being a boy. Don't let ridiculous societal programming control you, son."

"Mom, it's more complicated than that." He realized he hadn't thought of the entire situation for her to grasp when she'd snooped his thoughts; just that he'd felt inadequate being a virgin, and was apprehensive about his impending wedding night.

"You're a virgin. So what?" she continued. "That's actually great and wonderful. While most young boys are encouraged to be the biggest whores possible, you've refrained and now…"

"Now what? I won't know what to do," he groaned. "She'll expect me to know things, Mom."

"Well, that's on you. As long as you aren't forthcoming, she just might have expectations. Wait, what did you mean by *it's more complicated*?"

"I uh, I…"

"What?"

He couldn't form the words, so he uncloaked himself.

After listening, Jo sighed. "You watched this girl torture herself with agony and you said nothing? You're not the victim here."

He quickly shielded his thoughts again.

They simultaneously planted their hands on their hips, at an impasse.

"This world is so screwed up that virginity is considered a negative. That's sad, but it doesn't have to be. You two were made for each other and saved yourselves for each other. Be thankful for that, and be honest with her. It'll bring her peace and joy."

"You don't know Carly like I do, Mom. She'll be devastated that I kept this from her."

"And she has every right to feel that way. Stop stealing her choices away from her. Tell her! And tell her all of it!" She poked him in the chest.

He flew her back to Evan's arms and grabbed Carly. "Vik, I'll see you at home." A sonic boom exploded beneath him as he flew home to their terrace.

"Carly, um…I uh…"

"What? What is it?"

"I'm a virgin." He smacked his arms against his sides.

She remained quizzically silent for a moment before bursting into laughter.

"Okay seriously, Carly? Like, really?"

"Is this a joke because you said that with a straight face?" She giggled a bit longer until she noticed he wasn't laughing.

Adam's face remained stone, hoping to conceal his embarrassment.

"Adam, you slept with Lana. I already told you I don't care about that. That was before us."

"No, I…no, I didn't. I allowed you to believe what you wanted because I was too embarrassed to correct you."

"But at Josh's party," she stuttered. "In the bedroom…I saw…"

"It wasn't me, babe."

"Then who was —" her entire disposition shifted, and she covered her mouth in horror.

He lowered his head. "It was Dylan. I just didn't…"

"I don't believe you," she replied with squinted eyes. "You were standing near the restroom when I…"

"I was downstairs at first, but core energy pulled me upstairs. Might've been his or yours. I'm still not sure. But I was lingering and agitated because I was confused about why I was up there in the first place. That's when you exited the restroom."

"Jeez, Adam," she breathed. "You could've just told me. I made a fool of myself so many times. I…" she grew angrier with each second that passed.

"I know."

"All the thoughts I tortured myself with were unnecessary."

"I know."

"The jealousy, the anger, the frustration, the…"

"I know!"

"Well, if you know, why haven't you apologized?" Her LR flamed red and tears sizzled on her lids. The air grew inexplicably hot, and the terrace railing sizzled as it melted. "How much longer were you going to live this lie? Until our wedding night? Until you could no longer fake it?"

"I'm sorry," he whispered, overcome with shame. "I was going to tell you…"

"Sure, you were," she interjected. "You're only telling me now because your mom snooped around in your head and found the truth." She shook her head.

"Wait? How do you know?"

"Spare me! I'm not stupid, Adam!"

He cowered shamefully.

"You know, this is the first time I'm feeling grateful that Rye interrupted us before we made love for the first time. I would've regretted it!"

"Babe, no. I…" He reached for her but she snatched away.

"Just stop. I don't know how to look at you right now, so it's best I don't." She stormed away from him.

The air returned to its normal temperature. It was then he noticed he had lost his connection with Zsita while Carly was there. It terrified him as he drew in massive breaths of fresh cool air. When he mustered the courage to search for Carly in the house, she was gone. He jogged around the community knocking on doors, but she was nowhere to be found.

ADAM WOKE THE next morning with a dry mouth and crawling flesh. Evan's absorption was already causing him problems. This couldn't have come at a worse time with the wedding just two weeks away. He was petrified that Carly would call off the wedding or the relationship completely. His heart ached. He had to find a way to redeem himself.

Just as the thoughts spread inside his mind, Jo and Evan's voices downstairs seized his attention. He sat upright on the bed when Jo knocked.

"Adam?"

"Come in, mom."

She leapt onto the bed like a toddler. "Soooo, I'm guessing you told her?"

"Yes, I told her. And now look, she isn't here." He rolled his eyes and pouted.

"Well, well, well. If it isn't the consequences of your actions?" she shrugged.

"This is serious, Mom."

"Mm hmm, it sure is. Either sit here whining about it or get up try to make it right."

Evan moseyed into the room. "Good morning."

Adam jumped out of bed and plastered himself inside the bathroom doorway. "Stay away from me, Evan. Don't touch me, man. I'm serious."

Jo burst into a fit of laughter, rolling onto her back, holding her belly, and kicking her feet.

Evan's expression was somber. "I won't take your cloak without your permission. I was just joking around yesterday. I completely forgot about your mother's…I had no idea about uh…that…"

"That's the whole point of privacy," Adam bit back. He knew Evan sometimes let it slip his mind that Jo could hear thoughts because she couldn't hear his, but Adam was soured just the same.

"Adam, chill," Jo said. "Now that you understand how it feels, I expect you won't pirate other people's memories without their permission."

"I won't, okay. Just keep him away from me." He cowered inside the doorway.

"Wouldn't the same rules apply to you, honey?" Evan asked Jo.

"Mine is involuntary. I wish everyone could shut their thoughts off when I was around, but Adam's snooping is completely voluntary." Finally, she and her son were equal. It hadn't been fair that he could invade her memories anytime he liked without her consent.

Now Adam was getting a taste of his own medicine, and he didn't like it one bit.

disjecta membra

val

VAL SKIDDED INTO Carly and Adam's driveway on a perfectly luminous Saturday afternoon with plans of shopping until the daylight escaped them, and the stores closed down. She'd never given up hope of healing their friendship because she truly loved Carly like a sister. She had done an awful thing by allowing herself to be led into a lustful situation to please Ksenyia. She was now a better person for accepting her wrongdoing without excuses, and changing the thought processes and feelings that guided her into that shady behavior.

Adam and Carly were her family, and she'd do anything for them. She hoped today would give her more time to allow Carly to feel the love and remorse pouring from her heart. She gazed up at the numbers in their address, *511411*, before gliding from her custom, reinforced, purple Phantom, and gently rapping on the decorative, two-toned, scarlet and gold door.

Carly stepped out immediately, wearing large dark sunglasses, light-denim jeans, a delicate ivory blouse, white tennis shoes, and a crossbody purse.

"Hey, Val."

Val stood a bit awkwardly, wanting to hug her. "Hey, you ready to spend some money?"

"Let's do it."

They headed toward the Promenade as a prelude to mall shopping.

"So, you're really getting an entirely new wardrobe?" Val asked as she parked the luxury car on the street of the Promenade.

"I kinda feel like everything I currently have is for a high school girl. Soon I'll be a college student, and *probably* married."

Val smiled. "I totally get it. I'm excited for you. Wait…probably?"

"I'm just annoyed about a lot right now. It's nothing worth ruining our day though, trust me."

"Oh, okay," Val nodded, not wanting to pry.

They quickly explored the normal Promenade shops before heading to the mall. They stuck close together as they shimmied in and out every store on every floor, only pausing to tuck bags away in the car when Val noticed they were being tailed by mall security. She thought it was just happenstance initially, but she was now convinced, as the two security guards turned toward each other, whispered, and darted their eyes suspiciously. She instinctively shadowed Carly without alarming her. It took Carly over a year before she even spoke to Val again, so she refused to taint their great time when the rent-a-cops may likely just gossip and go away.

"I'm thirsty," Carly announced.

"Lemonade?"

"Wouldn't be a mall trip without it," Carly beamed.

"May as well add a buttery pretzel to the mix."

"Oh my gosh, yes!" Carly rubbed her stomach.

Val eyed the mall security officers intently as they attempted to disguise their shadowy surveillance.

When they finished their shopping and made their way to the car, local police had also parked near the exit. Carly obliviously stuffed her bags into the overflowing back, and then buckled herself into the front passenger seat. She leaned towards Val, who lingered outside the driver's door. "Val, everything okay?"

"Yeah, everything's fine." Val pulled out of the parking structure and intentionally drove slower than usual, as she noticed the police tailing them. She wondered why they didn't just stop them if that's what they intended.

Carly snapped a few selfies and text messaged Jo about her recent purchases when the police siren blared.

Val pulled the car over and rolled the windows down, not lost on them waiting until they were in a deserted area before initiating the stop.

"What the heck is going on?" Carly asked. "What did we do?"

"We didn't *do* anything," Val snidely replied.

Two male officers flanked Val's car.

"License and registration, young lady," Officer Skaarsgard demanded of Val, with his hand firmly on his weapon.

Val didn't speak. She simply handed him her documents and continued facing forward.

"What's the problem, officer?" Carly asked of the cop on her side.

"Shut your mouth and do as your told. Won't be no problems," Officer Wilkes barked at her.

"Don't speak to me that way. You're not my parent. I asked what the problem was. Why have you stopped us?"

"Just let them play their little game, Car," Val whispered, knowing the mall security reported them, Carly specifically, because of her complexion.

"No, Val. We have the right to know what we've been stopped for."

"You have the right to do as your told," Wilkes boomed. "Where's your identification?"

"I don't have to give you anything. I'm not the driver and this is a traffic stop," Carly snapped back.

"Alright, step out of the vehicle," Wilkes ordered. "Both of you, now!"

Skaarsgard pocketed Val's documents, drew his weapon with his right hand, and pushed Val onto the hood of the police cruiser with his left. Wilkes followed suit by forcefully shoving Carly onto the hood.

Carly groaned aloud when Wilkes slammed her stomach against the grille. Val's LR flamed fuchsia.

"Val, I'm okay," Carly mouthed. "Don't." She shook her head.

Val snapped her eyes shut and breathed deeply until her LR returned to its normal hue.

"Put your hands behind your back and keep em there," Wilkes demanded of Carly. "Whose car is this?"

"It's hers," Carly replied. "You'd know that if you did your job."

Val sighed. "Okay, the two of you have had your fun. Run my license, check my registration, and get on with it. This is unnecessary."

"We got a call from mall security regarding suspicious behavior," Skaarsgard finally divulged.

"What was suspicious about us shopping at a *shopping* center?" Val asked. "And don't touch me. Don't touch either of us."

Skaarsgard dug his elbow into her back, slammed her face down, and handcuffed her. "Well, we believe you've got a car full of stolen merchandise here, which is probable cause."

"A few receipts would end your unfounded accusations, but that's not what you want, is it?" Val said with an eerie blank expression, mustering every ounce of patience she could gather.

"Shut up! See if that one has any drugs or weapons on her. She looks like the type," he said to Wilkes regarding Carly.

"Type to what?" Val growled.

"Check her," Skaarsgard repeated.

Wilkes groped and prodded Carly. She squirmed uncomfortably with her hands handcuffed behind her back. She glanced over at Val with tears in her eyes. Val's LR flamed even brighter, and she took no precautions to conceal it this time.

Wilkes hurled over, grabbed his crotch, and wailed like a wounded animal. "Oh my God!" he screeched.

Carly couldn't see what was going on behind her, so she turned around.

"Wilkes, what going on? What'd that bitch do to you?" Skaarsgard yelled, pointing his firearm at Carly.

Within seconds, Skaarsgard crumpled to his knees, and dropped his weapon. Their dark-blue uniform trousers were drenched in blood.

"Val, what'd you do?"

Val didn't respond. She continued calmly severing their members with a blank expression.

Carly used her energy to unlock their cuffs and softly grabbed Val's bicep. "There are cameras, Val. They have body cameras. Cruiser cameras."

Val just stared at her vacuously.

Carly ashed all the cameras and rendered the officers unconscious. "Come on, Val. Get in the car." She delicately escorted her into the passenger seat and drove off.

They rode silently for a few minutes.

"Val, you have to control your temper."

"He was touching you."

"I know that but…"

"It was wrong. You didn't do anything wrong."

"This is the world we live in, I…"

"He was hurting you, Carly!" Val whipped her head Carly's way.

"I would've been fine but now we might've been exposed."

"I'm not sorry! They were assholes and I'll never be sorry! I only wish I permanently removed their hands so they'd never touch another woman without her permission ever again." She folded her arms across her chest.

Carly softened. "Thank you." She touched Val's knee.

"Don't mention it."

"Did…something happen to you?" Carly probed.

"It's nothing. Like you said, it's the world we live in, right?"

"It is, but we can change it. I'm learning that. Talk to me, Val."

Val loathed the memory that changed her in a way she could never come back from. "There was this guy I thought was nice when I was a freshman in college. He gave me a tour of the campus when I was a fish out of water and we became fast friends. One night we were walking back to the dorms from the library, and we made a detour just to talk. We hugged me and then tried to kiss me. I leaned back and apologized for apparently giving him the wrong idea. That wasn't good enough. He wouldn't let me go and wrestled me to the ground. He…he pinned my legs apart and…I punched and scratched but nothing deterred him. When he stole his way into my body, I blipped, and before I knew it, his body parts were everywhere. I ran back to the dorm, drenched in his blood."

Carly pulled the car over. "Oh my gosh, Val. I'm so sorry." She hugged her from the driver's seat. "I'm sorry I chewed you out back there. I didn't know."

"No one knows, not even Ksenyia, and I never want anyone to. I'm nobody's victim."

"You're too kick-ass to ever be anyone's victim."

They shared a smile and squeezed hands.

Carly sat back and replayed every memory of Val with greater appreciation.

"Disjecta membra," Carly whispered.

"Huh?"

"It's a term I learned from poetry and reading classes back in Silver Springs. It's essentially what you do when you rip people apart."

"Disjecta membra," Val repeated. "Sounds weird, but regal," she chortled.

"You're a regal being, Val. Not that you need me to ever tell you, but if anyone ever touches you without your express permission, disjecta membra, and never regret it." She flashed her crimson LR.

Val flashed her fuchsia LR in return. She knew Carly could've stopped that cop from groping her, but she likely would've caused global damage. Not only that, she knew Carly never wanted to hurt anyone, and she loved her for being that person.

They held hands the way home.

carly

CARLY LEVITATED HER dozens of department store bags onto the terrace before hugging Val goodbye. She paused as her core spread from her head to toe, and seemed to be trying to remove itself from her body completely. She paused and closed her eyes.

"Car, are you okay?" Rye asked, as she had blipped over without warning.

"I'm fine. Just felt a little weird, but I'm okay now." She wondered why Rye had shown up the way she did.

"I have to tell you something. Or some things, rather that I've been meaning to." She gulped and sighed.

Carly held her hand. "Whatever it is, it's okay." She attempted to give Rye her undivided attention, but her core continued to tug and pull. She fought it and steadied herself while Rye continued.

"I wasn't always able to port out of the galaxy. Something happened to me.

Many decades ago, when I was 14, I was pulled through a portal as I slept. When I woke, I was in a strange place. Not Earth."

Carly told herself she was actively listening, but she was truthfully overwhelmed with the strange pulling, pending nuptials, Adam's omissions, missing her parents, and starting college.

"I was in the Makovian Universe on the Mother Planet."

"I thought Makovia was a galaxy."

"It is. It's both."

Carly inadvertently frowned in confusion and exasperation.

"You see…"

Carly dropped her bags and doubled over.

Adam gazed down from the railing with a concerned and confused expression on his ridiculously gorgeous face. "Carly?" He swooped down and gathered her into his arms. "What's wrong? Are you hurt?"

"I'm fine," she wriggled free. "I'm sorry, Rye. Can we talk later? I'm a bit exhausted."

"Sure, of course. I'll look in on you later." Rye hugged her before blipping out.

Carly swiveled around Adam, and went upstairs into the bedroom.

"Wow. Looks like you bought the whole mall," he nervously chuckled.

She rolled her eyes at him without responding.

"I cooked dinner. Are you hungry?"

"I guess," she shrugged. "Need a shower." She snatched off her blouse.

"Babe, what's that on your shirt?" He pointed while approaching her.

"What?" she looked down at the blood transfer she hadn't seen on the back of her shirt.

"Looks like blood," Adam said.

She had no intention of lying to him simply because she was angry and disappointed in him. "Oh, it's not mine."

"Whose is it?"

She sighed. "Val and I were stopped by Piure PD."

"What? Why?"

"They thought we were stealing. At least, that's what they said."

"Why—wh…blood," he stammered.

She bounced onto the bed to remove her shoes. "Val said mall security was following us around from store to store. The cops said they reported us for suspicious behavior. Val thinks we were racially profiled. Well, me, specifically."

"Okay, then what?"

"We drove out of the mall parking lot and the cops pulled us over in a deserted area. They refused to tell us why they'd stopped us, and they got mad because I demanded to know. They made us get out of our car and shoved us onto the hood of their police car, even pulled their guns on us."

"What!" Adam knelt in front her, indicating he was anxious for the entire story.

"Then they cuffed us. One of the cops said to check me for drugs and weapons because I looked like *the type*." She exaggerated air quotes with her fingers.

"One of the cops…he started groping me, and I…felt his disgusting erection against me, and Val…reacted."

"Reacted how?" Adam growled through clenched teeth.

"She castrated them." Carly shrugged and tried to get up from the bed.

"Whoa, whoa. You mean she?"

"Yes, and I support her a thousand percent."

"Who were these cops?"

"Wilkes and Skaarsgard, I believe," she blurted, again, attempting to get up.

"Which one touched you?"

"Wilkes."

"Mm," is all Adam managed before moving out of her way.

"Don't go doing anything crazy. Val already took care of it. They'll never grope or profile any other innocent women ever again in life. So there, it's done."

"What about their cameras?"

"I ashed them. What's for dinner?" she asked while swinging her body away from him, refusing to allow him to think everything was fine and dandy after he'd lied to her for years.

He breathed loudly and stood up. "Ratatouille."

"Great. I'll be downstairs after I shower."

"Okay." He moved the shopping bags from the patio into Jo's old bedroom down the hall that Carly had converted into a wardrobe.

The moment Carly was alone and underneath the running water, she allowed herself to cry. She scrubbed herself so ferociously, her skin flushed red all over. Her parents had always protected and shielded her, so she'd never experienced this level of hatred. What angered her was that she had been oblivious to it. It was yet another growing pain she was experiencing without her parents.

She simply had to thicken her skin and accept that ugly situations like those were probably waiting for her and Adam in adulthood. She couldn't allow herself to get so emotional or bitter that she lost control of her core the way she did when Rye blipped over. Somehow, she knew that could've been bad for everyone, everywhere.

strands

carly

CARLY HAD CALLED Crystal shortly after Adam confessed. She didn't believe Rye would understand, Jude wouldn't care, Val was Adam's bestie, Kane was out of touch, and Jo and Vikki would be biased. Crys was a normal girl, and being a college freshman, Carly figured she'd likely have the best advice to offer.

This morning, she had hastily dressed and raced to Crystal's college dorm. She knocked slightly.

"Hey you!" Crys flew into her arms.

"Hey, I've missed you like crazy," Carly said.

"Miss you too! Come on in."

"I'm so sorry my first visit since your move-in day is under these circumstances," Carly lamented.

"Don't you worry about it." They plopped down on the single bed. "So, what's going on? You sounded really upset on the phone. The wedding's still on, isn't it?" Crystal folded her legs.

"Yeah," she breathed. "For now, anyways."

"What do you mean?"

"He lied to me, Crys."

"About what?"

"He let me believe he wasn't a virgin this whole time. Turns out, he is."

"What do you mean by letting you believe? How exactly did he do that?"

"Well, my first semester at Keetering, we went to Josh's party and I saw him outside of the bedroom where Lana was naked under the covers."

"Okay, and?"

"I saw that someone was under the covers with her, and then suddenly, there was Adam standing outside the bedroom door."

"I can see the implication, but how…"

"When I had insinuated about it, he never corrected me. I have literally brought it up like a half-dozen times and he never denied it. Now he tells me years later that it never happened."

"I see," Crys sighed. "I can see how upset you are, so you might not wanna hear anything that doesn't support your anger, but the truth is, I understand why he never corrected you. He's a scared young man who's still finding his way."

"But we had a pact, no more secrets! And he broke it."

"That's definitely not cool. Did he apologize?"

"Yeah, after I pointed out that he hadn't."

"That boy was always stubborn."

"He still is, for sure. Drives me insane with it."

Crys gazed into Carly's worried eyes. "I sense this goes way deeper than what you're telling me, but if you ever want me to know, I'm here. Until then, your wedding in less than two weeks away, so you have to decide on forgiveness in a hurry. Do you want to forgive him? Or do you feel too betrayed to ever trust him again?"

"He's scaring me, Crys. I'm scared to vow to be with him for a lifetime when he's too stubborn to be honest with me about little things."

"I completely understand, but everyone we love will hurt us sometimes. Not saying it's okay or to even expect it. It's…we're all human and we're just now learning about life for the first time ever. I don't know about you, but that can be scary most of the time."

Carly didn't bother to correct her on the *human* part because they were, after all, part human.

"My parents tell me all the time that no matter how hard I try to be perfect, I'll hurt someone I love, and I can only hope for forgiveness if I've been good to that person. Adam's been good to you for longer than he's made this stupid mistake. I believe he can redeem himself. As long as he accepts full responsibility, and truly expresses his understanding of how he hurt you."

They interlocked fingers as a tear dropped from Carly's eyes onto her jeans.

Crys tenderly wiped it away. "Hey, look at me. Relationships of all kinds are hard because there's a whole other human besides ourselves that will aggravate us to infinity. Not everyone is worth the aggravation, but I really believe Adam is worth it, for you. I've never seen two people mesh so cohesively."

"I just want to…punch him in the gut sometimes." She almost said burn his body hair off, but stopped herself.

"Yeah, but that'd be abuse," Crystal laughed. "We all have a limit. You'll just have to find out what yours is, and pray Adam doesn't exceed it."

"Thank you, Crys." She hugged her tightly. "I finalized my admissions forms and will be joining you in Fall semester. So, tell me about these college guys you're surrounded by."

"Oh my gosh," Crys squealed.

They spent several hours discussing college life and parties before Carly left.

CARLY NEARLY DROVE home, but took a detour. She just wasn't ready to be around anyone else's energy. She desperately needed to focus on her own. She had left her cell phone behind on the night stand that morning to prevent anyone at Meridian from tracking her.

As she drove, she struggled with the years of anguish Adam caused her by allowing her to think he'd slept with Lana. On one hand, she understood, but then there was the unavoidable fact that he'd allowed her to keep bringing it up without correcting her. Though this wasn't insurmountable, it hurt her just the same. She also couldn't figure out what was going on with her core and why it was suddenly going berserk. It tugged, it pushed, it pulled, it pulsated, it expanded…it was scaring the life out of her.

Emotionally exhausted, she parked and trekked to a dense thicket at the Piure-McIntyre city borderline. She gazed at the digital strands of the Hex barrier, and ran her fingers across them like guitar strings, knowing there was no reason why she should be able to see the fibers of a biokinretic barrier. And here they were, crystal clear. They existed within her, outside her, and were oddly movable. As tears streamed down her cheeks, her core rumbled ferociously, imploding, exploding, and tugging in every path of existence, beyond the four cardinal directions humans knew of. Similar instances had occurred in the past, but she'd simply forced it down until it stopped. Not this time.

"Scionian Carly," an androgynous voice echoed in her head. *"Mother of Suns and Light."*

She shook her head wildly, and doubled over. Her breaths grew labored as her frustrations mounted, attempting to bury her, until she let go of it all. She released an ear-piercing yelp as her LR flamed crimson; it rotated clockwise, then counter-clockwise before overtaking her pupils completely. The ground shook and split.

She was tired of fighting her body, fighting her pain, and fighting eventuality. She rested her lids, lifted her arms, and allowed the eruptions to overtake her. She muted all thought and fear. Innumerous explosions simultaneously shredded and rebuilt her. She didn't know what was happening and she didn't care. For every obliterated nucleus, a new cell sprang up — a new strand, a new her. She felt aflame, but she was radiating light, incased in energy so bright, the average human wouldn't be able to stand the sight.

When she opened her eyes, she merely moved the Hex strands aside and walked through. When she looked around, she was gliding on air, and had no idea how. She crossed back over into Piure and spun in the air. Within seconds, she lost consciousness.

SHE AWOKE TO the comforting sounds of psithurism, trilling insects, and chirping birds. The susurration confused her, but they subsided as she became fully alert. She sat for a moment, and remembered that she still wasn't ready to return home just yet. She glanced over at the Hex, but didn't see the strands, so she presumed she had dreamt it. Once she regained her bearings, she dusted herself off and ventured deeper into thickets of Piure's outskirts, avoiding the obvious places Adam would search for her.

9

moirai

adam

ADAM PERUSED THE Promenade, eager to find the perfect gifts for Carly to at least break the block of ice crystalizing between them. He was clueless what to get because she'd just nearly purchased every item the town had to offer over the weekend. When she left, left her cell phone, and didn't return home for an entire day, he knew he'd messed worse than he ever had before.

Flowers just weren't enough but they were a sweet gesture that usually softened her a bit, so he grabbed a bouquet of poppies. He wanted to give her something grand that no one else would think to give her or even could. He stopped walking and text messaged his financial manager about it. He then shoved his cell into his back pocket, and angled his body toward the Book Haven when he caught sight of a familiar figure in the distance. He walked briskly over to a small crowd of young boys following a fleeing woman.

"Jessie?"

"Adam, hey." Jessie darted her eyes in a pendulum fashion.

"Are you alright?" he asked, gazing angrily at the three teenagers.

"She's fine, bro," one of them blurted.

Adam dropped his bags. "She doesn't seem fine. I suggest the three of you run along and leave her be."

"Adam, it's okay. My car is just up the street," Jessie pointed out while attempting to walk to it.

One of the boys moved into her path, forcing her backwards. "Yeah, and we'll escort you, cutie," the Brendan snickered as the others leered.

Adam was a man of little patience. After Carly and Val's encounter with the police, his tolerance level of women being harassed and not feeling safe anywhere in public, plummeted into hell. He snatched Brendan by his jacket so forcefully, he'd nearly thrown him into the wall. "Listen and listen well, leave her alone…hell, leave all women alone and take your punk asses home." He shook the boy with each word before throwing him down.

"Hey bro," a second boy growled, stepping closer to Adam.

Adam glowered so fiercely, the boys jumped back before smartly running away.

He'd felt his eyes grow hot, and could only hope his LR hadn't activated. He blinked a few times before turning to Jessie. "Kids," he shrugged. "Are you okay?"

"I'm fine, thank you," Jessie breathed. "This new batch of high schoolers are much more aggressive than I remember."

"They look like freshmen."

"That's even more troubling. You look great, by the way. How have you been?"

"I've been…okay, in therapy," he openly confessed.

"Oh, that's very responsible of you."

"Here, let me help you to your car." He grabbed her bags.

"You don't have to do that."

"It's my pleasure." He'd wanted to say he *did* have to, but thought better of it.

She walked briskly to her car and unlocked the doors. Adam presumed it was to avoid uncomfortable conversation. He tucked her bags into the trunk and closed it.

"I really appreciate you intervening back there, but you're not responsible for me. I just want you to know that."

"It's…"

"You don't have to save me. It won't bring — just, you're not responsible. Thank you." She patted his hand and hopped in her car.

He closed her door and watched her drive away with an aching in his heart. "It's fate," he'd whispered, staring after her, knowing he'd be her lifelong protector whether she wanted it or not, asked for it or not.

"It's such a beautiful thing to see you and Carly together and happy," Evan confessed.

"Thanks, man. I can't even categorize it as happiness because it's so much more than that. It's…it's indescribable."

"I completely understand. I feel the same way about your mother."

A silence thickened the atmosphere.

"Adam, you're the most important person in your mother's world. She talks about you all the time. Really, she brags," he chortled.

"Brags? I've messed up so much, that's hard to believe."

"Everyone does something others disagree with and we sometimes hurt the ones we love in the process. You're an awesome young man. Never forget that," he said while patting Adam on the shoulder.

Okay, wow. That felt very fatherly to Adam, and Evan had never given off that vibe before.

"Adam, I'm in love with your mother. Well, more than in love, really. I can't imagine life without her. I…I'd like to ask her to marry me, but I'd like your blessing in doing so."

Adam knew Evan had already asked, but he didn't know if it was okay to reveal that. Perhaps Evan thought he'd gone about his proposal the wrong way and wanted to take a different approach.

Adam gazed blankly to the sky. The whole thought of giving his mother away triggered his defenses, but Dr. Blake had warned him that being over-protective impeded her happiness, and his healing. He wanted her to be happy, and she deserved to be. He just didn't know how to believe in Evan after Mark had betrayed her the way he did. The pain she had experienced when Mark broke her heart was maddening. He had to let the past go.

"Evan, you already know my mother and I have a very close relationship," he stuttered, hoping not to come across as obsessive.

"I know."

"What I mean is she's my only parent and even if she weren't," he sighed, "I would be just as protective of her because she's…delicate."

"I understand."

"No, I need you to hear me. Mark destroyed her heart with his infidelities, then had the nerve to make her feel crazy for it. He gaslit her like crazy. Put her on psych meds. Threatened to take me away from her. Through it all, she was there for me. She held it together for all of us. She deserves someone who won't lie, or cheat, and will put her life before their own. A protector. I've always been that person."

Evan lowered his head as if he was preparing for a no.

"But I can't be everything to her."

Evan's head popped back up.

"It's selfish of me to deny the love you two share. I don't think I have ever seen her truly happy until you came into her life. Not like this. She's joyous and complete with you, and I want her to grow deeper into that. So…you have my blessing."

Evan jumped up with relief in his eyes. "Thank you! I promise you, I will spend the rest of my life making your mother happy."

"You'd better," Adam warned him with a firm hand shake.

Evan's face turned serious. "I'd die for her."

The gleam in his eye translated his deep devotion. They understood each other.

flowers for her hair

carly

THE WEDDING WAS two days away, and Carly had no clue what to do with herself. Grief was isolating, but she had to find a way to bridge the massive gap between pain and joy. She sat on the bed for a spell before deciding to march over to Rye and Evan's to have a showdown with Kane. She'd grown tired of the stale air and uncertainty between them.

She closed the front door and started over, presuming that if she wasn't proactive, their friendship might just cease completely, which unnerved her. She wondered if he ever thought to visit or text message her, or just spend all his days and nights with Rye. She fixed her attitude before ringing the doorbell.

Rye opened the door. "Hey, Car. What's up?"

"Hey, is Kane with you?"

"Yeah, he's upstairs."

"Is it okay to go up and see him?"

"Really, Car? Of course. I'm not his mom. Go ahead."

She jogged up and knocked gently. "Hey."

"Hey, Carls!" He jumped up and bear-hugged her. "It's so great to see you."

"You too." *It's not like we don't live around the corner from each other,* she thought.

"What's up?" He fidgeted a bit.

"I just…wanted to see you is all," she breathed, hoping he didn't notice her aggravation.

"Yea, I think about coming over all the time, but I don't…I don't want to be in the way."

"In the way of what?"

"Oh, with the wedding and all the planning. I'm sure it's a lot for you two." He nervously cleared his throat.

"You wouldn't be in the way, Kane." *It's called moral support.* She refrained from rolling her eyes.

"I know it may sound weird, but I'm still learning how to be a better friend to you…to be the friend you deserve. I might overthink sometimes, but I'm working on that too," he laughed.

She stared into his eyes with a blank expression, knowing there was more to it than what he put off.

"So…"

"Kane, I love you." *I'd never hurt you.* "You're still my best friend, and you're the best friend of my best friend. I see Rye every single day. But you?"

"Can you look me in my eyes and tell me you've forgiven me for what happened senior year?" he demanded.

"Forgive you for wha…oh." She finally smirked and grabbed his hand. "There's really nothing to forgive, Kane. It was a kiss. We were sixteen at the time."

"Yeah, I know, but the look in your eyes…"

"I was just surprised by it."

"So surprised you slapped half my face off. I hurt you and made you uncomfortable…and I don't know how to…" His hands trembled.

She saw he was afraid of her. Her heart splintered, but she held it together.

"Kane, you need to forgive yourself because I made peace with it a long time ago." That kiss never really bothered her long-term. It was the way he had ditched her that had hurt her feelings.

"I don't know how to do that."

She took his hands into hers to calm his nerves. "If you don't find a way, you'll keep yourself from me, which hurts me more than any little mistake ever could. Our friendship will be…over."

He exhaled a gust of air from his lungs. "No," he shook his head. "I'll never let that happen."

"You're already letting it happen." Tears glazed her eyes.

"I'm sorry." He wrapped his arms around her. "I'm so sorry, Carls. I promise I'll do better." He buried his face in her thick curly hair.

They shared sighs of relief.

"I must confess, I did come over with an ulterior motive."

"Oh boy." He steadied himself.

"Will you walk me down the aisle?"

He grabbed her up in the warmest embrace. "Of course, I will, Carls. Of course. I'd do anything for you. You're my best friend, forever."

She beamed at him.

"Soooo, I kinda need your advice too," he said in a lowered tone with his eyes darting suspiciously towards the room door.

"Sure, what's up?"

"Well…" he pulled a velvet box from his pocket. "I want to ask Rye to marry me."

"Oh crap," she laughed heartily. "It's like a chain reaction! Wow, oh my gosh. Let me see that." She opened the box to the sparkling diamond ring.

"What do you think?" Kane probed.

"I think you already know."

"Do you think she'll say yes?"

"Uh, yeah," she chortled. "You two are nearly one person."

He smiled in relief and shoved the ring back into his pocket.

"I'm so happy for you, Kane."

"Thanks, Carls. I only hope I can make her happy for as long as I live."

"Hey, don't do that."

"Don't do what?"

"I heard your tone change on the *long as I live* part. It's normal to age and grow," she reminded him.

"It's like, I knew that my whole life before meeting her and learning your world. Now, for some reason, I don't want that. I don't want to get wrinkly while she stays…"

"She'll age too, Kane."

"Just not as fast as I will. I worry I won't be able to satisfy her like…"

"It's a natural concern to have. If we all walked around feeling immortal or believing in eternal youth, what would we appreciate? We'd be arrogant and ungracious. You're not that kind of person, and you should never aspire to be." She rubbed his hand.

"You're right, but getting old isn't something anyone actually wants. We just don't want to die young, so getting older is the consolation prize."

They shared a familiar laugh as Carly massaged her chest in discomfort.

"You okay?" Kane probed.

"Yeah, just felt like…I don't know, a pulling feeling. Weird."

He bounded to his feet. "I'll get Rye."

"No, no. It passed. Might have been heartburn from the *light* meal Vikki cooked for me."

"What is her version of light? Because she seems rather intense most times."

"She is, but in a good way. She's truly a gem of a human. Like you." She smiled.

"Like me, but with superpowers."

"Kane, I love you this way."

"Weak and ordinary?"

"You're neither of those things."

"Sure," he responded unenthusiastically.

"Look, I know these *abilities* are seductive, but they come at a great cost. You just can't imagine the cost until you're paying up every day."

"Nothing can be worse than being inadequate, knowing you'll become useless to your partner sooner than later."

"Having your parent kidnapped, tortured, and executed just for existing is worse than sharing everyday with someone you love eternally," she interjected. "Waking up every day next to them. Holding them, being with them. This isn't a movie, Kane. This isn't some scenario you can safely judge from a movie theatre seat while eating popcorn. These people want us dead. What sane person would want that lurking after them for the rest of their life? All for smooth skin?" A tear escaped her.

"Hey, hey, I'm sorry. I didn't mean it that way. I guess I allowed my greatest fears to make me ungrateful. I didn't think of it that way. I'm sorry."

"It's okay. I know you don't know, but I also never want you to find out."

meridian

JULY 31st

Everyone bustled about the community decorating and preparing for the ceremony. Adam was at Evan's while Carly sat in front of her vanity table, surrounded by Jo, Vikki, Val, Rye, Ksenyia, and Jude. She had disassociated herself from the scene and focused on Adam. That way, she wasn't a panic attack away from ruining the day.

Jo and Rye took turns styling her hair, Vikki and Val primped her gown, while Ksenyia and Jude readied her accessories.

Jo kept rubbing her shoulders every few minutes, likely snooping in on her thoughts, which she didn't want at all today. She just wanted the ceremony to be over so she and Adam could progress into the next phase of their lives.

"Forever. Forever with Adam," she thought repeatedly.

After Vikki had made her face over for two hours, she swiveled around towards the mirror.

"Oh my," Carly gasped.

"Do you like it?" Vikki anxiously probed.

"I love it," Carly warmly replied. The delicate pinks and lavenders danced softly against her glowing sienna complexion in a way she never thought they could.

"Your shoes," Jude said as she bent down to slide them onto Carly's feet.

"And garter," Rye added with a mischievous wink.

Carly flushed as Rye slid the garter onto her thigh.

"And now, for your crown," Jo said as she placed a floral tiara atop Carly's pin-curls.

Carly stood and faced them. They cupped each other's waists, with their gold and scarlet gowns touching the floor.

"Awww," they collectively chimed, clutching their chests.

"Please, don't cry, you guys," Carly pled.

"You're just so…so perfect." Jo patted her heart as her cheeks grew a dewy rose.

"Jo, you promised," Carly reminded her.

"I know, I know, but look at you!" Jo turned her towards the full-length mirror.

Carly was stunned by her transformation. She was eager for a moment alone to reflect. "Thank you all so much. I can't believe you've made me look…so beautiful."

"You're always beautiful," Rye sang.

"You're officially becoming my real sister today," Vikki tearfully added.

Val pressed her palms together before folding her arms embarrassingly.

"Oh my gosh, you guys," Carly blushed. "I think it's time to switch off and check on Adam."

The ladies shuffled out of the bedroom.

"If you need to empty your bladder, now's the time," Jo reminded her.

"Definitely," Carly agreed as she handed Jo her bouquet and dashed into the restroom.

Just around the corner, Evan, Krill, Sage and Kane fixed their bowties in front of the mirror. Adam's bowtie was a scarlet- gold swirl, complete with a gold handkerchief. The other's bowties and cummerbunds were scarlet.

Kane fidgeted as if he were the man of honor. "Bathroom break." He absconded up the staircase.

The others patted Adam on the back.

"Is the garden ready? Rings? Luggage?" Evan asked Krill.

"How many more times will you ask?" Sage teased.

"Everything is good to go. Just waiting on the bride," Krill boomed in his deep rumbling tone.

"Can't believe I agreed to a surprise honeymoon, courtesy of Rye," Adam said to Evan.

"She can be sweet when she wants to be," Evan huffed. "I think this occasion is one of those times." He touched Adam on the shoulder reassuringly.

Adam smiled at himself just when all the ladies entered the house. "Mom, you look beautiful." He embraced her. "Is everything okay?"

"Yes, son. Everything is fine. Carly's fine. The rings are fine. The garden is fine. Vikki's fine, and I'm fine." She cupped his face.

He grinned, trying not to worry about Carly not being with them.

"She's the bride, Adam. Her entrance is to be grand." She kissed him on the cheek. "Everyone, we should head over to the garden."

They filed out of the house where decorated white silk tents awaited them just a bit off into the distance. Upstairs, Kane sat on the bed with a solemn expression.

"Pssst."

Kane popped his head up and looked around just when the French bedroom windows flew inward, and Carly floated in.

"Carls," Kane breathed as he helped her move her gown aside. "You scared the daylights outta me. Why aren't you at the garden?"

"Probably the same reason you aren't."

He silently gazed at her exquisite beauty. The flowers braided into her hair sweetly scented the air. The last time he'd seen Carly dressed in womanly attire with makeup was prom. A time when he was still hopeful that she'd choose him. A time when neither of them knew themselves or what the future held.

"I needed a quiet moment is all," she confessed.

"I did too. I wanted to be by your side, but that would've been weird for the others."

"I'm sure Val felt the same way. You guys should've traded off," she snickered.

"I can't believe you're getting married and *I'm* walking you down the aisle. Me. I kept thinking it should be Evan. He's more of…"

"He's a lot of things. Fatherly even, but he's not you."

"It seems surreal," he whispered.

"Remember the first day we met?"

"How could I forget? Mr. Brent's class. I sat on your desk, chatting you up, thinking I was enchanting you," he laughed.

"Haha, your vibe was immaculate from the second I met you."

"Immaculate, huh?"

"Truly."

His eyes glazed over and heat rushed into his face.

"You did this same thing the day I interviewed at McIntyre Foods."

"What same thing?"

"Blush."

He dipped his head. "I'm sorry, Carls. I'm just that kinda…"

"I know, and I love you for it," she gleamed.

He took her hands into his and they shared a tender moment of reflection before heading to the garden together.

"See you in a minute," Kane said as he kissed her on the cheek and joined the wedding party.

Jo rushed over to her. "Are you ready?"

"I am."

The tents were full of food, refreshments, and stunning décor, but it wasn't lost on Carly that everyone there were without loved ones — cousins, parents, etc. There were eleven people, in total, not counting the clergyman. Crys couldn't attend due to college schedule conflicts.

Carly's parents were no longer among the living. Adam's father had passed away, along with many relatives of the other Descendants. She swallowed the absence for the present.

Get it together, Carly.

Jo escorted her to her marked spot before joining the others.

When the delicate music began, Carly entered the main tent. The first set of eyes she met were Adam's, moist and glossy. All her apprehension and sadness instantly melted away. She saw no one and nothing but him. The earth itself disappeared and they floated among the cosmos, hands adjoined.

Everyone stood and Kane offered her his arm. She secured him tightly and they marched down the aisle of white silk, with poppies scattered about. Each step she took brought her closer to their eternal love. Adam's tears flowed freely and he opened his hands right when she took her last step, joining him.

THEY SWIFTLY ESCORTED the clergyman off Meridian grounds before the reception began. She and Adam shared their first dance as the drunken sun lowered in the western sky.

"I love you, Carly Norah Wit-Rozovsky."

"I love you, too, Adam Angel Caspian-Rozovsky."

They shared a tender kiss before Krill changed the playlist. "Let's get this party started!"

"Uh oh," Carly chuckled.

"And so it begins," Adam laughed.

Hugs and laughter circulated throughout the reception tent as Carly excused herself to change into her reception gown.

"My daughter!" Jo screamed from the entryway.

They embraced long and hard as they swayed to the beat of the blaring music.

"Ready for some food?" Jo asked.

"I'm famished."

"Woohoo!" Jo kicked off her heels and escorted Carly back into the reception tent where the others wasted no time popping refreshments.

Krill and Jude were on the dancefloor, each grasping a bottle of beer. Val and Ksenyia soon joined them. Sage was standing alone, watching on, as the others mingled.

Adam had removed his bowtie and blazer. Carly stared at him from across the way. Somehow the shiny wedding band on his finger made him even sexier. She couldn't wait to have him all to herself.

After several hours of food, cake, speeches, dancing, and drinks, the time had come to wrap up the evening.

Carly spotted Rye blipping in and out of sight, porting their luggage to their secret honeymoon destination. She suddenly worried a bit about leaving Jo and Vikki at Meridian. She knew Evan wouldn't let anything happen to Jo, but Vikki had no one to protect her.

"Hey, married lady." Kane snuck up behind her.

"You're up next, buddy," she teased.

"If, *if* she says yes."

"The longer you take to ask her…"

"Yeah, yeah, yeah." He put his arms around her. "Can't believe you're all grown up and leaving me," he mimicked in a fatherly tone.

"Kane, cut it out. We'll only be gone for two weeks."

"Two *magical* weeks. Wink, wink."

"Shut up already." She flushed crimson.

"I…oh my God in heaven. You're a…you've never…"

"Shhh, shut up!" she whispered loudly as she pulled him out of the tent.

"I never would've guessed that you two…"

"Well, you wouldn't have to guess if you ever spent time with me."

"Ouch," he whined through his tipsy haze.

She folded her arms across her chest. "Next year I'll be 20."

"You say that like 20 is old."

"I feel old sometimes."

"Carls, what's up?" He instantly sobered up.

"I'm scared."

"Scared of what?"

"Of…you know…*it*. Doing *it*."

"Ohhhhh."

"I always thought I was ready after I fell in love with him, but now that I know it's gonna happen, I'm scared I…I won't be good enough." Her breathing grew ragged.

"Whoa, whoa. Calm down." He steadied her with both his hands on her shoulders. "It's okay. It's totally natural to be nervous. Especially when you're thinking this far ahead. Stop doing that. Stop over-thinking. It doesn't even have to happen tonight or the next. Just enjoy spending time alone with your new husband and everything else will fall into place."

After a moment, she calmed herself. "Wow, Kane. I never knew you were so full of wisdom."

"Well, you'd know if you spent time with me."

She gut-punched him.

Adam ducked outside. "I was wondering where you snuck off to. Time to say our goodbyes."

Kane stared after them as they entered the tent and made their rounds.

Jo hugged Adam until Evan peeled her off. "Alright, honey. It's only for two weeks."

She sniffled and squeezed the bride and groom's hands one last time before joining the others in a circle.

Carly instantly caught the brewing animosity between Sage and Vikki, and thought they should honeymoon somewhere close by.

"Are you two ready?" Rye asked, interrupting her thoughts.

Adam reached for Carly's hand. "Yes," they answered.

As the Descendants threw poppy petals into the air, Rye grabbed their hands, and they were moving through space. When they opened their eyes, they saw the moon and its radiant casted glow over the rippling waters. The moon was so close, Carly instantly knew they were no longer on Earth.

"Your luggage is inside, there's enough food to last a year, and everything else you could possibly need is stocked."

"Is this even Earth?" Adam asked.

Rye simply smiled at Carly.

"Wait, I know this moon. We're on Sharen," Carly confirmed.

Rye had ported her to Sharen in the RIP Galaxy when they'd first met. She'd fallen in love with the moon and Rye had promised her a return visit one day.

"Holy cow," Adam breathed.

"Don't be alarmed by the noise you hear behind the house. It's just the generator," Rye informed them.

"Wow," Adam whispered again while gazing at the life-size moon.

"Well, this is where I leave you," Rye said with a shrug. "I'll be back every three days to check on you."

"But, what if…"

"Bye." She blipped out before Adam could bombard her with any more questions.

"What if she doesn't come back, Carly? We'd be stuck here forever."

"Babe, calm down. Look around. We have an entire planet to ourselves to do whatever we want."

They gazed at the massive pastel moon.

"To ourselves," he repeated in awe, a wistful smile spread across his impossibly gorgeous face.

When he took her hand into his, nothing else mattered but her. The longer they stood in perfect silence, the more he didn't ever want to return to the chaos and pain earth housed with a vengeance, as if it were its purpose.

He turned to her.

Her heart beat so furiously, she thought it'd burst from her chest.

Without a hint of hesitation, he scooped her up into his arms, and kissed her breath away before carrying her into the cozy cottage.

honeysun

adam

ADAM AND CARLY woke in each other's arms with the kindest suns warming their skin. No alarms, no cell phones, no television, no impending doom.

When she sat upright, he pulled her back under the covers.

"How do you think Mariah put all this together?" he asked in a sultry morning voice.

"I honestly have no idea, but she's been porting for decades before we ever met her. As far as we know, this is *her* getaway."

"Smart girl. Anyway, enough about her." He pummeled her with kisses everywhere until they decided to get up.

Carly blushed at herself in the bathroom mirror. She had spent the night making love with Adam until they fell asleep in each other's arms. She blinked slower because she was afraid she'd wake up from this fantastical dream, and she never ever wanted to. She swiftly showered and joined Adam in the kitchen where he stood, shirtless.

"Hungry?" he asked.

"Starving."

He scavenged the fridge. "Eggs and toast?"

"Sounds great." She plopped down in the barstool.

"What do you think there is to do out here?" He ransacked the cupboards for glasses.

"Um, oh…what does that paper say over there?" Carly pointed.

He snatched it up from the counter and gave it to her. He poured them some orange juice as she read over the note.

"Well?"

"According to Rye, we can hike, snorkel…oh, and even ice-skate if we're willing to travel out far enough."

"Cool, sounds like fun to me."

Carly grinned, knowing her husband was still a misanthrope, no matter how hard he tried to be selectively social. "Let's get out there and see what there is to see. I mean, after all, you can fly," she reminded him.

"I can, can't I?" He nuzzled his nose into the nape of her neck.

They scarfed down breakfast and dressed in jeans and hoodies. They stepped outside into the unknown and gazed up at the sky, where the sun and moon were on equal footing.

"This is amazing." Carly radiated with joy.

They interlocked hands.

"It truly is. You ready?"

"Yup." She climbed onto his back and they jetted off into the skies of Sharen. "Wooo," she yelped as they twirled around.

"I can't believe how much water there is on this planet," Adam yelled. "Like how?"

"Who cares! It's ours right now."

He turned them upside down and flew them in circles until they spotted crashing waterfalls.

"Are you wearing a bathing suit?"

"Nope," she replied.

"Even better." He grinned and landed on a cliff near the edge of the rushing falls.

"Last one down is a rotten egg," she taunted as she stripped down to her undies.

Before he could get his jeans off, she dove into the roaring waters.

"Cheater!" he called after her.

She swam backwards towards the edge.

"Babe, be careful."

"What?"

"I said, be careful," he yelled. "We don't know what's on the other side."

She playfully rolled her eyes at him.

He swam closer to catch her.

She grinned before allowing the tide to carry her over the edge. "Wooooo!"

"Carly!" He floated above the waters, past the fall's ledge. "Carly!" The fierce foamy waters blocked his vision, and he lost sight of her.

He flew down and went under, popping his head up every few seconds. "Carly, this isn't funny anymore."

After a few more dives, he flew into the sky and summoned the waters from the ground. He had never attempted to move a large body of water before and doubted he even could. With the water rippling in the sky, he easily spotted Carly, nestled inside a nook. He sighed when he realized she was playing hide and seek with him behind the waterfall. He rubbed his forehead, owning his overreaction. He guided the clouds from the skies, revealing the trio of blazing suns, released the waters, and rushed back down to her.

He slowly entered the cave, where Carly awaited him, radiating more heat and warmth than a million suns. The waves rushed and whooshed behind them. She leaned her back against the wall, closed her eyes, and opened them with her flaring LR rotating.

"Well, I guess you're the rotten egg." She bit down on her bottom lip.

He rushed into her. They devoured each other and laid facing the waterfalls until the sun began to retreat.

"HOW ARE YOU two sapheads doing?" Rye asked as she tip-toed through their mess on the floor. "Not that I need to ask from the looks of it," she mumbled.

"Rye!" Carly screamed as she flew into her arms.

"Hey, Mariah," Adam beamed, catching her off guard with a hug.

She jerked back a bit, ready to stop him from messing her hair. "Looks like Sharen has done you two some good."

"We love it here!" Adam exclaimed.

"Glad to hear it," Rye smiled.

Adam stared with a carefree look in his eyes. "How's my mom?"

"She's just fine."

"How's everyone else doing?" Carly asked.

"Same ole, same ole," Rye shrugged.

"I don't know if that's good or bad," Carly replied.

"No one's fighting, so that's good."

"Oh, thank goodness. I was worried."

"About who?" Rye asked.

"Sage and Vikki seemed to have some bitterness between them." Carly just wanted to be sure.

"Oh, them. Vikki's been staying at home since you left."

"Wait," Adam interjected. "She's not even going to the gym?"

"She hasn't left the house."

Carly glanced at Adam.

"Hey, hey. None of that," Rye stated. "Those are all adults back there. Let them work their own problems out. You're on your honeymoon."

"She's right," Adam quickly concurred.

"I just came to check on the generator, make sure you two were alright, and see if you needed anything that wasn't already here."

"We could use a cell phone signal," Carly said.

"Yeah, I never cared to do that. When I come here it's because I don't want to be in touch with anyone," Rye told her.

Adam nodded.

"I get why *you* wouldn't need it, but I sometimes wanna text you, and I feel weird not being able to." Carly poked her bottom lip out in a puppy dog fashion.

"We can look into it AFTER your honeymoon, and that's if you ever care to come back here."

"Oh, we will," Adam sang.

Rye snickered. "Alright, you two, I'm out."

"Hey, tell Kane I miss him and tell Jo we love her," Carly added.

"Yeah, yeah, yeah." She put up the peace sign and blipped out.

"I don't know how I keep forgetting that girl can pop up while we're in the middle of doing…*things*." Adam grinned wickedly.

"I'm sure she has better *things* to do with Kane."

"Then we shouldn't waste a second of not doing *things*."

They smiled and flew into each other's arms.

THEY'D SPENT THEIR honeymoon soaring the skies, exploring the planet, and each other. With the fiercest regret, the time to return home was nigh. Tomorrow, they'd return to Earth, and Meridian — reality. The moon shone nearly as brightly as the sun as they laid clinging to each other in the moonlit darkness.

Carly sprang up from her sleep, breathing heavily, clawing at her chest.

"Babe, what's wrong? Are you okay?" Adam clung to her.

"Yeah," she breathed, "yeah, I'm fine," she whispered as she leaned into his kisses on her neck and shoulders. "Just a nightmare. Let's enjoy the last night of our honeymoon. Go back to sleep."

"Honeysun," he murmured.

"Huh?"

"Not honeymoon, honeysun. You're the sun, every sun. My sun."

He pulled her so taught and snug, she may as well had been part of him. For added measure, he wrapped her in his arms like an octopus. She rested in his familiar comfort, which overtook her until she eventually succumbed to it.

meridian

RYE PORTED THE newlyweds to their front door and disappeared. The turned happily towards each other, rosy-cheeked and glowing.

Adam levitated the door ajar before scooping Carly into his arms, and carrying her over the threshold. "Welcome home, Mrs. Rozovsky."

"And now, let forever begin," she whispered with interlaced fingers around the nape of his neck.

They swayed inside each other's arms in the foyer for several moments before closing the door.

"I'll get started unpacking our bags," Carly told him.

"I'll be up to help in a bit. Just wanna check on Vik."

"See you soon," she gleamed with a kiss.

She bounded up the stairs and attacked the suitcases Rye had lovingly delivered. Before she was able to empty out the first suitcase, Adam returned, hysterical.

"Vikki is gone!"

"What do you mean she's *gone*? She's an adult, so she's allowed to…"

"She's gone, babe. She left this." He shoved a piece of paper at her.

Hey bro. You can't be surprised by this. It's what everyone wanted anyway. I doubt anyone even notices I'm gone until you check my room. I'm so sure of it that it hurts. No one deserves to live a daily reality of contempt. I also have demons I must slay and I aim to do just that before moving on with the rest of my life. I wish you and Carly the very best because you've both been kind to me. Thank you for trying your best to love me. I definitely love you and I hope to see you again one day. Love you, brother. — Vikki

"Oh no," Carly said.

"I'm going to find her."

"Adam, calm down. She's been begging you for some time and space so she can work through her emotions. Maybe you should honor that."

"I'm all she's got, Carly. She can work out whatever she needs to, but I won't abandon her when she clearly needs me the most. She needs to know she's loved."

Carly gazed back down at the note, re-reading the slaying demons part again.

Adam was emotional, but wondered if Vikki had made her way back to Russia to find Nikolay. With Vikki's new abilities and how proud she was of having them, Adam knew in his gut that's exactly what Vikki would do.

"You've been showing her, but it's up to her to believe it. You could reverse time for her, but she still needs to heal to allow herself to be loved, Adam. Let's give her some time and see if she reaches out."

He breathed loudly and deeply to express his reluctance and disagreement.

She cupped his face. "We just got home from our honeymoon. Our honeymoon. We're actually married and this just can't be our first day back home."

He gazed intently into her smoldering eyes before acquiescing. "Okay. Alright. I'll give her some time."

1:15 legacy

adam

Two weeks had lapsed fairly quickly and life went on for the Descendants at Meridian. Most moved about as if Vikki's absence meant nothing to them. Many Descendants showed more outward concern about the Afrax Panel's disavowal and revocation of visitation privileges.

Jude's disdain was most obvious, but Ksenyia's aggravated disposition alarmed Adam when she'd told him she'd never intended to permanently separate herself from her family, and would not have agreed to the Hex if she'd known where it could lead. He promptly relayed the information to Carly, who quietly mulled over it.

With regular woes woe-ing, the newlyweds took every opportunity to venture away from Meridian, including this warm Saturday. Adam and Carly grabbed ice cream cones and joked about who was the strongest between them as they held hands in the Promenade. Carly blatantly adored his unwillingness to submit as they mushed their faces together, giggling like school children. They locked pinkies and strolled around without a care in the world, still on cloud nine from their honeymoon.

When they were within steps of the Book Haven, tremors rocked their cores. Adam dropped his cone and protectively shoved Carly behind himself just as a burly, melanated stranger rounded the corner.

"Descendant of Dauma Wit," the man bellowed in a thick British cadence, pointing at Carly.

"Who's asking?" Adam didn't allow Carly to go around him, though she stole a full glance at the man.

"I didn't ask."

As the man inched forward, the more Carly's expression morphed from wary unknowing to familiarity. His facial features were unmistakable, causing her to shudder in disbelief. Her defenses completely melted away when her chest hummed harmoniously. She calmly maneuvered around a crouching Adam.

"It's okay, Adam. I think I know him."

"It's been far too long." The young Adonis with the glistening bronze complexion smiled warmly.

"Are you my?"

"Yes, I'm your PawPaw."

She gasped at the bomb thrust upon her.

"What the hell did you just say?" Adam frowned.

"Young man, all will be explained, but we must get out of sight. Is there somewhere safe we can go?"

"Carly isn't going anywhere with…"

"…it's okay, Adam. Yes, there is." She phoned Rye for immediate evac.

Within seconds, they were in Meridian's meadows.

"Car, you better be right about this." Rye's eyes swarmed across the stranger's face.

"I would never put anyone here in danger." She scowled at the man she vaguely remembered from childhood, signaling him to start talking.

"My name is Charro. I am Dauma's greatest grandfather by over eight generations, and one of your eldest living ancestors." He was considerate enough to make eye contact with them all instead of only his beloved descendant.

"Why are you here? How did you find her? She's never mentioned you before." Adam remained stone, prepared to disbelieve anything the man said.

"I haven't seen him since I was 4. He just disappeared and I…I thought he was dead all these years. I mean, he had to be." Carly turned towards him. "Where have you been?"

"As you know, it is unwise for Descendants to reside in clumps. The last time I saw you, I'd specifically traveled to meet you — the pride and joy of your mother's life. I could not allow traditions to…well, I had to hold you in my arms. Even if only once."

Rye, on-guard, circled him as he spoke, prepared to drop him on the inhabitable ice planet of Origa, which was nothing short of a death sentence.

"Perhaps if we sat, this would be easier to digest." Charro squatted on the grass.

Carly followed suit, with Adam close by. Rye refused and remained standing protectively near them.

"I understand your minds'll likely remain closed, but I assure you, you'll change them."

"We're waiting," Rye snapped.

"My name is Charro Konstantin Wit and I am the only biological child of Emebet Etea, or as I have been dubbed, a Legacy Descendant."

"What the hell is a Legacy Descendant and who is Emebet?" Adam's patience was shorter than the Kármán line inside a blank mind.

"Adam," Carly pled. She clearly, and desperately desired to hear what Charro had to say.

"A Legacy Descendant is a firstborn of the 7 women who birthed a batch of abnormal children in Sintashta — the beginning of what you all know as the ancient bloodlines."

Rye fidgeted and swallowed impatiently, choking back the sarcasms that usually flowed effortlessly.

"That's rather impossible, PawPaw Charro."

"I gather it would seem so, and you can just call me PawPaw, little one. You always had a difficult time pronouncing PawPaw's given name. I see very little has changed in that department."

Carly inadvertently smiled while Adam and Rye's blank expressions remained cemented.

"You all may call me Ro, for short."

"Well, Ro for short," Adam quipped, "keep talking."

Carly patted Adam's knee to calm him. "My mother would have mentioned this, if…"

"No, little one, she would not have, as it was long decreed before your existence. Your mother, if nothing else, was wise and strong. It seems that she still is." He extended his palm towards her chest and it vibrated toward him. "Yes, she remains. Little ones, hear me when I say this truth is finally required. With the strongest of us lacking physical form, we'll fight an uphill battle. Nevertheless, we must press on."

Dauma had alluded to her age before her merger with Carly, which included three centuries. Now Ro was suggesting he had lived a millennium, while maintaining the appearance of a man in his late twenties, at best.

Charro angled his head sentimentally before allowing a long-withheld story to pour from him.

"Mother would speak of a foreign man that I would never meet," Ro began, "my father. His name was alleged to have been Verdapok Ākrid, and according to Mother, he was not of this world, but of one she'd referred to as Makovia."

Carly glimpsed Rye's gaze drop to the ground.

Adam sighed while slapping his hands against his thighs, unable to contain himself. "Aliens? If that's what you're here to say, just save it."

"Young man, you will listen. Belief or disbelief is the choice you have, but you will listen." His entire pupil glowed a glorious amethyst, the same hue as Dauma's LR.

Adam was so taken aback by it, he took Carly to the side. "Why didn't you ever tell me he existed?"

Carly squinted her eyes into slits so sharp, they sliced right through Adam's core.

"Okay, you're right," is all he offered, rescinding his audacity. He knew she would end him in that moment, and he dared not test her patience any further.

Rye had resorted to sitting, as though she was burdened by a guilty conscience. She sincerely appeared to be intrigued.

"As I was saying, the tales Mother told were just stories, as far as I was concerned. On one hand, he was the love of her life. On the other, she hated him for breaking her heart. My biological father was nothing more than a myth. The other mothers refused to speak of him, as if we Legacy children didn't share the same lineage. Our *abnormalities* were attributed to a chemical reaction, though no one could explain how it seemed to only affect the specific women who'd come into contact with the same stranger."

They remained quietly entranced by Charro's story.

"The Legacy children grew very close and protective of each other as time passed. I was the first to reach puberty. One day, my dearest friend, Mureet, had broken her leg. Her ankle had become trapped between two boulders and she'd moved too fast, twisting it completely backwards. Her leg, well she was to lose it. Then an infection spread and she'd grown sick. She'd wept like I had never seen. One night, as I comforted her, a purple dust poured from me and found its way into her skin. Her tortured cries summoned the neighbors, who gawked at the freak who was believed to be killing an innocent girl.

"Even when Mureet appeared the following day, miraculously healed, there were no apologies from the parents who had banished and shamed me. Mureet knew what I had done and thanked me. Mother, on the other hand, forbade my contact with anyone, especially Mureet. She'd effectively shut me off from the outside world, categorizing me as a danger to myself and others, when really, she'd wanted my power at her disposal. She hounded me every second of every day until I was able to produce the dust at will.

"Slowly, I came to accept Mother's resentment. She loathed absolutely everyone and everything. She hated me and all that I was, but refused to let me go. Especially as the other Legacy children's abilities grew. We were half-siblings, so our cores did not synch as yours seem to. Abominations, is what Mother called us. Eventually, I ran away. We all did.

"The first of us disappeared within a century after we'd left. A pattern quickly emerged and we recognized we were being hunted. We developed a code of contact and decided it was safer if we separated, but Mureet refused to leave my side, right up until we were the only Legacy children remaining. One day, we couldn't pull away from each other. We had pledged that if we were to die, it would be together, but we were afraid our kind would perish with us. We believed our kind were the next step in the evolutionary chain and should live on. I asked for her hand in marriage and she accepted. Soon after we wed, she'd become pregnant." His voice cracked.

"Weren't you all half-siblings?" Carly thought. *"They couldn't have synced, if so."*

"One day I came home and she was…gone. Never to be seen or heard from again. My unborn child…I knew she'd not gone willingly. Though she'd taken my last name, the Rozovsky blood in her veins ran deep."

Adam snatched his head up, now more interested in Charro's story than ever.

"Though I knew I'd likely be captured, I went in search of her and the unborn child we had named Daphni. All I found was this." He removed a small booklet from his inside jacket pocket and handed it to Carly.

She opened it and read the first few sentences to herself. "Mureet's journal?"

"Yes. It is common practice now, but Mureet was the first. I learned the importance of journaling because I'd never had known of her tortures without reading it. After more centuries passed where I failed to age, I was faced with a choice of life or walking death. I knew what Mureet would have wanted, so I chose life, eventually remarrying and producing heirs."

Carly clutched the journal against her chest.

"I won't tell you what it contains. It is your birthright to read for yourself."

"This still doesn't explain why you've resurfaced," Adam reminded him.

"500 years is a very long time to live in hiding, watching your descendants spread about the Earth until eventually being captured and killed. Well, Mureet's journal sent me in search of answers…and answers, I found," he sighed before continuing. "We have an origin, as does the Iksha."

"There are several glaring abnormalities that can't be ignored, Charro," Adam interjected. "How are there Descendants from other bloodlines if you were the only remaining Legacy child?"

"The others mated and produced heirs before their capture. This, I learned later."

"How can half-siblings sync cores when my half-sibling repelled me?"

"Legacy children were half-siblings by alien DNA, as it were. Is your half-sibling perhaps a full-blooded human?"

"Okay, well if you're the only Descendant of Emebet *Etea*, how is it that you came under the Wit umbrella of lineage?" Adam continued.

"Ah, well…Mother was not born in Sintashta, but Ethiopia, princess of Guangabi and heir to the throne. She was discarded in Sintashta when she was 15 years old because her sister conspired against her to reign in her place. A bitter seed was planted inside of her early on. She became spiteful and full of hate because she was abandoned in a foreign country with no friends, family, resources, or way to fend for herself. She could not return home or she would've been executed on site. She was eventually taken in by a poor family; the Wit's.

"She said her dark skin made her stick out like a sore thumb in a town that was ripe with those with pale skin, eyes, and hair. Most ridiculed and mistreated her. While vulnerable, she'd said a strange man with marble skin and weird eyes approached her. She would steal into the night and he would tell her tales of a world where people were different, strong, and giving. Where food was plentiful and there was no sickness. She'd quickly fallen in love and become pregnant, bringing shame upon the family who'd graciously taken her into their home. Alas, the war of Wit's was born. Etea lineage versus the untainted, although another Wit became pregnant, allegedly by the same stranger. Of course, we'll never know."

It was unbelievable how he'd answered every burning question Carly ever had as to why Wit's seemed to be indescribably disjointed. However, there were always tales of seven women, not eight. Something was missing.

"To make a long story short, the Wit's labored to secure Mother a husband before her shame could permanently ruin any reputations. Mother was too bitter to allow me to grow to accept her husband as my father. It was imperative to her that I knew I was inferior, lest my complexion beat her to it," he laughed. "To answer your question, I have come because I can no longer ignore what must be done and what is required to do it."

"Which is what?" Carly gently asked.

"My mother must be stopped."

There was absolute silence. His implication shocked them all into pause.

"PawPaw, are you saying that…"

"…yes, little one. With a heavy heart, yes. The founder and leader of the Iksha is none other than my very own mother — your eldest living ancestor."

"Wait," Carly stopped him. "She's human. Is she not?"

"As born, yes."

"Then how can she still be alive?" Adam demanded.

"I am likely the reason, but I can't possibly remember every tiny thing from the last thousand years. I am part human, after all."

"Then, allow me," Adam insisted, ready to grab ahold of Charro's forearm.

"Excuse me?"

"PawPaw, Adam can access memories. He can see what you've forgotten."

"Amazing," he whispered. "Will I see them as well?"

"No," Adam swiftly answered. "Not unless you recall them on your own. I can't help you to remember. I can only view them as they are."

"So, then I must trust you'll tell me the truth of what you find?"

"Just as we must find a way to believe the story you've thrust upon us."

Charro openly mulled over Adam's statement before agreeing. "We're on the same side. Give it a go." He shoved his bare arm towards Adam.

After making contact, Adam remained stooped on the grass for what seemed like an eternity. Usually, he was done within seconds, but a thousand years of memory was quite a longer movie to watch.

Adam's core temperature increased and beads of sweat riddled his skin. He frowned and murmured several times while grasping Charro's arm.

"Well?" Charro inquired.

"Your mother has been telling you stories of her childhood since before you could understand. Emebet was not the sole heir to the Guangabi throne. She was the youngest of thirteen siblings. eleven sons, two daughters. It was believed that neither she nor her sister would ever inherit the throne with eleven male siblings. As disease ravaged the family, the males and parents perished one after the other. It was believed that Emebet, or Emmy, as her siblings called her, and her sister Amashi, possessed some sort of immunity. After your mother's exile, Amashi ruled for a few years before dying of what was believed to be the same plague.

"After learning of Amashi's death, Emebet believed she could return to Guangabi and rule as Queen, leaving impoverished Sintashta behind forever. However, Emebet was forbidden to ever return. Guangabians had decided she must have poisoned her entire family for the throne. Once she accepted her fate, her bitterness turned her."

He took a few deep breaths before continuing.

"Sickness was rampant in Sintashta as well, but Emebet never fell ill, so eyes turned to her, again, as the culprit until…"

"Until what?" Rye asked, anxiously.

"Until she became pregnant with Charro and exhibited signs of illness, seemingly proving that she had not poisoned anyone in Sintashta. Mother and child were to die, but Charro, you healed her while still in the womb.

She saw her pregnant belly illuminate with lavender light. She'd repeatedly absorbed your amethyst crystals before you were ever born. Long story short, after that, you became her infinite supply of V."

"V?" Charro asked.

"The Iksha calls the serum they harnessed from the Wit Bloodline, Vechnyy."

"An eternal fountain of youth," he mumbled to himself in disbelief. "That's why she kept me prisoner. To harness what she could not replicate, and what no one would ever believe existed."

They sat silently for a moment, allowing Charro time to absorb what he'd heard.

"I was just a thing to her. We're all just things to her. But if she's dedicated to our destruction, then that must mean she's harnessed all she desires and requires our existence no longer."

Carly jumped to her feet, solution oriented, as usual.

"We need the journals," she declared.

"Which ones?" Rye asked.

"All of them. Every single one from every Descendant, everywhere."

"Why? What are you cooking in that brain, Car?"

"The only way we're going to know which abilities she's harnessed is to read every journal."

"What difference does that make?" Adam interjected. "Isn't that a bit beside the point?"

"Not if we identify bait to lure her into the open," Carly informed him.

Adam folded his arms across his chest before acquiescing.

"Dylan did tell me the Iksha's main priority was to harness what they didn't have," Carly continued. "Not to study, but to possess. Emebet must've discovered she could never destroy the abominations without becoming one of them. She'd never have stood a chance while human. But something's not adding up." She tapped her chin.

"In what way?" Rye queried.

"Yes, how exactly?" Charro joined, with scrutiny blazing in his eyes.

"I can't imagine it was terribly difficult to terminate what could have only been a few dozen Descendants at some point. So, why didn't she? What stopped her?"

"That, I do not know," Charro replied.

"We need to tell the others immediately. We can't hold this back from them." Adam knew the other Descendants must be informed of this revelation.

"Not before I meet with Jo," Carly whispered.

Adam nodded, unwilling to reveal any of his mother's abilities to Charro. "Let's go now, then tell the others asap. We cannot sit on this."

"PawPaw, please stay here with Rye until we return."

"Of course, little one."

Adam grabbed Carly and flew them to Evan's.

"Adam, we're going to need to allow Jo and my PawPaw to communicate. We don't have time to conceal her abilities from him."

"As much as I don't like it, I understand. We need to do this quickly so we can make our rounds at Meridian. The last thing we need is further dissension between the Descendants."

They all agreed. Adam, Carly, Jo, and Evan returned to the gardens swiftly.

The moment Charro stood on his feet, Jo's demeanor changed immediately.

"Colossians 1:15," Jo randomly blurted out.

Charro's eyes glazed over as if he'd come into the presence of a long-lost love.

"Legacy Descendants were decreed as Colossians 1:15 beings by the Kremlin, but abominations by Iksha," Jo continued.

"Several centuries after our creation, yes," he confirmed.

"Don't you mean *the* Iksha, Jo?" Carly asked.

"No," she responded with glassy eyes. "Iksha is the name Emebet had given her alter ego."

"It is your mother who is speaking, little one," Charro clarified for Carly.

Carly smiled but wondered aloud why Adam hadn't mentioned Emebet referring to herself as Iksha.

"Because it wasn't in Charro's memory," Jo spoke. "It's from mine and buried deep inside my daughter's core."

"Mom, how could you know when Emebet's son didn't?" Carly asked in disbelief.

"He did. He's just willed himself to forget the thing he couldn't bear to accept. Merging with our ancestors blessed me with some of their memories, including those of his firstborn son, Kāto."

Charro lowered his head in shame. "How would you react to discovering your own mother wanted you dead? You'd want to forget."

"But you couldn't have forgotten your mother wanted you dead if you came here to tell us," Adam insisted.

"That's not what he's willed himself to forget," Jo added. "It's that his mother's power grew from…"

"Dauma, please," Charro pled. "Allow the little one to read from Mureet. Not us."

"Very well."

"I'm still confused at how teenagers ran around loose in Sintashta with blazing LR's without being rounded up," Adam said.

"The Legacy children left Sintashta when they were 17 to avoid persecution," Jo revealed as if she was reading a book. "Centuries later, Emebet employed the Kremlin to assist her in locating them. But they merely wanted to harbor the Legacy children and their Descendants for scientific study, so she came up with better plans. She'd deceived the Kremlin by pretending to assist them, only to betray them, since she already had a supply of Charro's healing crystals inside her. Once she'd harnessed the first trait of self-regenerative healing, she could not be killed, and they grew to fear her. Ultimately, she'd convinced them that all the 1:15 beings were dead. They eventually closed their case files and Iksha silently grew from one head, to dozens, to hundreds."

"Just because we can heal ourselves doesn't mean we can't be killed," Carly corrected.

"Read the journal, baby girl," Charro said.

"I…I need to go home," Carly informed everyone.

"Are you okay?" Adam asked before anyone else.

"I just feel dizzy and tired. You guys tell the others what's going on, but leave Jo out of it."

Truth was, Carly could vomit and she didn't know why. All of this was just a bit much for her. She couldn't enjoy a few days of peace with Adam before Descendant drama sucked her back into its blackhole.

early

CARLY LAID ON her stomach, on her bed, reading where Emebet had come into the most powerful ability early on in her quest to procure Descendant abilities. She'd harnessed it from Mureet and Charro's offspring, Daphni. She possessed cellular regenerative powers beyond that of simple healing, and reverted cells to their optimum state of youth. It would seem that Daphni was the origin of Vechnyy, the evolution of Charro. Daphni, the first known Descendant of Rozovsky-Wit combined bloodlines.

According to the journal, scientists studied Daphni for decades and discovered that the Wit and Rozovsky bloodlines carried unique markers that, when combined, could produce an unconditional invulnerability trait, which terrified them. Emebet couldn't risk anyone else possessing eternal youth nor the ability to be withstand all attacks, so she'd changed her primary directive to slaughter the Rozovsky Bloodline, saving the Wit's only for scientific purposes — the V.

musical chairs

adam

Adam paced the flooring of his Meridian living room, staring at his cell phone, patiently waiting for Vikki to respond to his dozens of text messages. He thumbed through the thread where he'd messaged her incessantly.

Vik, if you need time, I understand. Just let me know you're okay.

Hey Vik, text me back. I'm worried.

I miss you, lil sis. Please come home.

Home isn't the same without you here. Please message me back.

He'd decided that Carly, being an only-child, would never understand this dynamic. Not only that, everyone who knew Carly, loved her. She clearly could relate to grief, but he wasn't grieving Vikki. She was alive, which meant they still had time to be in each other's lives, and he was done wasting those days waiting. Regret seemed childish and avoidable because he had breath in his lungs. He intended to go in search of her.

"Hey, babe," Carly greeted him from behind.

He casually shoved his phone into his pocket. "Hey."

"Everyone wants to meet at Evan and Rye's to discuss Mureet's journal and what our next move will be."

He masked his anger, and wondered how the others could nonchalantly plan everything else in the world, but never even mention Vikki's name, as if she didn't exist.

"When?" he asked.

"Now."

"Okay."

They walked briskly to the next block, where the Solomin's front door was open, with Ksenyia and Val already inside.

"Hey," Carly waved.

"Hey," Ksenyia swiftly replied. She rubbed her tiny triceps to express her discomfort with Adam's presence, though it was her idea to have a three-some with him a few years back that landed them in the awkward predicament in the first place.

"Hey, guys." Val was no longer uncomfortable because she had done the emotional labor required to heal and redeem herself, whereas, Ksenyia had refused. It was causing a disconnect between them.

Adam ignored Ksenyia, and any indirect vibes she casted. He plopped down in a chair, and folded his arms across his muscular chest.

Carly grabbed them a bottle of lemonade from the fridge as other Descendants piled in.

When they all were present, Evan orchestrated. "Let's move below, shall we?"

They tarried into the immaculate and well-stocked basement. Each Meridian home had basements and tunnels underground that led to an outing at the city line.

Sage splayed a map across a huge round table, grabbing everyone's attention. "Based on the journal, there's a facility in Menorca, Spain. I've printed out a map."

Everyone gathered around it.

Rye sighed. "Before this gets drawn out, let's start with the most basic question, are we planning to go there to investigate?"

"We're not sure what language is even spoken there," Evan added. "We'll need to communicate with at least a few people to get around."

"They probably speak Spanish since it's in Spain, but it doesn't hurt to research it," Evan suggested.

"Catalan and Spanish," Kane replied, descending the basement staircase. They all turned to look at him.

Jude sucked her teeth and rolled her eyes.

"Kane, you shouldn't be here," Adam said as gently as possible.

"Excuse me?" Rye became heavily defensive. "This is *my* home."

"Rye, you know what he meant. This is too dangerous for him," Carly implored.

"Well, he's involved because we're in love and nobody can change that."

"It's alright, babe. Carls is right. I'll be upstairs."

Rye flashed a resentful glare Carly's way that softened under glistening tears. "I'm really tired of Kane being left out. It forces me to split my focus while you all get to have your mates by your side 24/7. I mean, how fair is that?"

Adam was eager to debate. "But that's because…"

"Save it, Adam! Your mother isn't a Descendant either, but she's affected by her affiliation with my brother. Meaning, their love made it okay for everyone to look the other way. What makes Kane so different?"

"I'm tired of playing musical chairs with this enigma," Carly said.

Adam would always side with any situation that made his mother happy or was beneficial to her. This was an unnecessary struggle, and Kane was indeed a big boy. If he wanted to be part of a dying species, he was prepared to vote to allow him. "You're right, Rye. He's part of your life and we all accept that."

"Are you *mad*?" Jude exclaimed. "So, we're just allowing anyone and everyone into our circle now? First Vikki, the ass-hickey, then the Legacy stranger, and now Kane? We're trusting any old person now, is that right? Not to mention we're banned from Afrax! I thought we came here to be safe and live free. At this rate, we may as well shout it to the whole world!"

"Jude, that's not what this is and you know it. And the Legacy *stranger*, my greatest-grandfather, is *your* ancestor as well. Or does that not matter to you?"

Jude's opposition became the national anthem of all meetings because that's who she chose to be in every situation.

"That's exactly what this is. Jeez!" Jude's face flamed. "And we don't know anything he tells us is the truth. How do we even know?"

Carly frowned at her. "You seem the most unhappy with being here. You don't have to be. At least PawPaw Ro is choosing to be."

"PawPaw Ro," Jude sarcastically huffed. "As far as we know, the Iksha, a.k.a. his mother, by his own admission, sent him here to infiltrate and destroy us!"

"Whoa," Sage said, attempting to calm things down.

"No, Sage," Jude shot back. "I don't get to choose my ancestors or my bloodline, so never mind about that right now. But Kane wasn't born into this. He shouldn't have a group of strangers voting on whether or not he dies!"

"You all aren't strangers to me, though I may be considered a stranger to you. You're like my family." Kane calmly added.

"*Like* family isn't family!" Jude screeched. "You have no idea what you're saying. You don't know our history. The torture, the death, the hiding. If you did, you wouldn't be so eager to join this life."

Val sighed at the swelling argument. Trained to think clearly in chaotic situations, she offered the most logical point. "Rye's distraction is one we cannot afford. If her thoughts are torn, someone could die."

"Maybe we should just take a vote and be done with it," Evan proposed. "Kane's a person, not a thing. We can't just look through him like he doesn't exist. None of us would be alright if something happened to our partner. Rye's feelings need to be respected."

They grew silent, but many of them nodded.

"Those against including Kane?" Evan posed.

Jude raised her lone hand and was furious when she saw she was being outvoted.

"Those in favor?"

The others voted in favor of matriculating Kane.

"Boom, done," Evan said. "Sage, please lead off."

Adam truly desired to see how many of their relationships would exist if not for the BK core sync, especially Jude's. He was starting to believe Jude wouldn't bother with any of them if she wasn't synced with Krill. Only Kane and Rye's relationship existed on simple choice, which he admired. They choose to love each other and that beauty inspired him. Besides, if Kane isn't some complication to be kept separated from the community, perhaps he and Carly could spend more time as friends again.

After the vote, they got back to business, with Kane standing off near the fireplace until Carly scooched over to make space for him.

"Whew," she breathed with her hand over her stomach."

"Babe, you alright?" Adam asked her.

"Yeah, breakfast isn't sitting well with me right now, but I'll be fine. Kane, how do you know what languages are spoken there?" she asked, changing the subject.

"My family is originally from Vitoria, Spain. We've visited all the surrounding islands dozens of times. Menorca isn't but a boat ride away from Vitoria. We traveled there many times during my vacations. I spent every summer in Spain growing up until the end of sophomore year when I got hired at McIntyre Foods."

"Oh, I never knew that," Carly divulged.

"Yeah, I haven't been for a few years, but if what you say is there is actually there, why have I never seen it? I mean, wouldn't I have noticed a regime this complex?"

"The Iksha is highly skilled at existing in plain sight. They probably masqueraded as local police or something."

"Oh, well that makes sense."

Next, they discussed accommodations and travel, with their main lodging agreed for Barcelona.

"I'll search for hotels," Ksenyia offered.

"I think we should rent a house versus a hotel," Kane stuttered. "You know, so we encounter less people."

"Smart." Val beamed at him.

Ksenyia swayed her perfect model frame around and searched for a home rental instead.

"To further lessen contact," Kane added while pointing at the map, "we should book a private ferry from the mainland, rent a jeep and dock in Ciutadella, where most tourists dock. We can travel from Ciutadella to Maó-Mahón and into Punta Prima. Should take about an hour or 90 minutes." He traced his index finger across the map from end to end.

The gang suddenly leaned in close, heavily intrigued by Kane, who hadn't previously spoken much. With Kane's intimate knowledge of the island, the Descendants easily agreed with his plans versus a port without adequate cover.

"Am I tagging along?" Charro asked.

"That wouldn't be wise, PawPaw," Carly said. "I imagine you are at the top of Iksha's list, so you should remain here, where you're safest."

He nodded in agreement.

"Someone will need to remain here to monitor Charro and the operations until we return," Adam said, refusing to trust Charro just because he was Carly's alleged kin.

"I'll stay," Jude anxiously offered.

"Gee, I'm surprised," Carly mumbled.

Jude rolled her eyes, which Carly dismissed.

Adam leaned quietly against the wall, anxious for the journey.

adam's ale

adam

WHEN THE DESCENDANTS boarded their private roll-on/roll-off ferry, the captain informed them that a storm had come through years prior that had destroyed the island.

"Va ser tota una anomalia," he explained. "Per què els turistes americans volen visitar una illa deserta quan les altres illes són boniques i animades?" He squinted his eyes.

"Yo crecí allí. Es sentimental para mi," Kane offered.

"Què?" The Captain frowned quizzically.

Kane simply slipped him a wad of euros to cease his questions.

"Ahhh, veig." The Captain bowed repeatedly, and promptly returned to the wheel.

Since Rye planned to port them back to the mainland, the captain's skepticism became background noise to the Descendants as they clambered into the rented jeeps on the ferry for readiness, and extra privacy.

Kane wistfully leaned over the edge and gazed out at the island drawing closer. Carly joined him as Adam quietly looked on from a respectful distance.

"The storm the captain was talking about had to have happened right when I got hired at McIntyre Foods," Kane said.

"That's the same year I moved to Piure," Carly added.

"Heck of a coincidence, isn't it?"

"Definitely seems that way," she whispered thoughtfully.

The moment their private ferry docked, they all swiftly drove off, and glanced around at the abandoned island. Nothing seemed to be left but marshy lands and a few people who appeared to be scaling to rebuild.

They drove for miles, hoping to come across the slightest clue. By the time they reached the other end of the island, they'd given up hope. They hopped out the jeeps and glanced in every direction.

"Whatever was here, is gone," Rye said, bored of the empty island.

The others shrugged, but continued to look around. They each went in various directions, chattering, and pointing at what they believed might be clues.

Adam turned when the colossal Mediterranean Sea relentlessly tugged at his core until he acknowledged its presence. It, like Zsita, refused to be ignored. Obeying its call, he slowly strode into the water, allowing it to cradle his every curve. Each of his steps were silhouetted by a Gaelic caim-like barrier, preventing a euxinic demise. Before anyone noticed, he was fully submerged.

He trekked through, the same as he would've on dry land. The water, as if greeting an old friend, guided his path, jet-skiing him lower, into a darkened flooded facility.

Bioluminescence from various organisms provided scarce lighting, so he energized for better sight. He glided forward, down a long hallway of numbered doors. He yanked on a few of the handles until a door opened, and a lifeless body floated out. He recoiled, shocked to his core, but bravely continued on. More floating bodies with symbols branded into their forearms bumped into him. He glared around at Dylan's carnage, believing his brother gained his freedom at the cost of all these people's lives, but he couldn't find it in his heart to hate his brother. He was sure every choice Dylan was faced with was horrible.

Adam continued discovering the rest of the facility, looking more carefully at each deceased Descendant, searching for Alexandra —his bio-mom—, having seen her face for the first time in his twin's memories the day he shook his hand.

He paused to reminiscence as Dylan's repressed memories seized his vision. He allowed them to replay from childhood to puberty.

The hazel-eyed boy felt the waters for as long as his mind could retain memory. He just didn't know he could control them. Enduring routine torture taught him to keep his mouth shut and learn through observation. He had watched his mother be drained 'til she was near death, only to be healed and drained again. All because she exhibited a useable trait. They were nothing more than a Descendant cattle farm. The Iksha tortured everyone regardless, so he had decided in his case, it'd be for nothing because he refused to give them another weapon by developing any abilities. He began plotting an escape but had no idea how he'd overcome a million short tons of water atop his head.

In the meantime, he grew to please Iksha personnel, playing their wretched game and even snitching on other Descendants until he gained enough of his captor's trust to trade for regular surface sessions with his designated scientist, Dr. B. He was rewarded with warm sun, fresh air, television, reading materials, real baths, hygiene supplies, non-patient garments, snacks, and occasional large meals. The once tiny frail boy had actually gained a bit of healthy weight.

When Dylan reached BK puberty at the tender age of 13, he sensed what he didn't know was Adam's existence, but remained confused, believing he was somehow fantasizing his long-held desire to be free. However, his connection to water was undeniable. During a routine torture session where militants sprayed him with high velocity hot water, hoping to incite a trait surge, the water sensed his desire not to be harmed and responded by creating a barrier, cooling its temperature before hitting him. Dylan simply pretended to be injured. He writhed on the floor, begging the militants for mercy. After they left the room, he grinned and thanked his new best friend, Navū; the water.

Another day, while taking a rare earned bath, he became overwhelmed with curiosity of Navū, so he bravely leaned back and submerged himself. He was initially afraid to inhale until the entire tub of water burbled. He stopped holding his breath to find he could breathe perfectly fine, but he wasn't inhaling liquid. He was somehow contained inside a bubble-like field. When he moved his limbs, the water cradled him.

The foot vibrations of approaching Iksha militants alarmed him and he quickly emerged from the water, with a dry head.

Adam sat up inside the bathtub, realizing he was physically reliving Dylan's past. He gazed around the flooded room before floating upward to a black dot on the ceiling. Using his energy, he extracted it. It was a camera. The Iksha was monitoring Dylan's every move and knew of his abilities, even though he'd faked them. It was likely they had anticipated the tsunami and moved the most powerful Descendants to a different facility.

Adam's mind and body continued to relive Dylan's every memory and emotion as if he had experienced them himself. More of them surfaced, revealing that Dylan had formed a close relationship with Dr. B, and she helped plan his escape, even suggesting Piure, California as the only place where the Iksha would never find him.

"What's so special about that place?" Dylan asked.

"There are people who are responsible for you being here. They are the real beasts who started all this."

Dr. B went on to tell him what he had to do to maintain his freedom and keep the Iksha off his back. Each time he went to see her, she frosted a new layer. He eventually became obsessed with a new free life, fascinated by the stories she'd tell him. He grew more anxious to escape by the day. She became his close confidante, teaching him how to speak and act around others. He was eager to see her every chance he got, versus dreading sessions where one wrong word would land him in the black-hell chamber, starving for weeks. The companionship quickly spoiled him, and he pledged his loyalty to her.

When Dr. B suggested the deluge, Dylan didn't want to disappoint her with his reluctance, but he didn't want to kill anyone, especially his mother. He'd die before harming her. He just couldn't agree until Dr. B promised him that Alexandra and a few others would be transferred to a convalescent facility for conformed patients, whose abilities were adequately documented and preserved. Only then did Dylan agree.

The day Alexandra was transferred, Dr. B arranged a farewell meeting between them. They converged in a darkened hallway, conversing in Russian.

"My son…"

"Mother, you'll be safe now, somewhere you can rest."

"My baby boy, the only day I'll rest is the day I die. The day it all dies."

"Don't say that. I'm saving you. We'll be together again."

"No, I want you to stay away. Stay free. I will be alright."

"I won't leave you to rot." He refused to put his faith in the other's long-contrived plan of destroying their captors. They'd been beaten down so badly that none of them were strong enough anymore.

She caressed her dear boy's cheek, wanting to warn him, but knowing their every move was being watched and every word, recorded. He, on the hand, had never been a believer of the Descendant-captive's resistance plans anyway, so he didn't care as much about what The Iksha militants saw. He'd always been a little rogue bird, determined to go his own way.

"Believe nothing and no one but the part of you that is good," she reminded him.

Of all the things she could've said to him, she chose to mention the brother he'd never met. She didn't say she loved him nor to be safe. She told him to believe in a stranger. His resentment for this long-lost brother of his deepened. The part of him that's good implied she believed him to be bad when all he'd done was love her as best as he could. Perhaps a lifetime of captivity had slain her ability to love a child who constantly reminded her of a cursed existence, whereas his brother was a symbol of hope and freedom.

When they embraced, she whispered in his ear.

"Find him."

Dr. B returned with a vial of V, urging him to take it and leave immediately. "Your travel supplies and documents are waiting for you in Barcelona. Remember, do not stop on any of the Balearic Islands."

"I remember. What about you, Dr. B? They'll kill you if they find out you helped me."

"Don't worry about me. Just get out of here. This place, and everything in it, needs to die."

They shared a quick embrace before she scurried out of site with Alexandra. He walked out of the back door of the surface housing unit and stoically approached the shoreline in disbelief that the day he'd dreamt of his whole life had finally come. He never imagined it would come at such a tremendous cost.

He gazed up at the disappearing chopper that was carrying his mother away, then down at the crashing waves and clear vial. He pocketed the vial and considered abandoning the plan. The thought of drowning any remaining captives turned his stomach. Then he remembered how they were living as cattle, tortured and ravaged daily. They were watched so aggressively that they couldn't end their own suffering if they wanted to. Convinced he was freeing them of their hell, he let the warmth in his chest grow to a boil.

"Boy! What are you doing there?" an Iksha militant demanded of him from a distance.

Never having wielded Navū on a massive level before, he was afraid he'd fail and be returned to his underwater cage, but he was out of time and refused to ever be anyone's prisoner for as long as he drew breath. He closed his eyes and forcefully commanded Navū, gathering the waters from as deep as the seabed, filling the skies with a translucent wrecking ball.

The militant tried to escape, but there was none. Dylan blanketed the entire island in seismic waves, destroying the buildings, boats, stone monuments, and any moving bodies. Now immersed, he sent bone-shattering torrents throughout the subaquatic facility until every nook and cranny was filled with liquid and the screams were silenced. After thirty minutes of tidal waves, he pushed debris in every direction before allowing the sea's current to carry him away.

Having no sense of direction, Dylan pled for a break from submerged travel and Navū delivered him to the dry grounds of Port de Pollença on Mallorca. He punched himself in the head and screamed, sending crushing liquid into the sky and splashing back down. He ignored the screaming tourists. Instead, he sat on the bank crying until the part of him tortured with painful regret died, and he went blissfully numb.

Twenty-four hours later, he was in California.

When the visions subsided, Adam mourned Dylan more deeply, wishing Carly had never merged them because he now believed Dylan deserved to live free after being tortured for so long.

"Navū, return me to the surface."

Adam majestically reemerged from the ocean, arid and solemn.

Carly flew into his arms. "Oh my God, Adam! Are you okay? I thought you flew away. What were you doing down there for so long? And how are you dry?"

"I saw his childhood, Carly. His whole life. He wasn't a bad person. He didn't deserve to die."

"But…he didn't. He's part of you forever."

"Just as your mother is part of you but you'd rather have her in your arms." He choked on the words, wanting nothing more than privacy to feel without judgment.

She saved her response for another time, held his hand, and regrouped with the others for return to the house.

When they were finally alone at their rented home in Barcelona, Carly sat next to him on the bed until he was ready to talk.

"They're all dead. He flooded the island and the underwater facility."

"Oh my gosh," she gasped. "How could he…"

"He was duped by some doctor who pretended to care about him. He didn't want to. Not only was he torn about it, it broke him." Adam's mind splintered. Something about Dr. B was oddly familiar, but he was too emotional to think more deeply about it.

Carly squeezed his hand.

"Being free our entire lives, we can't judge the decisions any captive has ever made. We can't imagine what it's like to have our flesh slowly peeled from our bones, only for it to be regrown and stripped again." Tears escaped him as he mourned his brother, his father, and every life taken at the hands of their enemy.

Images of Dr. B flashing her fake wicked smile at a trusting Dylan hadn't fully subsided. The water in the toilet bubbled up into a frozen glob as his pain and regret peaked.

"Babe, look at me." Carly pulled his face to hers, forcing him to focus on her. "We're going to end this, one way or another, but to do that, we need to keep our heads clear. We can do that together. I'll help you and you help me, okay?"

He swallowed his jagged emotions over and over. They sliced his insides but wouldn't go down. He could've had a brother, but Dylan was destroyed in ways it would've taken a lifetime to heal from. The night they battled, Dylan did try for a truce. He obviously wanted a relationship and tried to express his desire for one, but was too damaged to show it in a way Adam could understand.

"Adam, baby?"

He stared blankly ahead as the ground rumbled, and droplets of water began seeping upward from the floorboards, breaking them apart.

Carly looked around in fear. She threw her arms around him to fully blanket him in calm. "I love you, Adam. Eternally, without bounds. I need you, and I'm sorry," she whispered in his ear.

He reluctantly expelled a burst of air he was holding captive. His fingers unfurled from the fist he had fastened. His eyes met Carly's.

Just as he was about to speak, Rye blipped in their bedroom wearing a bath towel, soaking wet, with lathered shampoo in her hair, babbling about frozen shower water, busted pipes, and earthquakes.

"I'm sorry," he whispered.

He pretended to be fine, but he was not. He saw how worried he had made Carly. He wanted her to forget everything he'd told her before she went Victorian on him. Besides, there was nothing she could say that would change the past or rescind his anger. Those Descendant captives were dead, his brother was deceived into killing them, and he knew Dr. B was still alive and well somewhere…likely wherever his bio-mom was. He planned to find Vikki first, and Dr. B second. And when he found Dr. B, he planned to kill her.

aftershocks

adam

Still in Barcelona at the rental home, the weight of the past and the revelations hung heavily in the air among the Descendants and Kane. The atmosphere within the group was tense, their individual thoughts swirling like storm clouds. It was Carly who broke the silence that had settled upon them.

"Adam, I know this is incredibly difficult for you," she began softly, "but we can't let anger and vengeance consume us. We need to focus on finding a way to stop the Iksha and put an end to their tyranny."

Adam clenched his fists, his knuckles white with suppressed rage. "I know, but seeing what my brother went through, how he was manipulated and used... It's hard to just let go of that anger."

Carly reached out and took his hand; her touch, soothing and warm. "I understand. And we're not letting it slide, we're channeling it into action. We need to be strategic about this, to find their weaknesses and lure them."

Rye nodded in agreement. "Car's right. We can't let our emotions blind us. We've got to be smart and careful."

Adam took a deep breath, his chest heaving as he tried to calm the tempest within him. "You're both right. I just need to find a way to focus on the mission and not get lost in my own feelings."

Carly smiled gently. "We're in this together, babe. We'll support each other, keep each other grounded."

Rye gave a determined nod. "And we have the skills to take down the Iksha. We just need to work as a team."

With their resolve renewed, the Descendants began to formulate a plan. They gathered around a table in the house's living room, maps and documents spread out before them. Rye and Kane had been working on hacking into the Iksha's communication systems, trying to gather any information that might give them an advantage.

"Fact is," Rye began, "we have found several Iksha facilities and eliminated them, which has kept us twirling in circles. We've been working from the presumption that if we can pinpoint their headquarters, we can eliminate them. But we've been wrong. Charro revealed that *The* Iksha is just Iksha — an individual we need to find. Not a place." Her fingers danced across the keyboard as she conducted web searches for Emebet Etea at lightning speed.

Carly gazed down at the maps with her arms folded across her chest as if she were trying to hold her heart from falling out.

Adam noticed. "Babe, you okay?" He embraced her.

"Yeah," she breathed. "I'm fine."

As they continued to brainstorm and strategize, a knock on the door interrupted their discussion. Kane entered the room, concern etched across his face. "Hey, I couldn't help but overhear. Are you all okay?"

Carly gave him a reassuring smile. "We're working on an end-game to eliminate the Iksha. Join us."

Kane nodded, his expression serious. "I'm with you all the way. We can't let them continue hurting people."

"We won't," Adam replied more harshly than he likely intended. "But we need to get back to Meridian. We've been exposed here long enough. Rye?"

"Yeah, yeah, yeah," she said. "Get everything packed and I'll make two trips. I'm ready to go home. Barcelona is boring."

"It's only boring because we didn't get a chance to explore it," Kane said in a soft tone, wrapping his arms around her from behind.

"Next time?" Rye whispered over her shoulder, kissing him.

"Next time." Kane inhaled her scent and sighed.

"Oh, for the love of," Adam whined.

Carly couldn't help but laugh. "Leave the lovebirds alone. That's probably how they feel when we're all over each other."

"Exactly," Rye said, sticking out her tongue.

meridian

OVER THE NEXT few days, the Descendants immersed themselves in research and prep. They sharpened their combat skills, studied the Iksha's patterns and vulnerabilities, while Adam stood off to the side, silently listening. Carly noticed every time, knowing he'd only tell her what was going through his mind when he was ready, and not a second before.

One evening, as the sun set over the horizon, painting the sky with hues of orange and pink, Carly found Adam sitting by the edge of the cliff she and Adam had jumped off together when they were seventeen. She sat down beside him, and watched the waves crash against the rocks below. He took her hand into his.

"I know you're still struggling with everything you've learned about Dylan," Carly said gently. "But we can't let his choices define us or our mission."

Adam sighed heavily, his gaze fixed on the distant horizon. "I know. It's just... hard. I never got the chance to know him, and now all I have are these memories that aren't even mine...but they feel like mine, like I've lived this life."

Carly rested her head on his shoulder, offering him comfort. "Remem-

ber, you're not alone in this. We're here for you, and together, we can make a difference."

Adam turned to her, his eyes filled with a mix of determination and vulnerability. "Carly, I don't want to lose sight of what we're fighting for, but I do miss Vik. She's out there alone. Might be in trouble…just, I can't focus on any one thing and it's driving me nuts."

"I'm here." She rested her head on his shoulder as they gazed out the eternal waters.

As the Descendants continued their preparations, Adam found himself spending more time with his mother. He had always admired her strength and resilience, and now, with the weight of his newfound memories, he felt an even stronger connection to her.

One evening, as the sun cast a warm glow across the horizon, Adam and Jo sat on the Solomin's porch, gazing out at Meridian's gardens. The psithurism lolled them into a state of living peace and contentment.

"I've officially accepted Evan's proposal, and we're going to apply for our marriage license."

Adam's eyes widened in surprise. "That's wonderful, Mom!" He embraced her. "I'm so happy for you."

Jo chuckled. "Thank you, son. We'd like you and Carly to accompany us."

Adam's curiosity got the better of him. "Have you guys set a date?"

Jo nodded. "We're planning to do a small ceremony in a few weeks."

Adam grinned. "That sounds perfect. You know Carly will want to help."

"Of course, and I'm looking forward to it," she gleamed.

Adam briefly reminisced about his parents' relationship before it all went south.

"Mom, do you miss Dad?"

"Every day," she whispered.

They sat until their side of the Earth twirled away from the sun.

ADAM, CARLY, JO, and Evan drove to the local government office to apply for the marriage license on a quiet Thursday afternoon. Carly beamed while

Jo blushed. Adam sat with a curious gleam in his eyes as Evan parked in the lot. Inside the government office, Jo and Evan filled out the necessary paperwork and approached the counter.

The clerk greeted them with a smile. "Congratulations on your upcoming marriage."

"Thank you," they chimed in unison.

"Now, let me review your documents. Please, confirm your names for me."

"JoAnn Marie Ivan," Jo stated.

Adam jerked his head upright.

"Evan Solomin," Evan added.

"Any middle name, Mr. Solomin?" the clerk asked.

"No, ma'am."

"Alrighty," the clerk replied as she scribbled notes, checked off boxes, and turned to her computer.

As the clerk typed their data into the computer, Adam leaned over Jo's shoulder to whisper to her.

"Uh mom, what is this name, Ivan?"

"It's my maiden name, son. Maiden means…"

"Mom, I know what a maiden name is. On my birth certificate, it shows Caspian as your maiden name. How? Why?"

"Your birth certificate was amended, son. The adoption—"

"Miss Ivan, is it?" the clerk asked, interrupting them.

"Yes."

"I'm showing a previous marriage to a Mark Caspian?"

"Yes, ma'am. That's right."

"I don't see a divorce decree on file…"

"He is deceased," Jo added, clearing her throat.

"Oh, I'm so sorry," the clerk said. "So, a widower," she uttered as she turned around to continue typing.

"So, the adoption is why your name is different on my birth certificate?" Adam resumed.

"Yes, son, yes."

"Isn't Ivan a man's name? What is —"

"It's actually a Croatian surname. We can talk about it more at home." She patted his hand and turned into Evan's awaiting arms.

"It's just a name, babe," Carly said as she put her arm around him.

"I just feel a little…weird…I mean, I never knew the name she was born with. I'm her son. How could I have lived my entire childhood without knowing something as simple as that?" Adam expressed his displeasure in discovering something he believed he should've always known *after* Evan likely had already been told.

As they left the government office, Adam walked alongside Jo, his mind still processing. His mother's maiden name was Ivan. She said it was Croatian, but Adam wasn't so sure about that, or anything for that matter, since she'd never told him. Technically, didn't tell him today. She had simply let him discover it on a happenstance fluke.

He was frustrated about everything, and he wouldn't allow not one more thing to pile on his lap before resolving what was already there. He decided in that moment to retrieve his sister from wherever she may be, and he didn't need anyone's permission or approval to do that.

amplified

carly

As Carly stretched and yawned on a sunny Saturday morning, she felt for Adam before opening her eyes. When she realized he wasn't there, she called out for him.

"Adam?"

He didn't respond so she went into the bathroom to freshen up. She then jogged downstairs, thinking he was cooking breakfast or watching TV, but he was nowhere in the house. She didn't worry. She shrugged her shoulders and fixed herself a bowl of cereal that she didn't eat. Just jabbed at it with her spoon. After a beat, she headed over to the gym for a morning sesh.

It was gloriously empty, so she went right into her workout. After thirty minutes, Sage joined her.

"Good morning, Sage," she breathed.

"Morning. Early start, eh?"

"You know it. How are you feeling?"

"Bored, actually," he responded, as picked up twenty-five-pound dumbbells.

"Why are you bored?"

"Descendant duties aren't the only thing in life I wanna do. I want a social life, to have fun, go out for ice cream, skydive, ski, snorkel."

"What's stopping you?" she asked.

"Honestly, preferring to share those activities with a…partner," he confessed. "I'd feel pretty lame going alone."

"You shouldn't, Sage. Besides, you never know who you might meet on your excursions. Don't lock yourself away in Meridian. Don't let it become a prison when it's only your home."

"I miss her," he said, dropping the weights.

Carly paused her workout and turned to him. "Vikki will be back after she —"

"Fenyx," he corrected. "I miss Fenyx."

She gulped. "I'm know you do, and I'm…I'm so sorry, Sage."

"You have nothing to be sorry for. It's not your fault she up and left without saying goodbye." He frowned, but the pain blazed in his eyes.

Carly didn't want to add insult to injury by lying to him, so she simply remained silent and touched his forearm.

He patted her hand. "Thanks for listening."

"Of course," she smiled.

They continued their workout in silence before Carly showered and visited Val, expecting Adam to be there.

"Hey, Val. Have you seen Adam?" She hugged her in the doorway.

"No, I haven't seen him today. Want some breakfast?"

"Some orange juice would be awesome," Carly replied.

"Hi, Ksenyia," Carly greeted.

"Hey, Carly. How's it going?" Ksenyia gracefully and elegantly sashayed about the kitchen, scraping scrambled eggs onto white ceramic plates.

"Everything's great, for the most part. Have you seen Adam around?"

"No, not since yesterday."

"Hm," Carly replied as Val sat a glass of juice in front of her. "Thank you."

She pulled out her cell phone and called Adam. He didn't answer so she text messaged him.

"I'm sure he's fine. Likely flying around town for sport," Val offered.

"That is his thing to do when he's bored," Carly agreed. "Thanks for the juice. Enjoy your breakfast, you two." She hugged them both and walked over to Rye's.

When she saw Adam wasn't there, she stayed and helped Jo iron out her wedding plans before heading home, exhausted. She stopped along the way and leaned over to catch her breath.

"Whoa," she uttered to herself, bent over. As she took several breaths, her chest whirred and pulled again. "What the heck is going on?"

She stood upright to center herself. When she focused, she was able to stabilize. She shook it off, dashed home, and jumped right into bed.

CARLY SLEPT AS peacefully as she could, though she tossed and turned with anxiety. Adam normally would've grabbed her close, but he still hadn't returned. In her slumber, the toil of existence and expanse pulled her into its depths.

An indescribable pulling of disconnect jolted Carly closer to an unreachable consciousness. The only feeling she registered was Rye's flesh…until it was cruelly ripped from her. Her lids refused to allow the blaring light inside, though it threatened to slice through. Several whirling nightmarish eternities passed before tiny foreign electrical charges connected to her core.

Had she been ported to Afrax?

Feeling it was safe enough to wake from her nightmare, she opened her eyes and gawked at an unbelievable sight. Convinced she must still be asleep, she blinked rapidly while pinching herself. Neither changed the scene. The faces surrounding her weren't the human ones she had experienced for a lifetime. Hundreds upon hundreds of onyx ovular eyes punctured her long-standing reality.

"This is it. I've finally lost it," she murmured.

Diamond arabesque skins crowded the space she and Rye had somehow been thrust into. She gazed over at the frightened, though knowing, expression on her best friend's face. Terror oozed from Carly's pores because she'd never known Rye to be afraid of anything or anyone.

They simultaneously scrambled onto their feet, with Rye lending a helping hand to assist against the dense gravitational weight.

"Rye, where are we?"

Her susurration seemed to alarm the strange beings. Lashing timbres rang out in undecipherable lexemes and foreign tones.

Rye grabbed her hand and squeezed. "Remain quiet."

Following an additional string of piercing yelps, Rye dropped back to her knees and pulled Carly down with her.

Carly knelt while glaring upward, confused.

Rye slowly lifted her chin to speak. "My companion does not understand. May I…"

"SILENCE!" a cloaked towering figure blared. "Your tongue is merely one of millions. We will ask. You will answer, for the penalty of insolence and disobedience is cellular cessation."

Rye shrunk herself so low that Carly no longer recognized her.

"You," the being pointed, "you are the one called Car-lee?"

Carly was so shocked that words failed her. Rye tugged her arm.

"I…I am."

"Stand."

She complied without releasing Rye's grip.

"Have you any idea why you have been summoned before us?"

"N-no."

Scattered lexemes flurried about. Their long grimacing faces turned toward one another.

"You there, stand!" they commanded Rye. "You were entrusted with a duty, of which you have failed."

Rye gulped but didn't respond with the quintessential sarcasm she was known for.

"You," the tallest figure growled while pointing a long-tie-dyed finger at Carly, "do you have any concept of where you are?"

"No," she mumbled.

"SPEAK!"

"No." Her fear and shock were quickly morphing into impatience and annoyance.

"You are now on the Mother Planet of Apricity — the Originating Light of Life that is Makovia," he informed her in a clickity tone.

She remained confused, so she kept quiet until asked a question.

"This one here beside you was to ensure your kind understood the boundaries and rules of the Metaverse. Instead, it seems our warnings and instruction were wasted, as now, we are forced to determine your fate."

"I don't understand," Carly said.

"Of course, you do not. Scionian Mariah Solomin of Ancestor Verdapok lineage has failed you."

The figure stood. "I am Tanjuetti, Elder Makovian Ancestor, and primary representative of what you may refer to as the Panel of Life. We are your creators, and as such, are responsible for all that you do and do not."

Carly's pulse ran the gamut and her inner embers inadvertently flickered. The other Makovian beings fearfully shuffled in response to her charging core. His revelation was overwhelming but not completely unbelievable, as she'd long believed the existence of Descendants was beyond Earth's matter. She yearned to question Tanjuetti, but was afraid of offending their ways of life in a way that would cost her, her own.

"As you have been led awry, you may ask your questions," Tanjuetti granted, hearing her thoughts. "But I warn you only once to control your sunfire."

"I do not understand what you mean when you say that you are our creators. What is a Panel of Life?"

Tanjuetti glanced over to another, nearly identical, but shorter, being next to him before reclaiming his seat. "For this, Ancestor Nanzaki shall respond."

"I am the one they call Nanzaki. The language and tones you hear among us is Giwaza. You are of the Scionian species, a reflection of the Originating Light of Makovia. Scionians were doomed to rebellion when your Light returned."

Sensing her confusion, Nanzaki lifted his palm to quiet her anticipated questions. "All will become clear if you empty your mind of questions and listen only with the intent to understand. Release your denial, Scionian Carly. All life is the existence of disbursed Light, of which, Four Macrocosms, compiling the Metaverse, now exist. Makovia, Scionia, Apexia, and Seer. You are now on the planet Apricity, Galaxy and Universe of Makovia. Makovia is the true Originating Light," he announced with reverence. "Apexia is the Light, Absorbed. Seer is the Light, Transmitted Through, and Scionia is the Light, Reflected."

"What is Scionia?" Carly asked.

"What you call Earth is, in fact, Scionia."

"A specular? Earth is a specular of…"

"Listen, and you will learn all," Nanzaki replied. "Ancestor Verdapok was once our Eldest, strongest, and wisest. He alone is responsible for your current tainted existence, as opposed to the raw Scionian we had all decided were required for the balance of the Metaverse. Verdapok believed differently and decided that Makovian Ancestors were cruel to abandon Scionians without the inherent divine heritage. These abilities you possess are therefore, considered to be abominations by many of us."

Sensing an impending threat, her core disobeyed and her eyes flamed. Tanjuetti was instantly on his feet, hastily dismissing the spectating Makovian beings from the hippodrome. "She's pulling on Nivval," he shouted.

"Control your sunfire, Scionian." Nanzaki maintained a calm disposition, though aware of the Scionian's ability. He decided to distract her with knowledge.

"What is Nivval?" Carly demanded, her LR flaming and rotating.

"Car, don't," Rye urged.

"It is the name of our sun, Scionian Carly. Now please, calm yourself. We mean you no harm," he pled.

After a brief spell, Carly closed her eyes, and quieted her defenses until the heat inside her chest cooled. She rescinded her energy before glaring back at him.

"Although Scionians refer to their universe as Laniakea, its given name is Scionia," Nanzaki continued.

"If Makovia is our creator, who is yours?"

"You ask a question, expecting an answer you will understand, but you will not. Not yet."

"Does that presumption disqualify my right to know?" she bit back.

"Your species remains entitled. Entitlement is a disease which continues to rot your very cores. You are not owed more than you've been given. The creator of all life is the Light, which sustains us."

"So, this Light is our God?"

"Who Scionians refer to as God is the Light. Creator of all of life. So, yes. But since your light is merely reflected back, it is no more than a duplicate of its original. Therefore, many Makovians have long debated over Scionia and Makovia being equally Originating Light."

"If we are duplicates, why do we look different?" Carly surprised herself with how well she followed what Nanzaki told her thus far.

"There are only slight differences in the important features of Makovians, Apexians, Seerians, and Scionians. Originally, Scionians were identical to Makovians in most ways."

"Most?"

"Yes, certain Makovian conditions cannot exist within your universe and galaxy. For instance, your suns emit forms of infrared that our skin and eyes have minimal tolerance for. Your original design was purely that which the Light had granted. Your current condition is genetically evolved in consideration of your suns."

"Are we named for our suns?" she continued, as Rye silently looked on.

"No, for mammalian lifeform. Your galaxy is the singular space where it is permitted to originate and exist."

Carly logged a mental note on his distinction of origination versus existence. "Permitted by the Light or Makovia?"

"Both. Scionian lifeforms are unpredictable in ways that have caused too much damage to ignore, and predictable in ways that have brought us insight. A collapse is a catastrophic event that we will avoid by any means required, including the complete cessation of your kind."

"You'd kill us all?"

"Yes. Your species is about power, control, possession and fear, which is why your entire nature is self-destructive. You destroy that which you fear may cause you harm before discovering if harm is the intent. You enslave one another to secure supply of sexual pleasures and to elevate the ego of superiority above one another — self-importance. You harm innocent children for sexual gratification, yet do not punish such depravity on the highest level. Your only redeemable quality of love has been retooled, clouded and diluted, tainted and rebranded. There is very little selflessness left of your kind."

It saddened her greatly to hear another species tell her what she'd learned by living. "I know humanity sucks, but we don't all deserve to die. Why not just terminate the bad ones?"

"All life granted by the Light deserves to flourish, but not at the cost of any other life. Scionians have caused the collapse of the Magnomium…"

"Magnomium?"

"I forget that you refer to your galaxy as Milky Way. Scionians caused the collapse of the Magnomium — or Milky Way, as you call it — several millennia ago. The rippling effects were and continue to be, eternal. If your kind refuses to respect all existence, then your existence must cease."

"So much is demanded of us, but so little is given by way of knowledge," she mumbled, still confused about data that's been programmed into her since birth.

"Some of you were given the knowledge, including the one standing beside you."

"Mariah can't be held accountable to spread a single message across an entire planet," Carly defended.

"Yes, she can, and yes, she will be. Her task included enhanced abilities to assist her in sharing the proper awareness."

"But the dinosaurs…E.L.E…how?" Carly interrupted, changing the subject.

"Reptilian lifeform was a result of the Light replacing what once was. However, in consideration of the Scionian suns, the Light decided to revert back to its original intent and cleansed the foundation in preparation. Walk with me." Nanzaki waved at Tanjuetti as he began to stroll the hippodrome, with Carly and Rye by his side.

"What does Magnomuium mean?" Carly was immersed in learning all she could, even it was a dream.

"Great sun."

"Oh."

"You see, there are many suns in existence. Billions. Most of them are larger than the ones The Light has bestowed upon Scionians, but larger isn't the equivalent of more powerful. The Scionian sun, Sol, is the second most powerful sun in the Metaverse, which is why it cannot be disturbed. Without stable sun, solar systems collapse. When solar systems collapse, the balance of Light immediately seeks to correct itself by ending life or beginning it. In our experience, it's usually the former."

"The problem may be that humans don't know non-human lifeforms exist," Carly reasoned. "The majority of us back on Earth, or *Scionia*, believe we're the only lifeforms in all existence."

"That belief is immaterial and incorrect." Nanzaki was resolute and emotionless.

"How? Why?"

"Scionians know other Scionians exist and have even domesticated non-human lifeforms. If they refuse to respect their own existence, no other existence can matter. Death and destruction are death and destruction, and those cannot be permitted to spread. Not ever again."

Humanity sucks, she thought, releasing a sigh.

"Things have changed, Scionian Carly, which is why you have been summoned. Your heritage has evolved into a paradox — a great unknown."

"How so?"

"Scionian wars have begun to bleed out in ways that they have in the past, and we've seen what happens next. Violence is apparently part of your nature, which is why the divine heritage was denied you after the Cleanse. When Verdapok interfered, he'd unwittingly given you the tools to global destruction. These are tools we'd determined you should no longer possess for the safety of the Metaverse."

"I don't mean to interrupt you, Nanzaki, but humanity has long since created nuclear bombs to destroy ourselves. The biokenretic gene isn't…"

"…yes, yourselves. Should your kind wish to die, your bombs will only kill your kind. divine heritage doesn't exist for destructive purposes as your bombs do, but do contain the power to obliterate planets and…galaxies."

She began to understand, though no Descendant had exhibited such power, to her knowledge. "Ancestor Nanzaki, no Scionian Descendant wields enough power to destroy an entire planet. They can barely…"

"…there is no force in your universe, nor ours, more powerful than your sun," he repeated. "I'm sure you believe you're burning or cremating persons, but you're actually disintegrating their cells from existence."

"Excuse me? That's imposs…"

"…Scionian Carly, you possess more power and energy than Sol or any singular sun because you call upon them all. Every form of energy in existence is at your command. When you called upon the suns in Greenland, your instinct to protect kept the energy from destroying the planet. That same instinct is also blocking your natural telepathic and telekinetic abilities."

"H-how do you? Th-that's something I would know. I set things on fire. I..."

"You are the product of generations of merged Scionians; an ability only witnessed once before. After your mother merged with you, you've since called upon the energies of all existing suns effortlessly; something never witnessed before. Disintegrating your cells only allowed them a fresh start but with a dozen of the strongest lifeforms resting within you, coupled with divine heritage. You've been…irreversibly amplified." Nanzaki awaited her response.

As she processed what he'd revealed about her being irreversibly amplified to call upon all suns in existence, in one sentence, he'd enlightened her on why she should be executed. "Once before?" she probed.

"I will teach you of Ybia another time."

She barely registered his statement because she'd moved on to other questions. "If that were true, the Earth…"

"You're not just one sun, Scionian Carly. You're all suns. You call to them all." *"All stars, matter, and energy,"* he thought. *"The Scionian still has no idea she can close her telepathic frequency. These omissions feel wrong."*

"Do as you are commissioned," Tanjuetti telepathically communicated.

She was simply unwilling to accept that because it meant she could supernova and end all life, which made her a threat, though his revelation implied her mother once posed the threat, and Konstantin before her.

Listening to her thoughts as she formed them, Nanzaki corrected her.

"No, that is incorrect. The threat materialized the moment Verdapok lay with Scionian Emebet. It only increased from there. None were so great that we hastily agreed to exterminate. But you, my dear, were a materialized prophecy, and now…" He pointed towards her midsection.

"Now what?"

"The new life you carry."

She ceased her stride and turned to face him. "Excuse me?"

"You cradle a child inside your womb, who will be the first of its kind. Consanguineous."

"I'm…pr…pr…pregnant?"

"Yes, pregnant is the Scionian reference."

Tears of joy escaped her lids as she wrapped her arms around herself, wishing Adam had shared in this moment.

"Oh my gosh, Car," Rye exclaimed, embracing her tightly.

Once Carly's thoughts regrouped, she descended into defense. "What do you mean first of *its* kind? That can't be right because my mother was a merged Descendant and she gave birth to me."

"Yes, she was and yes, she did. She'd married a man who carried no divine heritage, and yet, you stand before me, more powerful than any lifeform in existence. Your merged state coupled with the child's father's core that was once split, presents quite a problem. Imagine the unborn life, with full heritage, born of generations of merged Scionians, and an evolved father. It is an unknown we will not ignore."

Murderously protective from the implied threat, she retreated.

"Tame your sunfire. No harm will come to you or the Consanguineous, for this is genesis. We are not as your Scionian barbarians and corrupt panels of government. Your fate will be decided by the entire Metaverse, as this decision far exceeds our mandate." *"It is unfair that we cannot share her immortality with her just yet,"* he thought.

"Genesis?"

"The start of an evolution that may save your humanity from cellular cessation. When the Light had not cleansed the Scionian Universe, as before, the Metaversal Panel of Life decided there must be purpose to your existence. Perhaps the unborn can be your redemption. Here, I will remove the blocks you have in place." He touched her frontal lobe with his elongated fingertips and her brain waves exploded.

First buried memories resurfaced, then sensations and voices spread about her. A history she'd never known became her childhood. All the damage she had allowed her cells to retain out of fear, regenerated and multiplied. Once she calmed the open frequency, her strength amplified.

Her thought processes increased faster than she'd ever imagined. She instantly recalled Val telling her how the Iksha feared a mating of Wit and Rozovsky bloodlines. Adam was a core once split, but the Iksha's fears had to have existed prior to Adam since they'd killed off most Rozovsky Descendants before he was born.

"Yes, it is true. Adam Ruslan is a product of the Scionians' closest successful attempt at altering its DNA."

They now conversed telepathically, which left Rye in the dark.

"If our universe was once destroyed, how did it regrow itself?"

"Cleansed," he corrected. *"There are four. Never more nor less. That is the essential organic balance of disbursed Light. We do not suppress nor control it. It will not allow for less than four."*

"But you said Scionia was once cleansed and…"

"We can clean house without destroying or building it."

"Can you do it without ending all life?"

"Yes."

"Then give us that chance."

"We have and you have failed."

"We were tampered with. One human failure should not doom us all. We are worth preserving."

"You'll have but one opportunity to convince the Panel. I suggest you do not fail." He flashed his Crescent limbal ring.

She cradled her stomach. *"I will not."*

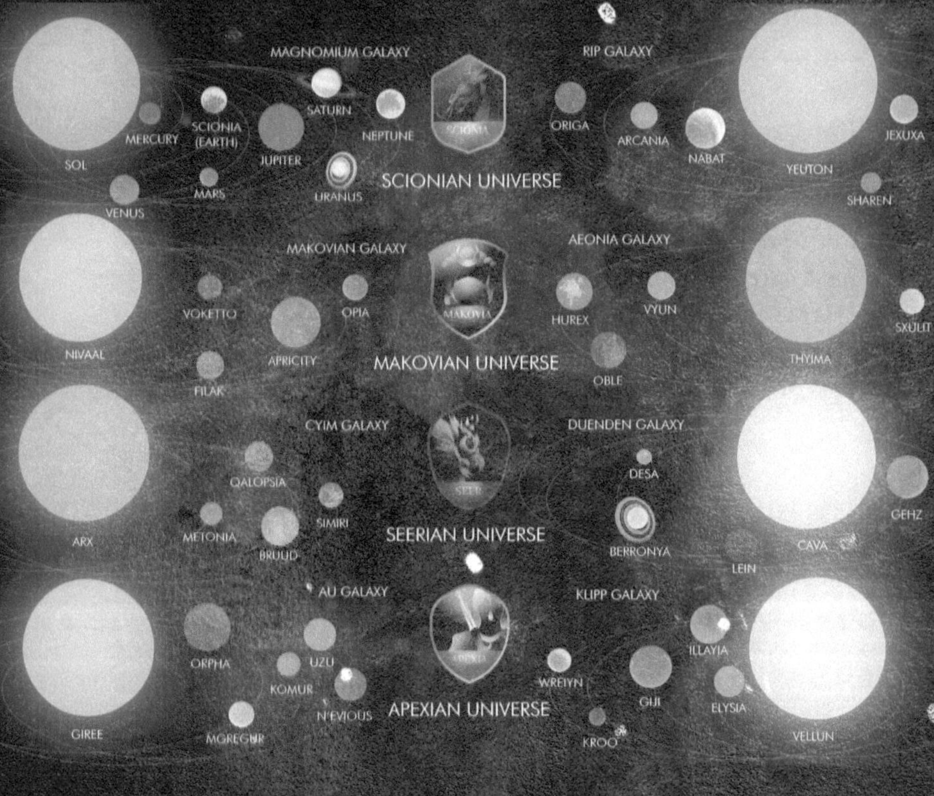
MAGNOMIUM GALAXY
RIP GALAXY
SATURN
SCIONIA
ORIGA
ARCANIA
JEXUXA
MERCURY
SCIONIA
(EARTH)
NEPTUNE
NABAT
YEUTON
JUPITER
SOL
URANUS
SHAREN
MARS
SCIONIAN UNIVERSE
VENUS
MAKOVIAN GALAXY
AEONIA GALAXY
MAKOVIA
VOKETTO
OPIA
HUREX
VYUN
SXULIT
NIVAAL
APRICITY
THYIMA
MAKOVIAN UNIVERSE
OBLE
FILAK
CYIM GALAXY
DUENDEN GALAXY
DESA
QALOPSIA
GEHZ
SIMIRI
METONIA
BERRONYA
CAVA
ARX
SEERIAN UNIVERSE
BRUUD
LEIN
AU GALAXY
KLIPP GALAXY
ILLAYIA
ORPHA
UZU
WREIYN
GIJI
ELYSIA
KOMUR
N'EVIOUS
APEXIAN UNIVERSE
KROO
VELLUN
GIREE
MOREGUR

the metaverse

carly

CARLY STOOD, TINY among the giant beings, before the Makovian Panel of Life on Apricity. Rye remained still and silent beside her.

"There is much you do not know, and must, before any further discussions will be tolerated," Tanjuetti stated from his high chair.

"This is not up for debate. Therefore, please withhold any responses. Arrangements have been made," Makovian Elder, Relve, added. "Nanzaki, if you'll please?"

Nanzaki nodded before turning to Carly and Rye. "Your minimum history lesson will begin immediately on Seerian planet, Gehz."

He touched their wrists, and they arrived in a massive structure, filled with a variety of beings, who clearly were not all of the same species, but also not human.

"Welcome, Scionians," Seerian Persa greeted with restrained delight. "Please, come forward and have a seat, so we can begin."

Carly exchanged a brief glance with Persa, as the Seerian's voice was oddly familiar to her. Nevertheless, she and Rye inched forward, clutching each other, and sat down in the empty elongated chairs near the front of the structure. Nanzaki joined other Makovians who were already present, including Tanjuetti and Relve, who had obviously ported themselves mere seconds after them.

Androgynous and towering, Persa summoned images from the archives and moved them around the room while speaking. "The Metaverse is the divine infinite space where all lifeforms exist; sentient and insentient. There are Four Macrocosms compiling the Metaverse: The Originating Light, one in which Light was absorbed, one transmitted through, and one reflected back — also known as Makovia, Apexia, Seer, and Scionia.

"There has been an ensuing Metaversal debate over Scionia, the Light Reflected. The cornerstone of the controversy is Scionia being believed, by some, as no more than an unauthorized duplicate of its original, leading to Makovians and Apexians discounting Scionia as part of the divinity of Light."

Apexian Maw shuffled, revealing his annoyance and impatience. *"In my opinion, Scionian matters were best disposed of without their presence."*

Carly glowered his way. "Seems everyone has a negative opinion of us," she mumbled.

Maw squinted at her, wondering if she had intruded on his private thoughts, as some Makovians had an annoying tendency to do. He tapped a button on a small device attached to his carpus called an Aeger. Apexians had engineered Aegers to block telepathic frequencies, which he resented using, as it gave him a headache after thirty minutes of usage.

"Please, refrain from solidifying your opinions and judgments until you learn it all," Persa pled. "You haven't even learned a fraction of our history."

Persa began the lesson with their own universe. "Seerians are wise, prophetic, visionaries who maintain the balance of the Verses with foretelling. Our ocular sight allows many of us to see across the Metaverse without use of tool or teleport. We are the keepers of history and graceful fighters who only draw weapons when necessary. We are Agender beings and reproduce asexually."

Persa went on to tell of how Seerians were largely humble and calm, but some were slightly haughty due to their gift of sight. Haughty Seerians were mostly rebellious youth, who were admonished for it.

"A megaannum ago, it was a Seerian who first received the debated Scionian vision, the Prophecy of Light, and was tasked with overseeing the Scionian evolution, leading to your conception, and the Consanguineous you bear." Persa nodded at Carly before moving on to Apexia.

"Apexia is the Originating Light, Absorbed. Apexians are brute, forceful, prideful, egotistical, warriors who predicate their existence on their physical abilities. Their lifestyle and truest joy are in battle, so they regularly hold tournaments of hunt, game, and swordsmanship."

Maw and other Apexians breathed sighs of pride as Persa continued.

"They're abnormally swift, agile, and possess the most heightened senses. They also have masterful engineering, navigation, and mapping skills. They are physically appealing, arrogant, and manipulative. Since its Cleanse, Apexians grew shrewder and largely keep to themselves, as they believe themselves to be the object of all envy." Persa's eyes fluttered upward in annoyance.

Maw snorted, and a smug grin spread across his gorgeous face.

Persa sighed and continued to the next Universe, spreading images across the hall like a deck of cards.

"Makovia is the Originating Light of all sentient existence. The first spark of life began with Makovia. Makovians are modest regal beings who pride themselves on being master-of-all-trades, but also the moral authority for all sentient lifeforms. Makovians are gifted with telepathic, telekinetic, psionic, and teleportation abilities. They are uncharacteristically strong, but are reluctant to use their gifts, and do so sparingly."

"Idiots, they are," Maw interjected in a cadence similar to a Scionian-Scottish one.

"Yet, Apexians were doomed to an existence of greed when your Verse absorbed the Light." Persa flashed a glare of warning. "We are all born of the same spark of Light. It's what we do with that light that determines our fate."

He cleared his throat, allowing them to continue.

"Apexians view Makovians as snobs, but we all respect their strength, power, and versatility."

Nanzaki and Tanjuetti both nodded in unison. Apexians were obnoxious but recognized their inability to fully conquer every Makovian warrior in hand-to-hand combat. In Tanjuetti's opinion, until Apexians could defeat them all, their sarcasm was ignored.

"Scionia is the Originating Light, Reflected. As the last of the Verses to complete its cycle of creation, Scionia is known for its vast sources of energy and Light, but also for its mammalian and reptilian lifeforms. Scionians have been historically regarded as abominations and less divine than the other Verses, per Makovia and Apexia," Persa clarified, ensuring Carly and Rye understood that Seerians did not share the asinine belief.

Carly paid special attention.

"This belief has led Scionians to be abandoned and left out of Metaversal matters. As a reflection of the Originating Light, Scionians possessed telepathic, telekinetic, psionic, and teleportation abilities just as Makovians. However, Scionians are also gifted with energy manipulation, regeneration, and merging capabilities. These massive gifts have always frightened the other Verses."

"Now wait a minute!" Maw interjected. "We're not afraid of anyone or anything!"

"*That explains a lot,*" Carly thought.

"Your fear or lack of it, as you claim, has led your kind to vote in favor of withholding their heritage and Cleansing their Magnomium Galaxy." Persa awaited his retort.

He defiantly bit down on his bottom lip. "That wasn't fear. It was logic. No organic being of flesh should possess a power great enough to destroy us all."

"The Light decided differently," Persa reminded him.

"The Light, the Light," he mocked, throwing his hands up in a fit of exasperation. "The Light has no voice. It doesn't speak, and you can't go around spouting off what you think it's trying to say!"

"If we were biased or unworthy, Apexians would not be here. It was the Seerian vote which allowed your species redemption."

"The Makovians summoning the Light to do its dirty work isn't the same as the Light organically Cleansing," Maw countered. "Pick a *divine* course of action."

"We may have summoned the Light, but we did not make the decision on our own," Tanjuetti reminded him.

Carly was full of questions, and wondered how the Light could be summoned. She instantly became obsessed with discovering the meaning.

Makovians and Apexians continued to bicker until Persa quieted them down. "We are not here for that today. We are here to welcome Scionians, and factually share history. Please, save your debates for a Panel of Life conclave."

Nanzaki and Tanjuetti haughtily dismissed the Apexians with a flick of their wrists.

Persa dove into the Seerian part of the Metaversal debate. "Seerians believe that because Scionia was the last to receive a choice, it was left with none, and that has been Scionia's existence since inception. Apexians despised Scionia for receiving what they believed was the greatest disbursement of Light, and it had the audacity to reject it."

"And that is why we don't believe the Light is what you all believe it is," Maw added. "Why would it distribute two identical portions of energy? Where one portion grew exponentially and the other did not? You never have been able to answer that have you?"

"You should be more concerned with why an inorganic space absorbed the portion of Light it was granted and was hungry for more instead of accepting its gracious disbursement," Persa calmly replied.

The Makovians sighed dramatically. They were in no mood to hear the Apexians whine about their disbursement of Light for the billionth time. They were greedy beings who wouldn't be satisfied no matter how much Light they were given.

Persa's extended fingers pointed upward to a map of the Metaverse where the ceiling had once been.

"Seerians foresaw the vast merging and expansion Scionia manifested as the Light's correction of the Metaverse's inability to humble itself. Of course, we remain outvoted on that," Persa stated plainly.

"And you shall forever be," Maw finalized, revealing the Apexians iconoclastic nature.

"Your greed and arrogance continue to blind you, even from a fate changing before your eyes," Persa added with pity.

"Well, wouldn't we now have a vote?" Carly asked.

"Yes, certainly," Persa confirmed while still glaring at the obtuse Maw. "However, it seems that we are faced with an even number of votes with your presence. Therefore, much change must occur to maintain fairness and balance throughout the Metaverse."

"How was it fair before?" Carly furrowed her brow.

"In truth, it was not, but voting could be weighed in favor or not in favor. Now with the four Verses actively present, we must find another way."

"The Panel of Life could've found another way before instead of excluding us and judging us without a voice," Carly flared.

"I agree," Persa said. "We proceeded in the best way we saw fit without resulting to violence. Seer has been the outvoted Verse in all MPOL conclaves regarding Scionia's inclusion. But the Light has brought you here now, confirming us and our abilities once again."

Carly was skeptical of any of them being on Scionia's side. If the Light truly brought her and Rye there, why hadn't it done so before? She was more inclined to believe something else forced the Makovian's hands.

"We *all* need to learn of this history," Carly said. "Not just Mariah and I."

Makovians and Apexians turned her way.

"The two of us can't decide for the entire species. All Scionians should know of their history, their origin, and what's at stake."

"We agree to an extent," Tanjuetti said as he stood. "Only those of you who have been *spliced* with divine heritage are permitted." His disgust was apparent. "The lesser of you are banned, so it will be your responsibility to represent them. That is the reason we are all here at this moment. To the MPOL monitoring this, the Makovians move to *require* the inclusion of Scionians in Onus Lyceum training."

There was an immediate uproar in the hall. Carly and Rye clung to each other as the others argued loudly.

"Why should we arm them with more destructive power when they've proven themselves to be highly unstable?" Maw asked.

"We all can be," Tanjuetti replied. "And even moreso when we don't know why we exist nor that other beings exist. Furthermore, the Metaverse has continuously suffered based on our decisions to exclude them. It is time we decide differently."

"I agree," Persa added. "Whether you believe in the Light or not, you cannot deny your own existence nor the existence of others. Scionians belong with us. They are not enemies."

"And as long as they are treated as such," Nanzaki began, "their course of action will remain until another catastrophic event befalls us."

"Fine," Maw conceded. "But we wholly reject all Scionians being included. Only those with divine heritage should be permitted to attend Onus training."

"I literally just said that," Tanjuetti replied.

"Why?" Rye asked.

"Because they would not survive it," Maw stated matter-of-factly.

Carly knew that was true, and she also knew Rye asked because she didn't want to be separated from Kane. Without Descendant abilities, Carly was certain non-Descendant humans wouldn't stand a chance against evolved beings.

"Rye, they're right," she whispered.

Rye nodded reluctantly.

"We agree."

"Well, that's good because the MPOL just passed their ruling and Scionia's inclusion in Onus Lyceum is now mandatory," Persa said.

"What is the MPOL?" Carly asked.

"The Metaversal Panel of Life," Persa answered. "A Panel of the strongest, wisest beings in the Metaverse who ultimately decide Metaversal Law, policy, and procedure."

"Lastly, should your kind fail the Onus training, cellular cessation shall immediately follow," Tanjuetti added like it was nothing at all.

"What?" Carly bolted to her feet. "As you have stated yourself, that is a decision you cannot make alone, and unless I'm missing something, this is a history lesson, not a Panel of Life *conclave*."

"Tame your sunfire," Nanzaki pled. "Tanjuetti, she is right. Now, think rationally, Scionian Carly. If Scionian, *Descendants*, as you call yourselves, fail Onus training, you will unequivocally prove yourselves to be a danger to the entire Metaverse. The MPOL *will* vote in favor of your cessation, and this is something I can declare with utmost confidence."

"By failing, Scionians will essentially reveal that their divinity — their power of Light — should be rescinded," Persa added.

"Then rescind it, but don't kill everyone!" Carly's heat spread about her.

Rye clung to Carly's nightshirt, wrapping her arm around her waist, hoping to calm her.

"If they were born with the heritage, revocation can only be achieved by cellular cessation. If their heritage was forced into them after their birth, it can be extracted without ending the lifeform. Unfortunately, this is non-negotiable," Tanjuetti finalized.

Carly had no idea if their Onus training was rigged for their failure nor what it entailed. There were too many unknowns to commit everyone's fate.

Nanzaki telepathically communicated with her. *"Scionian Carly, Onus training is a gift and all Metaverse beings are subjected to it, as they all have heritage. If it were rigged, our species wouldn't be as plentiful. Please, concede. Your people cannot continue running around without accountability,"*

"Scionians should want to be trained on how to use their abilities responsibly and safely," Persa added. "Rejecting the opportunity to learn the best ways to be safe is a threat to the entire Metaverse."

Carly thought long and hard, while reminding herself to find a way to keep Makovians out of her head. If Adam's theory was right, that all humans would eventually become Descendants, then their batch should lead the way — ethically and responsibly. "We will comply."

When her temperature receded and the bubble of heat carrying her hair deflated, everyone reclaimed their seats. She glanced around at the fear in everyone's eyes, aimed her way. It saddened her because she wasn't anyone's enemy nor would she harm any of them without defending her own life and the lives of her loved ones.

Maw and other Apexians grinned smugly, anxious for the opportunity to weigh themselves against Scionians in Onus training.

"It has been decided," Tanjuetti concluded.

"Onus Lyceum training shall commence in three Scionian days' time," Persa declared.

"After your initial meet with the POL on Apricity, you'll be returned to your home planet to make your selections," Nanzaki stated. "You will then return here, from here you are then ordered to report to planet Gehz in the Duenden Galaxy for twenty-one Scionian days."

"Three weeks?" Carly asked.

"Eh, yes," Tanjuetti confirmed. "Unless you have more pressing matters to attend to that are more important than the fate of your species?"

"No, it's just…"

"Just what?" Tanjuetti demanded.

"Nothing," she glared at him with defiance blazing in her eyes.

He haughtily turned his back and sharply gathered his intricate robes.

Carly silently allowed multiple thoughts to pummel her, yet she wasn't overwhelmed. She worried the Descendants wouldn't agree to return with her. She assumed they wouldn't believe her nor Mariah's account of what had transpired. She was afraid of what the Iksha would do in their absence from the planet. She had no idea where Adam was and absolutely refused to travel across the Metaverse without him.

Most importantly, she was determined to find out what Seerian prophecy Persa had mentioned, as that seemed to be an underlying theme to all that was transpiring.

Without warning, she and Rye were ported back to Apricity.

enlightenment

adam

BLOCK-CHUNK ICE THREATENED Adam with eternal imprisonment. Each biting step, he sank into the frozen thicket. Zsita howled and whistled in his ears, begging him to turn around. Bitter white flurries obscured his view. The skin on his cheeks was ravaged so viciously by the relentless gusts, it was all but burnt off. He adjusted his goggles and pressed on, believing this was the only way to save them all.

Traits that could rescue him from the freezing hell were forsaken for possibility because the Iksha could be watching him right now, examining his every move, and he'd decided it was wisest to present himself as Dylan. No one knew Dylan was gone except the Descendants at Meridian.

Endurance was a must, and failure was nonexistent. Oddly, the piercing pain didn't deter him from taking another step forward. It inspired him not to turn back. He refused to waste the remainder of his life battling for his birthright to peacefully exist, living on the edge of fear, accepting that any second of any day some stranger may snatch a loved one from him.

He didn't know or care why his ancestors never had before, but today he was fearlessly crossing the line, and walking into the unknown, believing he'd walk out, into his wife's arms.

When he approached the facility, he remained cloaked by the thicket, watching Iksha militants and Descendant captives scurry about. He sucked in several breaths before ensuring his cloak was intact. He then activated his aero-invisibility, marched right to the main door, and walked in behind a militant. When the huge metal door whooshed closed, the militant suspiciously gazed around, as if he sensed Adam's presence behind him.

Adam wasted no time casing the facility. He eyed Descendant captives slave away while enduring abuse. Their eyes were hollow, and they were severely underweight. Most had mangled matted hair, and were dressed in heavily soiled, ripped, beige rags, while a few others were visibly clean, with fresh garments, and brushed tresses.

He bent several corners before a slight change in core vibration captured his attention. He scanned the room until he located the source. There she was, Alexandra, his bio-mom, tall and graceful, even under the horrible conditions. He knew it was her because he had seen her face in Dylan's memories. Her light-brown eyes with winter-green freckles had the audacity to sparkle as she spoke to a fellow captive she called Ulyana. Her long blonde hair was stringy, lifeless, and thinning, but brushed backward into a ponytail.

She was gaunt, but her skin was dewy, and smooth. Adam stood in awe, overwhelmed with emotions he never knew he'd have because he never thought he'd ever meet her. A cloaked figure crossed between them, temporarily blocking his view. He was so annoyed by the brief disruption that he searched for the figure's face out of curiosity. It was none other than Vikki, disguised as a captive.

Alexandra suddenly snatched her head up and glared directly into Adam's eyes, as if she saw him.

"Impossible," he mumbled.

planet apricity
MAKOVIAN UNIVERSE

carly

CARLY AND NANZAKI strolled along the most abundant garden she'd ever seen.

"Each of you are powerful. With power, comes obligation, and accountability. What you do, not only affects those nearest to you, but also those farthest from you," Nanzaki warned.

"Those within our circle are responsible with their abilities, though I've ended two lives with great regret, as I'm sure you're aware, since you've been watching from afar. It's the Iksha who present the problem."

"That is quite incorrect. Those embracing dark Light shall perish, for they covet and steal, but never possess. There is only but one of you who presents the greatest threat to the Metaverse."

Carly paused and turned towards him, praying he didn't categorize Adam as a threat.

"No, it is not him. It is you, Scionian Carly."

"Me? But how? Why? I'd never hurt anyone I didn't absolutely need to."

"That, I believe, as it is quite subconscious. However, Scionian emotions are anything but predictable. Your kind lacks structure and training. Your inability to separate necessity from desire is a threat to the entire Metaverse. With your emotions, comes the Suns, their Light, and all energies."

"What does that mean, exactly?"

"You are the Mother of Suns, my dear. The most powerful tangible force in existence. More than heat, fire, energy, and matter."

She stood frozen, confused, and in disbelief.

"You are the only living being who possesses the ability to supernova an entire galaxy. That ripple could reverberate well beyond the Magnomium. It is the unknown that Makovians do not favor."

"I've never energized even close enough to supernova. Our plan—"

"…another misconception. Scionia does not belong to your species, though natural selection has entrusted you with its care."

She scowled as he educated her.

He blocked their telepathic line, and refrained from informing her that she was organically Guardian of all.

"With several of the most powerful Scionians known to have existed merged inside of you, you are able. There is no energy source in your universe more powerful than your Suns. None, besides you. Imagine the implosion. That is our greatest concern. These scientists and militants you fear, you should not."

"But they're killing us," she reminded him.

"Because you allow it." When he placed his thumb and forefinger against her head, connection to her core became obstructed. He had previously partially unblocked her, but now with Onus Lyceum approaching, and her species entire existence hanging in the balance, he thought it was time to help her completely free herself from her own restraints.

He, other Makovian Elders, and Seerian Overseers had witnessed her organic heritage freeing itself where she had immediately suppressed it once again. It was then Persa and other Seerians urged Makovians to force-port her and Mariah before her efforts to contain the Light failed her.

After streams of light sparked inside her eyes, she simply turned towards him. She thought for several moments. If she was deemed a threat, they may choose to kill her. She cradled her belly.

He turned and continued walking. "We are not soulless. Your species is quite fearful."

She relaxed a bit, unsure if she feared for the safety of her unborn child or for anyone who tried to harm her family.

"They could've been neutralized long ago," he said of the Iksha.

"They've spread. If we destroy their known facilities, what of the unknown?"

He huffed. "That is the right question. You'll meet with the Makovian Panel, here on Apricity. If you want your husband, go and retrieve him. When you do, you will return to us. I'm sure I don't need to warn you of the consequences of ignoring our commands?"

"No, Nanzaki. I will return."

"Correction, you will return with your most trusted cluster who possess the heritage."

She gulped.

There was something more in his eyes, his voice. There was something more he wasn't saying. She probed and crawled through his thoughts. If it had anything to do with her abilities, it was always better to know than not. She'd learned that the hard way.

"You seem to be the wisest among them," he said, after she had failed to penetrate his telepathic block.

"For our sake, let's hope I am. Take us to the Panel. We're ready."

"Mariah Solomin will likely receive punishment," he reminded her.

"I'm ready," Rye said from a distance.

"Very well." Nanzaki pulled Rye to them, then blipped them into a white ovular drome, where several Makovians awaited them.

Immediately upon their arrival, Tanjuetti bolted upright. "Nanzaki, you were not granted permission to restore her!"

"Indeed, I was, Elder," Nanzaki reminded him. "No being's heritage can be obstructed in any form during Onus Lyceum training. It has long since been decreed."

Tanjuetti huffed and heaved, clearly afraid of Carly, even moreso now that Nanzaki had removed the psychic blocks and cellular suppression she had placed upon herself.

Carly squinted, wondering why she heard dozens of murmuring lashes and clicks of voices without any mouth movement. Even more alarming, she understood them.

"Very well, let's move forward," Makovian Relve declared. "Scionian Mariah Solomin, please approach."

Rye squeezed Carly's hand one last time before walking towards the towering beings.

"You stand accused of failing to fulfill your duty of spreading awareness of the Metaverse, ensuring the captivity of rogue and threatening Scionians with divine heritage, and reporting back to us in a timely manner," Relve declared. "Do you deny any of these allegations?"

"I do not," Rye sadly and quietly replied.

"Very well, then it is the judgment of this Panel that your bestowed amplification be rescinded — suspended, pending your successful completion of the three integral segments of Onus Lyceum training. Should you fail any segment of the training, cellular cessation shall immediately follow. Any questions regarding our decision or punishment?"

"I have questions," Carly announced strongly, stepping forward. "What amplification was bestowed upon her?"

"Mariah Solomin's teleportation abilities were discovered several Scionian decades ago," Relve began. "She was detected traveling back and forth between the Magnomium and RIP galaxies at such a rapid speed, it threatened the continuum. At such time, a Makovian POL Elder was tasked with retrieving her. Once she was brought to Apricity, she was warned to restrict her ports to the Magnomium and to reduce the speed at which she traveled. She was defiant and desirous. At which time, the Panel had offered to amplify her abilities to port the Verses without obstructing time, under the conditions previously stated. She failed to fulfill the conditions."

"So, you employed her to spy on our species, control them, report back to this planet, and single-handedly eliminate all Descendant threats?" Carly asked.

She was recruited because the Seerian prophecy was nearing materialization with the growing power of your mother, a Makovian Elder thought in their native Marra tongue.

She jerked her shoulders back, preparing to respond to the absurdity of that.

"She agreed to the terms and conditions," Relve reminded her, abducting her focus.

"It would seem that you delegated your own duties to a child, who clearly was just learning how to use her abilities, and had no clue about any divine heritage nor the implications of exploring her natural organic state. Your punishment is far harsher than it needs to be."

"Car, it's okay," Rye uttered.

"No, Mariah, it isn't." She turned back to the Panel of Elders. "To threaten her with death if she fails to complete a training course that should have been available to Scionians since our inception, is ludicrous."

The Elders shuffled.

"All beings face cellular cessation if they fail to successfully pass Onus in four cycles," Relve stated.

"I reject your imposition on her behalf," Carly finalized in Marra.

"You what?" Tanjuetti asked in disbelief.

Rye gasped in amazement at Carly speaking in Marra.

"I respectfully request a reconsideration of the punishment you're imposing on her. She deserves better than death looming over her head during every aspect of training. Our kind has been lied to, denied our history, and made to believe we were alone, when all along, you were watching us be tortured and murdered."

"We are not —" Tanjuetti attempted to counter.

"It was *your* Elder who traveled to our planet and laid down with our women for his own pleasure." Carly pointed her finger. "Regardless of whatever his self-righteous reasons were, he derived pleasure from us without educating us, and then left those women to their devices, to watch their children be crucified and slaughtered. Verdapok was *your* responsibility and *you* failed. You failed us long before we could ever fail ourselves. What was your punishment?" she demanded with a piercing gaze.

"Car, it's okay, really," Rye pled.

"No, Mariah. I won't let you bear the responsibility of a Panel with the power to end an entire species, avoid their own damned consequences of action and inaction while preaching that crap to us. No."

After several layered voices, they turned back to her.

"Very well. It has been decided that Mariah Solomin will not face cessation should she fail portions of Onus training. However, what we cannot do alone is change the laws of the Metaverse, long since decreed by the Metaversal Panel of Life, who overrules the Makovian Panel. Therefore, any Scionian being who fails Onus Lyceum training in its totality, after four cycle attempts, shall face cessation. Mariah Solomin shall have one cycle. Her amplification is hereby rescinded." Relve elongated his finger toward Rye.

"Scionian Carly, please step aside," Nanzaki ordered.

"It's okay, Car. I remember this and it doesn't hurt so bad." Rye bravely lifted her chin.

Nanzaki flanked his fingers along her rib cage. Within seconds, Rye grunted, and hunched her shoulders. Carly raced back to her side.

"You okay, Rye?"

"Yes, just more boring than I've ever been," Rye replied with tears glistening on her lids. "Now I can only travel between two galaxies." She sniffled.

"Then how will we return three days from now?" Carly asked the Makovian Panel.

"*You* will teleport your selections," Tanjuetti said with annoyance dripping from his clickity tone, as if she was supposed to understand everything he said.

"What the he—" Carly began before correcting herself. "What are you talking about? I'm not a teleporter, and you just disabled the only one we have!"

"What's the point of you restoring her if she will continue to be this dense?" Tanjuetti screeched at Nanzaki. *"This Prophecy of Light doesn't seem believable the way she behaves. Though she's but a child, she presents an obtuse weak one,"* Tanjuetti thought.

Carly frowned. *"Older than Mariah was when you swindled her into accepting your consequences at the cost of our entire species,"* she bit back in thought.

Nanzaki dismissed Tanjuetti. "Scionian Carly, once again, you are mother of all suns, all energy. There is nothing you cannot do. No one will hold your hand these next three Scionian days, so I highly suggest you search yourself, unobstructed, and return as ordered."

"Fine," she spat, jerking away from him. "Send us home, please. We're ready to go."

He sighed with hesitance. *"Every divine being of heritage manipulates energy, but she is energy, and does not seem to feel her power. Our every trait is no more than a sub-trait. An extension of her,"* he thought.

"Now," she demanded.

"Have patience with her," he thought as he opened a gateway.

Carly took Rye's hand, and they walked into the portal together.

insipience

early

Adam hastily crossed the room, anxious to yank Vikki by her arms, and shake some sense into her.

Before he could reach her, a militant yelled out. "You there! What is your name?"

Adam froze. Perhaps his aero-invisibility had worn off, and he had been spotted. The crooked-toothed militant approached Vikki and aggressively snatched the hood from her head. Vikki mischievously glanced up at the militant, and smirked as if she were enjoying herself. Her blue eyes sparkled with wicked pleasure.

The militant grabbed her forearm and flipped it over, in search of something. Adam glimpsed other Descendant captives, who had stopped to watch. They all had a symbol branded into their left forearms, same as the deceased he saw underwater in Menorca. Once the militant realized Vikki didn't have one, he reached for his weapon. With a slight push, Vikki flung him across the facility, into a wall, where his head splattered.

Chaos exploded.

Alexandra gazed Adam's way again as if she saw him. Before he could spring into action, he found himself at home, in his bedroom, with Carly scowling at him.

"Carly?" Adam asked, looking around quizzically.

She slapped him across the face. "You left me. You left me when you promised you never would," she said, upset because she refused to tell him she was pregnant under negative circumstances, so she would simply wait.

"I-I didn't leave you. I just wanted to retrieve Vikki before something bad happened to her."

"And while you were out trying to save someone who didn't want or need to be saved, you left us all alone to worry about you. You have no idea what I've been through or what's going on! The Iksha is the least of our problems! Not only that, I was ported off planet!"

"Babe, I'm so sorry, but Mariah has to send me back! Right now, right now!" he pled, ignoring everything she said.

"Rye didn't port you."

"I gotta go back, babe! I found Vikki *and* my bio-mom. Even Mariah and Evan's mom is there…. wait what?"

"What are you talking about? You need to slow down because you aren't making sense." She was frustrated with all she was shouldering.

"I found Vikki in her hometown, the same facility where Alexandra was initially held when she was pregnant with me and Dylan. Vikki returned there. She was discovered and a fight broke out right when I was ported. Now what do you mean Mariah didn't port me? How did I get here then?"

"I brought you home," she said, exasperated.

"You? How?"

"It's a long story that I don't even understand, but right now, let's get Vikki."

"And Alexandra," he added.

She sighed loudly, grabbed his wrist, and focused. She inhaled and exhaled for a few minutes.

"Babe, are you sure you didn't imagine it? I know you've been under a lot of stress lately, and—"

Before he could finish, they were back at the facility. Descendant captives were cowering while Vikki smashed and crushed militants like a hulk.

"Run! Go!" she yelled at captives who were too afraid to attempt to run. She glanced to her left. "Adam? Carly?"

Alexandra made her way over.

"You two shouldn't be here," Vikki warned. "I don't plan on making it out of here, but neither will Nikolay."

"You don't even know if he's here, Vik. As far as you know he's dead by now," Adam said.

Alexandra approached from behind. "Son," she whispered with a hand on his shoulder right before going limp.

Adam caught her before she hit the ground.

Carly knelt beside them.

"They have weapons that suppress the BK gene," Vikki warned as she flung metal tables around to shield them from the onslaught of BK darts.

"We don't have time for this," Carly declared, rising to her feet.

She stood erect, closed her eyes, and channeled the planet's energy, intentionally refraining from summoning Sol's power. Her hair was suspended and she split the energy bubble around her to protect Adam, Alexandra, and Vikki.

Vikki gazed around in disbelief at the BK darts disintegrating when they hit her bubble.

Carly swiftly identified militant from captive. She then spumed a minimal burst of energy, atomizing all militants within a five-mile radius, while encapsulating everyone else inside protective energy domes.

She calmly turned and opened a portal near Afrax. "Everyone, leave this place. Go home. Your loved ones are waiting for you."

They whimpered.

"This is Alexandra's *other* son," Ulyana told them. "Not Dylan. It's okay, let's get out of here. It's our only chance."

One by one, they entered the portal. Once they had all passed through, Carly turned to Adam.

There were so many questions burning in his smoldering eyes, but she remained focused.

He gazed down at Alexandra. "She should come with us."

"We don't know her, Adam. She can't right now."

"Why not? I've waited for this moment my whole life." He anxiously cradled an unconscious Alexandra in his arms.

"You'll understand later. Right now, she needs to go to Afrax."

"She's right," Ulyana concurred from the edge of the portal. "She should be with us right now."

Adam reluctantly handed Alexandra over to Ulyana and two others, who carried her into the portal. Carly swiftly closed it behind them. She bent over, and held her belly.

"Babe?" Adam rushed to her side. "Are you okay?"

"Yeah, I just wanna go home. Been a long day."

"Okay, let's go home." He looked around for Vikki, but she was gone. "Dammit!"

"Adam, she's a grown and very capable woman. She knows how to find us. And after I talk to you about my day, she'll want to come home. Believe me." Even Carly knew Vikki that well.

He cupped her face and kissed her tenderly on the lips in the way that always melted her. With locked eyes, they returned home.

meridian

ALL THE DESCENDANTS paced around the training facility in their pajamas, except Rye, who sat. Charro eyed everyone with his arms folded across his chest. Kane remained by Rye's side, just as Jo was in Evan's arms.

"Mariah, why are we here?" Ksenyia asked.

"You snatched us up in the middle of the night like it was an emergency and no one's saying anything," Jude added.

"Just wait for Carly and Adam," Rye patiently replied.

Just then, Carly and Adam walked in.

"Hey, guys," Carly started, "I'll get right to it because we have no time to waste." She cleared her throat. "Mariah and I were ported off planet the other night."

Murmurs erupted immediately.

"What do you mean?" Val inquired.

"Please, let me finish, and I promise I'll answer every question you all have. Mariah and I were ported to a planet called Apricity by beings who call themselves Makovians. Apparently, they are our creators."

"Creators?" Charro asked.

"Yes. We've all wondered how we began as Descendants and I'm about to tell you. There was a Makovian being named Verdapok—the same one my PawPaw told us about— who ported to Earth and mated with several women in Sintashta. Makovians are not humans. They possess telepathic, telekinetic, psionic, and teleportation abilities. When Verdapok made children with human women, he spliced our ancestor's DNA with divine heritage." Carly sighed.

"Divine heritage? Like, what?" Krill expressed his utter disbelief.

Rye sat quietly, with her head partially down.

"I know it's a lot to digest, but this isn't the half of it. Divine heritage is what we call biokenreyis. Iksha scientists labeled our abilities using whatever little name they made up, meanwhile, we're simply part of a Metaverse of evolved beings." She went on to tell them the history, as she had been taught on Gehz by Persa.

The room fell silent when she finished the history portion. She wanted to allow them time to absorb that before dropping the bomb of Onus Lyceum training on them.

"Mariah, say something," Evan implored. "This can't be true, can it? You would've told me about this long ago if it were true."

"Not this, brother," Rye responded. "It's all true. I just didn't know how to tell anyone about it without being categorized as crazy, and being institutionalized. I already had enough threats of death and imprisonment swirling around me. I was a child, Mom and Dad were gone, and I desperately needed some freedom. I was suffocating."

Evan's eyes glistened with restrained tears.

"So, now that everyone knows how we began, there's a more pressing matter," Carly resumed.

"Who did the Iksha abduct now?" Sage asked.

"Iksha is the least of our worries," Carly replied, capturing everyone's attention, especially Charro's. "We're required to report to the planet Apricity, in the Makovian Universe, in three days' time, of which, one day is gone, to undergo Onus Lyceum training."

"Onu-who?" Jude probed.

"It's basically Descendant training, and it's non-negotiable."

"You've got to be kidding me," Ksenyia whined. "This is just too farfetched."

"Onus Lyceum is a three-week process, and every single one of us is going, except for Kane." Carly had every intention of force-porting them if she had to.

"And what do you mean it's non-negotiable?" Jude stepped forward with her arms crossed. "I know you're not saying we have no choice like you're the boss of us. I just know that's not what you're telling a group of free adults."

Carly glowered down at the five-foot-tall Jude, unbothered. "If you refuse, we all die. Or did you miss that part? I won't let you or anyone sentence our entire species to extinction."

"So, three weeks of learning ways to control and enhance our abilities from the very beings that pioneered us? I'm down," Sage said.

"Me too. I'm in," Val added.

"Babe?" Ksenyia directed at Val. "Just like that? You believe this?"

"Why would Carly and Mariah lie to us?" Val replied. "Why can't everyone see how much sense this makes?"

"It actually makes more sense than anything else we've ever learned our entire lives," Adam said, finally speaking up. "We know our abilities aren't from this world. If they were, everyone would have them. How much longer do you want to live in the Iksha's shadow?"

"I'm going," Krill announced.

"Krill!" Jude bulged her eyes.

"And so are you," he told her with a pointed finger.

"I…"

"We're both going," he concluded. "You can be as bitter and jaded as you want, but you're doing nothing but making yourself miserable, and it's driving me away. Is that what you want?"

"Of course not," Jude said in a soft tone.

They locked hands.

Ksenyia wasn't quite sold yet. "Val, babe, I don't know about this. We're just taking their word for it without any proof at all."

"You've taken the Afrax's Panel's word for it for decades without pushback, and now you're faced with the opportunity to free your mind and yourself. You're telling me you aren't willing to find out?" Val eyed her intently.

"Off planet though?" Ksenyia continued. "We could be trapped there."

"We're already trapped here," Val rationalized. "I personally would rather strengthen and learn of myself from my creators versus the beasts of this planet who're dedicated to assaulting us, imprisoning us, torturing us, and murdering us out of fear and lust."

Ksenyia opened her mouth, but no words came out.

"I'm going, K."

After a beat, Ksenyia acquiesced. "I'm going with you. I'd never let you go alone."

They smiled and bumped foreheads.

"What about me?" Jo asked. "I'm not a Descendant."

Carly sighed. "Everyone, there's something I need to tell you, about…Jo."

Adam squeezed her hand.

"When Adam and Dylan were infants," she began, "their bio-mom secretly slipped Jo a full dose of V when she retrieved Adam from the orphanage."

"Great, more secrets you've been keeping from us," Jude screeched sarcastically.

"It wasn't a secret. Just none of your damned business," Carly bit back. "And given your horrible attitude towards everything, I never believed Jo could be safe if everyone knew because of the special circumstances surrounding her condition. You're acting the same Chandler did before he attempted to kill us all. So, the real threat in this community is you!"

"Calm down, Car," Rye said, standing. "You shouldn't be upset. Here, sit down." She offered Carly her seat before turning to Jude, and walking up to her, chest to chin. "Now you listen to me, you little pipsqueak, you're out of line, you don't contribute anything useful anymore, you complain all the time, but never have any solutions, and you will NOT attack Carly anymore!" She mushed her forehead with her index finger. "When was the last time you and Krill had sex, huh?"

"Excuse me?" Jude clutched her collarbone. "That's—"

"None of my business, right? Exactly my damned point."

"Those two things are nothing alike!" Jude exclaimed. "My sex life doesn't affect anyone here, but Jo taking the V, does!"

"You don't listen well, do you?" Carly muttered, exasperated.

"Jude," Adam interjected. "My mother didn't take the V. It was forced on her. She had no idea what had happened to her nor could she explain why she was experiencing what she was experiencing. She's innocent."

"Jude, that's enough," Krill boomed. "Carly mentioned special circumstances a minute ago. We all saw what happened with Vikki after she took it, and worse, Chandler. What special circumstances happened with Jo?"

Everyone was all ears.

Carly breathed loudly. "For starters, every human known to have ingested the V has had negative side effects at some point, often hastening their death. Jo is the only living human who not only survived it long-term, but developed abilities similar to those of, what we now know, are our originators. Based on the tests, the V has permanently bonded with her cells."

"What abilities, Carly?" Val gently asked. "And what tests?"

"She can hear people's thoughts," Carly divulged.

Everyone gasped and began talking over each other. Val stared at Carly for a while, and she knew it was because she didn't answer her second question, nor would she throw Sage under the bus.

"So, this whole time, she could hear all of our thoughts?" Ksenyia probed.

"The whole time we've known her?" Sage added.

"Yes," Carly replied. She leaned back and allowed them to say all they wanted to, but waited for them to calm down.

"Why would you think she wouldn't be safe if we knew that?" Val asked.

"For starters, Jo ingested a different strain of the V than Chandler did. His strain was apparently tainted with something harmful. Second, the presence of it was destroying her relationship with her son, so I planned to extract it from her, but I didn't want to risk her life. And lastly, the strain of V that Vikki ingested originated from Jo; the only living human who has survived the V long-term without any negative side effects. And I didn't want anyone even suggesting that Jo be used as a lab monkey to produce any V." Carly was tired of secrets and splitting her thoughts between what to say and what to keep hidden. It was time everyone knew.

"So, she can hear what I'm thinking right now?" Ksenyia asked.

"Don't talk about her like she isn't here," Adam replied. "She can speak for herself."

"*This is all clearly bullshit,*" Ksenyia thought, shaking her head.

"I wish it were," Jo responded.

Ksenyia popped her head up. "Fluke. You saw me shaking my head." *"Adam is freaking distracting, looking at me with those eyes of his."*

"Ksenyia, you have a lot to work out with Valentina, and I think you should talk to her immediately," Jo said, not wanting to out her for the thoughts she was harboring about Adam.

Val snatched her head in Ksenyia's direction. Ksenyia dipped her eyes shamefully, tucking her rogue copper strands behind her ear.

"I'm thinking of number 1,342,883," Sage thought.

"1,342,883, Sage, and can we please not do this?" Jo begged. "It's not something I asked for, but it's done now. It's a permanent part of me, just as it is for all of you. None of you asked for it either. Please, don't hate me. I love all of you."

Sage smiled. "I think it's pretty darned cool, Jo. I'm sorry for testing you." He had previously known about Jo being the V because he had tested her blood, but they never told him she could hear thoughts. He gave her a huge hug.

"Everything is making sense now," Krill said. "That's why Carly always took Jo with her when visiting Afrax. It was so you could hear the thoughts of the Panel."

Carly nodded. "And also, because if I left her here, and anyone did anything to harm her while I was gone, I'd ash them without hesitation."

"Bad ass!" Krill bumped fists with Carly.

Jude released a jealous grunt and sat farther away from the group.

"What about Vikki?" Krill asked in a low enough tone that Jude couldn't hear him. "You think she'll be alright since she took a strain that originated from Jo?

"It looks that way," Carly replied.

"Where is she?"

"I called her, but she hasn't responded," Adam told him.

"Likely because she doesn't know what's going on," Krill surmised.

Carly touched Rye's forearm, sharing coordinates. "Rye? Can you…"

"On it," Rye said. She blipped out and back within thirty seconds, with Vikki in tow.

"What the hell, Adam? I told you I had plans and I was in the middle of something important. I need to do this, so I can be whole again!" She turned her palms upward.

"Vik, trust me," Adam replied. "There's nowhere else you'd rather be right now, than here. Krill can you debrief her?"

"Sure thing," Krill bellowed.

Jude flew back to his side with the reemergence of Vikki.

"Little one," Charro started, "are you sure this is the best course of action? If we port off planet, who knows what travesties will befall our people in our absence?"

"All I know is what *will* happen if we refuse," Carly said. "Iksha is nothing compared to these beings…and they're right about this training. We all desperately need it." She rubbed her forehead in fatigue, hearing so many voices echoing everywhere. They were bickering and she hadn't even told them about the Descendant captives they'd just freed.

Jo glanced her way.

"Please, don't read my thoughts right now, and don't tell ANYONE anything you've heard," Carly thought.

Jo's eyes bulged, but she kept quiet, and tucked herself inside Evan's arms.

"I'll get you some ice water, Car," Rye offered.

"You're doing the right thing, baby girl."

Carly bolted onto her feet. "Mommy?" she whispered with tears trickling from the outer corners of her eyes.

Jo flung around. "Your mother said you're…"

"Doing the right thing," Carly finished.

"You heard her?" Jo whispered.

"I-I did," Carly gleefully mumbled.

"Oh my gosh," Jo silently mouthed. They embraced and rocked back and forth.

Rye returned with the water. "Drink this."

She gulped it down. "Thank you. Can you and Ev come by the house tomorrow morning? I'm exhausted." Carly breathed.

"Of course. Car, go be with your husband. I've got this here," Rye lovingly suggested.

Adam wrapped Carly inside his arms. "What's happening, babe? You're changing. Everything's changing."

"Tell him, Карли."

"Our future is unfolding before us. Let's go home," she whispered before blipping them out.

irrevocable love

carly

CARLY GUIDED ADAM onto their rear patio deck, facing the gardens and skyline. She'd told him the basics of what had happened on Apricity in the Makovian Galaxy before the meeting, but this was more important, by far.

"I'm still in a state of shock over all this. From you teleporting, to aliens, to Ulyana…" He'd maintained the fiercest poker face during the emergency moment in the training facility.

She took his hands into hers, and gazed intensely into his smoldering, breathtaking, hazel eyes. He tucked her fluffy curls behind her right ear before touching her face.

"Adam, we're pregnant."

He paused for what seemed like an eternity to her. Tears poured from his before he released a woosh of air from his lungs.

"We…you…us," he stuttered. "I..I love you more than my own life!" he exclaimed, wrapping his arms around her waist and pulling her body to his.

"You're my everything, and I absolutely promise you, on my life, I'll never leave you. I'll take care of you and our child for eternity," he whispered into her ear as he sniffled.

She squeezed him as hard as she could.

"I'm so sorry I wasn't here," he whimpered, descending into full-on crying.

"Shhh." She placed her fingers on his lips. "The past is over. Our little miracle," she said while touching her stomach, "is the future."

They embraced again as Adam floated them upward.

"Consanguineous," she whispered while gazing down at Meridian from the sky.

"What?"

"It was the Makovians who first alerted me to the baby. They called her or him, Consanguineous."

"What does it mean?"

"Our ancestry. But she or he is also considered our genesis, and is the only reason they didn't just kill us all without warning," Carly told him as they hovered.

"They sound…severe," Adam chuckled.

"They definitely are." It felt good to finally smile after all she'd been through.

"Hold on," he said as he drew her close and flew them to the poppy field. "I forgot you can't pass straight through. But you can port now."

She blipped them to the other side of the Hex, they landed, and immediately spread out on the grass. She laid her head on his chest as they gazed up at the stars.

"This is the most amazing moment of my life, aside from the second you entered my life," he confessed. "I always knew. Always."

"Knew what?"

"That there were other beings out there and we weren't from here. A part of me refused to let that go, and our unborn child likely is the one who beckoned them to reveal themselves." He put his on her stomach.

"There's so much to learn and I'm excited for all of us," she said, touching his hand.

"Okay, so tell me, how can you teleport and hear your mom now?"

"I don't really know, but there's apparently some Seerian prophecy about it, and…"

"Prophecy?"

"Yeah," she laughed.

"This is theeee best day of my life!" he grinned from ear to ear. "Tell me more."

They laid in each other's arms until the dawn discussing the Metaverse, and their unbelievably exciting future.

CARLY WOKE A bit later than she usually did. She jerked upright and waited until she blinked enough times to convince herself she was really home. The toilet flushed, the water ran in the sink, and Adam appeared in the bathroom doorway.

"Good morning, gorgeous," he drawled.

Her cheeks flushed warmly. "Good morning, beautiful."

He flew into her arms. They pummeled each other with endless kisses when her stomach growled.

"Yes, ma'am," Adam said to her stomach.

Curly laughed heartily. "Could be a him."

"No, *she* couldn't." He kissed her belly. "I'll make us some breakfast and look in on Vikki."

"Okay, I'll be down in a bit."

They kissed dozens more times before tearing themselves away from each other. The doorbell rang as he glided downstairs. "I'll get it he yelled."

She swiftly freshened up before joining him downstairs.

"Good morning, Car," Rye said with an embrace. "Did you tell him?" she whispered.

Carly nodded happily.

"Yaaayyyy!" Rye hopped up and down. "I'm going to be an auntie," she clapped.

"Sounds like you told her," Adam said, dipping his head out from the kitchen.

"I did." Carly winked at Rye. "Is Vikki awake?"

"I'll get her up in a bit." He joined them in the living room.

"Good morning, you guys, and congratulations," Evan said.

"Thank you," they chimed.

Evan wore an expression of worry as he sat on the sofa. "When do we need to report to the Makovian planet?"

"Tomorrow," Carly replied. "Just that fast."

"Great, I'll go get your mother," Evan told them before heading towards the door.

"Kane too," Rye reminded him.

Evan nodded and closed the front door behind him.

Adam went into Vikki's room to wake her, then returned to the kitchen to start breakfast.

"Still unbelievable," Carly shared with Rye.

"I don't even fear Onus Lyceum. I'm ready to conquer it and learn new things. I'm more fearful of what could happen while we're away from Earth."

"I personally think the planet will survive without us for 21 days. I'm anxious to find out what that Seerian Prophecy is all about. Did you notice how they kept going around the specifics of it?"

"Yeah, it's weird how intentionally vague they were. You wanna know something?"

"Of course, I do."

"I haven't felt this animated, excited, and alive since I was a teenager. Shhh, don't tell Kane," she giggled.

The two of them squeezed hands and cackled like school girls.

"What are you two so happy about this early in the morning?" Vikki asked from the hallway leading to her bedroom.

"There's so much to be happy about," Carly beamed.

"Such as?"

"You're back home, dozens of Descendants have been freed after decades of captivity, we've discovered our true origin, Adam and I are becoming parents, and we're all going to travel across the Metaverse to perfect our abilities."

"What the what?" Vikki marched over to the couch. "You and Adam are what?"

"You're gonna be an aunt!" Adam exclaimed, grabbing her by the neck from behind and messing her hair.

She playfully pushed him away. "Oh my goodness, congratulations!" She leaned down and hugged Carly, then turned and punched Adam in the gut.

"Where is the love?" Adam said, out of breath.

"I'm gonna be an Auntie," she said to herself. "I have so much stuff to buy!"

They all smiled and hugged each other before going into the kitchen.

"Here," Vikki snatched a barstool from under Adam's pending bottom and scooted it towards Carly.

Adam hit the floor. "Hey!"

Vikki ignored him. "Sit down, Carly. I'll get you some juice."

Rye laughed out loud.

"Rude," Adam said as he scrambled onto his feet.

"Apple, orange or cranberry," Vikki asked with her head shoved into the fridge.

"Apple is fine, Vikki. Thank you," Carly smiled. She gazed around at her family; happy and growing. She'd protect them all with her life, and was ready to master Onus Lyceum.

"Knock, knock," Jo said as she, Evan and Kane entered.

Rye flew into Kane's arms as if she hadn't seen him in weeks. Carly beamed brightly. Adam embraced her from behind just when the doorbell rang again.

"I'll get it," Adam said.

He returned with Sage.

"Hey, good morning, everyone," Sage nervously waved while eyeing Vikki.

She put her hand on her hip.

He approached her, lifted her chin with his left forefinger, and kissed her. "I'm in love with you, and I never want to be apart from you ever again." He gently raked the tips of his fingers across her face and cheek.

She closed her eyes and inhaled his scent, speechlessly.

The others grinned and clapped in the background. Carly's heart simply leapt with glee.

Adam sighed. "Bacon anyone?"

"Yes!" they all chimed and began scrambling about.

They shared a hearty meal and delightful conversation, as a family.

meridian's garden

EVAN AND JO'S simple wedding ceremony was pushed up to today, given their departure to Apricity the following day. Catered food and other refreshments were delivered to Meridian's gardens, as Rye zipped around, erecting canopies and modest décor, all while wearing a pink silk gown and seven-inch stilettos. Kane looked on in amazement while lending his hands anywhere he could.

Carly and Adam planned to announce their pregnancy to the community during the reception, with Jo and Evan's blessing. After everyone helped the bride and groom with their preparations, they gathered in the gardens, and mingled.

Sage and Vikki walked around with interlaced fingers, happier than anyone's ever seen them. Charro was the only one present who wasn't paired, so he quietly looked on with a smile. He paced with his hands clasped behind his back, dressed impeccably.

Carly sat beside Adam, quietly conversing with her mother, which filled her where she had felt nothing but anguish before. "I'll go check on Jo one more time."

"Okay," Adam kissed her. "I'll go get Evan."

Carly pranced over to the rec room. Just before she reached the entryway, murmuring voices slowed her stride. Val and Ksenyia were engaged in a heated whisper battle. She listened intently because she wanted to know what "him" Val was referencing.

"He's my best friend, my brother, my family, K. He's off limits. We've discussed this. You said you understood and you were over it," Val whispered through clenched teeth.

"I am over it. All I said was there was some lingering attraction because it wasn't Adam I experienced. It was Dylan," Ksenyia explained.

"That really doesn't matter anymore because it was a mistake regardless. One I'll never make again. There's 3 billion men in the world to experiment with, but he's not one of them. Now tell me you understand, or do we need to end this?"

Carly didn't realize until this moment that she hadn't fully forgiven Val, because she was unsure if she could trust her. But now, she absolutely did. She remained still to gather the whole of it as she learned that Ksenyia was indeed the aggressor.

"End us? You'd leave me? Over him?" Ksenyia's eyes glistened with tears.

"K, it wouldn't be over him. It'd be over you disrespecting boundaries and other people's relationships. If you want to still experiment with other people, we aren't a good match for each other." *You already know the answer, it just hurts to accept it,* Val thought.

Carly made her presence known, not wanting to snoop anymore of Val's thoughts. "Hey, you two. Just came to check on Jo. Ceremony is about to start."

"Oh, we'll head over then," Val said, taking Ksenyia by the wrist and leading her away.

"You look…heavenly, Jo. Like an angel," Carly wooed.

Jo spun around gracefully. "With all of your help, I think I clean up well," she laughed. "Come here." She opened her arms wide and Carly raced into them. "I knew from the moment I met you, I'd love you forever."

"I love you too, Jo."

"Oh my gosh, I'm supposed to be the one crying, but I don't wanna mess my face up." She wiped Carly's pretty tears and exhaled. "Well, let's get me married."

They held hands and marched out the door.

"Rye, the bride is in route," Carly alerted Mariah with a quick phone call.

As Jo approached the silk-lined runway in her shimmery pearl gown, Evan cast an illusion of Jo's favorite view; the galaxy. His eyes soon overflowed with tears of joy. The two exchanged vows under the skies, among their friends, and family.

The reception was in full swing and everyone danced about. Charro stole Carly from Adam for a few whirls, while Adam twirled Jo around until she returned to Evan's arms. The clinking of silverware to champagne glass captured everyone's attention.

"Everyone," Evan began, "thank you for joining my wife and I on this joyous occasion, but we have more wonderful news to share."

"Don't tell us you've got a bun in the oven already?" Krill jokingly asked.

"Not quite," Evan replied. "But my son-in-law and his new bride does. Glasses in the air. Congratulations to Adam and Carly on their new life adventure of becoming parents!"

"Congratulations, son!" Jo yelled and clapped.

Adam and Carly blushed and thanked everyone.

As the festivities wound down, the Descendants gathered in the garden to discuss Onus Lyceum training.

"So, we're really leaving, not just the planet, not just the galaxy, but the universe," Sage said in disbelief.

"My concern is Kane being safe while we're gone, since he's the only one of us not permitted to go," Rye added, her anguish apparent.

Kane tilted her chin upright. "I'll be alright, babe. I promise."

"You can't promise me that." She glanced away with pain in her eyes.

Carly looked on, knowing Rye will be distracted from Onus Lyceum by the torture of separation and fear. But there was nothing she could do to change Metaversal Law.

"Hey, guys. I'm going to change out these clothes, use the restroom, and I'll be right back," Kane announced before dashing off.

"*I won't be torn away from her,*" Carly heard Kane thinking as he jogged away.

The others remained to chat with each other. A mixture of anxiety and excitement swirled in the air.

"Why did you choose me to go?" Vikki asked Carly. "I mean, I wasn't born with the divine heritage you mentioned."

"Because you have it now," Carly replied, "and it isn't destroying your cells or cycling out of your system like the previous V Nikolay gave you. Most importantly, you're our most skilled combat fighter, and you belong with us." All of it was true. Vikki's reaction to the V was definitely due to the source…Jo.

Just when a thought formed in Carly's mind, a piercing scream rang out.

"Kane," Carly whispered.

Rye blipped out with Carly right behind her.

They arrived at the Solomin house to find Kane, writhing in pain, on the bedroom floor upstairs.

Rye dropped to her knees, cradled his head, and caressed his face. "Baby, what's wrong?"

Carly knelt and retrieved the culprit from his clasped palm. "He took it, Rye." She held the empty vial in the air.

"Oh my God," Rye uttered. "Why did you do that, Kane? I told you…I told you," she croaked with tears streaming down her cheeks.

"I'll never let us be apart," Kane managed through strained grunts and convulsions.

Adam arrived first, bursting through the front door. "Carly!"

"We're up here," she calmly replied.

Adam rushed through the bedroom door and pulled Carly into his arms. "You okay?"

"I'm fine. It's Kane."

"What happened to him?"

Carly gave him the empty vial.

"Oh no." Adam gazed down at Kane.

Frantic footsteps echoed right before everyone else arrived upstairs. Val, Sage, Evan, and Jo entered the bedroom, with the others crowding the doorway.

"What happened to him?" Evan asked.

"He took V," Carly told him.

"How'd he get his hands on V?" Val frowned.

"It was a left-over lab sample from Vikki's testing," Adam divulged.

"But how did he get it? Or even know what it was?" Val probed.

"It was my fault," Rye cried. "I stole it from Adam's jeans without him or anyone knowing because…because I—"

"It's okay, Rye," Carly soothed. "You didn't give it to him. He took it himself."

"I would say it should've been locked away, but that wouldn't really matter with the abilities we all have," Jude offered, to everyone's surprise.

"Adam, why did you have it in your pocket?" Val quietly asked him.

"Because it was my mother's blood and I didn't want it out of my sight."

Val nodded and stood back.

"Let me have a look at him," Sage said, bending down to check Kane's vitals.

"Is he okay?" Rye asked anxiously.

"Well, he's unconscious, and his heart rate is elevated. Same as Vikki's when she took it," Sage said. "Let's get him in bed."

Sage cradled his back while Adam grabbed his legs. They placed Kane on the bed. Rye immediately covered him with a blanket and curled up beside him.

"Only time will tell how his body will respond," Sage said. "All we can do now is let him rest."

"Rye," Carly whispered while stroking her hair, "I'll be right downstairs if you need me, okay?"

"Okay," she smiled weakly.

Carly kissed her forehead and they all trekked downstairs.

"Let's take it into the basement," Evan suggested.

They gathered in the basement and collective sighs filled the space.

"So, what are we gonna do?" Krill asked.

"Yeah, we can't leave him now because he could die and Mariah would never recover," Ksenyia added.

"Well, like Carly said, he wouldn't survive the Onus training, so we can't take him," Jude said.

"We don't know how his body will respond to the V," Vikki interjected. "So, we shouldn't decide so hastily right now. How much time do we have left?"

"End of day," Carly answered. "That would be exactly 72 hours from the moment Rye and I returned home, though we should bump it up."

"I agree," Adam added, squeezing her hand. "I don't know about any of you, but I'd rather not risk being late, even by a second."

They nodded.

"We cannot leave the boy behind," Charro said. "I know that I am new among you, but I am eldest of the bloodlines. Unless one of us are designated to remain, we should take him."

"What do you think, Dauma?" Jo thought.

"Take him. He will recover," Dauma replied.

Carly sighed while Jo frowned.

"Dauma, if you're there, we need you," Jo thought before turning to Carly. *"Why can't I hear you or your mother?"*

"Later," Carly silently mouthed. The moment her core was unobstructed and she returned home, she instinctively learned how to shield herself. Jo was effectively banned from her thoughts, but Carly could hear Jo's. The only thoughts she still couldn't hear were Adam's.

"Is anyone going to stay behind with him?" Sage asked.

"None of you can stay behind," Carly reiterated. "We all need to go. Our best course of action is to sleep while Kane is unconscious and hope for the best for him."

"What if he isn't well when it's time to go?" Val inquired.

"We will have no choice but to take him to a hospital," Carly stated sadly, angry that Kane was willing to risk his life and everyone else's. She knew that his feelings towards Rye might change if he survives the V and that terrified her. What bothered her most was disagreeing with her own mother.

"Okay, then." Val breathed.

"We should all get some sleep and meet in the gardens at 3:00pm," Carly suggested.

Everyone agreed and dispersed to their homes, with Charro taking up temporary residence in Carly and Adam's guest bedroom for the day.

Carly peaked in on Rye and Kane one last time before she and Adam headed home for the biggest night's rest of their lives.

onus lyceum: proem

carly

"**R**ISE AND SHINE, beautiful," Adam gently whispered.

Carly's full ebony lashes fluttered before she came to. "Good morning," she beamed as a stream of sunlight warmed her cheek through their curtains. She gazed into his seductive, impossibly beautiful eyes, communicating her eternal love.

He caressed her face. "It's afternoon, but I'll take it," he shrugged with the sincerest smile and kiss.

She jerked upright. "Crap! Is it time already?"

"No, no," he soothed. "I know how important this is to our survival, so I wouldn't allow us to be late. We still have a few hours."

She rested her head back against the pillow and breathed a sigh of relief. "We should go check on Kane."

"Shower water is already on." He kissed her.

She jumped out of bed and into the bathroom. After she dressed in her mother's favorite outfit, she ported them to the Solomin's doorstep, not wasting time on walking.

Adam rang the doorbell.

"Son," Evan greeted him with a hug. "Come on in, you two."

Adam led the way. He glanced back at Carly as they both mouthed "son" simultaneously.

"Kane's upstairs with Mariah, and your mother is in the kitchen making sandwiches for everyone before our trip. How are you feeling, Carly?"

"A bit anxious, but otherwise, good."

"And how's…"

"They're fine," she beamed, patting her belly.

"They?" Adam nearly shouted.

"Meaning, we don't know if they're a he or she yet, babe. Calm down," she chuckled.

"Oh, oh, right." Adam exhaled.

Evan giggled.

"I'll check on Kane and Rye. Has anyone seen them yet?"

"Mariah won't let us in the bedroom. She said she's waiting for you and no one else," Evan shrugged.

Carly shook her head and walked towards the staircase.

"I'll be in the kitchen helping my mom if you need me," Adam said.

"Okay, tell her I said hi, and I'll see her soon." She made a beeline to the bedroom door and knocked. "Rye? Rye, it's Carly."

Rye cracked the door and peaked through the slit before pulling Carly inside.

"Is he?" Before she could finish, Kane exited the restroom, shirtless, and smiling.

"Carls!" he beamed, grabbing her up in a bear hug the way used to years ago.

"Kane, put her down," Rye demanded. "You have to be careful how you squeeze her right now."

"Oh right, I forgot. I'm sorry. Are you okay?" He inspected her for damage.

"I'm fine," she shooed his hands away. "So, has anything happened?"

"Nothing's happened," Rye confirmed. "He hasn't developed superhuman strength or beamed us into space."

"How are you feeling, Kane?" Carly probed.

"I feel better than I've ever felt in my life!"

Carly noticed he looked a tad younger, but not much. "Why haven't you let Evan or Jo inside the room? You know Kane will need to be evaluated by Sage before any decisions can be made."

"I don't give a damn what they say or think. I was waiting for you," she blurted without formality. "I remember what Nanzaki said about your abilities. Plus, your mom had bio-scan, so I figured maybe you do too now."

Carly figured she'd know by now if she could analyze Descendant's power levels. "Rye, I'm not sure about any of that. I.. I don't—"

"Now's not the time to doubt yourself, Car. Please, try. Otherwise, I'm staying behind with Kane no matter the consequences."

"Mariah."

"I mean it, Car. I will not be separated from him when there's a possibility I'll never return."

Carly debated with herself for a minute because there'd be an all-out Metaversal war before she'd let anything happen to Rye, or to the planet because Rye was forced to choose herself. "Okay. I'll give it a try."

"Thanks, Car."

Carly wrung her fingers, inhaled, and exhaled a few times. "Okay, Kane, take a seat on the bed."

"Okay." He sat on the edge of the mattress with his palms on his knees.

"This will hurt, but I'll try to keep you calm," Carly warned him.

He inhaled and exhaled. "I'm ready."

Carly positioned herself in front of Kane. "Give me your hands."

He extended his hands, palms up. Rye angled herself to get a better view.

"Unlock the door, and do not, under any circumstances, try to prevent Adam from getting through it," Carly warned.

"Okay, Car." She unlocked the door and returned to the bedside.

Carly expelled a large breath before sinking her thumbs into the center of his hands. Rye covered her mouth, anticipating his cries of pain, but they never came. After forty-five seconds, Carly withdrew her thumbs, summoned her healing crystals, and went to the bathroom sink to wash the blood from her hands.

She closed the door and leaned onto the sink to allow herself a moment to process what she believes she sensed. This was all new to her, so wanted to be sure. Until she was, she'd limit her responses to them both. The bottom line was, Kane would be just fine. However, he was already reading at Level One; meaning, he could levitate objects, but likely didn't know it yet.

"Car, are you okay?" Rye asked through the door.

Carly immediately exited the bathroom. "Yeah, I'm fine. So is Kane. We should all meet up in the garden in thirty minutes to prepare for travel."

"Thank you, Car." Rye threw her arms around Carly's neck

Carly squeezed back just as hard. "You're welcome, babe. See you both in the garden in thirty."

"We'll be there," Kane beamed.

Carly went right into the kitchen and hugged Jo.

"Hi, baby girl. How are you feeling?" Jo asked.

"I'm actually great."

Adam cupped and caressed the nape of her neck. "How's Kane?"

"He's doing well. I did a bio-scan on him."

"You what?" Adam choked on the lemonade he had begun sipping. "I remember your mother performing one on me. How do you even know how to do that?"

"I honestly don't know, but I did it."

"Did it work?" he asked anxiously.

Jo and Evan had moved closer.

"Yes, but I'm not really sure about the results right now. I just know he's fine, his cells are adapting, and it's safe to take him to Apricity with us." She had no intention of being scolded over abilities she was new to. Their only options were to believe her or not.

"You're incredible. Do you know that?" Adam gleamed.

"You truly are the best of us," Evan added.

They group hugged.

"Well, let's pack these sandwiches and juices up," Jo said.

The four of them wrapped and packaged the food, and headed over to the gardens. They plopped down amidst the beautiful purple flowers and waited for the others to show up.

"I'll actually have my sandwich now," Carly announced.

"Turkey, ham, or veggie?" Adam asked her. "Darn. I don't know where my mind is," he said while reaching for the veggie.

"Turkey."

"Woooow," the three of them chimed because Carly generally doesn't eat meat.

"Let the cravings begin," Jo sang with a grin.

Rye and Kane were the first to show up. Before long, the entire community gathered. Sage immediately checked over Kane, giving him a thumbs up.

After devouring their sandwiches and chugging their juice, they girded their loins.

Adam helped Carly from the grass.

She dusted off her bum. "This is it, guys. It's time. Since Kane is coming with us, we won't have to worry about leaving anyone behind."

Krill cracked his neck and hopped up and down. Sage followed suit. They gathered into a circle and grabbed each other's hands.

"Everyone," Carly began, "I know this isn't easy to believe or commit to. You're all my family, and I love you. I'd do anything to protect you. Although we didn't ask for nor start any of this, we'll certainly finish it. Together, we go. And, together, we will return."

"I love you, Carly," Jude said first. "I know I've been a bit bitchy, but I still love you, and I'd never hurt you."

"I love you, Carly," Ksenyia followed in her British cadence.

"I love you and I'm proud of you, little one," Charro added.

I love you's swirled about.

"Let's do this," Adam said with a wink.

Carly opened a portal, and within seconds, they arrived at the hippodrome on Apricity, where an arena of Makovians, Seerians, and Apexians awaited them.

Adam gleamed and slowly spun around, with twinkling eyes. "Babe, I'm living out my lifelong dream. All thanks to you." He kissed her.

"Carly," Jude whispered, "I must admit that I didn't believe you, but I'll never doubt you again." Her eyes bulged.

"It's like, I'm gonna wake up in any moment," Kane uttered to Rye.

Rye's eyes sparkled with anticipation.

The Descendants gawked and turned every which way to absorb everything they could. Jo squeezed Evan's hand so tight, the blood drained from it. Vikki and Sage clung to each other. Krill's grin spread wider than it ever had. Val and Ksenyia were stone-faced in disbelief.

Tanjuetti stood. "Thank you for returning, and welcome."

"I knew you'd come, and I knew you'd master the art of teleportation," Nanzaki thought, with a pleased smirk.

Carly grinned.

"Introduce yourselves," Relve demanded. *"Though unnecessary, Scionians seem to require such formalities to feel comfortable."*

"Yes, because most Scionians can't hear thoughts, don't communicate telepathically, nor have ocular sight across universes," Carly thought sarcastically.

Apexians leaned forward, analyzing the Descendant's physical attributes. Maw squinted his eyes at Krill, then Vikki.

Seerian Gehzlings looked on with their crescent limbal rings, which signified their extensive ocular gifts. Persa leaned back elegantly with glee while other Seerians silently observed.

Each Descendant introduced themselves by name and bloodline. Jo, Vikki, and Kane made their introductions last.

"Onus Lyceum will begin on the Seerian planet of Gehz, and consists of three segments," Tanjuetti announced. "Proem, Avant, and Guardian. You'll learn more of the components of each segment on Gehz. You will be required to successfully complete each segment. Failure is not an option. Failing any segment is failing the entire course. You are dismissed."

Thankfully, Carly had secured Rye a pass on that part.

Several portals appeared across the drome. Nanzaki opened a massive gateway and slightly bowed towards the Descendants. "If you'll please?"

The Descendants walked through, with Adam bravely leading the way.

When they arrived at the Gehzian ovular-shaped aerodrome, Carly and Rye guided them to where they should sit, along the back rows on the left, behind the Makovian Neophytes. There were dozens of unfamiliar beings spread throughout. Carly presumed the more youthful, quizzically eyed beings were present for Onus Lyceum as well. The drome had been modified to include Neophyte sections, with floating spectator seating above the floor.

Apexians were easily identified by their Aeger devices, which cast an emerald light from their wrists to their rectangular heads, and triangular pupils. Makovians' diamond-arabesque skin glistened under the lighting. They adorned intricate robes, bedazzled with crystals, and sat so erectly, one would think they were incapable of relaxing. Seerians, were androgynous,

tall, sophisticated beings with elongated fingers, disk-shaped eyes, and lux-
urious raven tresses.

Persa, as a familiar, took to the dais. "Greetings, Neophytes. Welcome to
this cycle's glorious convocation. Makovia, Seer, Apexia, and Scionia. Given
the vast and exciting change in dynamic, the common Scionian tongue shall
be spoken throughout, which you all have learned since birth. No other
tongues are permitted this cycle, due to the unique circumstance of Scionian
inclusion for the first time in Metaversal history. I am sure many of you have
questions, most surrounding the recent inclusion of Scionians. I assure you,
your queries will be addressed throughout."

"I wonder how they found us," Makovian Neophyte, Margol, uttered to
her friend in Marra. "I thought they were forbidden to ever come here." *"And
why can't hear him?"* she thought regarding Adam.

"I heard they're telepaths like us," another Makovian Neophyte, Hindru,
said, glancing back at the Descendants with distinct curiosity in his eyes.

"Yeah, but they look too stupid to control it," Makovian Neophyte, Laspi,
snorted in a pompous tone.

Carly merely glowered, not caring for Laspi's energy. She rolled her eyes
at him and looked forward.

Though he did not understand Marra, Adam was familiar with negative
energy. He flashed his LR at the Makovian Neophytes, pulled Carly's leg
closer to him, and returned his attention to Persa.

On the adjacent side of the floor, Apexian Neophytes were seated in the
front rows, with Seerian Neophytes behind them.

"I shall now yield to our most gifted Liege, physicist, astronomer, histo-
rian, and prophetic visionary, Noluh." Persa bowed out, dimmed the lights,
and took their seat in a hovering cathedra.

"Greetings, Neophytes. Among many things, please be aware that it is forbidden to disclose your cycle placement or station before, during, or after
Onus, until you successfully complete it. I shall begin with basic Metaversal
history, which most of you learned during your initial rearing and educa-
tion. Please, be patient with those who are learning for the first time," Noluh
said as they displayed multiple holographic images across the drome. "The
Metaverse is the divine infinite space where all lifeforms exist; sentient and
insentient," Noluh went on, repeating all of what Persa had taught to Carly
and Rye on their visit.

The Descendants were enraptured and not one of them uttered a word during the lesson. Val's eyes lit up when Noluh mentioned the Seerians' agender existence with asexual reproduction. Noluh listed each of the galaxy's system suns: Duenden's Cava, Cyim's Arx, Magnomium's Sol, RIP's Yeuton, Makovia's Nivval, Aeonia's Thyima, Au's Giree, and Klipp's Vellun.

"We shall make no mention of galaxies where neither sentient nor insentient life-forms exist, as they are infinite. The two occupied galaxies within the Seerian Universe are Cyim and Duenden, with Duenden housing the most sentient life," Noluh continued. "I originate from the planet of Gehz, in the Duenden Galaxy. Gehzian culture is centered not only around ocular sight and foretelling, but all Gehzians are equally committed to the immense responsibility of raising and educating all Gehzlings. Therefore, we live as a planet of a singular family unit."

"Wow," Carly muttered in sheer amazement. "Humans could learn a thing or two."

"Or a million," Adam concurred. He smiled at Jo, on his right.

Noluh informed them of the other occupied galaxies before moving on. "Now that we've covered the rudimentary facts of the Metaverse, let's move on to the segments of Onus Lyceum." Noluh summoned more holographic images from the archives. "Onus Lyceum was established a decamillennium ago, after a megaannum of violent clashes between the Verses, coupled with sporadic eruptions, resulting in irreparable damage to the Metaverse, and monumental loss of life. The Metaversal Panel of Life, MPOL for short, then unanimously decided that all beings would be required to learn control and skill on how and when to wield their divine heritage or face cellular cessation."

Sage thew his hand up in the air. "What is cellular cessation?"

"Death," Noluh replied. "Save your questions because most will be answered by simply allowing the lesson to continue, uninterrupted."

"Sorry," he uttered.

"Psh, we know," Laspi snorted.

"Is there a problem, Neophyte Laspi?" Noluh asked.

"There is not, Preceptor Noluh," he politely, but sarcastically, replied.

"Very well. To continue then," Noluh dismissed the arrogance and privilege of the pedantic Neophyte. "Onus Lyceum is not only a mandatory scholastic program, it is also Metaversal Law. The three segments of Onus Lyceum are Proem, Avant, and Guardian. Proem, which is co-managed by Makovians and Seerians, consists of history, heritage scan verification, physical exam, interplanetary travel, artifacts, energy sources, astronomy, engineering, mapping, and navigational skills. Avant, co-managed by Makovians and Apexians, consists of heritage guidance, discipline, and growth, hand-to-hand combat, dance, swordsmanship, and tournament. Guardian, wholly managed and overseen by the MPOL, consists of limitations, pairing, responsibility, and placement. Each segment spans seven days, each day the equivalent of a singular Cava axis. At the end of each segment, you will be tested by MPOL on the totality of what you learned and how you apply it. Your pass or fail rating, as determined by the MPOL, shall be final."

"What else is new?" Margol sneered.

"Gehz is the only planet where time lapses identically across the Metaverse, which is why the MPOL is stationed here. Meaning, time increments are the same here as they are on any and every planet in the Metaverse."

And why Onus is held here, like everything else, Margol thought.

"Explains why you thought you were gone for a day while on Apricity, when it was actually three days," Jo whispered to Carly.

"Proem begins now," Noluh continued. "Neophytes, follow me."

The trainees filed out of the aerodrome. Collective gasps abounded from the Descendants, along with a sprinkle of Makovians and Apexians who had never physically experienced Gehz.

Muscular Apexian Drudge elbowed his fellow Apexian Neophyte, Wolmyn, for openly gawking at the majestic crimson and cream swirling atmosphere. "Stop acting like you've never seen the archived images before. You literally won the Onus lottery, being the coveted selected alternate of three Verses, and you embarrass us the first chance you get." He shook his head.

Wolmyn cleared his throat and straightened up. "It's just different up close is all."

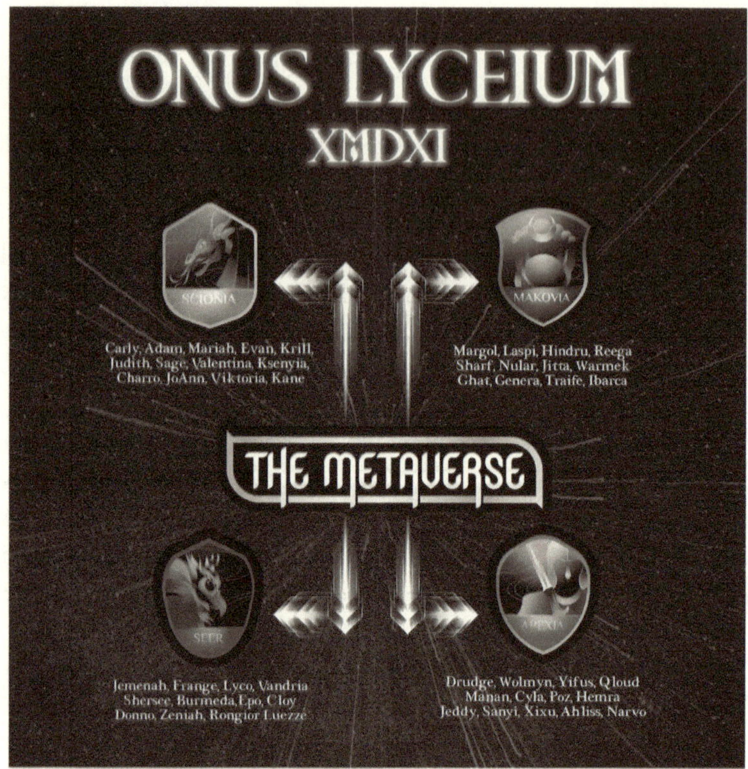

"You know you are not his parent, Drudge?" Apexian Neophyte Yifus said, challenging Drudge. "You're not a Merser yet either. You're a Neo just like the rest of us. Go on, Woly, stare all you like."

"He's humiliating our species in front of these Scionians," Drudge growled.

"No, your misery is embarrassing," Yifus countered. "Just mad he was selected on his first cycle and you weren't. You're still here so lighten up."

Carly gaped at the red cindered land and magnificent creamy sun. She couldn't believe her eyes nor her luck.

"This is utterly incredible, babe," Adam said. "I just can't believe this is real." He gripped her hand, and she returned the gesture.

"Same here," she replied through a grin.

"Quick, pinch me," he teased.

"No way. If this is a dream, I'd rather not wake up for a long while."

"Are Scionians this…dependent and vulnerable?" Drudge asked with disgust dripping from his tone. "You may as well accept cessation now and save yourself the exertion."

The winds whirled. Adam waved them away effortlessly before he turned.

Many Neos gasped at his mild display of heritage. Carly sensed their excitement, which maintained her calm. The other Descendants remained protectively near.

Adam shielded Carly from Drudge's view. "I've only been around Apexians for a few hours, but you seem dedicated to a miserable existence."

Yifus sniggered. "We never miss an opportunity to tell him he's way too serious. He doesn't represent us all. My name is Yifus, everyone calls me Yif."

Adam extended his hand, and the Apexians jumped back, preparing to fight.

"What is this gesture?" Yif inquired, lowering his defenses.

"On my planet, we shake hands when meeting someone for the first time. I'll show you." Adam slowly took Yif's wide hand into his and demonstrated a hand shake.

"Amazing," Yif said with a smile. "I love to learn new things."

Adam experienced no memories of Yif's, and Carly, knowing him best, chuckled at his guised disappointment.

"This is Qloud, Manan, Cyla, Poz, Hemra, Jeddy, Sanyi, Xixu, Ahliss, and Narvo."

Qloud eyeballed Carly intently.

"We're traveling to the laboratory by foot to initiate the heritage scan and physical examination," Noluh informed them. "This way," they pointed.

Everyone trailed behind the Preceptor, into a massive, towering, white, sleek structure. Several lifts elevated them to a higher level at lightning speed. They stepped into a room lined with a dozen life-sized white pods, transparent screens, and Seerian bio-engineers.

"When I call your name, step forward," Noluh commanded. "For those of you who do not have them on your home planets, these," Noluh pointed, "are divinity capsules, designed to detect, measure, and catalog your heritage and overall health, as well as check for any abnormalities or obstructions. It is wholly painless. Refusal is the equivalent of failure."

Adam fidgeted.

"It's okay," Carly soothed. "These seem similar to the Afrax corridor, and mom's bio-scan."

Adam touched the faded scars in the center of his palms from Dauma's scan of him. "Uh huh."

Noluh blankly eyed Carly before calling upon the first dozen Neos, which included Kane. He exhaled sharply before throwing his shoulders back and proceeding to his designated pod. The others swiftly entered their pods as well. The bio-engineers tapped a few icons on their crystalline tablets. The pods glowed, but emitted no audible noise. Carly's core, however, detected a mild hum. Within fifty seconds, the process was complete and the pod shields opened.

Noluh called upon the next dozen, a nice mixture of each Verse, including Jo, and Vikki. Carly immediately noticed the pattern. They were first testing those they believed either had low levels of heritage or were obstructed.

"This one is quite bright," Noluh intentionally thought, while eyeing Carly. Makovian Neos followed Noluh's line of sight to Carly and Adam, who were holding hands.

"Who?"

"Which one?"

"Which one is the Preceptor referencing?" Laspi thought, with his arms crossed, darting his eyes suspiciously between Carly and Adam.

Carly tilted her head to the right while quieting all the Neo's thoughts to focus on Noluh's, realizing she hadn't heard any Seerians' thoughts before now.

"Yes, Scionian. Seerians aren't open books as Makovians, Apexians, and Scionians. We rarely require thought, and our primary processes aren't cerebral." Noluh smirked.

Carly was thoroughly intrigued.

"Seerians are quite exquisite beings," Dauma hummed.

"Mommy, you've met them before?" Carly queried.

"Focus, baby girl."

Before long, she and Adam were called upon in the final group. Adam kissed her on the lips before settling inside his pod. If he so much as squirmed uncomfortably, she'd level the entire building without hesitation. She clambered into her pod, laid back, and closed her eyes. Atomic sparks connected to every cell in her body, blanketing them, crawling through them. She was tempted to resist the invasion, but opted to relax as they worked their way through her.

As the zeptoseconds lapsed, heaviness she hadn't noticed weighing her down, was lifted. When the pulses made their way to her womb, she opened her eyes. Her LR flared and she wanted out of the pod before any harm was caused to her unborn child.

"Remain calm, Scionian Carly. No harm will come to you or the Consanguineous," Noluh told her from beside the closed pod.

"She's nervous," Adam said, alerting her to the fact that he was out of his pod.

"Adam? Why am I still inside?"

"It's because they're evaluating both of you," he replied.

When her stomach jerked, she was over it. "Release me right now or I'll—" the pod shield opened, and Adam grabbed her into his arms.

"You were only inside thirty seconds longer than the others," Noluh informed her.

Carly didn't believe it because it felt like no less than five minutes.

"Feeble," Drudge snorted.

Carly glared his way, with her LR flaming and rotating. He nervously cleared his throat and looked away. With all forty-eight Neos tested, they were escorted into an adjoining auditorium.

"The remainder of today, you'll learn to map and navigate the Metaverse. For this, I'll yield to Apexian Preceptor, Qiar.

The stately gladiator of a being appeared from behind a wall with his Aeger active and glowing. "I am Qiar. Let us begin."

He went on for four hours teaching them how to measure space and time before delving into the basics of navigation. A loud beep sounded.

"It is now time to rest for an hour," Noluh announced. "Refreshments await you in the mess hall on the level below us. Enjoy, and return promptly."

The Neos walked briskly to the lifts and descended. They wasted no time filling their upturned plates with a mixture of alien foods aligning the counters before sitting. Each Verse stuck together in groups.

"It's weird to come all this way, just to isolate ourselves," Val said.

"I agree," Sage replied. "Should we spread out?"

"Definitely," Krill bellowed.

They grabbed their food and walked towards the other Neos. Krill, Jude, Sage, and Vikki went to the Apexians. Charro, Rye, and Kane joined the Makovians. Carly, Adam, Jo, and Evan, went to the Seerian tables.

"May we join you?" Jo asked.

"Yes, please," soft spoken Jemenah answered as they scooted to make space.

"My name is Jo. This is my husband, Evan, my son, Adam, and my daughter-in-love, Carly. It's such a pleasure to be here. Your planet is so beautiful."

"We are not all from Gehz, but thank you. I'm from Qalopsia. We've heard so much about you," Jemenah said. "We are all…uh, *ecstatic*, for this."

Carly imagined it was quite a feat for them to speak in a language they had no use for until today. She wondered if they'd heard good or bad things about them. She knew humans weren't collectively nice people.

Jemenah introduced everyone. "Frange is from Simiri. Lyco, Vandria, Shersee, Donno, and Burmeda are from Gehz. Zeneah is from Metonia. Epo and Cloy are from Berronya. Rongior is from Bruud, and Luezzé is from Desa."

"Amazing," Carly beamed.

"What is it like on your planet?" Frange inquired.

"The planet itself is beautiful, mostly," Jo answered.

"It's so blue and green, while your sun is yellow," Frange said.

"In visions, your liquids are rather transparent," Jemenah added.

Other Seerian Neos nodded their heads, with their bright eyes trained on the Descendants.

"I once had the same questions as a young boy," Adam replied with a kind smile. "Drove my parents and teachers crazy with it. Well, our trees are green, which provide oxygen to our atmosphere, and our sky is blue due to a process called Rayleigh scattering." He patiently went on describing the scattering of blue light, which delighted them.

Over her shoulder, Carly spotted Val gazing over at them longingly. *"They're so beautiful,"* she thought.

"You are quite the gentle flame," Jemenah told Carly.

"Yes, very harmonious," Frange smiled.

"Your eyes are different than the Prophecy of Light visions we—" Jemenah stopped when Lyco elbowed her. "I'm sorry, I have over-spoken. What of you, Evan?"

"I'm a mellow, fun-loving guy," he said with his signature charming grin. "I'm here to learn and contribute to the peace and tranquility of the Metaverse."

His answer seemed to please them, while Carly's determination to learn of the Prophecy of Light swelled.

The Descendants made very pleasant conversation before returning to the auditorium for another excruciating four hours. When the first day of Proem drew to a close, Noluh returned to escort them to their housing structure.

"I'm sure you're all exhausted, so Preceptor Qiar will teleport us to the dormitory."

When Qiar nodded, his long, thick, twisted strands fell across his almond-shaped eyes. They arrived at the expansive building a nanosecond later.

"Your quarters are preassigned. Simply find your name. I suggest you rest tonight, as tomorrow is dedicated to interplanetary travel, which can be exhausting for many," Noluh told them before Qiar blipped them both out.

The Descendants regrouped.

"Okay, let's find our rooms," Val said.

The Neo's inched down the long hallway, breaking off into rooms as they found their names.

Vikki's was the first of the Descendant's names they crossed. "Well, this is me," she said. "Looks like they're separating and scattering us."

"I think it's so we get to know other beings," Sage offered. "Let's all see what the rooms look like inside."

Vikki searched for a doorknob or key slot, but found none. It was completely blank. "How do I open the door?" she wondered aloud.

A crystalline panel appeared to the right of the slate door.

"You must've said a key word or there's some voice recognition of some kind," Sage suggested.

The silhouette of a palm illuminated in red on the panel. Vikki cautiously placed her hand on it and the door slid to the left.

"Welcome, Scionian Viktoria." the AI chimed.

Impressed, they all entered slowly. The motion-activated lights glowed, brightening the massive quarters.

"This isn't a dorm room. It's a loft," Adam said as he scanned the space.

"And the loft is lofting," Carly added as she glimpsed the appliances, transparent screens, and stairs to an upper level. "It's huge enough for Sage to stay in here with you."

"Well, that's definitely gonna happen," Sage chuckled. "But something tells me I'm supposed to check into my own little suite before staying here with Vik tonight."

"I'm sure you're right," Krill said. "These are advanced beings, and I imagine they're keeping track of everything we do during this training."

"It's like a resort," Jude said while running her fingers along the exotic plants.

"Well, I suppose we should all go find our own," Ksenyia shrugged. "I don't know about you guys, but I'm beat."

"I'm more intrigued than fatigued," Charro chortled. "So, after we check into our quarters, I plan to roam the halls for a bit."

Sage kissed Vikki. "See you in a bit."

The rest of them continued down the hall and entered their rooms, one-by-one. Carly and Adam noticed their names were together on the right side of the door above the palm screen.

"I wonder why we were housed together, while the others were separated," Adam said.

"The only logical answer is because they knew beforehand that you and I were a wedded pair. They only learned of the other pairings when we all arrived together," Carly answered.

"That makes perfect sense. Well, let's see what we've got." Adam placed his palm on the screen, opening the door.

Their quarters were the size of a quaint home. Carly immediately descended into comfort, saving the sight-seeing for another day. Her thoughts swarmed around the Prophecy of Light, how Makovians, Seerians, and Apexians were so savvy with their use of common English, and why they were more focused on Carly than the others. Something was going on and she wouldn't let her guard down for a second.

Adam called Carly into the restroom. "How do you suppose we shower without nozzles or spouts?"

She figured everything was voice-automated. "Shower on?" she said, unsure.

The water flowed from the ceiling like a botanical waterfall. They stripped and showered together, climbed into bed nude, and sank into an exhausted slumber.

22

prophecy of light

carly

ABRIEF SIREN WOKE them.

"You have thirty minutes to report to the mess hall for breakfast. Thirty minutes," The AI voice announced.

Carly quickly hopped out of bed, with Adam right beside her. They searched for clothing before Adam sighed. "Clothes," he said, unsure.

The far wall shifted, revealing red and orange pressurized jumpsuits. Their names were on the breast pockets.

"Well, I guess we know what to wear every day," Carly shrugged. "What about undergarments?"

Two drawers opened near the hanging jumpsuits. They smirked, hurriedly dressed, and made their way into the hall, where others were rushing towards the cafeteria for breakfast. After the Descendants reconnected over a delicious meal, the alarm blared again, followed by an AI prompt to report to the shared living space for transport.

Noluh and Qiar awaited them.

"Good morning, Neophytes," Noluh greeted. "I hope you slept well. Today, we will travel the Metaverse to view all planetary atmospheres, landscapes, and artifacts. As we are all have different genetic markers, some of us require different forms of oxygen to survive. Therefore, if you'll notice, on your left sleeve, there is a button. When pressed, a nano-shield, will be deployed around your head, sealing your suit, to supply life-sustaining oxygen. Your entire suit is equipped with several different forms of protection. It will self-deploy in any atmosphere it detects the presence of harmful elements or lack of breathable air. You are not permitted to remove your suits, unless instructed by a Preceptor. Is that understood?"

"Yes, Preceptor," most chimed in unison.

"Very good. We will begin with the mother Verse of Makovia. Qiar, if you'll please?"

Qiar opened a large portal, and crossed over first.

"Please, grab a knapsack for travel," Noluh pointed.

Seerian Neo's obediently began grabbing their knapsacks and walking through the portal, while others slightly hesitated.

"The sooner, the better," Noluh urged.

Carly grabbed Adam's hand and led the way.

When they all arrived on the other side, Noluh continued her lesson. "We are now in the Makovian Universe, galaxy of Aeonia, on the planet Sxulit. MPOL Magistries may teleport in and out at any time, and they're monitoring your every move. Due to the time differential, we can only spend a maximum of one hour on each planet, so please pay attention. Vyun shall not be visited."

They spent thirty minutes each on Sxulit, Hurex, and Oble, visiting key sites and appreciating their various gravitational pulls before moving on to the Makovian galaxy, with planets Apricity, Filak, Opia, and Voketto. Carly's core reacted differently to each sun, Thyima and Nivval. She'd noticed the change when she Rye were first ported to Apricity, but hadn't realized it was her proximity the suns. They welcomed, warmed, and charged her nicely. She looked forward to experiencing them again in the future. Moreover, after each planetary port, her center felt a bit heavier, which attributed to varying gravities.

After returning to Gehz, many Apexian Neo's began to vomit.

"Turn your darn Aegers off," Noluh suggested. "They don't mix well with frequent teleportation. Aegers pressurize the brain unnecessarily, which disrupts the flow of vital fluids in your bodies. I'm quite sure the Makovians couldn't care less what thoughts you're harboring when their very lives depend on passing Onus." Noluh shook their head.

"Got that right," Margol snorted, with the other Makovians joining in with sniggles.

"One hour lunch and rest period before we move on to Apexia." Noluh walked away.

"That was fun!" Rye exclaimed.

"I saw your eyes sparkling the whole time," Carly said, hugging her.

The Neo's crowded the mess hall and piled their trays high with food. The Apexians chugged all the liquids they could, and even had turned their Aegers off. Carly was disinterested in their miserable thoughts, but Jo snooped away as they sat at a table near the far wall.

"Boy, that Drudge guy doesn't let much light in, does he?" Jo said.

"I met dozens like him in high school," Adam replied while shaking his head.

"Hmph, seems he's high off being from an elite family on his home planet of Kroo," Jo whispered. "But he's bitter over not being selected during first cycle drafts among his age class for Onus when he reached puberty. The MPOL selected others, setting him back a cycle, which is a year."

"I wonder why that's such a bad thing for him," Evan wondered aloud.

Carly gazed stoically at the Seerians. "I'll be right back."

"Wait, I'll come with you," Adam offered.

"No, babe. Enjoy your food. I'm fine. Just wanna chat with them really quickly." When she stood, the Seerian Neo's immediately took notice and moved aside to make a space for her. "Hey."

"Hello, Carly," Jemenah sang in a tiny voice. "How are you enjoying Onus so far?"

"It's actually pretty wonderful. I'm very curious about the Prophecy of Light."

Their gorgeous eyes darted every which way as they nervously nibbled on their food.

"What exactly is it?"

"Only the original Seer can tell you. It is their birthright," Frange informed her. "We are forbidden."

"Who is the original Seer?" Carly probed.

"Persa of Gavaleed," Frange divulged.

"I understand. Thank you. Thank you so much. Enjoy your meal and we'll chat again soon." Carly beamed a sincere smile before returning to the Descendants.

"Is everything alright, little one?" Charro asked.

"Yes, PawPaw. Everything is great. I'm ready to explore the Apexian Universe."

"They actually have me quite intrigued as well," Charro replied. "Many of them are outwardly grumpy, but I'm sure there's more to them than that."

"That's what I've been thinking," Sage added. "They're clearly very young, and the younger you are, the more pressure is on you to do what a carved society says you should."

"Facts," Adam concurred.

"I'm sure it's to help them avoid many unnecessary pitfalls of life," Jo interjected.

"Based on history, their entire culture is grounded in violence," Krill said. "And they've been eyeing me like they wanna try me out or something."

Vikki sniggered. "That'd be epic."

"Heck yeah," Krill responded. "They did say Avant involved combat and tournament. Can't wait for that bit."

Vikki nodded in agreement.

"Meanwhile, the Makovians are blatant snobs," Jude snorted. "We're supposed to be a reflection of them? Psh, I think not."

"You got that right, babe," Krill agreed.

"The Seerians seem to be the most civil, harmonious, and welcoming," Val said. "And I'm utterly falling in love with Gehzlings. I hope to explore the planet more."

"Me too," Ksenyia said. "Hopefully, we don't have curfews where we can't go out after training hours like children."

"I wanna venture as well," Carly said. "We should ask Preceptor Noluh about it."

The AI announced a ten-minute courtesy before training resumed. They finished their meals and reported to the lobby for transport.

"Well, off to the Au galaxy we go," Noluh declared before Qiar opened a portal.

They explored Mgregor, Komur, Uzu, Orpha and N'Evious in two hours flat. They then ported to the Klipp Galaxy, starting with Illayia, Elysia, Wreiyn, Giji, and saved Kroo for last. Drudge paraded around, proudly pointing to several monuments and statues of prominent Kroo Merser Warriors who had set records for swordsmanship, hunt, and game. The Descendants had never seen the young Apexian so animated. Drudge actually smiled, which shocked them all.

Qiar ported them back to Gehz.

"That is all for the day," Noluh announced. "Tomorrow, we'll complete our travels with the Seerian and Scionian Universes."

"Preceptor Noluh," Val called. "Are we able to explore the outdoors or must we remain inside this structure?"

"Oh, you are free to roam the lands, within the Rossur city parameters. I will simply caution you to limit such excursions to conserve your energy stores for Onus. You are not prisoners," Noluh smiled. "However, we Gehzlings are very protective of our family and culture. Educating yourself on our laws will help you to abide by them, lest you're sentenced to cessation unnecessarily. Good night to you all."

Qiar blipped them out as the Neo's scurried down the hall.

Val and Ksenyia turned to each other and gleefully grasped hands.

"Carly, you coming with us?" Val asked.

"Yeah, I think I will. Adam, will you stay here or go out with the guys?"

"I'm not sure yet, but we'll figure it out. Please, be careful. I love you." He kissed her.

"Always," she blushed. She adored the confidence he'd settled into since their marriage. Though he was still madly protective, he didn't attempt to smother her or prevent her from living life.

"Let's see if Jude, Jo, and Vikki wanna come along," Ksenyia proposed. "Make it a full-on girl's trip!"

Carly smiled as she followed behind them. Her mind was on getting to Persa. She would take in the sights afterwards.

The six of them exited the housing structure into the open swirling winds.

"You guys go on ahead of me and I'll catch up," Carly said.

"Carly," Jo warned, "now you know Adam will literally kill me anything happens to you."

"Nothing's gonna happen. I'm only going to the main drome right over the hill there."

"How will you find us without a cell phone?" Val asked.

"I don't need one. I'll find you, trust me," she winked.

They all hugged and parted ways. Instead of porting to the aerodrome, Carly enjoyed the burgundy and cream swirls on her trek. She gazed up at Cava, buttery and magnificent in the sky. She was surprised how she captured the scent and warmth of its core. She took her time walking, using it to practice the art of pulling energy from the universe into her core faster than she expelled it, so she's never depleted. After a while, she arrived at the drome.

"Hello?" she called out as she entered. Her voiced echoed through the vacant lobby.

"I've been waiting for you," Persa said from the shadows.

"You have?"

"Yes, for quite some time, in fact."

"H-how old *are* you?"

"Seerians typically live an average of three thousand cycles. I'm nearing the end of mine, and wondered when or if our paths would cross."

"I don't understand why you—"

"The Light doesn't reveal all, Carly. If it did, we'd have no reason nor reward to have any faith."

"What is the Prophecy of Light?"

"Join me inside," Persa extended her arm to the ovular auditorium.

Carly walked ahead. When she entered, images and videos were on all the walls, ceilings, and transparent screens. "What is this?"

"This is you."

"I-I can see that, but how did you—"

"You already know that answer. I'll share with you what you do not. An Eon ago, the Light had dimmed, and stopped communicating with sentient beings. Before your species' well known extinction level event 65 billion years ago, there was another, more devastating event, caused by Scionian Ybia."

"Who is Ybia?"

"Ybia was the most powerful Scionian being in your universe, and she'd unwittingly drew upon a catastrophic amount of energy from all the Scionian suns. She was unaware of her ability to do so, and was overwhelmed with human emotion. The Supernovae she caused, irreparably destroyed planets and abnormally merged others. This is why there is only one habitable planet in the Magnomium Galaxy, where the planet of Jupiter was once three separate, smaller, habitable planets. The damage affected the closest universe — Makovia, ending all sentient and insentient life on Vyun. The reason why the damage didn't completely destroy the Aeonian Galaxy was due to Verdapok's ancestor, Hith. Sensing the impending blast wave, he swiftly projected absorptive shields, teleporting at a rate of speed never seen before at that time, to protect the planets, suns, and solar systems."

Carly gasped and tears glistened in her eyes. With that tiny drop of knowledge, she immediately understood why Verdapok did what he did, yet her flesh sent her into denial. "B-b-but the planet Sharen is habitable. I've been there. We're not like Ybia, I'm not like her. We're different. We've evolved. We—"

"That is merely Metaversal history," Persa soothed her. "You need to know your past in order to understand your present. Sharen is in the Scionian RIP Galaxy, which is why your friend, Mariah, was forcibly summoned by the Makovian POL on Apricity. Not only was she quickly approaching a dangerous rate of speed, she threatened to spread the unstable Scionian species to another galaxy before it had been decided that Scionians would be included in the divinity and attend Onus Lyceum."

That made so much more sense to Carly than what the Makovian Elders had put off. With humanity being as progressively violent as it was, it shouldn't be allowed to spread across the universe to destroy anything else. She understood with more clarity how important Onus was, but wondered if her instance in Greenland was indicative of history threatening to repeat itself.

"Now, Ybia was simply a Scionian being who lacked the proper control, training, and knowledge — but with an expansive ability to harness. You, however, are more. You embody every attribute the Light required to manifest itself among us. When I received my first vision of you, I was but fifteen cycles in age, and you had not been conceived in the flesh quite yet," Persa chuckled. "This, I did not know, and required guidance from my Elders. What I had received was the vision of visions. The Light had chosen me to reveal itself materializing in the flesh, where its presence was vital. My Elders taught me that it was my duty to prepare a safe space for you, to oversee and protect you. Successful, unchallengeable Seerian culture had decreed it."

Carly ogled Persa stoically, entranced. "Why was Ybia without the tools she needed?"

"Because Makovia, as a whole, arrogantly resented Scionia for its perceived rejection of its disbursement of Light, believing Scionia was a pilfering disobedient child of Makovia. Even after Ybia proved to other Verses that Makovians were the direct cause of the supernovae by voting alongside Apexians to exclude Scionians, it took several thousand years more before you were born, and the Prophecy of Light began to unfold precisely as it was foreseen."

Carly wasn't lost on the plurality. That meant Ybia did more than supernova Sol. More importantly, how does her existence change anything?

"You were born Light, Carly. Meaning, you required no enhancements, mergers, or tampering to realize your full deity. Therefore, your merger with your mother, which included the energies of a dozen others from your bloodline, altered my original vision. You had effectively exceeded the power of Light, and continued to do so once you were with child."

"Nanzaki told me my sync with Adam also altered my abilities."

"That is his, and other Makovians, presumption. However, Seerians have disproven this. When you underwent divinity testing, your sources were revealed and none linked to your husband, Adam. His presence calms you and brings you joy, not power. The Scionian core sync only exists in your universe. While away from your universe, pairing is utter free-will."

Carly was alarmed and intrigued.

"You, Carly, do not rely upon a Scionian core as the others do."

"I set things on fire, and boil water, mostly," she nervously chuckled.

"Fire is a lower, more rudimentary, level of energy. The highest form is Light. Light is the embodiment of life. From molecules to cells. Light embodies the ability to deconstruct, restructure, and merge lifeforms. Carly, you did not cremate the Iksha militants. You disintegrated their cellular structure, atomizing them."

"I did what?"

"We watched you in Greenland, from here. Saw you bind JoAnn's cells with extracted divinity. And watched as you rejoined two beings who were abnormally split, as embryos, in their mother's womb. That's quite a bit more than *boiling water*, wouldn't you say? Most beings have a one-dimensional body, which limits their abilities, as they should be. You, however, can atomize and rebuild cells."

"What the what?"

"You're still in disbelief? Even after you have already achieved it?"

"I absolutely do not believe I have achieved it. When? Where?" She surely wanted to know when she allegedly killed someone and brought them back.

"Here, I'll show you." Persa flicked their elongated finger towards the wall.

Carly watched herself floating, as a ball of energy, towards Adam and Dylan, before she rejoined them. She had thought she was simply aflame, but that didn't explain how she'd reduced Dylan to a ball of pure energy. She was doubting the Prophecy, and herself, because the power terrified her.

"You must, at all times, respect the power you wield. Respect involves the acceptance of your power's existence."

"I would *never* supernova …"

"For you, it would be a Supranova, not supernova. Supra is an explosion of *all* suns. The end of all life everywhere."

"I didn't ask for this, and I don't think I want it. I'm becoming a mom. I just got married. I'll be starting college next Fall. I…" she cried when she thought of her unborn child, whether they would be a boy or girl…and how their life would be affected by all this. She instinctively cradled her womb.

"Do not fear for her, she is the Consanguineous descendant of…"

"She? H-how do you?"

"Divinity testing, my dear."

"I'm having a daughter," she tearfully muttered.

"Of course. Your lineage has no Y chromosome, and therefore, cannot pass it."

"Adam created this child with me and he has it. What about Charro and Konstantin Wit?"

"Simply put, your genetics supersede Adam's. You were not descended from Charro's line, but the other woman in the household in Sintashta."

"But, Emebet…her Ethiopian heritage. My mother…"

"The Wit bloodline was chosen for its direct link to Mitochondrial Eve, the first Scionian, descendant of Ybia, chosen to seed Scionia after the reptilian cleanse."

Carly knew Persa was referencing the extinction level event that killed the dinosaurs.

"The reason the Wit's were the only family who welcomed the exiled Emebet is because they were the only Scionians *of color* in Sintashta." Persa openly expressed their dislike of the term. "Your unborn child and husband are the evolution of Scionia."

"This, this is too much. Adam's got a shield, which couldn't be the ability of the millennium. And, and…and my mother would've told me if Charro were not my direct ascendant." Carly shook her head. Her temperature rose and the seats in the drome began to melt. She rebuked the responsibility of all life. It wasn't fair, and she hadn't asked for it.

Persa changed the flow of the conversation. "The reason the suns seem never to shine the same when someone dies is because they dim from transition of life. But they are re-energized when the life force is recycled back through them. Every life is recycled through the suns, which is Light as we know it. Also, why the Wit/Rozovsky bloodline has always been the pairing to revere on your planet. We Seerians see, but have only interfered once, and that one time was in your regard."

"By porting me to Apricity while I was sleeping?" The conversation effectively distracted her and the room cooled.

"That was the Makovians, but at our insistence, and…that moment was the viable instance of your pregnancy. Makovians had watched all Verses, and wondered if a Makovian, Seerian, or Apexian would fulfill the Prophecy of Light they doubted so fervently. The foretelling that the Light would manifest itself in the flesh. It was like a competition. They had doubted Seerian's ocular foresight, though we had proven ourselves an infinite number of times, and could not completely dismiss the vision where you were born Scionian. However, manifestation of the Light was more than they were willing to wholly believe. But you are that manifestation."

"No wonder the Makovians and Apexians hate us so much," Carly mumbled. "They each wanted the Light to manifest in their species, but it chose Scionia. A universe Makovia already resented to the point of exclusion. They're jealous for no reason because we're all one of the same. Different abilities, but the same sentient species."

Persa beamed and nodded. "I knew you'd understand. It only took minutes for you, where millions of years have lapsed for Makovians and Apexians."

"They understand. They simply refuse to accept it. It's a delusion we call racism back on Scionia."

"I am familiar."

Carly shook her head.

"The Metaverse is watching you, and our very survival depends upon your completion of Onus Lyceum. Without basic control, structure, and willingness to respect the Laws of the Metaverse, a war would be inevitable. You don't need to sit upon a throne. Simply learn the required control, master your emotions, and show everyone they have nothing to fear."

"They have nothing to fear from me."

"I, and other Seerians, know this, but we're gifted visionaries. It's different when you can see what others cannot," Persa sighed. "You should explore the city with your friends and family. We'll speak again." Persa turned to walk away. "Oh, one more thing. Truth is everything. Ybia did not die during the supernovae. She faced her justice when she was summoned before the MPOL."

"If she didn't die, then…"

"Indeed, Carly. She didn't die during the Supernovae. She lived a long while before transitioning, but she is the direct ascendant of your species. More directly, Adam's."

"There's no possible way. Just no way my mother, of all people, missed that."

"She did not miss it," Persa shrugged. "She simply did not tamper with fate because she knew it could be the end of us all. Dauma never interfered, which was very trying for her. She is one of the greatest, and most respected, Scionians to ever exist. She was the one Scionian we've seen exhibit Seerian tendencies."

Carly's mind zipped and zoomed. She immediately wondered if there was a way to restore her mother. If she was as powerful as Persa claimed, then she should be able to. After a few moments, she decided she still did not want the responsibility.

"I just want to live my own life. I'm only 19."

"The Light and all its energies chose you before you were conceived. Many genetic defects that previously proved a life as undeserving (narcissism, sociopathy, psychopathy, Y chromosome) were absent in your genome. The merged lives before yours could not sustain the ultimate power of the Metaverse. You were chosen and there is no giving it back."

"But...I..."

"These scientists your people fear, demand cessation. Your planet would be consumed and devastated by violent wars that would destroy most lives in an effort to vanquish the one segment that is the future of your species. Those self-proclaimed scientists are hellbent on extracting divine heritage for their own nefarious purposes. You could change all of that in an instant. Either accept your gifts and responsibility or risk hurting the ones you love."

Carly swallowed her resentment.

"Your gifts know no bounds, but you do have a choice." Persa intentionally thought.

A lone tear trickled down her left cheek. "I've gotta go."

She blipped over to an outdoor lounge, where the others awaited her. She embraced them, and they enjoyed the remainder of the evening exploring the city, and bonding with Gehzlings.

heritage analysis

DAYS LATER, THE Neos gathered at the aerodrome for testing to culminate Proem. So many nervous faces crowded the auditorium, as POL spectators hovered about, watching on. MPOL Magistries watched from protected quarters off-site.

The most nervous of all present, was Rye. Carly sensed her anxiety and fear, so she gripped her hand tightly.

"Thanks, Car," Rye exhaled.

"You'll pass," Carly reassured her.

"But what if I don't?"

Carly held her gaze. *"Even if you didn't, you will not die. I will not allow it,"* Carly thought. "You will."

"Mariah, you will pass. I'm rarely confident about tests, but this time, I am," Adam added.

Rye half-smiled.

"I don't know how to worry that you won't because something in me tells me you will," Kane said. "I don't even know what it is, or why, but you will pass." He held her gaze for the longest time before kissing her tenderly.

A tear gathered in Carly's eye. She sizzled it while imagining if the Light had selected any of the other beings to manifest itself in, how powerless she'd be to protect her family and friends. She was chosen for a reason. She had responsibilities.

Noluh announced commencement of the examination, and explained how it would be administered. Visual, auditory, written, and Kinesthetic. "There is water stocked at your desks. You are free to stand and stretch, when needed. If you require use of the restrooms, a Proctor will escort you. Communication between Neophytes is forbidden during testing. Sharing clues, answers or notes of any kind is forbidden. You will have six hours to complete the assessment. If you finish sooner, Proctors are automatically notified, your tablet will be confiscated, you will exit the testing area, and report to the Scoring and Review room, located down the hall. Any questions?"

"How would they know or stop us from communicating telepathically?" Margol thought.

"Why would you want to cheat?" Carly communicated.

"Mind your business and stay out of my head." Margol frowned. *"It's not something we can just shut off. Most of us are born this way."*

"I'm only trying to help you. Some of the Proctors are Makovian."

"You can shut up now," Margol hissed.

"I highly recommend my Apexian Neophytes deactivate your Aegers during testing, as they do compress brain waves," Noluh added.

"Then how do we keep them out of our heads during testing?" Drudge asked. "They could easily cheat and get answers from us."

"Quickest way to fail," Laspi thought.

Other Makovian Neo's chuckled.

"No two tests are alike. All they'd do is waste their time being distracted by your thoughts, which will have no bearing on their own exam. A quiet mind, I'd say, puts Apexians at an advantage."

Laspi's pompous grin evaporated.

"Any other concerns before we begin?" Noluh glanced around the room. "Very well. Good luck to you all. You may start now."

As the hours lapsed, Neo's gradually disappeared from the test area. The last group to finish included Carly, Rye, Kane, Jo, Wolmyn, Yif, Hindru, and Jemenah. Carly had long since completed the exam, but she didn't submit her answers, preferring to remain with Rye, Jo, and Kane. When the six hours ended, their tablets were confiscated and they reported to the SAR room, where the other Neo's were immersed in discussing the test and their worries.

They mingled for thirty minutes more before Noluh, Persa, Qiar, and Makovian Preceptor Miendrin entered holding crystalline tablets.

"You will now be divided and assigned to a Preceptor to discuss your scores," Noluh announced.

Preceptor Qiar was the first to call his list of Neo's. "Xixu, Kane, Hindru, Qloud, Sanyi, Lyco, Manan, Judith, Hemra, Cloy, Ksenyia, and Warmek."

Preceptor Persa followed. "Drudge, Viktoria, Margol, Jeddy, Krill, Reega, Adam, Burmeda, Donno, Ghat, Traife, and Genera."

Preceptor Miendrin barely looked at his tablet. "Valentina, Jemenah, Yifus, JoAnn, Vandria, Shersee, Epo, Nular, Charro, Rongior, Ibarca, and Narvo."

Preceptor Noluh called the rest. "Carly, Frange, Mariah, Cyla, Sharf, Evan, Poz, Jitta, Zeneah, Luezzé, Ahliss, and Sage. Please, report to your designated Preceptor now."

When the Neo's gathered around their assigned Preceptor, nano walls enclosed each of the four groups.

Carly glanced around the sterile room.

"Regrettably, one of you did not pass, and a few of you struggled," Noluh informed them.

Rye's breathing became staggered, so Carly gripped her hand firmly.

"Poz, I am afraid your journey ends here for this cycle. Please, report to the main drome area. You will be ported home from there."

Poz dropped his head and walked right through the nano wall.

Carly released Rye's hand with a reassuring smile before turning her attention to Noluh. "I thought if Neo's didn't pass, they were…"

"Each Neophyte has four eligible cycles in which they will return to attempt

Onus. There are variables which can alter those predetermined cycles. Such as, a full roster for the cycle, which doesn't count against their eligible four attempts."

Evan, Mariah, and Sage were also learning this for the first time.

"Sharf, Luezzé, and Jitta — you came dangerously close to failing the exam. Therefore, you will be provided a refresher opportunity over the next two days before Avant begins. The rest of you did well. I will see you all in two days' time. You are dismissed. Well done." Noluh congratulated them with a singular clap before dissolving the nano walls.

When they reemerged in the main SAR room, Adam's group was waiting for them.

"We all passed," he told her with an embrace. "A few were advised to take a refresher over the weekend, but we're all good."

Vikki and Krill high-fived Carly and Sage while Evan nervously tapped his foot on the floor.

"She passed, Ev. Don't worry," Carly assured him.

He opened his mouth to respond in a typical manner before smiling warmly. "Thanks, kiddo."

"And from the looks of it, so did you, squirt." Adam threw his arm around Rye's neck.

For the first time ever, she didn't shirk him away. "Yeah, I was a nervous wreck. I'm better now. Worried about Kane." She glanced around.

"One in our group didn't pass," Carly told them.

"Who?" Vikki asked.

"Poz from Komur in the Au Galaxy," Sage replied. "It was a little sad, but they said he gets three more attempts in the future."

"Yeah, Preceptor Persa gave us the rundown on that process too," Adam said.

"It must be nice to have so many tries," Rye added sarcastically.

Kane's group reemerged. Rye flew into his arms.

"We all passed," he reassured her.

"Thank goodness," she sighed as she buried her face in his chest.

Preceptor Miendrin's group were the last to return. Evan immediately wrapped his arms around Jo. "You worry too much, old man," she teased.

"Anyone who didn't pass?" Evan asked her.

"Rongior," Jo whispered.

Carly wondered how a Seerian wouldn't pass Proem unless they simply didn't want to, and preferred to go home.

The Descendants exited the drome together, with Apexians right on their heels.

"I imagine you think you're better than us because one of our people failed," Drudge growled.

"Dude, nobody cares," Adam responded dismissively.

"What is dude? I am Drudge."

Adam sighed. "This isn't a competition or a game."

"Aren't you more concerned with being executed for failing?" Carly asked. "Poz has three more attempts, and I'm sure he'll pass next…"

"You just got here, so you don't know Apexian culture," Drudge spat.

"Calm down," Qloud said. "Like you said, they don't know and it's not their fault that they don't know our ways of life. Back off." He blocked Drudge.

"We're really tired of asking you to calm down," Yif added. "Poz will be fine. And perhaps these old ancient traditions need to change."

"Definitely," Cyla agreed.

"Yeah," Ahliss breathed. "I'm tired of conforming and not making choices for my own life and future."

"We all are," Jitta said, joining them. "Makovians also have outdated expectations and societal norms that only suck the joy out of living."

"Oh, go cry to your plentiful Quarry fund," Margol said.

"Quarry isn't everything, Margol," Jitta replied.

It amazed Carly how every species shared many of the same problems. She shared a knowing glance with Adam and the other Descendants while the other Neo's joined in on the discussion.

"Individual planetary traditions are a problem," Zeneah agreed, "but Onus is absolutely necessary, and there's no denying that. So, while we're here, we should focus on the importance of that."

Carly wondered how some of them, like Zeneah, spoke with accents similar to British ones.

"So, you actually believe the history we're taught here?" Drudge challenged everyone.

"I do," Carly answered.

"You would," he huffed. "You only believe it because Ybia was allegedly Scionian, which alludes to your stupid Verse being the most powerful."

"How dumb are you?" Adam countered. "Why does something like that even matter to you?"

"It's fear," Evan offered. "He's young, and afraid of being inadequate among his people. You've been overly programmed, but you seem strong enough to break free from it."

"Don't patronize me. We all have to go home after Onus concludes, where our lives, laws, and traditions will resume," Drudge said. "Apexian history was portrayed as wicked and weak, and we're far from both."

"Listen to yourself, Drudge," Qloud urged. "Learning self-control is the very essence of why we're here, and you're having the hardest time with that basic necessity."

"No one should care more about perception of fact than the fact itself," Lyco said, finally speaking up. "As Seerians, it's very difficult to deceive us."

"But not impossible," Drudge opposed.

"Your obsession with becoming a Merser blocks your ability to think clearly, logically, or even happily," Yif pointed out while shaking his head.

"No, but then hierarchy of logic is employed," Jemenah delicately took over, "If there is a possibility of altered facts or omissions, then one should proceed with their decision based on the opposite being true. If Ybia hadn't destroyed all life in the Scionian Universe and part of the Aeonian Galaxy…"

"Vyun is only one planet," Drudge interrupted."

"Is it not part of that galaxy?" Jemenah earnestly asked.

Drudge rolled his eyes defiantly.

"If Ybia did not supernova," Jemenah continued, "If Apexians were flawless faultless beings who were the strongest, wisest, and most powerful… how would you proceed?"

Everyone fell silent as the swirling winds propelled sand into their faces.

Drudge guiltily glanced at his Aeger to ensure it was still working properly before he replied. "I'd still agree with the requirement of Onus and attend willingly."

"And why would you make that decision?" Jemenah inquired further.

"Because Apexians *are* the most powerful, and we'd still need to practice discipline and control," Drudge forced through gritted teeth.

"There, that wasn't so hard, was it?" Jemenah sang.

Carly grinned smugly as the others sniggered.

Ksenyia scowled at Val's flushed cheeks.

"So," Val croaked as she cleared her throat nervously, "are we going out again or what?"

"Maybe we could show you around Rossur this time," Vandria offered in a fluid tone.

"Is co-ed alright with you ladies?" Evan asked.

"Let's make a night of it," Jo exclaimed.

The Neo's trotted over to their living quarters for refreshments before heading out on the town. Carly was entranced with the entire experience of exploring the life and culture of different beings on another planet. She kissed and squeezed a cheery Adam infinitely as they scurried from place to place until dawn.

onus lyceum: avant

carly

CAPRICIOUS SANDY EDDIES pirouetted majestically across the dorm windows in the outskirts of Rossur, where the now heavily integrated Neo's were gathered in the cafeteria to congregate about the start of Avant. A storm of excited chatter vibrated the walls between gulps and munches, mingling with the fresh scent of anxiety.

"Thankfully, we've had the opportunity to watch recordings of the last one hundred cycles of Onus," Wolmyn breathed.

"I still wonder why the Guardian segment is some big secret," Laspi thought. Carly's facial expression didn't change at learning his perplexity.

"Yes, we've been studying and preparing since birth," Drudge added.

"Wow," Carly whispered. She imagined how much healthier and safer Scionia would be if the planet shared the same culture of discipline, awareness, and learning. She swallowed her resentment.

"How old *are* you, if you don't mind sharing?" Ksenyia inquired with a coy gleam in her eyes.

"Nineteen cycles," Drudge replied hesitantly.

The air grew thick with the obvious sexual tension between the two.

"Well, what is this segment like?" Adam asked, slicing right through it.

"Plainly," Margol drawled, "traits are pitted against traits, skill against skill, and you're guided on how to safely harness and wield your abilities throughout. But, together, as a cohesive force." She exaggerated air quotes.

Carly giggled because she thought that was strictly a human thing.

"*A farcical gesture,*" Margol thought with a half-grin. "*The best part, and why most even care to participate, is having any subconscious or biological obstructions removed during divinity testing.*"

Carly refrained from nodding, but she understood the lure of that among youth.

"*Farcical describes your entire disposition,*" Laspi thought with his muscular arabesque arms folded across his chest.

Margol sniggered.

Oh, she smiles. Carly was delighted by it.

"Sounds exciting, if you ask me," Vikki said.

"Of course, it does," Sage giggled while patting her behind.

"I'm curious about your heat," Qloud said to Carly.

"Bro, what?" Adam jerked upright.

"Calm down," Yif urged, darting between them. "Qloud hasn't mastered the tact of context. He meant, he's curious about her ability to burn because he harnesses the energy of clouds."

"I meant no harm," the young Neophyte offered. "I have never met anyone with an ability to test my own."

"It's quite alright," Carly replied with an earnest grin. "Somehow, I knew what you meant."

"*Somehow,* he was gonna get his lips smacked off his face," Adam mumbled under his breath.

"Pardon?" Qloud touched his mouth questioningly.

Vikki slapped Adam on his back. "You really need to control your temper, little brother."

"Yeah, okay," Adam replied impassively while reclaiming his seat, and continuing to grumble to himself.

The dorm siren blared. They emptied their trays, disposed of their waste, and assembled in the main living space.

"Good day," Noluh greeted.

Qiar and Persa simply nodded.

"Good day, Preceptor," the Neo's chimed in unison.

"Let's get right to it. Qiar, if you'll please?"

A portal opened inside the space and everyone passed through without hesitation, right into a massive open stadium.

"Your first lesson of this segment is," Noluh began, "Avant is the most challenging and arduous. This is usually where half of Neophytes fail due to their own abstrusity, need for accolades, advancement and recognition, and vanity. Onus exists for the safety of the Metaverse and no other reason."

"This is especially important to my fellow Apexians," Qiar added. "Dismiss your need to uphold our culture while you're here and focus on the needs of all existence."

Persa nodded in agreement. "Your second lesson: Divine heritage is quad, as the Metaverse. Your abilities are grounded in four essential elements; space, time, energy, and matter. All shall be explored, and all shall be measured."

"Combat during Onus may, and has, resulted in the cessation of Neophytes," Qiar informed them.

Worried mumbles of the Neo's fluttered.

"It is an unfortunate, and natural, consequence of learning one's limits," Persa added.

"Since lethal force isn't encouraged," Noluh continued, "Aegers are strictly prohibited during Avant." With an elegant finger twirl, all Aegers evanesced.

"How do we keep our opponents out of our heads during battle?" Drudge asked anxiously.

"Strength and discipline," Noluh answered as she and the other Preceptors approached the center of the field. "Gather into a circle. We will begin by identifying our sources. Your source may be elemental, celestial, or etymological."

"Preceptor?" Rye interrupted. "What is etymological?"

"It means your immediate source of divine heritage is unable to be sourced. Now, everyone, concentrate."

"What's the point of this if they tested us during Proem?" Laspi thought.

Carly gathered Laspi didn't understand the concept of introspection or observation.

"This isn't about external thought or belief. Focus. Do not worry of *exerting* too much energy right now. Think only of your source. Find your spark and ignite it," Noluh said.

"Reminds me of our first day at Afrax," Adam whispered into Carly's ear before charging his core.

Carly glanced around at the bowed heads of the Neo's and piercing gazes of the Preceptors. She had always been taught that this process was called flowering because she believed she had a biokenretic core. Now being told something different, she didn't know where to consciously pull from. Before closing her eyes, she sighed in amazement at the beautiful rainbow of circular and crescent Limbal Rings in the circle of Neo's. The Descendants gaped and gawked at their surroundings. Jo, Kane, and Vikki openly expressed their gratitude just to be part of something so phenomenal.

She swiftly and lazily flowered, pulling from a part of her she always had in the past. Her eyes grew warm and the galaxy of sparkly stars replaced everyone's flesh. She smiled and squeezed Adam's hand.

"Why don't these Scionians display a spectrum of heritage as the others do?" Nular inquired, pointing to Jo, Kane, and Vikki.

"And why do only *your* eyes rotate?" Jitta asked Carly and Adam.

"We haven't really figured that out for certain," Adam replied.

"Focus only on your own energy at this time, Neophytes," Persa reminded them. "You're already unnecessarily distracted. Where do you feel? What do you feel?"

"What do you sense? Follow it," Qiar added as a green tint slightly sheathed his melanated muscular frame.

"Take the time to follow the changes you experience when channeling," Noluh instructed. "When you believe you've found your source, step forward."

Several Seerian Neo's began stepping forward. Persa approached each of them individually. "When you feel your source, connect with it. Employ your empathy, and be kind to it. Do not attempt to drain it for the sake of possession or vanity. When you draw upon more energy than required, your source will eventually become reluctant to lend, and you will slowly become powerless."

Apexian and Makovian Neo's gradually entered the diminishing circle.

"Never just focus on the power you feel," Qiar gently bellowed. "Always communicate with, and be considerate of, your sources."

Nearly all Neo's had stepped forward, saving only Carly, Adam, Jo, Evan, Rye, and Kane.

"It's okay, Adam," Carly soothed. "I know you're communicating with Zsita and Navu. I'm okay."

Adam released her hand and joined the other Neo's.

"Kane," Rye began.

"Go, Mariah," Kane replied. "You aren't leaving me. I'm still here." He smiled and she stepped forward.

Jo nodded at Evan and he joined the others.

"Kane," Carly said while facing him and planting her palm on his chest. "You may feel something here, which is most common, as you've seen with the others. But you can feel differences anywhere in your body. Try not to allow anything or anyone inside your thoughts. No matter what, we're all here."

He smiled tenderly at her before bowing his head. After several moments, he hunched his shoulders. Carly did not step forward, but remained by Kane's side.

Persa smiled her way.

Qiar approached them. "Have neither you touched your source?"

"I'm unsure if I have a source, Preceptor," Kane responded.

"We all have a source," Qiar boomed "Don't give up searching, young Neophyte." He patted Kane on the shoulder. "And you?" he asked of Carly.

"Identified, but I will remain by his side," she replied, calmly and firmly.

Qiar nodded and returned to Noluh and Persa's side.

Charro glanced back at Carly with pride beaming from his eyes.

"You may all now return your channeled energy to its source," Noluh instructed. "For the next exercise, you will be strategically paired with a fellow Neophyte."

Drudge openly perked up. "Finally."

Yif rolled his eyes upward.

Ksenyia flushed pink.

Qiar stepped forward. "Lethal force is not encouraged, but unintentional use is not against the rules. The purpose of this exercise is learning how much energy is required and summoning no more."

"You may not be disqualified for inadvertently ending a Neophyte's life, but you will be permanently failed for intentionally and maliciously doing so," Persa added. "Meaning, cessation for failing Onus will be on the MPOL's docket immediately versus failing after four cycles and having a hearing."

"You two," Qiar pointed to Wolmyn and Warmek. "Step forward. Everyone else, fall back."

"Interference at this stage is forbidden by Neophytes," Noluh informed them. "The goal of this exercise is to learn how much energy to summon and when to stop. Learn the limitations of your channeling ability through your opponent and yourself."

"So, are we battling each other?" Wolmyn asked.

"Not quite a battle," Qiar explained. "More of a lesson, but a fierce one. Your lesson ends when your opponent has become powerless against you."

"Subdue," Persa added. "Subdue your opponent."

"This exercise will repeat until every Neophyte has entered the arena," Noluh said.

Apexian Wolmyn and Makovian Warmek nodded.

"A process of elimination," Adam whispered to Carly.

"Similar to Dagaal," Carly replied.

"Begin!" Qiar announced.

The two Neo's locked eyes of uncertainty and began circling each other. Wolmyn was the first to visibly summon from his source. He ejected a forcefield at Warmek, locking Warmek's arms at his sides.

Drudge sighed with pride. *That's right, go primary. End it quickly.*

Carly disagreed with Drudge's thoughts on Wolmyn's approach, but she returned her focus to the center of the coliseum.

Warmek struggled briefly before closing his eyes. Loud pings, akin to shattering metal, filled the arena as Warmek freed himself from Wolmyn's prison, sending Wolmyn hurtling backward with a burst of energy. Warmek immediately pounced atop Wolmyn sending a surge of painful shocks through him, until Wolmyn yielded, screaming for mercy.

The Preceptors patiently looked on as Warmek ended his assault and retreated.

"Well done," Qiar told Warmek while levitating a depleted Wolmyn to the side. "Remember, the goal is not to *win*. Sage, approach."

All the Descendants leaned in close as Sage casually strolled onto the field. Once Qiar announced commencement, Warmek launched into his attack. Sage seemed to allow himself to be stricken by Warmek's flurry of shocks because he didn't attempt to dodge them. Sage grunted and dropped to his knees before inhaling. His LR flashed Mindago green seconds before the first ectoplasmic ring formed in his left hand. He angled it to where Warmek's shock energy was blocked.

Warmek's fear was apparent as he sent out another chaotic burst of shocks, which failed to penetrate Sage, who began shielding himself with rings. He rose from the ground and wielded the rings like hula-hoops before meshing them.

Vikki fidgeted nervously.

Carly instantly feared that Sage would kill Warmek with that amount of energy.

"We can't interfere," Jo reminded her.

"Sage, you don't need that much power to subdue him. Please," Carly thought.

Sage shook his head briefly before splitting the rings and imprisoning Warmek, by pinning him to the ground. A dripping Sage staggered forward and stood over Warmek as he writhed in pain. Any longer and the rings would melt through him, so Sage released him.

The Neo's clapped. Carly truly wished they understood how close Warmek came to death, and perhaps, they did. That was the purpose of Avant.

Qiar attempted to pat Sage on the shoulder, but he jumped away. "You will burn yourself."

Qiar nodded.

"Well done, Sage," Noluh said.

"Thank you. May I have assistance with drying myself before I am matched?" Sage asked.

"You may."

"Carly," he called. "Can you dehydrate me, please?"

Carly jogged over and placed her fingertips on his shoulder. The sizzling from the contact alarmed Qiar until he saw the moisture evaporating from Sage's skin and clothing.

"Thanks, Carly."

"Of course." She smiled before jogging back over to Adam.

"Jemenah," Qiar called. "Sage, are you ready?"

"I am."

Sage and Jemenah's exposition quickly became intense as they bested each other time and again, to the delight of everyone. Jemenah's abilities were similar to his, but Sage had perfected his technique for a longer time, locking himself inside Afrax's training room daily for years. Eventually Sage got the better of Jemenah, and the Neo's cheered as if they were being entertained.

Jo, and Kane were swiftly subdued by their opponents, given they had very new and limited heritage. Vikki put up far more of a fight and bested her opponent for three rounds before she was subdued.

The exercise continued until twelve Neo's remained; Adam, Carly, Val, Laspi, Margol, Jitta, Drudge, Qloud, Sanyi, Frange, Lyco, and Zeneah. Lyco was currently on the field, and Margol was summoned forward. She strode confidently towards Lyco and immediately powered up with a lopsided smirk on her lips.

Upon commencement, Margol sent an earth-shattering blast at Lyco, slamming him into the stone stadium seating, knocking him unconscious. Jitta, Sanyi, Lyco, and Frange were quickly subdued by Margol as well. Laspi was up and he excitedly faced her head on, communicating telepathically with her.

"You ready to lose in front the Metaverse?" Laspi thought.

"In your dreams," Margol teased.

"They still think this is a game they can win," Carly thought disdainfully.

"Begin," Qiar yelled.

The two Makovian Neo's immediately began besting each other, though Carly quickly sensed Margol's extreme hesitance. After toying with Laspi for a while, Margol eventually subdued him with minimal effort. They playfully slapped palms before Zeneah was summoned forth.

Zeneah reluctantly treaded onto the field. Margol sneered with understandable confidence. After all, she had just subdued several of the most powerful young beings in existence. Carly detected reluctance in Zeneah, though Zeneah's thoughts were either cloaked or they simply had none. As a Seerian, Carly understood Zeneah would be a being Margol could actually learn from.

Margol quickly employed her primary trait, which Zeneah effortlessly deflected. This caused Margol to summon more power. When her attacks failed to subdue Zeneah, she channeled such a massive amount of energy that her eyes glazed over. Zeneah glanced around with uncertainty pouring from her because everyone fidgeted with concern over the amount of power Margol was about to deploy.

When the blast struck Zeneah, everyone gasped and began making their way to her to administer aid. However, when the dust settled. Zeneah stood erect, and untouched, just as Jude had during her turn.

"Do you think Zeneah's invulnerable like Jude?" Adam asked Carly.

"No, I don't think so. I think she's an absorber." Carly squinted because the energy Margol had expelled hadn't dissipated.

Without warning, Zeneah blasted Margol with a mixture of the original blast, coupled with new energy. Margol flew violently into the stands, knocking her unconscious.

"I only summoned a small amount from my-my own source…my foresight really," Zeneah nervously offered. "The energy…it…it was…hers."

"It is quite alright, Zeneah," Noluh said. "You were gauged to be appropriate."

Carly was amazed by Zeneah's use of her Seerian foresight to help her predict Margol's actions before they'd happened. Apparently, this gift isn't as common among Seerians as she had thought.

"Valentina, come forth," Qiar summoned.

Carly grabbed her hand. "Don't disjecta membra."

Val winked at her and marched onto the field.

Carly knew very well that Val was saved for nearly last because her abilities were bloody and gruesome. She had witnessed Val dismember, but never reattach.

"Begin!" Qiar bellowed.

Val quietly flowered and awaited Zeneah's attack. When it didn't come, she opened her eyes.

Zeneah stood perfectly still, revealing her fear.

"Zeneah's afraid of hurting Val and Val doesn't want to hurt Zeneah," Carly muttered.

"Well, someone has to do something," Adam said.

Val tinkered with Zeneah's joints and ligaments until it became too painful to bear. Zeneah sent a medium blast Val's way. She went down without fight, feigning defeat.

Carly breathed a sigh of relief.

Neither Qiar nor Noluh were convinced.

"If you came to fail, then move aside for others deserving of the space," Noluh said.

"Preceptor Noluh. May we all exchange words?" Persa requested.

Qiar, Noluh, and Persa huddled several feet away. When they reemerged, Avant was resumed.

"Drudge, come forward," Qiar called.

"Adam," Carly whispered. "It seems they want to see us battle each other."

"I noticed, but they'll be sorely disappointed," Adam replied while gripping her hand.

Qloud stood by with apprehension oozing from his pores. Meanwhile, Drudge strutted onto the field and faced Zeneah head-on. Their exercise commenced and Zeneah awaited Drudge's attack. Drudge wasted no time encapsulating Zeneah in a death-grip energy field. Zeneah wailed and cried out to the point where Adam nearly interfered, until Carly restrained him.

Zeneah dropped to her knees when her bones began to break. Iridescent teal-colored blood leaked from her nostrils, and her head drooped. Drudge didn't seem to have any intention of stopping until Zeneah was dead, and none of the Preceptors would interfere with his choice.

"Killing Zeneah is suicide," Carly transmitted telepathically to him. *"Stop. Stop now."*

Drudge immediately ceased his attack. Zeneah fell to the ground and was whisked away by other Neo's.

"Carly," Qiar called.

"Babe," Adam said in a low voice. "He may be horrible…"

"Don't worry," she assured him with a kiss before calmly walking right past Drudge and Qiar, to the injured Zeneah. "Please, back away," she asked the group before summoning her healing dust.

Zeneah writhed and whimpered before settling into a deep sleep. Carly turned and glided onto the field. Drudge smirked right before Qiar commenced their exercise. Carly remained straight-faced. Drudge attempted to encapsulate her, but his pressurized energy field evanesced before his eyes.

He tried a few more times before switching to energy blasts, which also didn't affect Carly.

She simply watched him deplete and exhaust himself without doing anything.

He bent over, out of breath. "Are you just going to stand there and do nothing?"

"You were going to kill Zeneah just to prove a point," she said.

"No, I wasn't. I was testing the extent of my heritage is all. Just like we were instructed to do," Drudge managed between breaths.

Carly knew he was lying, and wanted no parts of his negative energy.

"Why are you questioning—" Drudge went limp and fell straight back.

Qiar stood over him. "He's unconscious, but alive."

Persa sighed deeply with contentment.

"Qloud, you're up," Qiar said.

Qloud nervously shuffled centerfield. Carly eyed him curiously. Sure, she could move this exercise along swiftly by rendering him unconscious, but she wanted to test her abilities out with him.

He summoned energy into a misty ball around himself and stared into Carly's eyes. "Burn me."

Without hesitation, Carly turned up the heat.

Qloud didn't flinch. "More."

She was careful to only call upon the required amount of energy to subdue him.

"Hotter," he demanded. "Burn me!"

The Preceptors looked on with wild curiosity.

Carly attempted to ash him, but felt her heat being absorbed by his mist. She smiled from ear to ear, having found someone she couldn't burn. She played with her temperatures for a while before deciding to try different sources. "What else you got?"

"What do you mean?" he asked, believing his victory was nigh.

"Can you do more than absorb heat?" she sent a simple blast his way.

He absorbed it into a static ball before creating a thunder storm around himself. Adam gazed on with heightened interest.

Carly decided that she understood the source and limitations of his abilities, and had no interest in embarrassing or hurting him. She saw all she needed to see. She amplified his static ball, and braced herself for contact.

Adam's feet lifted from the ground just as the blast approached her chest. Before she could exhale, Adam was there, shielding her, and deflecting the blast.

"Adam, you know this isn't allowed," she reminded him.

"Neophyte Adam," Qiar boomed. "Interference is against the rules."

"When was the last time you had a pregnant Neo in Onus?" Adam demanded, fully prepared to give his life to protect his wife and unborn child. "I won't allow any harm to come to them, and I'm willing to die to protect them."

Persa approached them. "You have no idea of your wife's abilities."

"I know she'd rather allow herself to be harmed before harming anyone here, and I won't—"

"She and the Consanguineous are perfectly safe, and your interference will be excused this one time," Persa concluded.

"Carly, you are excused," Qiar said. "Adam, it is your turn."

Adam faced Qloud, anxious to see how Zsita measured up.

Qloud summoned his electrical mist. Thunder and lightning raged around him, forcing the Preceptors backward.

Adam took flight, hovering, and pacing himself. Before Qloud could expel an attack, Adam simply dehydrated his mist and redirected into the atmosphere. He twirled himself into a vortex as Qloud watched above in horror.

Carly smirked, knowing Adam was showing off, but completely understanding of why. None of them have ever been allowed to fully explore their abilities without fear of detection. In Onus, they were instructed to do just that.

Qloud steadied himself as Adam descended upon him, engulfed in a tornado of vicious wind and water. Carly's grin began to evaporate when Adam didn't slow down or stop, but began tearing through Qloud at rapid speed. Qloud's screams echoed, but he was engulfed in Adam's vortex. The Neo's covered their mouths in horror as they floated away into the sky, out of sight.

"Do you think he killed him?" Rye asked Carly.

"No," Carly replied. "I can still feel them both."

When the storm returned, Qloud fell from the sky and landed on his back. Qiar immediately assessed him. He nodded at Noluh.

"Today's exercise has concluded," Noluh announced. "We will discuss the outcomes tomorrow before the next exercise."

Persa gazed up at Adam, hovering above.

Qiar opened a portal. The Neo's began to limp and walk through.

Adam landed and took Carly's hand. "He's extremely powerful, but he doesn't know it."

"Why'd you take him away?"

"I wanted to see his memories and learn the raw truth of his life, his people, and his planet. There's something about the Apexians that rubs me the wrong way, and I don't want us to be caught off guard."

Carly shook her head as they entered the portal together.

dilation

carly

Carly laid in Adam's arms with her eyes wide open. A whirl of painful negative energy clouded her. There was something going on back home, but she was so busy with Onus training, she hadn't made time to focus on what it could be.

When the alarm sounded, she and Adam moved about their quarters in perfect sync with each other.

"Have you noticed the weirdness going on between Val and Ksenyia?" he asked her.

"Ksenyia has always been a flirt since we've known her," Carly answered.

"This seems to be more than simple flirtation. I really feel like the two of them have lost their sync or something."

Persa's words rushed back to Carly about syncs and how they only existed on Scionia. She wondered for a moment if that's what was happening. "They'd been having some issues for a while."

They moved into the kitchen area.

"Issues," he huffed. "Issues are leaving the orange juice out of the fridge or not helping around the house. Ksenyia's actions are completely disrespectful, in my opinion. I don't understand why she doesn't break up with Val if she wants a polyamorous relationship because I can tell you that Val does not."

"Have you talked to Val about it?"

"Haven't had a chance. Onus has us all in a chokehold every day."

"I'm sure they'll work it out," Carly said.

Adam rested his palm on the counter. "Thing is, I don't think they will."

Carly had no idea what to say because she'd sensed Val's mangled heart finally moving away from Ksenyia when they'd arrived on Gehz. She wondered what would come of their little family community if the two of them separated.

The second alarm sounded, so they rushed into the cafeteria to grab food. The Neo's were mixed, mingling, and the chatter rebounded off the walls. Adam and Carly sat beside Rye, Kane, Jo, Evan, Val, Frange, Margol, Laspi, Zeneah, Qloud, Drudge, and others.

"So, we're all in agreement that yesterday's exercise was nothing more than a test?" Val said.

"Everything in Onus is a test," Drudge offered.

"They want to see what we will do before teaching us what we should do," Frange added.

"Right," Jitta said. "How else to know one's character if they aren't allowed to follow their organic instincts?"

"It's a precursor to the coveted Guardian segment," Margol said.

"It's so we have no idea what we're walking into from moment to moment," Jemenah added.

"Lessens the likelihood that we planned our actions," Qloud said. "Makes sense to me."

"The order they called us is what I'm most curious about," Ksenyia drawled while tapping her forefinger against her lips.

"I've been thinking about that as well," Warmek said as he approached their table. "Did they call upon us from presumed weakest to strongest?"

"I don't think so," Carly replied.

"I agree," Adam concurred. "I think many of us have similar abilities, whereas others have traits that are incomparable."

"There's logic in that," Frange began, "but I don't think they'll ever disclose their strategic reasoning."

"That's so we can't go home and share that information with future Neo's," Zeneah said in a soft cadence that was akin to a British one.

They all looked her way since she rarely ever spoke.

She shrugged. "Think about it. If Neo's went home and told all future attendees exactly what was to happen from start to finish, they'd do nothing more than practice and rehearse everything from their words to their actions. Anything rehearsed doesn't require much thought or logic. Just mindless repetition."

They all chimed and nodded in agreement.

"Preceptor Noluh said we'd discuss yesterday's exercise today, and I, for one, am anxious for it," Margol said.

The final alarm blared. They emptied their trays and assembled in the main living space, where Noluh, Persa, and Qiar awaited them.

"Good morning, Neophytes," Noluh greeted. "Qiar, if you'll please?"

Qiar opened a portal back to the stadium. Once everyone traveled through, Noluh continued.

"You will be separated into four teams today, and you shall, in every way, join or face each other. The successful Neophytes will have the ability to make choices in the Guardian segment that others will not."

Margol's hand went up. "What kind of choices, Preceptor Noluh?"

"The kind that lessens one's chance of complete failure," Noluh answered.

"For those of you on your fourth cycle, you understand just how detrimental that small edge is," Persa added.

Several Neo's looked around at each other, wondering which of them was on their fourth cycle.

"Don't waste your time trying to figure out what cycle anyone is on because that information is forbidden from being disclosed, as stated on your first day, if anyone was paying attention," Noluh explained. "There are very few rules. One, you may not opt out or quit. Two, lethal force is not encouraged, but may be an unfortunate consequence to completion of the assigned task. Three, external assistance from Preceptors, MPOL, and any non-Neophyte is strictly prohibited."

Carly stamped her resentment down, still angry about Rye only being granted one life or death cycle, where everyone else received four.

"I shall now divide you into your teams," Noluh continued. "And before anyone asks, yes, we will discuss yesterday's exercise after you're assigned to your team."

Carly doubled over while holding her chest. Thousands of unknown voices rang in her head — some shouting and swearing; others merely speaking, but as if they were directly in her ear. She was still learning to quiet most while listening to others. But right now, it was if the entire Metaverse was talking at once. And she saw something, a woman.

Adam was on his knees instantly. "Babe, what's wrong? Are you okay?"

"I just…I don't know. I saw something, felt something." She shook her head and exhaled a few times.

"What did you see?" Adam whispered.

"Neophyte Carly?" Persa called. "Are you well?"

"Yes. Yes, I am. First trimester issues," Carly breathed.

"Are you able to continue?" Qiar inquired.

"Yes, I'm fine. Please, continue," she insisted while quieting the voices.

"The four teams are Diamond, Oval, Pyramid, and Prism," Noluh stated. "Each represent space, time, energy, and matter — the Metaverse."

"Do not allow your thoughts to dwell on which team characteristic you are placed within," Qiar added. "They are all interchangeable."

Noluh nodded. "What should concern you most is the fact that you will face each other, friend, foe, lover, and stranger. Nothing is of higher importance than the safety of the Metaverse.

> TEAM DIAMOND: Adam, Mariah, Margol, Ahliss, Jeddy, Yifus, Shersee, Frange, Genera, Traife, and Hindru.
> TEAM PRISM: Carly, JoAnn, Jitta, Kane, Donno, Viktoria, Epo, Wolmyn, Luezzé, Vandria, Ghat, and Reega.
> TEAM PYRAMID: Krill, Valentina, Drudge, Laspi, Zeneah, Manan, Narvo, Sanyi, Lyco, Cloy, Burmeda, and Warmek.
> TEAM OVAL: Sage, Evan, Ksenyia, Judith, Cyla, Xixu, Hemra, Qloud, Charro, Sharf, Nular, and Ibarca."

Once they had all been separated into their respective teams, they glanced around at each other. Carly received huge waves of concern from the majority of the Neo's, fearful they were grouped unfairly.

"Onus is not a competition. These are all teaching exercises," Persa emphasized.

"Then why is there a reigning team who will win a prize?" Laspi inquired.

Noluh had not stated such, but the Neo's clearly had presumed a negative.

"No prize was mentioned nor offered. Over the many cycles of Onus, Neophytes have proven time and again that responsibility, knowledge, strength, and wisdom aren't sufficient motivators of empathy, moral and ethical behavior," Noluh answered. "The segments are occasionally modified."

"So, you move the goal posts as it suits you?" Jude asked.

"It doesn't suit *me*. I have successfully completed Onus training and am very much in control of myself and actions. I am intimate with, and respectful of, my sources. I am skilled at harnessing the required amount of energy and wielding it with absolute control. Your individual perceptions are key factors in determining your every action," Noluh replied.

Bored of the piddly complaints, Yif required different brain food. "May we now have some insight regarding yesterday's exercise?"

"Yes, of course," Noluh began. "Yesterday was a first-time live approval for you to utilize your abilities as you saw fit, without restriction or consequence. The Preceptors and the MPOL needed to see the choices you'd make, how you'd touch your source, and which abilities paired and grouped cohesively, versus those which are incomparable."

"Incomparable?" Carly asked.

"Yes. Incomparable abilities are those requiring no assistance nor can they truly be amplified beyond their organic state of existence," Persa responded.

"It was not without consequence," Drudge interjected. "You told us that lethal force…"

"Why would you *want* to cease another being's existence, Neophyte?" Noluh probed.

"I…I didn't…wouldn't want to. I was just saying that it wasn't without consequence because…"

"You're openly expressing your resentment regarding not being able to cease another's existence, Neophyte," Qiar clarified.

"No, I'm…"

"Of all the questions or concerns you could've had, this was your chosen topic of query," Qiar continued. "You also were the only Neophyte who nearly ended the life of another Neophyte."

"No, I…" Drudge stammered.

"Mind your desires, future warrior," Qiar warned.

Drudge pursed his lips and dipped his head.

"Moving forward, the goal is to complete a singular or set of tasks in order to solve an ultimate problem," Noluh handed out coded digital DataPads to each team. "I suggest you designate a leader, but it is not a requirement."

The Neo's stood around, holding the DataPads, awaiting instructions.

"Upon instruction to do so, and you activate your DataPad, you will have exactly one day, twenty-four Gehzian hours, to solve your ultimate problem. A time clock will remain on your DataPad throughout, and can also be found in the helmet of your body suits. If interplanetary travel is required, you must find your own way to carry out such travel. Your DataPad provides access to all Metaversal history archives. Your DataPad will inform you when your task has been successfully completed. You will not receive any assistance from Preceptors, though you may assist one another, teams notwithstanding." Noluh paced. "You will be monitored at every turn, and your actions will be recorded."

"How?" Margol asked.

"That data is confidential to prevent tampering and sharing with future Neophytes, which could compromise the integrity of Onus," Noluh said.

"If you have any questions, now is the time to ask them," Qiar softly boomed.

Rye lifted her hand. "I'd like to confirm that a reigning team doesn't mean the other three teams fail, is that right?"

"This is but a part of the entire Avant segment," Noluh confirmed. "Your failure or success shall not be wholly predicated on this singular exercise nor upon anyone else's action or inaction. Only your own."

Rye breathed a sigh of relief.

"Any other questions before we begin?" Noluh asked. A full beat of silence passed. "Very well. Please, activate your DataPads."

The four Neo's holding the D-Pads —Carly, Adam, Drudge, and Sage— anxiously tapped their fingers against the screen. The devices illuminated and required each team member to submit to a retinal scan before it revealed their assignment. Coded messages appeared:

An energy surge threatens to disrupt the digital fabric of the Metaverse. If harnessed incorrectly, this energy could be weaponized for destruction.

PRISM: *Map the energy flows within the Metaverse. Using data analytics and pattern recognition, predict the surge's path and identify critical nodes where energy accumulates.*
DIAMOND: *Construct a communication network to educate and prepare the inhabitants of the Metaverse for possible energy disruptions.*
OVAL: *Develop a real-time monitoring system. Create an AI that can provide live feedback on energy levels and predict potential breaches in security.*
PYRAMID: *Engineer a containment solution. Design a digital structure capable of withstanding and regulating the excessive energy without breaking down.*

The Preceptors had disappeared by the time the Neo's looked up. The countdown clock began on the D-Pads, sending a surge of urgency through the Neo's.

"Does anyone know what these cryptic messages mean?" Drudge asked everyone.

"They aren't cryptic," Val replied with a roll of her eyes.

"We should all join forces and help each other figure it all out," Carly suggested, wholly believing the ultimate goal of Onus was for Metaverse inhabitants to work together to ensure its safety and stability.

"Carly is right, but too many thoughts are focused on self," Jo thought.

"No way!" Margol yelped. "I don't know about you, but I'd very much like the advantage in Guardian, if you don't *mind.*"

Carly immediately heard Margol's screeching thoughts that she was on her fourth cycle and couldn't afford failure. Though she understood Margol's need to successfully complete Onus, she still believed they should join forces, as the Preceptors did not forbid it. Something told her that all of them should set their individual assigned teams aside and work as one singular unit. It wasn't in her to silently stand by and allow anyone to perish for failing a training course. Four attempts or one-hundred made no difference to her.

"Agreed!" Drudged yelped.

Drudge's enthusiastic agreeance with Margol didn't shock her one a bit. Without Aegers, she imagined she'd learn quite a bit more from the Apexians.

"Carly, baby girl, you must accept that evil exists as surely as good," Dauma communicated.

"Mommy, I know, but watching them be executed is something I know I'll have a problem with," Carly thought.

"May the best team win," Drudge smirked.

"Does he speak for all of you?" Frange asked.

"No, he does not," Charro responded. "No leader of Team Prism has been selected. I elect Carly."

"Of course, you do," Drudge quipped. "Well, I respectfully nominate myself."

"Of course, you do," Manan responded.

"Teaming up was not forbidden," Zeneah reminded them.

"Exactly. It would be to our benefit to work as one cohesive unit," Yif added. "What the Preceptors said is paramount. Let's just think about it for a moment."

"We don't have time for that!" Margol exclaimed.

"You don't know, Margol," Ahliss said. "As far as you know, the task could be completed in a matter of minutes."

"Oh, right!" Margol exaggerated. "Constructing a communication network to educate and prepare the inhabitants of the Metaverse for possible energy disruptions sounds like it'll take just a few minutes. Um, right. Hold on a moment."

"Margol, you're overly excited. Try to calm yourself," Adam pled.

"Don't tell me what to do when you're five seconds new to all of this!" She thrust her hands into the air. "You're not anyone's leader!" She puffed her chest forward.

Carly narrowed her eyes, in contrast to burning the immaculate strands of what she presumed was hair on Margol's pretty head. Margol's emotions were overwhelming her, so Carly approached her and extended her hand.

"What! Don't touch me!" Margol was mere seconds from a complete meltdown.

"I mean you no harm, Margol," Carly said quietly and softly as she patiently waited for Margol to make contact with her. She stood patiently, her hand hanging ambivalently in the air.

The Neo's looked on.

Margol smacked her hand away. "Mind tricks don't work on Makovi—" a surge of calm and relief washed over her when she made brief contact with Carly's skin, which paused her. She immediately clung to Carly, who embraced her without hesitation.

When the others witnessed Carly's calming influence, they eagerly made contact with her, each searching for an available piece of her skin to touch. Soon, most of them were gathered in a bunch with Carly in the center, as she graciously shared herself.

"Does this mean we're working as one team?" Drudge asked from the sideline with his arms folded across his chest.

"Absolutely not," Margol reiterated, withdrawing her hand from Carly. "If we were meant to be one singular team, they wouldn't have divided us."

"I agree," Laspi added. "I do think we should choose leadership," he directed towards his team.

Carly turned to focus on her teammates, who seemed to be anxious to get started, and the thoughts of the majority of the others were opposed to working together. "I don't think we should waste any more time than we have to. All those in favor of appointing a leader?"

Most raised their hands.

"Cool, great. Let's quickly choose, so we can get started."

"You already seem to be the logical choice," Ghat said.

"All in favor of Carly?" Vikki proposed.

Most swiftly raised their hands in agreement.

"We're all a team regardless. Never forget that," Carly reminded them. She glanced over at Adam.

He made eye contact with her before his teammates tore his attention away.

A red button illuminated on the D-Pad.

**BEGIN
TASK**

"Everyone ready?" she asked with her forefinger hovering over the button. They nodded in agreement and she tapped it.

*"The planet richest in divergent energy must
be shielded from outside pilfering."*

An astral map was displayed below the message.

"Seems to be coordinates to the energy-rich planet," Vandria said.

"It can only be Vyun," Jitta rushed.

"Vyun is reported to be uninhabitable," Donno added. "The atmosphere could kill us."

"Didn't Preceptor Noluh say our nano suits will automatically deploy protections in hostile environments?" Jitta reminded them.

"Allegedly, yes," Vandria interrupted. "But what if it doesn't?"

"We have to get to the planet in order to complete the task," Carly said. "Most of you can project force-fields just in case the suits fail. I'm willing to port there to find out. Alone, if I have to."

"Never alone," Kane said. "Which of you are skilled at navigation to confirm the coordinates?"

"I can do it," Wolmyn offered.

Everyone crowded around as Wolmyn calculated and decoded the astral map. "It is Vyun," he confirmed.

"Great. Who can teleport that distance?" Carly asked knowing the Makovians on the team—Reega, Jitta, and Ghat— could likely port, so she refrained from volunteering.

"I can," Jitta and Ghat chimed in unison.

"Awesome," Carly said. "But we need to have a plan of how to shield the planet's energy once we get there. Any conductors among us?"

"We'll likely need an amplifier as well," Carly added.

Reega and Luezzé volunteered to conduct.

"Any amplifiers?" Donno asked.

"I can do it," Carly truly began to wonder if yesterday's exercise was for the Neo's to witness each other's capabilities more than the MPOL.

"Shall we get going?" Wolmyn proposed.

"Where are the other teams?" Jo asked.

Team Prism glanced around at the vacant stadium.

"They must've gotten started on their tasks," Vikki said.

"As should we," Carly added. "Is everyone ready?"

Jitta opened the portal and Carly bravely walked through first. The moment her foot touched the barren surface of Vyun, her nano helmet deployed.

The others slowly trickled through, each anxiously feeling for their helmets.

Infinite sparks surged through Carly's body. She blinked and was back on Gehz in the stadium, where all the Neo's stood around discussing the exercise. She furrowed her brow, believing she was experiencing killer Déjà vu. She stumbled around, gawking at everyone mingling normally, as she waited for a sign to indicate the dream she knew she was trapped inside of. However, when she examined the scene more intently, the Preceptors' eyes were following her around.

She marched over to the trio. "What's going on?"

"This is post-exercise socializing," Noluh began, "and your fellow Neophytes are discussing…"

"Stop, you know what I mean."

"I'm afraid I have no capabilities to access your thoughts, Neophyte Carly."

"You seem upset. Are you well?" Qiar asked.

"No, I'm *not* well. This is a dream. It has to be and I'll just wake myself." Her breathing was labored.

"I assure you, this is no dream," Noluh said.

"Breathe, Carly," Persa soothed. "If you believe this has all happened before, you've likely incidentally traveled through a time rift."

Qiar and Noluh audibly gasped but gathered themselves swiftly.

"I do not believe it," Qiar hissed. "Time travel is a myth and I will hear no more of it."

"What did you see?" Persa probed.

"It was…tomorrow. You divided us into teams and…"

"She knows of the teams and we haven't announced them yet," Noluh interrupted. "The prophecy is true."

"Go on," Persa encouraged.

"We were divided into four teams. Prism, Diamond, Oval, and Pyramid."

Qiar and Noluh exchanged glances of astonishment. Every cycle the team names and tasks change.

"I was on Team Prism. Our first task was to shield the energy of planet Vyun, so we teleported there. Once there, everything changed. I…I skipped to the end of the exercise, and ended up back here. As if the last 24 hours never happened." Carly couldn't believe the words coming from her mouth.

"It wasn't a dream. You controlled time and traveled farther back than you intended," Persa said.

"If I am to believe you," Qiar stepped towards her, unknowingly triggering Adam's defenses across the field, "which team solves the problem? What was the intended goal?"

Her eyes narrowed into almond slits. "Collectively, we were all Team Apeirogon. A shape with infinite sides, all cycling back to the same point of origin. The same source, the same…everything. The intended goal was to ensure the safety and continuity of the Metaverse. Oh, and we battle each other tomorrow in non-energy, hand-to-hand combat, where Viktoria and Drudge are the ultimate victors, and thirteen Neo's fail Avant; Jeddy, Hindru, Jitta, Epo, Luezzé, Vandria, Reega, Manan, Narvo, Sanyi, Lyco, Xixu, and Sharf. And one is killed at the hands of Drudge; Traife."

Qiar cleared his throat because not even the MPOL knows the intricate depths of the exercises of each cycle, to maintain the integrity of Onus.

Further, Seerians do not house frontal lobe thoughts for telepaths to pilfer, and Qiar maintained his active Aeger throughout.

Adam began making his way over.

"Do not continue," Noluh warned. "It compromises everything."

"Why did it happen when we arrived on Vyun?" Carly anxiously asked, so she'd have some answers for Adam later, and for herself.

"Because the planet houses the most powerful and diverse energy sources in the Metaverse," Persa said. "It was once home to a low-energy derived species who existed solely to protect the Light within it. That is why it devastated the Metaverse when Ybia destroyed all life there. It was decided that it was best to leave it uninhabitable, but that decision has left the planet open to pilfering."

"So, our tasks weren't controlled?"

"Team Prism's task was not…is not," Noluh divulged.

"Why not?" Carly's temperature rose.

Adam took flight, tearing the Neo's focus away from their mindless chatter.

"Because of you, Carly. No one else can do what you can," Persa said.

Adam's arms were around Carly. "Are you okay?"

"I'm fine, babe," she flashed a glare at the Preceptors. "Just extremely exhausted."

"Can you port us back now?" Adam asked them.

"Certainly," Noluh answered.

Adam and Carly rejoined the other Neo's.

"This is going farther than intended," Qiar whispered.

"The MPOL is watching everything and they have not interfered," Noluh replied in a hushed tone.

"That means *nothing* right now. The Scionian seems to have time traveled," he growled under his breath. "Meaning, they could have *no* power to stop her or they would have, as it has been long-decreed as forbidden." He controlled his pacing because the Neo's eyes were trained on them.

"How can an alleged myth be forbidden?" Persa sarcastically queried. "My vision has been disregarded for thousands of years by all Apexians and many Makovians, though I have warned everyone relentlessly!"

"Yes, Persa," Noluh said, attempting to instill calm. "We are aware. Let us remain calm and discuss this with the MPOL after returning the Neophytes."

"If your…" Qiar began.

"You still have the audacity to say if," Persa huffed.

"Enough," Noluh interjected. "Qiar, open the portal now, please."

He did so without hesitation as Noluh informed the Neo's of what was to come the following day. When they crossed over, Noluh spoke briefly before the Preceptors disappeared.

Carly turned to Adam. "I need to lay down."

"Let's go." He took her hand and they walked towards their quarters.

"Hey," Vikki called. "What's going? Is she alright?"

"Everything is fine. She's just exhausted," Adam said while thrusting his palm into the air to prevent Vikki's approach. "Tell my mom she's okay, so she won't worry."

Vikki nodded and fell back.

metaversal panel of life

PLANET OF GEHZ

PRECEPTORS NOLUH, QIAR, and Persa approached the MPOL, located just beyond the city of Rossur, in Carch.

"Before you begin, we are aware of the enigma regarding the Scionian Carly," MPOL Makovian Magistry Brambor announced.

"Her time-travel capabilities are quite more than an enigma, Magistry Brambor," Qiar replied.

Brambor sighed, unwilling to share with non-Magistries that Scionian Mariah was the first being in existence to present a time disruption enigma, though only by a fraction of a second.

"The problem, Magistries," Persa began, "is the Scionian child has no idea of depth of her abilities and will continue to pose a threat so long as truths are withheld from her."

"This Panel has previously decided that informing an unpredictable Scionian being that it has the power to destroy all sentient and insentient life is unwise in the same manner as handing a murderer a sharp object," Apexian Magistry Clyfus said.

"Have we not learned the opposite?" Noluh posed. "Ybia, Magistries. Ybia is the reason Onus Lyceum exists. We've been shown an infinite number of times that failing to allow beings to deeply explore their sources and abilities lead to catastrophic and eternal consequences."

"Yes, Seerian Noluh," Magistry Clyfus responded. "However, a being with time dilation and other unfathomable power, has never existed before. Therefore, the same logic and principles cannot and should not be applied."

"Her time disruptions could cause a collapse of the Metaverse as we know it. She could kill us all!" Qiar boomed. "She hasn't even returned to the point of origin and is currently reliving the day, completely compromising the outcome of this cycle of Onus. She should be eliminated before she develops and sharpens her abilities. Once she does, no one will be able to stop her."

"This Panel will not sanction an unjustified cessation, Apexian Qiar. Most certainly not of an unborn innocent. You, of all beings, should appreciate that," Seerian Magistry Falani said. "Or have you forgotten your own origin story?"

"I have not," Qiar replied in a humble hushed tone, with his squircle-shaped head bowed.

"You cannot cease the Light," Persa warned. "Any attempts to do so may result in dire consequences for all. I believe it is best to train Scionian Carly in our ways, which presents the very best odds that she will share our values and beliefs. I've been pleading for this since before Carly was born."

"The Light would not have chosen her to manifest itself if she were not fit," Noluh reminded them.

"Yes, yes, we've heard your implorations before, Seerians Persa and Noluh," Magistry Clyfus said. "Until we discuss the developing matter further, and as we continue to watch the Scionian in Onus, our decision stands to reveal on required details, and allow her to successfully complete Onus. The Scionian is not exempt from the consequences of failing Onus Lyceum, nor are her counterparts."

"Magistries, please!" Persa begged. "You have unjustly stacked the odds against the Scionians by excluding them for centuries, then forcing them to pass in one cycle or face cessation. This will force Scionian Carly's hand. I do not believe this is the route —"

"It is not your decision to make, Seerian Persa!" Magistry Brambor roared. "So long as this Panel decides, so shall you abide. If you find that you cannot, we can discuss your removal. Are you in compliance?"

Persa sighed sharply. "I am."

"Very well. Dismissed," Magistry Brambor waved the Preceptors away.

onus lyceum: guardian

carly

Two days had lapsed since Carly had unintentionally chronoported. She and Adam sat beside other chattering Neo's in the mess hall of the dorm while awaiting the commencement of the Guardian segment. Carly was stoic and quiet as she relived the prior days for a second time, though the second was compromised by her experiencing the first. It had disappointed her to watch everyone make the exact same decisions again, and it hurt her to watch Traife die twice.

Adam chatted with the others while squeezing her hand.

Jo focused so intently on Carly that Evan took notice.

"Babe, are you alright?" he asked. "You've been staring at Carly all morning."

"I'm fine, but something's different, and I don't know what," Jo whispered.

"Should I worry? Do we need to get her home?"

"No, no," she breathed while patting his hand. "We can't quit or stop. Everything's fine."

Carly briefly glanced Jo's way with vacant glazed eyes.

"Carly, can you hear me? If you can hear me, blink twice."

Carly simply glared at Jo with a blank expression.

Jo's breathing changed and her concern multiplied. The moment she rose to join Carly, the alarm blared. Everyone swiftly crowded the main living space where the Preceptors awaited them.

"Good day, Neophytes," Noluh greeted. "Welcome to the Guardian segment. Congratulations on making it this far. The Guardian segment consists of individual simulations designed to test your core characteristics. The simulation will be unique to each Neophyte as it presents a multitude of realities, based on decisions made throughout. Ending the simulation prematurely will result in failure of the segment. Only after successfully committing to a series of thoughts and decisions, will the simulator release you."

The only thought Carly lent to the situation was how vehemently she opposed this segment. She was disinterested and it seemed highly unnecessary for her.

"Is it timed?" Frange inquired.

"No, it is not," Noluh answered.

"So, we could potentially be trapped in the simulator indefinitely?" Margol queried.

"Also, no," Noluh responded. "It is not time constrained, but the simulator is designed to decide your core characteristics based on a series of decisions you will make. As such, the simulation averages between eight to twelve hours."

Carly's eyes darted back and forth as if she were reading a book.

Jo shuffled from side to side.

Adam caressed her palm with his fingertips. "What's the longest time the simulator has taken to process a Neo?"

"144 hours," Persa said, incidentally glancing Qiar's way.

"6 days?" Margol whined.

"Yes," Qiar answered. "You have 7 days left of Onus and nowhere else you should be. Does this probability present a problem for you, Neophyte?"

"No, Preceptor," she replied.

"Your mind and body won't know the difference," Noluh advised them. "144 hours in the physical simulator may be just a few hours or a day to you within the simulation. Creating anxiety-ridden possibilities in your mind beforehand will negatively impact the outcome."

Their voices were faint in Carly's mind as she splintered, with a focused mind, while traveling beyond the vast reaches of the expanse of the Metaverse, where beings shuffled about in their daily lives. Eventually, she found her way to Scionia — Silver Springs, Minnesota.

"What of the advantage you spoke of for the person who ultimately solved the problem, which was Carly?" Adam asked.

"She may choose to complete the automated simulation or have her traits tested out of the Simulation Pod," Persa answered.

Many Neo's grunted and groaned, expressing their wish to have the same option.

"The Simulator is streamlined, and faster. The fastest recorded simulation is recorded at thirty-two minutes," Persa continued. "Which shall you choose, Neophyte Carly?"

"The Simulation Pod," Carly replied monotonously.

"If everyone will follow Qiar into the portal, we will begin," Noluh said.

Carly snapped herself back to the present, blinked up at Adam, clutched his arm, and walked into the portal. They arrived in a vast white lab, lined with sleek white Simulation Pods. Proctors from Makovia, Seeria, and Apexia awaited them.

Qiar's energy disturbed Carly, so she spared a glance his way, and noticed him constantly checking his Aeger.

"If everyone would please disrobe," Noluh requested. "Gowns will be provided. The nano suits are not permitted inside the SimPods."

The Neo's swiftly changed into white iridescent gowns. They were escorted into their SimPods by the Proctors. Adam and Carly kissed before parting ways.

Carly had chosen the SimPod for solidarity. She briefly glared at the Neo's settled into their Pods.

"Neophyte Carly, if you'll please?" Persa gestured.

Carly climbed into her Pod and laid back.

"Relax, Neophytes," Noluh said. "This will be the same experience as eating breakfast with your family."

Within seconds, the Pods sealed them in. Carly slowly blinked once. When she opened her eyes, she was standing in a foot of snow, as the gusty stormy winds blew her hair in every direction. She glanced around, but there was nothing but ice in every direction. When she squinted through the storm, tiny bits of a familiar building captured her eye. She instantly knew where she was and made haste toward it.

She burst through the doors and glanced around at the expired snack items on the convenience store shelves. Without hesitation, she entered the secret passageway and hopped on the elevator. There were no buttons, so she awaited a monitor to quiz her. When no one said anything, she summoned her energy to move the elevator into descent. When she exited into the blank hallways, her memory kicked in, and she ran towards the security room she had remembered from when her mother had retrieved her and Adam years prior.

The security room was vacant and the television monitors were busted. The entryway to the corridor was open and dark. She swiftly ran down the strip and into the Afrax living space where lifeless bodies littered the ground. She gasped in horror as she scoped the facility. Everyone was dead. After she wondered how such a gruesome thing could've happened, she closed her eyes and searched herself. When she opened her lids, a replay of events unfolded before her.

She watched the vision as Iksha militants stormed the facility, killing everyone in sight. The voice of a woman giving instructions captured her attention. When she turned, the melanated woman walked past her, pointing at cowering children beneath tables. *"There,"* she'd directed the militants, who swiftly unleashed energy blasts, killing the children.

As Carly gazed on, she knew it was none other than Emebet herself. Charro's mother; her ancestor.

"This is absurd. Now is our perfect chance to eliminate the threat," Qiar's voice echoed in the distance.

She shook off the intrusion and rewound the scene displaying before her, revealing how Iksha militants gained access to Afrax. On Emebet's orders, Descendant militants energy-bombed the Hex the Levkin's had cast around the facility until it was compromised enough for her to absorb the remnants. Once down, her militants stormed inside and executed everyone in sight.

Carly sped through the scene and stopped upon a discussion between Afrax councilmember, Baxter Fokin, and Emebet. His life was spared at the cost of all the other lives at Afrax. Baxter had agreed to reveal the coordinates to the other Descendant safehouses once he was safely away.

"Am…am I free to go? I've done as you've asked," Baxter stammered.

"Though you and Leeailia Kashirin failed at securing the Wit Descendant, you've done well," Emebet drawled. *"The wretched city of Piure is next, and the other safehouses will follow."*

Carly's eyes flamed. She wouldn't allow it. All the innocent residents of Piure would be murdered, all so this evil wicked woman could finish something she started centuries ago out of pure hatred. No, she would not sit idly by. No.

The tiniest flutter nudged her from inside. She cradled her belly. "Can you hear me in there?"

"Mama," a tiny voice echoed in her mind, followed by tiny flutters. She smiled when she realized her unborn child had grown enough to form thoughts. Tears streamed down her cheeks. "I won't let this happen. I won't."

Inside the all-white room on Gehz, alarms beeped. The Proctors raced to the digital wall and frantically stared down at their D-Pads.

"What's going on?" Noluh demanded.

"Neophyte Carly…she's coming out of simulation statis," a Proctor said.

"That's impossible," Noluh mumbled as she grabbed the D-Pad. "A Neophyte should not be able to regain consciousness without completing the Simulation."

"And her unborn's gestation has accelerated as well," the Proctor supplemented.

"How?"

"Teleporting to different planets outside of Gehz," the Proctor said.

"I warned them," Qiar added as he frantically paced. "She cannot be controlled and should have been terminated while she was under!"

Carly heard him as she freed herself from the SimPod. She floated gracefully above, suspended in air like a dove. She radiated light and her LR glowed opal.

Persa fearlessly beamed up at her in prideful delight.

"Neophyte Carly…" Noluh began.

"Don't," Carly snapped. "There is a vital situation in progress on my home planet, and I will see to it."

"You cannot leave the training without express permission of the MPOL," Qiar warned.

With her hair and white gown suspended, her eyes burst of light. She angled her head his way. "I will protect my family."

"You will be expelled," he continued.

Carly didn't bother to respond, she blipped into the MPOL chambers where the Magistries sat, watching the scene unfold on their monitors.

"Welcome, Scionian Carly," Magistry Brambor said. "We've been waiting to meet you."

"Have you?"

"We have," Seerian Magistry Qisa said. "Most of us, very anxiously, and long before your flesh birth."

"Then why have you assigned a being to oversee me who wants me dead?" she demanded.

"Apexian Qiar's reactions and suggested courses of action do not represent this Panel," Magistry Brambor stated.

Carly glimpsed the chambers. The Seerian members were openly joyful of her presence. The Makovians were in disbelief and acceptance, and the Apexians were disgruntled.

"Nevertheless, I must tend to a threat unfolding this moment on my home planet."

"No Neophyte has ever been allowed to pause their training for any cause," Magistry Clyfus stated.

"My visit here is a courtesy," Carly replied. "And the segment isn't disrupted, given the simulation statis of the Neo's, and my awarded advantage."

"If they complete their simulation in your absence…" Magistry Brambor began.

"That's not my problem nor my concern. If there is a disposable planet in the Metaverse, now is the time to disclose it."

"What?" several Magistries echoed in wonder.

"Origa," Seerian Magistry Qisa divulged without hesitation.

"Qisa," Brambor wailed in disbelief.

"We can continue this discussion upon my return." Before any of the Magistries could object, she was gone.

"Do you think we should tell her *now*?" Magistry Falani asked. "If she discovers a truth we could simply share with her, she'll be angry, feel betrayed, and will be unwilling to trust us or believe anything else we tell her."

"The Consanguineous being purported to be unconditionally invulnerable changes very little, Falani," Magistry Clyfus said.

"This Panel is making less and less sense. And being that we are looked upon as the wisest and most all-knowing in the Metaverse, we need to do better," Magistry Qisa added.

Brambor sighed with his two of his four fingers against his frontal lobe.

"The Scionian has clearly demonstrated herself as being the Light incarnate," Qisa continued.

"And how has the Scionian accomplished this?" Magistry Clyfus rhetorically asked. "By exhibiting the rarest trait? Let us not forget that Scionian Mariah Solomin unintentionally was the first being to time-travel. Is she too the Light incarnate?"

"Your unwillingness to believe in the Light and the Prophecy is obvious," Qisa replied. "However, Scionian Mariah exhibited only one divine trait of the Light, whereas Scionian Carly has exhibited them all."

"We likely would've thought the same of Scionian Ybia had we physically existed to witness her destructive abilities," Magistry Clyfus added. "Instead, we rely upon Seerian projections."

"And biological evidence," Qisa added. "You're clouded by your determination to disbelieve the Light. All Apexians have demonstrated that fault in their existence."

The Magistries bickered.

"This gets us nowhere," Magistry Brambor interrupted. "We need to focus on the matter at hand. The Scionian has time traveled at a distance never achieved before. She has exhibited a level of power that has never been witnessed before. Regardless of whether we believe in the Prophecy, we need to proceed on the basis of what we have physically witnessed. The bottom line is she possesses enough power to destroy us all with little to no effort. The majority has agreed that her power alone isn't sufficient reason to destroy her nor her unborn. So, let us focus on how we can help her."

"Helping her and allowing the child, which is believed to be unconditionally invulnerable, to be born, is not an act we can undo," Clyfus reminded him.

"We can't undo any sentient being the Light has prescribed," Falani said. "I don't think I need to remind the Apexians that Qiar was once among one of the life-or-death enigmas. Not one Apexian Magistry voted for his cessation."

"We do not vote for the Scionian's cessation now!" Clyfus said. "We simply need to proceed cautiously."

Carly ported just north of the McIntyre-Piure border. Hovering above, she easily spotted the Iksha's motorcade on approach. She landed several feet ahead of them on the road.

"What the hell is she doing out here in the middle of nowhere?" the driver asked.

The driver swerved to a stop in the middle of the dirt road, and the rest of the motorcade followed suit.

"What is the problem? Why have we stopped?" Emebet demanded.

"Madame, you'll want to see this," her driver said.

Emebet sighed in bored exasperation before staring out the front window at a radiating Carly. Emebet slowly exited the backseat and approached. The moment she did, Carly evanesced the motorcade with a flick of her wrist.

Emebet glanced back with a calm wry expression. "That's a nice ability. Who are you?"

"Carly Wit."

With a contorted expression, Emebet grumbled, "Abomination."

"Your self-loathing, vengeful heart, and resentment of your own son has motivated you to exterminate your own Descendants and their innocent kin." Carly detected Emebet's attempts to suppress her.

"You know nothing!" Emebet circled her. "That beast of a child killed his own sibling inside my womb before he ever drew breath. My biggest regret is not terminating him before he was born." She attempted other silent traits to inflict damage upon Carly.

"He didn't kill his twin because he never had one. What you thought was another fetus, was nothing more than the darkness you'd put inside him that he rejected. He was better than you before ever laying eyes on you."

Emebet hurled a blast of black lava at Carly, who simply ported to the other side of the road. Emebet whipped around. "You're not the first tele-porter I've encountered."

"Oh, I know. The first was the father of your only child…Verdapok Akrid."

Emebet openly expressed her displeasure in Carly knowing such intimate details of her past. "I'm impressed you know so much. Which can only mean, you've met the abomination that once occupied my womb. The only one of the Legacy offspring who escaped me."

"After all this time, you still blame him for something he had no control over? He saved you from death time and again. He's the reason why you haven't died yet, and you still want to harm him?"

"Yes! He should not exist, nor should any of you!" She pulled every trick and trait out of her BK goodie bag, but none pierced Carly's bubble.

"What of you? You kill us all, then what? You get to go on doing what exactly? Ruling the world? Killing innocents? What is your end game?" Carly pried.

"I was born naturally to this world. Chosen. Exalted. My existence is required to ensure the likes of your kind never spring up again like weeds. Verdapok told me the history. I know there are others like you in other universes, and at some point, they'll come here again. Lowly and lustfully seeking to derive their sick pleasure from us. And when they do…"

"You have no idea why Verdapok did what he did," Carly began. "Our species always existed with abilities that you find to be abominations. Well, unless, of course, *you* possess them. All Verdapok did was give our species our heritage back."

"I don't care why he did what he did! Listen to what the hell are you even saying! That having sex with naïve young women was a noble act?" Emebet laughed in disbelief. "That abandoning us with his seed to fend for ourselves alone was a gift? Spare me! He didn't even bother to stick around to help raise the children he created!"

"Because he couldn't, Emebet. Makovians cannot withstand our sun, which is why he only went out at night."

"Don't you ever speak my given name as you are not royalty!" She expelled a massive blast Carly's way.

Carly deflected it and watched it explode in the distance. "Iksha, what he did cost him his life. He was executed upon his return home. He knew his life would be forfeit for what he had done, but if you knew the whole story, you'd understand why he could no longer watch us exist defenselessly."

"Enough, child. You will not change my mind with some sob story of nobility, and the militants you killed, there's millions more where they came from."

"Millions," Carly thought. She'd suspected as much.

"I will fulfill my purpose, so it is best that you step aside, and I'll spare your life."

"You still don't get it." Carly shook her head.

"Here's what you do not know: I was pregnant by Verdapok twice. The first child disappeared inside me. Verdapok returned and laid with me again, determined to give me a child. The entire time, the first child merged with me, granting me regenerative abilities. I was already born with a rare genetic immunity to sickness and disease. I've harnessed every Descendant trait known to have existed. Serve me or die, right here, right now." Emebet powered up.

Carly looked on at the woman who had killed hundreds of innocents just to possess a power she wasn't born to wield. "I don't want to kill you but I don't want anyone else to die. Please, don't make me do this. All you have to do us leave us alone."

"You cannot kill me, you arrogant beast! I am the one true eternal being!" Emebet launched into her attack.

Carly did nothing more than duck, dodge, and avoid her blasts, while sending a few of her own, hoping empathy would magically grow inside Emebet's heart. She had no interest in battling, and had no more time to spare. Her unborn child fluttered about her stomach, reminding her of the importance of the safety of the innocent.

"Please, don't make me do this. All you have to do is abandon this absurd quest for revenge against a being who is long dead and forgive your son, who has done nothing but love you. Please, leave us alone."

"You know nothing about the abomination who dares to call itself my son!"

"Please, don't make me do this," Carly repeated.

"Do what?"

"Kill you."

"That's laughable."

"I know something you don't know."

"Doubtful but do entertain me with your final beliefs."

"The body you're in wasn't created for the energies you've forced into it."

"You are correct, it has been upgraded, thanks to your bloodline."

Carly glowered at the woman who had murdered dozens of her ancestors for a selfish cause. In that moment, she accepted with finality that Emebet had made her choices, which left Carly with only one. She sighed. "Doesn't matter what you do to it, it will always be what it was born to be."

"And what's that?"

"Temporary." Carly summoned the power of Light. The energy of all one-hundred-seventy-six billion suns and stars awakened at her command. The child within her womb expanded its elastic concealment to protect all life besides the one their mother sought to end.

She lifted the imagery she'd cast for Emebet's sake, revealing that she had ported them to Origa when she'd first landed on the dirt road. Emebet watched in horror and disbelief as the green world around her slowly morphed into an ice-ridden desolate plane with scarce oxygen and little heat. She shivered as the double-digit negative temperatures stabbed her.

With one singular push, Carly atomized Origa into scattered intergalactic dust, leaving her floating in wide open space. She glanced around, again afraid of her ability to destroy on the highest level. Before she was able to contemplate floating there ambivalently forever, she was pulled back to Gehz.

"Now that you've destroyed your enemy, you can restore Origa," Magistry Qisa informed her. "It does not need to be gone forever. You have the power, Scionian Carly. Use it for the good of life."

Carly ported back to the space where debris from Origa continued scattering throughout the galaxy until she commanded its return. Once gathered, she reassembled and restored the planet to its former whole state.

She remained afloat within a ball of energy to protect her lungs from erosion, while allowing the reality of what she had done to settle over her. The energies of the galaxy blissfully communicated with her as she circled its sun, Yeuton.

"Thank you," she whispered to it. It glowed its gratitude.

When she rounded planet Sharen, sweet memories of her and Adam's honeymoon warmed her. The baby jumped, which tickled her. "I can't wait until you meet your father."

"*Dada,*" the tiny voice echoed.

Carly chuckled in happy tears as she enhanced her vision to see all she could.

"*Light.*"

"You can see the Light?"

"Light, light."

"Light," Carly repeated, deciding their baby had named herself that swiftly. "Mommy, you'd be so proud of me right now," she whispered.

Dauma didn't respond. She sighed. Once she was satisfied that the only permanent damage caused was the lives of those ending innocent lives, she ported back to MPOL chambers.

The moment she arrived, she ensured Adam was safe, then reduced her energy levels, restoring her sources to their full power. The Magistries clapped as she caught her breath, with many of them standing in their applause. She didn't understand what she had done to deserve such an ovation because she had just ended sentient lives.

"Scionian Carly, you have hereby successfully completed Onus Lyceum training," Magistry Brambor announced.

"Huh?" She wondered if she was still trapped inside the simulation the entire time. "How?"

"What every other being requires the simulator to determine, you have demonstrated in real time," Magistry Qisa said.

"Then what is the point of the simulation process?" Carly queried.

"Every sentient being in the Metaverse who successfully completes Onus Lyceum are assigned overseer responsibilities, commensurate with their core traits," Magistry Clyfus informed her.

"And how has that worked out for the Metaverse without Scionians?" Carly demanded with slit eyes. "And how could you have seen what just happened out there?"

"We too possess divine heritage, Scionian Carly," Magistry Qisa said. "I am gifted with enhanced ocular sight and projection, allowing my sight to be shared with others."

That made more sense to Carly than anything else they've told her. She groaned and leaned forward. "I'm returning to my husband."

"The majority has voted, and you've been assigned Guardianship of the Metaverse, Scionian Carly," Magistry Qisa announced.

Carly instantly stood upright. "Excuse me? What exactly does that mean?"

"It means," Magistry Clyfus cut in, "that despite several of us dissenting, you've proven yourself to embody the Light in the flesh, and therefore, overseer of the Metaverse."

"Thanks, but no thanks. I'm becoming a mother, and I just got married. I have no interest in being any ruler of the Metaverse."

"Are you foregoing this divine appointment?" Magistry Clyfus anxiously asked while leaning over the table.

"Scionian Carly," Magistry Qisa interjected. "Before you decide, you have the power to take on a lesser appointment. I beg of you not to reject all Guardianship."

Carly glowered as she attempted to focus on their thoughts. The many activated Aegers transmitted annoying static waves, which annoyed baby Light, so she instantly evanesced them, uncloaking all their thoughts. After listening, she understood Qisa's plea.

"What do you propose in place of me overseeing the Metaverse?"

"Guardianship of the Scionian Universe," Magistry Qisa said. "You have demonstrated your determination to keep your people safe the way no other being has ever done. As Guardian, other beings must acquire your permission to port into your Verse. This is a decision, you do not want in the hands of another, I assure you."

Carly thought for a moment and Rye came to mind. "I accept the appointment. Now, I will return to my husband." She bent over, feeling uncharacteristically heavy in her center.

"And the Consanguineous…" Magistry Brambor interjected.

Carly spun around with fire in her eyes. "What of my child?"

"It would seem they are coming forth, and we hope your people complete their simulation before," he said.

"And why is that?"

"I would imagine you'd want your Descendant to be born on your home planet. If the Consanguineous is born here, they will be regarded as Seerian," he continued.

"Which would be a delight for us," Magistry Qisa added gleefully.

"Er, thank you, but Light will stay put until we return home."

"Light?" Magistry Qisa inquired.

"Her name is Light," Carly informed Qisa.

"Oh my." Magistry Qisa and others exhaled sighs of joy. "Mother of Light."

Carly smiled, put two fingers in the air, and blipped back to the Simulation room.

Persa raced over to her. "Are you okay?"

"I'm just exhausted," she replied while making her way to Adam's SimPod.

"Don't worry. I kept watch over him," Persa said.

Carly placed her palm on the transparent pod covering. For a moment, everyone and everything was reduced to nothing as she communicated her irrevocable love to Adam. She then exhaled sharply and grabbed her belly. The moment she turned to find a seat, Adam's Pod opened.

He sat upright. "Carly." He leapt from the Pod into her arms.

They embraced and pummeled each other with kisses as the Preceptors and Proctors looked on.

"I had a dream, a simulation, that the Iksha had destroyed Afrax," he told her. "And...all I could see was you and our baby. I held her in my arms. I...I can't explain it, but I was with you as you destroyed Emebet. It felt so real."

She released a sigh of relief, fully believing she had somehow connected to Adam's mind while she was away. Something she had never been able to do, including now. "You'll have her in your arms soon enough," she said as she groaned and doubled over.

He swept her into his arms.

"We need to go home," she whimpered before releasing a shattering yelp and a shockwave of energy.

One by one, the SimPods opened and the Neo's stepped out.

"Did we pass?" each of them began asking.

Noluh checked the acrylic screen for any rejections or abnormalities. Green completion notifications appeared beside everyone's name. "You've all passed."

They cheered and clapped.

"We need to leave," Adam demanded. "Now."

"Car!" Rye raced over to her. "What's wrong with her?"

"I think she's going into labor," Adam said. "We need to get back home right now."

Carly feebly lifted her right index finger, opening a portal inside the Simulation room.

Rye spun around. "Are we free to go?"

"If you're okay with skipping graduation, then yes," Noluh replied.

"To hell with graduation, but we will be back," Rye said in a stern tone.

"Adam, let's go so we can get her to a hospital. You guys. We're leaving, let's go!" Rye yelled to the other Descendants.

Each of them passed through the portal, right into Meridian's gardens. Rye immediately ported them to the hospital.

Carly passed out from depletion.

26

mother of light

adam

ADAM DREW BACK the sheer curtains of their bedroom, allowing the morning sun to warm Carly and Light's skin. He truly couldn't believe his eyes as he gazed upon them in awe and admiration. A tear escaped him.

"Good morning," Carly croaked.

He swiftly wiped the rouge tear away and joined them on the bed. "Good morning, beautiful." He caressed her cheek, adored her face, and gently kissed her. "How'd you sleep?"

"Soundly."

He smothered one-month old Light in tiny kissed until she stirred. He scooped her from Carly's chest.

"Thank you because, my bladder," she giggled while making her way into the restroom.

Adam rested Light against his bare chest. "I love you Light Amuad," he whispered into the crown of her head.

She stirred, and her bottom lip shivered in the most adorable way. He inhaled and exhaled her intoxicating baby scent just when Carly returned to the bedroom.

She chuckled and stretched in front of the French patio doors. "I'm thinking of making a trip to Gehz soon."

"I kinda figured that. Val and Rye have both been anxious to go back."

"Yeah, I imagine so," she laughed. "Light's old enough to port now."

"I'd rather she remains here with my mom and Evan because if even a grain of rogue red sand scratches her face, I'll…"

"I agree, I agree," she acquiesced with a smile.

"Besides, now that Kane's quantum communication abilities are flourishing, we won't be out of touch for even a second," he said.

"Yeah, Vyun truly opened him up like a flower. I can't believe he and Rye are married."

"Right, just a minute ago, we were all high school students. Now, we're married," he breathed. He couldn't believe how happy and healthy his life and emotions were.

"And us, parents? Blows my mind every day."

"You can say that again, but I wouldn't have it any other way."

"Well, I'll get breakfast started," she said.

He floated onto his feet without disturbing Light. "Together."

"My goodness, you two are sappiest bunch of sapheads that ever sapped!" Vikki said from downstairs.

They chuckled while joining her.

"Good morning," she greeted while abducting Light from Adam's embrace. "How's my little ray of sunshine doing today?" She kissed her incessantly.

The doorbell rang.

"I'll get it," Adam sang.

Jo, Evan, Rye, Kane bounced inside. Cheerful warm greetings of hugs and kisses filled the house. Adam hugged his mom and rocked back and forth. Rye made a beeline Carly's way.

"How are you feeling, babe?" Carly asked Rye.

"Sleepy," she laughed.

"I can certainly relate," Carly beamed. "And how's my little nephew doing?" she asked into Rye's stomach.

"He's fine too."

Adam embraced Rye long and hard. "I can't wait to take my nephew hiking," he said while rubbing her tiny belly, proud and gleaming.

"You don't even hike," Carly teased.

"That's beside the point. We'll adventure together," Adam said with a twinkle in his eye.

"Can Dad come along?" Kane playfully added.

They laughed heartily and shared a nice quiet breakfast before retiring to get dressed for the day.

"I asked Kane to send a message to everyone for a town hall meeting today in an hour," Carly told Adam as she changed Light's diaper.

"They're gonna think something is wrong," he responded as he simultaneously worried about his bio-mom, and whether any of the others they'd rescued had survived the Afrax massacre.

"Maybe, but discussions are required."

"Indeed, they are," he breathed. "It's so surreal that we don't have to look over our shoulders anymore for the Iksha."

"Or the MPOL," she added. "We completed their training."

"Right. Like, we're finally free, Carly." He stood over her and nudged her head upward with a finger beneath her chin. "We dreamt of this moment for so long. You longer than me, but now…it's finally a reality."

"I know." She swaddled the baby and turned to him. "Adam, remember that Emebet told me there were millions of militants out there."

"But we had presumed as much. With their leader gone, what purpose could they have?"

"That's a question I'm afraid one of them may attempt to answer. That's the main reason why we need to have this meeting today. That and volunteers for the MPOL. I can't imagine who'd want to permanently leave their home planet and everything they've ever known." She sighed.

"We must be released from here," Dauma communicated to Carly.

"My mom said she and my other merged ancestors need to be released from their mergers," Carly shared.

He kissed and turned towards the patio. He thought of how unbelievable it was that during Carly's pregnancy, she couldn't hear Dauma at all. After the birth of Light, Dauma returned, regaling her on all the wonderful conversations had with her ancestors. Light apparently had hijacked Carly's ability to communicate with her mother, allowing the baby to know her maternal grandmother.

"That's impossible, isn't it?" he inquired, still learning of her limitless abilities.

"I know you don't really believe in the Prophecy of Light, but apparently, there's a way. I just need to find it, if it exists."

"I believe in you and our family," he affirmed. "I don't trust or believe anything those other beings said because they sat and watched us be tortured and slaughtered without interceding to simply unsuppress abilities we were genetically and organically created to have."

"I know, I know," she soothed. "But Ybia, babe. After what Ybia…did…" she trailed off in memory.

"Carly, you okay?"

"Yeah, yeah, I'm fine. Look, there's something I forgot to tell you. Please, don't be angry with me. With all that was going on, the baby, Onus, the Prophecy…"

He knelt in front of her and took her hands in his. "I promise you that I will not be angry with you. I promise you."

"Persa…"

"Babe…"

"Adam, stop. Please, listen. At least listen. Persa watched over you while I tended to Emebet. If they meant us any harm, it wouldn't have been difficult to end us while in Sim statis."

"Okay, okay," he acquiesced. He'd listen, but he wasn't as quick to believe the Seerians as Carly was.

"When Persa told me of Ybia and what she had done, they also revealed that Ybia hadn't died in the supernovae event."

"Okayyy…so, why wasn't that part of the Metaversal history lesson?" He already leaned toward disbelief of anything they'd divulged because it was even clearer how they omitted facts.

"You may not believe it now, but I'm convinced it's because of this very moment we're having."

"Say what? Carly…"

"She lived, Adam. You're already aware that she's the reason Onus even exists."

"Uh huh, so they've said."

"Think logically for a moment. If Ybia lived, what do you expect she did during her life span?"

"Skydive, hunt, fly…I don't know, babe. There're a million things she could've done with her life after killing everyone and everything in this universe."

Carly simply glanced Light's way.

Adam's furrowed gaze followed hers. "Okay, that's a given."

She nodded. "Adam, you're Ybia's direct descendant. Her only living descendant."

He silently gazed into her impossibly gorgeous eyes, loving how her eternal innocence balanced his willingness to acknowledge the darkness he believed existed inside everyone.

"I think that's the primary reason why Persa kept watch over you, and also why our child was of the greatest concern to them. They feared what she'd be capable of."

One thing about Adam, his logic had sharpened over time, and was now largely devoid of human emotion. He immediately thought of how little sense it made that he'd be Ybia's most direct descendant versus Carly, given her abilities. He was no fool. He recalled how Carly couldn't even pinpoint in her memory when she'd hit biokenretic puberty. He could, without hesitation. If all living Scionians were descendants of Ybia, then why would he be singled out as most closely related to her? How was Alexandra, his bio-mom, skipped over in that process? Unless they know something about her that he doesn't.

He processed several hundred possibilities in a matter of seconds and only one conclusion made sense.

"No, Carly. Ybia is likely *your* direct ancestor, if anyone's. Not mine. Look at your abilities versus mine. Although she, in one way or another, is presumed the Eve of us, Seerians aren't flawless."

"Are you suggesting Persa lied?"

"No, I'm suggesting that they don't know, and their logic led them to an incorrect deduction or that Persa was lied to. Moreover, it's logical that Persa needed to shift your focus since, based on what you told me, you refused their prophecy that you were the Light incarnate, and your energy levels were reaching threatening levels. Any of these are possibilities that should be considered."

"Mm," is all she managed while listening. "Rozovsky-Wit," she mumbled under her breath.

"They may have been afraid but wanted you to prove your divinity to yourself. You are quite stubborn, babe." He was so pre-occupied with convincing Carly not to be trusting of beings they'd just discovered existed, he'd completely missed her reference.

"Mm hm." She maintained eye contact with him.

"I mean, think about it. Why would one descendant be more closely related than any other after so much time has passed between?"

"We're not genealogists, so do we really know how it all works?" she proposed.

"Okay, well let's go with not knowing if any specific human can be genetically linked to Ybia…"

"Okay, where would that leave us?"

"It would leave us at why Persa told you that? What was their intention in telling you that? What did it accomplish? Why is it significant?"

"Mm." She silently mulled over his logic. "The only thing that makes sense is that their data is incorrect. Perhaps Seerian data has led them to believe you're the closest descendant, but it's really someone else."

"Uh huh, and what about why that would even matter? Like, why did they even mention it?"

"Mm hm, I'll think about it a little deeper," she said.

"That's all I ask, babe. I don't want you to have trust issues, but I do want you to question beings who have watched us perish for centuries when they had every power to stop it. I'll never try to make up your mind for you. I just want it to remain open."

"I love that about you," she beamed, kissing him. "We should get going."

"Yep." He scooped Light into his arms and they headed to the rec room.

Everyone was already there, mingling, and chatting.

"Hey, guys," Adam said.

Each one of them rushed over to coo over the baby, taking turns holding and kissing her.

"So, I gather we're here to discuss returning to Gehz?" Krill asked with Light cradled in his arms.

"Yeah, and something else that happened right before we left for Onus," Carly replied.

"What happened?" Ksenyia inquired.

"Well," Adam started, "Vikki had decided to revisit her childhood hometown to kill the man who killed her parents and deceived her. I went after her. When I did, I discovered several Descendant captives there, my bio-mom, Alexandra, among them. Vikki compromised the facility and Carly finished the militants off. Alexandra was hit with a BK suppression dart and I wanted to bring her back here, but Carly was against it."

"Good call," Krill said.

"With the militants dead, Carly opened a portal for the survivors to just outside of Afrax. Alexandra was still unconscious, so a friend of hers, named Ulyana, carried her through," he finished.

Rye and Evan glared at each other.

"Excuse me, what?" Rye asked.

"What was Alexandra's friend's name?" Evan pressed.

"Ulyana, I believe," Adam repeated.

"Our mother," Rye breathed turning into Evan's arms. "Our mother is alive."

"We've got to get to Afrax," Evan said.

"Um," Carly lowered her head. "While everyone was in Sim statis, I… ended Emebet — Iksha."

Charro jerked into a rigid stance. "Little one, are you alright?" He darted over and embraced her.

"I'm fine, PawPaw. She was so far gone, there was no other choice. Before I arrived, she'd penetrated Afrax and executed everyone there. I didn't see any survivors."

Everyone gasped in horror. Rye bent over to catch her breath.

"There's more. She told me she'd never stop until she'd killed us all. Us included all beings in the entire Metaverse."

"So, not only is the Hex not very effective, we no longer need it?" Ksenyia asked.

"It took a team of enhanced militants and Emebet to bring down the Hex at Afrax, so I believe we should leave it for now because…Emebet said there were millions of militants out there, and we have no idea how they'll proceed without their leader," Carly added.

"As far as we know, they may want revenge," Jude said. "We have to find them and end them before they regroup."

Carly dipped her head. "Just killing people really turns my stomach. We don't know if they were abducted against their will and given life or death alternatives. We just don't know enough to proceed with that course of action."

"Then how will we eliminate the looming threat?" Jude further inquired. "I just want to be free. We did everything we were supposed to do."

"I'm leaning towards agreeing with Jude," Sage said.

"I *fully* agree with her," Vikki added. "Look at what it took for me. Are we willing to drop millions of them in the Siberian desert with journals for deprogramming? What of those who aren't Descendants but were abnormally enhanced, just as Iksha was?"

"There are tons of unknowns, which is why we're discussing it," Carly answered. "If even one of them had zero choice but to join Emebet's ridiculous crusade or face execution, then they deserve a chance to abandon it and start over."

"I agree with Car," Rye said. "None of us know what it feels like to actually be abducted and forced into a way of life or be killed, except Vikki. It's easy to stand here, safe, free from duress and hypothesize what you'd do if it were you. But the truth is, you never know what someone would do until they do it. Until you're faced with the same, a little grace, mercy, and understanding won't hurt."

"Besides, once we identify them all, keeping track of them shouldn't be hard," Kane offered.

"I definitely agree with allowing them an opportunity to walk away from it all," Jo said.

"And let's be honest, if they refuse or lie, will we end them then?" Jude asked.

"Honestly, they'd be threatening our lives at that point, and we'd have no choice," Carly replied.

"At that point, I'd end them myself," Adam concurred. "You all are my family. We're growing and changing every day. We were literally off-planet a month ago with extraterrestrial beings! We have responsibilities now that can't be compromised because one human decides they want to exterminate an entire group of people. We have a duty not to allow a force like them to regrow or expand."

"Speaking of which," Charro began, "we did not stick around to receive our Guardianship duties."

"That brings us to the final reason for the meeting," Carly said. "It's time for us to return to Gehz."

"Good, I'm ready," Rye offered.

"I know you are, babe," Carly smiled. "Just remember not to port from Gehz to any other planet until you give birth. You saw what happened with me."

"I won't, but they need to restore me and remove this stupid suppression since I passed Onus. I'm tired of feeling slow and helpless."

"You aren't slow, babe," Kane said. "You're just used to moving *much* faster than everyone else."

"And I want it back. I deserve it back," she retorted.

Kane rubbed her arm and kissed the crown of her head.

"Also, we need to discuss the MPOL and Scionian representation on that Panel," Carly continued. "Before we return, we should decide here and now who is willing to volunteer."

"Not me. I love Earth…er, Scionia," Jude said first.

"Same," Krill chimed.

"I'll do it," Val said, finally speaking. "I've always wanted to be a part the biggest change life had to offer and this is my chance."

"I'll go too," Ksenyia added.

"So will I," Charro offered. "I feel I belong there, where I can watch over my descendants with the power to protect them…you, little one. And if there's a way to find out what happened to Mureet, I will gladly serve."

"That's three. Any others?" Carly asked. "We need a minimum of five."

"Perhaps we should return to Afrax to make sure there are no survivors," Rye suggested.

"I agree," Adam said. "Just because you opened the portal for them outside of Afrax doesn't mean they found their way inside."

"That's true," Carly replied.

"Well, let's get this show on the road," Evan said.

"Baby Light can't go," Carly reminded them.

"I'll stay here with her," Jude offered.

"I'll remain as well," Krill said.

"I'll stay behind too," Val chimed in.

"I'm going to tag along," Ksenyia said to Val. "My family was there."

"I understand, of course," Val replied.

"K, can you…" Krill croaked.

"Of course," Ksenyia replied.

The traveling Descendants gathered into a circle.

"If my child so much as—"

"Adam, I've got her," Val said with a smile. "We'll take the best care of her. I promise you."

"Mm," he nodded and kissed Light dozens of times before returning to the circle.

"Will you do the honors?" Rye asked Carly.

Carly nodded.

They all grabbed hands and blipped over to Minnesota. Carly led the way as they descended into the facility. The smell of decomposition saturated the humid atmosphere. Rye vomited immediately. Carcasses remained exactly where Carly had seen them in her dilated vision.

"Let's split into pairs," Carly suggested. "We'll clear the facility faster that way."

They agreed and went their separate ways. Adam and Carly began at the farthest west end and worked their way east, leaving no stone unturned.

"I can't believe they were left like this," Adam said.

"Baxter Fokin is responsible. He was the one who planned this with Emebet."

"When I get my hands on him, it won't be pretty," he growled. "And he almost had you. If you hadn't taken my mom with you…"

"I know. And who knows how many other unsuspecting Descendants he and Leeailia betrayed. We need to…"

"Babe?" Adam was worried that she had paused mid-sentence. "Are you alright?"

"The survivors we'd sent over, they aren't here. They're in an abandoned warehouse a few miles from here," she said.

"Great, I'll gather the others." He flew around, notifying the others.

They blipped over to a dilapidated building with shattered windows and peeled paint.

"What are we waiting for?" Rye asked, walking anxiously toward the building.

Evan and Kane caught up with her, with Adam, Carly, and the rest not too far behind. Rye raced inside.

Adam glanced around. "There's movement upstairs."

"Yes, I feel the embers of a fire burning," Carly added.

They wasted little time heading up.

"Mom?" Rye called out. "Mom, it's Mariah, and Evan. Are you here?"

When they entered the room, an abandoned fire burned inside a trash can in the middle of the empty floor.

"Where did everybody go?" Evan asked.

Carly grabbed her temples and winced. "They're afraid. They're hiding behind that wall over there."

"Mom, it's your daughter, Mariah, and your son, Evan. You don't have to be afraid. We've come to take you home." Rye fidgeted and tears filled her eyes.

"No one will hurt you. The Iksha have been destroyed," Adam added.

Only then did the wall covering shift. One by one, the former captives entered the main room. The moment Rye spotted her mother, she raced into her arms, sobbing. Evan quickly joined in the embrace.

Alexandra crept forward. "You are not Dylan Dmitry," she said softly. "But I…I feel still feel him here."

"I'm," Adam croaked before clearing his throat, "I am Adam. Dylan didn't make it."

Tears trickled down her cheeks at learning her son was no longer alive. She embraced him in a tight hug.

Jo silently watched with her hand on her heart.

Adam valiantly fought back his tears. "I'd like you to meet my mother," he motioned Jo over.

"You're as beautiful as the day I first saw you," Alexandra said.

"Thanks to you."

"No, thank you for giving my son, our son, a life I never could," Alexandra gushed.

The two women tearfully embraced.

"Has anyone seen my daughter?" a woman asked in a Russian-English accent.

"Who is your daughter?" Carly asked.

"Valentina. I am Zoya Osborn."

Carly gleamed. "Yes, she is alive and well. She is with us, back home in California."

"How do we know the Iksha has been destroyed?" Ulyana inquired.

"The Iksha was headed by a woman named Emebet," Carly began, "and I…I killed her."

"What of her followers?" Ulyana probed.

The eyes of the former captives oozed of fear.

"Many of her followers are still out there," Carly answered. "But we now have the upper hand. We will find them and neutralize them. You will no longer live in fear. We have much history to share with you, if you'll trust us enough to come with us."

"The others at Afrax were all slaughtered," Alexandra reminded her. "Betrayed by our very own. How can we be sure we are never returned to…"

"I will never allow any harm to come to you or anyone else here," Adam assured her. "That part of your life is over."

"What of the other safehouses?" Zoya inquired. "Have they been compromised?"

"They remain active," Carly said. "However, we should return home, to California, where you'll be safest and discuss our next moves from there."

"There's plenty of food, clothing, water, and medicine," Evan said.

"Mom, let us take you home," Rye pled.

Ulyana exhaled sharply. "Okay. I am ready."

Carly opened a freestanding portal, and motioned for Jo and Kane to walk through first. After everyone passed through, it closed.

The former captives gazed around at the colorful flowers and well-maintained lawns. Many of them kept looking up at the sky, smiling in disbelief.

"Let's walk over to the rec room," Rye suggested.

"I'll grab Val," Adam told Carly.

"No," Carly replied. "Stay with your mom and Alexandra. I'll grab Val and the others. I'll be back in five." She kissed him and ran off.

Adam led everyone to the rec room where the former captives were provided adequate beverages, food, fresh clothing, and blankets. Within five minutes, Carly arrived, cradling Light in her arms. Val rushed inside and made a beeline straight into her mother's arms. After everyone had an opportunity to reconnect and catch their breath, Adam reminded them that they had pressing matters to discuss.

"We all have been through a lot. Many of us more than anyone could imagine, but those of you who have lost time, we need to catch you up on what's happened and what's to come. Carly?" He motioned for her to take over, and he scooped Light into his arms.

Carly proceeded to debrief the former captives on all that had transpired over the last decade. Many had questions, and the Descendants joined in to patiently answer them. When she finally arrived at Metaversal matters, many expressed their disbelief in the existence of beings from other worlds.

"Why has no Descendant ever mentioned coming in contact with these beings?" Zoya asked.

"Because those who did, and bore the Legacy children that jumpstarted our bloodlines, have all passed away," Charro answered.

"I must admit, I am having a hard time believing you are of the first born from so long ago," Ulyana confessed. "It's all so confusing and unbelievable."

"I believe it," Alexandra said. "I believe you all and I believe it all. Iksha scientists abducted and tortured us in their attempts to extract and replicate abilities we possess. At no time were they ever able to explain how or why we carry such genetic traits. They had no answers because those answers were not of this world."

"She's right," Zoya breathed. "At some point, we've all thought the same. I won't waste any more time fighting the truth. I am ready to see and learn."

"We were required to complete a training program on a planet called Gehz in the Seerian Universe," Carly announced. "After successfully completing it, our species was awarded power to preside on the Metaversal Panel of Life, and we require volunteers."

"Do you mean, live off planet to sit on a panel similar to the safehouse panels?" Ulyana asked.

"Yes, that's correct. Val, Ksenyia, and Charro have already volunteered. Would any of you like to join them? We require a minimum of seven."

"I gladly volunteer," Zoya offered. "I will never be separated from my baby again."

Two others volunteered.

"I will go," Alexandra uttered.

Adam jumped up. "Are…are you sure? I mean, you just got here."

"Not only do I tire of this world, this is the opportunity for power to make the best changes, and I dreamt of it the entire time I was in captivity. I never thought I'd make it out alive, so I dare not pass it up."

Adam's heart was a mixture of sadness and joy. He wanted more time to get to know her, and wanted Light to know her paternal grandmother, but understood why she'd want to get away from humans and the planet entirely. "I understand."

"We can always visit, babe," Carly reminded him.

He breathed a sigh of relief when he remembered he was married to the Light incarnate.

"Well, now that we've decided who will serve, we should leave for Gehz before day's end. Lastly, we all believe Afrax should be restored and renamed. We can re-shield it for any of who wish to reside there. You are more than welcomed to stay here with us, or we can take you to one of the other safe-houses."

Many of them were eager to get to a safehouse because they felt overly-exposed and Meridian was above ground and without reinforced walls. All of the non-MPOL volunteers agreed with the restoration of Afrax, but were unwilling to make their home there. Ulyana was among the few who had decided to remain in Piure.

Sage led the way in assisting the newcomers with settling into their temporary digs. When the sun dipped in the western sky, the Descendants gathered in the gardens to port to Gehz. Val and Ksenyia arrived with packed bags.

"Is everyone ready?" Carly asked.

They all nodded.

"You sure you want to take the baby?" Val questioned.

"Those we trust the most are traveling with us," Adam answered.

"Say no more," Val giggled.

The distance was too far to blip, so Carly opened a portal. One by one the entered and exited inside the aerodrome in Rossur, where Persa and Noluh welcomed them with open arms. Together, they ported to the MPOL where Panel seats were assigned, and Guardianships were decreed. Most notably,

Kane being granted Guardianship of intergalactic communications, including his duty to spread the message Rye was initially given when she was just a child.

"It has been decreed by this Panel," Magistry Qisa announced, "that Scionia shall no longer be referred to as the Light, Reflected. With acknowledgment and respect for the ways in which Scionians have enriched Metaversal culture, Scionia is now the Light, Transformed."

Persa and Noluh unveiled the updated images. Applause reverberated off the chamber walls. The newly sworn Scionian Descendants dawned their robes.

"I can't believe you're leaving me, Val," Adam muttered.

"I'm not leaving you, best friend. I'm protecting you," she reminded him.

"I'll still miss having you near every day."

"I'll miss that too. Thanks to Kane, interplanetary communication will be the same as cell phone text messaging," she said.

They embraced tightly.

"Well, time for me to go be all political and what not," she giggled.

"Go get em," he replied with a wink.

They all spent the evening discussing Metaversal matters, the future, while baby Light was doted upon like royalty.

EPILOGUE

transformed

TWO YEARS LATER…

joann

J O LEANED BACK in a plush lounge rocking chair on Adam and Carly's back porch deck, overlooking the massive field of bloomed orange and yellow poppies, where Light and Rade romped and played. Their tiny little innocent thoughts echoed in her head. Adam had finally fulfilled his promise to build Carly her dream house amidst the poppy field where they fell in love. Of course, he didn't stop there. He'd purchased the entire city of Leighton to ensure their privacy and seclusion. She was so proud of the man he had become. She burst of such contentment and gushing joy, a happy tear slid down her left cheek.

"You're such a crybaby," Evan teased her from his own lounge chair right beside her.

"I know it," she giggled.

Light's thoughts faded in and out like a radio that couldn't quite stay tuned to station, just like Adam's once had. All she got were bits about flowers, candy, cookies, and Rade being careful.

Her curly brunette pigtails bounced with each hop. She plucked an orange poppy for herself and a yellow one for Rade. She glanced up at the sun, closed her eyes, and allowed it to warm her Saturn beige skin. "Come on, catch up, catch up," Light yelled out.

"Fa-fa," Rade stammered as he pointed his cute forefinger at the yellow poppy.

"Flower," Light enunciated, helping him learn with a kiss on his chunky cheek.

Carly bounced outside with a platter of lemonade and chocolate chip cookies. She beamed at the toddlers in the poppy field. "Those two. Do they ever get tired?"

"Not with all the snacks we give them," Evan said.

"You mean, the snacks *you* give them, uncle mayor," Carly teased.

"It's a tough job, but someone's gotta do it," Evan sighed, resting his hands behind his head.

Adam, Rye, and Kane joined them, each carrying sandwiches, chips, and veggies.

"Oh brother. This mayor thing is going to his head already," Adam laughed.

"Tell me about it," Jo said.

Kane embraced Rye from behind as they gazed out at the field where their tiny tot chased Light around, trying to catch her.

"*I can't believe this is real,*" Rye thought.

"*Our perfect little family. Such a perfect life,*" Kane reflected with a sigh.

Adam, Carly, and Evan's thoughts remained a glorious mystery to Jo, which made her days there so peaceful.

Dust flurries drifted towards the deck, capturing everyone's attention. Adam glanced up just as two black unmarked SUVs approached.

"Grab the kids," Adam uttered.

Carly grabbed Light and Rye scooped Rade. They rejoined the others on the porch just as the SUV's reached the end of the driveway. Adam, Evan, and Kane formed a protective barrier between the women and children, and the strangers.

Jo immediately thought that the situation Adam had confessed to her about Terry Ann Griffith was finally coming to a head as four suited men stepped out of the vehicles wearing sunglasses.

"Is this the residence of Carly Wit?" the balding man asked.

"Who's asking? And who are you?" Adam demanded.

"My name is Agent Freys and these here are my colleagues," he flashed his federal agent badge.

"Stay here," Adam instructed the women on the porch.

He, Evan, and Kane approached the agents. Adam eyed the badges intently. "Kane."

"On it."

"Well, uh, we're here due to an incident that occurred a few years back at the Piure Mall. Is this the residence of Carly Wit?" Agent Freys asked again.

"Carly's my wife," Adam answered.

"I'd need to speak to you wife, sir," Agent Freys said with an unsettling smirk on his weathered face.

"It's okay, Adam," Carly yelled from the porch. "Stay here with Nana Jo," she told Light. "Mommy will be right back."

"Valid," Kane uttered.

Adam nodded.

"What's going on? Is there a problem?" Carly asked while looping her arm around Adam's.

"We'd like to ask you some questions, starting with where you were the day of May 11, 2022," Agent Freys said.

"I'm not answering any questions of any kind, but feel free to tell us what this is about, since you are on our private property," Carly replied.

The other agents expressed their annoyance by shifting their body weight and placing their hands on their hips.

"Well, on May 11th, there was a rather gruesome incident near the Piure Mall where two local police officers were, uh, well…they were gelded."

None of the Descendants flinched or changed expressions.

"I'm very sorry to hear that, sir," Carly replied. "But what does that have to do with us?"

"Not them, you. You see, mall surveillance footage captured video of you and a female companion exiting the mall with what was believed be fraudulently obtained merchandise." Agent Freys opened his tablet to share CCTV footage. "See, this is you, and your friend loading bags into a very expensive vehicle. And there are Officers Skaarsgard and Wilkes tailing you out of the parking structure, intending to conduct a probable cause stop and search." He paused for Carly's response.

She simply kept her eyes trained on him, and neither confirmed nor denied any statements or allegations he made.

"Now, Skaarsgard and Wilkes were admitted to the hospital, with their members detached inside their trousers. Their body and dashboard cameras weren't present on the scene when help arrived."

"Why are you telling us this?" Adam asked.

"However, a few seconds of footage was captured and uploaded before they mysteriously went offline, and that's why we're here," Agent Freys continued. "You see, we can't figure out how such a ghastly thing happened without either of the officers being touched by anyone. Would you mind accompanying us to our offices to answer some questions?"

"No, thank you," Carly replied. "Anything further?"

"No, ma'am. You all have yourselves a fine day now," Agent Freys drawled before turning to walk away.

"Agent Freys," Adam said. "Thanks for coming all this way." He extended his hand for a shake.

Agent Freys foolishly took it. Adam swiftly sifted through his memories before smiling and suppressing the most immediate ones.

The pompous smirk on Agent Freys' face slowly faded. He glanced down at his hand inside Adam's and pulled away. He then turned towards his colleagues. "Why are we here? How'd?"

"Sir?" a fellow agent queried. "We were just leaving."

The Descendants watched the agents clamber back into their vehicles and drive off.

Adam turned to Carly. "Looks like we have a new problem on our hands."

"What'd you see?" Evan asked.

"They're on to us. They saw the footage of Val gelding the officers after they forcibly handcuffed you both and groped Carly. They saw Carly ash the cameras and now their secret agency wants to uncover Carly and Val's abilities to examine and exploit them for military weaponry."

"What's going on?" Jo yelled from the porch.

They all went inside the house.

"Federal agents saw footage of Val dismembering two Piure police officers and Carly ashing their cameras," Evan told them.

"Oh no," Rye cried. "What are we gonna do?"

"We don't need to do much," Carly ensured them.

"I've already suppressed one agent's memories of the incident," Adam added. "Though the others will likely just show him the footage again. I wanted to make contact with all of them out there, but I had a feeling their vehicles were equipped with cameras."

"I don't know about anyone else, but I'm not afraid nor bothered by this," Jo added. "Let's go back outside and continue enjoying our day. I don't wanna miss the sunset."

"Sounds like a plan to me," Kane agreed while scooping Rade into his arms.

"Mommy, mommy," Light called with her arms up in the air.

Carly picked her up, but she immediately leaned over into Adam's arms. He kissed her.

"So, we're not going to do anything?" Evan asked.

"We're going to live. Joyously and happily," Carly replied walking towards the back door.

"That's the decision?" Adam blushed.

"That's the decision," she beamed back at him.

They returned to the back deck, and enjoyed their meal over laughter as the children's giggles filled the air with love.

ABOUT THE AUTHOR

Calix Leigh-Reign is the author of the #1 Amazon Bestselling YA/ Sci-Fi series, the Scion Saga Series and Legend of Ore trilogy. She's a certified paralegal and a member of SFWA. Her earliest literary inspirations include Alice Walker, Larry Strauss, VC Andrews, and Stephen King. Calix enjoys discovering the minds of those who rebel against social programming, listening to and creating music, a great cup of coffee, exquisite ethnic cuisine, spending time with family & friends, attending movie premieres, traveling, and the arts. She spends her free time in the gym, fantasizing about story plots, and different ways of changing the world.

Read more at www.calix.co

THE SCION SAGA SERIES

opaque: scion saga book 1 (2016)

split adam: scion saga book 2 (2017)

specular: scion saga book 3 (2023)

OFFICIAL FAN CLUB:

ScionSaga.com

Facebook.com/ScionSaga

Instagram & Twitter:
@ScionSaga

MORE READS

amazon.com

THE DESCENDANTS
SCIONSAGA.COM

UP NEXT:

SCION SAGA: ORIGINS

ScionSaga
MERCH & SWAG

SCIONSAGA.COM

SCIONSAGA.COM

sovareign